The Bourbon Thief

TIFFANY REISZ

MIRA

The Bourbon Thief

MIRA

ISBN-13: 978-0-7783-1942-9

The Bourbon Thief

Printed in U.S.A.

First printing: July 2016
10 9 8 7 6 5 4 3 2 1

To Kentucky, my home

I

Paris

There wasn't much in the world Cooper McQueen cared about more than a good bourbon. In his forty-five years, not one single beautiful woman had managed to persuade him to set down his drink and leave it down. But when the woman in the red dress walked into his bar—a gift from the gods tied in a tight red bow—McQueen decided he might have seen the one woman on earth who could turn even him into a teetotaler. Her dress was tight as old Scrooge's fist, red as Rudolph's nose, and looking at her, McQueen had only one thought—Christmas had come awfully early this year.

Miss Christmas in July glanced his way, smiled like she knew what he was thinking and was thinking along the same lines herself, and McQueen figured he'd be leaving the bar early tonight and nobody better try to talk him out of it.

Not wanting to appear too eager, he continued to sip his bourbon—neat—as he kept her in his peripheral vision.

Christmas in July walked over to the bar and took a seat. He watched her study the menu and he smiled behind his glass. In one minute he'd go over to her, buy her a drink, let it slip he owned the bar, dangle out the bait, see if she was in the mood to nibble. He'd seen his fair share of beautiful women in his bar, usually too young—he had some pride, after all—but Miss Christmas looked a respectable thirty-five. A real woman. A grown woman. The sort he could sleep with without apology. She had dark skin and black hair that lay in heavy coils down her back and tied at the nape of her neck with a red ribbon he fully intended to untie with his teeth given the opportunity.

One minute up, he went to claim the opportunity.

It didn't break McQueen's heart to excuse himself from his current conversation with someone who was either an invest-ment banker or a venture capitalist. He had stopped listening the moment Miss Christmas walked in. He went over to her and sat in the empty bar stool to her left without waiting for an invitation. He owned the place. No reason not to act like it.

He didn't say anything at first. He let the silence linger and grow as heady as the muddy Ohio River on a hot night, the kind that made even the sidewalks sweat. Maybe he could talk the lady into a stroll over to the river while the night was still warm. Maybe he could talk her into something more.

"What can I get you?" Maddie, the pretty blonde bartender, asked the woman.

"How about a shot of Red Thread?" the woman said. "I like to match my drinks to my hair ribbon."

"Red Thread?" Maddie glanced at McQueen, a silent plea for help. "I don't think…"

"Red Thread's been out of business for thirty-five years," McQueen said to Maddie.

"Oh, good. Thought I was going crazy. Could have sworn

I knew every bourbon there was," Maddie said. "Any bottles left?"

"Not a one," McQueen said, not a white lie, not a black lie. A little red lie.

"What a shame," Miss Christmas said, although she sounded neither surprised nor disappointed. Christmas was right. Her voice had a frosty tone to it. She was cool. He liked cool.

"A damn shame. They say it was the best bourbon ever bottled." McQueen waited for the lady in the red dress to speak again, but she stayed silent, listening, alert, eyes only for Maddie at the moment.

"What happened to it?" Maddie asked him.

"Warehouse fire," McQueen said, shrugging. "It happens. You distill alcohol and store it in wooden barrels? Fire's your worst nightmare. Red burned to the ground in 1980 and never reopened. No one knows who owns it anymore." McQueen had tried to buy the old Red Thread property himself but had no luck. He'd gotten as far as finding the shell company— Moonshine, Ltd.—that owned the acreage and the trademark, but it didn't seem to have a human being behind its name. "I would know because I've looked."

"Isn't that interesting…" Miss Christmas said with the hint of a smile on her red lips, and he couldn't tell if she meant it or if she was being sarcastic. She spoke with a Kentucky accent, faint but recognizable to someone who spent half his time in New York and half his time in Louisville. Kentucky accents sounded like home to him and his ears always perked up when he heard one.

"Can I get you something else?" Maddie asked the woman.

"Four Roses, neat. Double pour."

"A lady who knows her bourbon and isn't afraid to drink it

straight." McQueen turned ten degrees on his bar stool toward her. "A woman after my own heart."

"I'm a Kentucky girl," she said with a graceful shrug. "And bourbon's like the truth, you know."

"How's that?"

"The first taste burns, but once you get used to it, it's the only thing you want in your mouth."

Miss Christmas brought the shot glass to her lips, took a sip and didn't flinch as she drank it. The bourbon didn't burn her.

"Tell me something true, then," McQueen said. "What's your name?"

"Paris."

"Beautiful name."

"Thank you, Mr. McQueen."

"You know who I am?"

"Everybody knows who you are. You own this bar," she said, nodding at the words *The Rickhouse, Louisville, Kentucky*, engraved on the mirror behind the bar, the image of a turn-of-the-century wood warehouse also etched in the glass. "I hear you're opening another bourbon bar in Brooklyn."

"You don't approve?"

"Leave it to white people to turn a beautiful drink like bourbon into a fetish. Find a way to make pumpkin spice bourbon, and you'll be a billionaire." She took another sip of her Four Roses, all the while looking at him out of the side of her eyes.

"I'll tell you a secret."

"Tell it."

"I'm already a billionaire. But I'm always looking for a new way to waste my money. Why not?"

"You need another business? You tired of owning your basketball team already?"

"I only own part of the team."

"Which part?" she asked. "I know which part I'd like to own."

McQueen laughed. "Tell me something, Miss Paris—what do you own?"

Now it was her turn to spin on her bar stool, ninety degrees, and she met him face on with full eye contact, fearless and shameless.

"I could own you by morning."

Her words rendered McQueen momentarily speechless. He couldn't remember the last time any woman had so thoroughly stupefied him. Bourbon on her lips and curves on her hips. He was halfway in love with her already.

"I would like to see you try," McQueen said. "And that's not a challenge. I really would like to see that with my own eyes."

"Shall we?" she asked, raising her eyebrow a fraction of an inch.

He had to know her. "Yes," he said. "Yes, we shall."

They left the bar together but drove separately to his house. As he wove his way through downtown traffic, he saw that somehow he'd lost her behind him. He'd given her his address and she surely didn't need to follow him to find it. An irrational fear took hold of him between the red light and the green, a fear she'd changed her mind, driven off, considered a better offer somewhere else with someone else. No, surely not. She'd wanted him, he knew it. He'd seen avarice in her eyes at the bar, and whether it was for his face, his money or his reputation as the richest man in Kentucky, he didn't care. They were all true, all parts of him, anyway. Whatever part of him she wanted, he didn't care as long as she wanted him. She did want him, didn't she? Irrational thoughts. Irrational fears.

Yet he couldn't shake the feeling that he must see her tonight, be with her. Anything less would be calamitous. A man needed wanting. What was the point of having wealth, power and the body of a man half his age if no one bothered to use him for it?

McQueen pulled into his driveway and saw a black Lexus already there and waiting. Self-respect prevented him from sighing in his relief, but even a self-respecting man was allowed to smile. She'd simply taken a different route. No big surprise. If she lived anywhere around here, she'd know about his house. Everybody in town knew about Lockwood—named not for the forest that surrounded the property he kept locked behind stone walls, but for the man who built it in 1821. Old by American standards, but McQueen's family was Irish. A two-hundred-year-old house was just getting comfortable by his grandfather's standards. And McQueen tended to judge everything by his grandfather's standards.

Lockwood was a redbrick three-story Georgian masterpiece with double-height white porticos protected by a twelve-foot-high wrought-iron gate. He and Paris parked in the circular cobblestone driveway in front of the temple-style porch. She emerged from her car all long legs and slim ankles and red shoes, and she didn't blink at the house. It seemed to make no impression on her whatsoever. Miss Paris must have her own money. The shoes, the dress, the Birkin bag that was nearly identical to the one his ex-wife carried? All that screamed money to him. No one was that unimpressed by money except people who have it.

Before entering the house, she paused on the front porch and glanced back at the gate.

"What?" he asked.

"Pretty fence," she said. "Traditional Kentucky rock fence."

"Glad you like it," he said, admiring the view from the porch. The perimeter of the Lockwood property was a rock fence built in the nineteenth century. "I had it built just for you."

"To keep me in or to keep me out?"

"To keep you surrounded by beautiful things. As you should be."

She raised her eyebrow slightly and without another word turned and walked into the house. If she hadn't been looking, McQueen might have patted himself on the back. Good line.

"Welcome to Lockwood," McQueen said, glad it was late enough all the staff but his security guard were gone. "Hope you like it."

"Very nice," she said, barely giving the opulent interior a glance. McQueen didn't mind that much. He'd rather she looked at him than his foyer, and she was definitely looking at him. Women considered him handsome, and even if they didn't, they considered him rich, which was usually enough to close the deal.

"I'm the fourth generation of McQueens to live here. My great-grandfather bought this house when he came over from Ireland," McQueen said. It was summer, warm, and she wasn't wearing a coat for him to offer to take. He wasn't sure what to do with his hands. At his age he should have his seduction skills down by now, but Paris made him nervous for a reason he couldn't name. "He'd planned to settle his family farther west, but the hills reminded him of home. So he stayed."

"And here we are. What would your great-grandfather have said about you bringing me to his home?"

"I'd like to think he'd have taken one look at you and said, 'Good job, lad.'"

"I'll be the judge of how good the job is done."

"Maybe we should get to work, then." He reached for her and kissed her under the crystal chandelier, which before today had looked elegant to him, but tonight seemed ostentatious compared to the elegance of this woman in her red dress. She tasted of apples and bourbon when he kissed her and she was right—it did burn, but once he had his first taste, she was all he wanted in his mouth.

McQueen pressed her back against the banister of the spiral staircase that led upstairs. He hooked her leg around his hip, slid his hand up her long bare thigh. She had panties on, but they weren't enough to keep his fingers out of her. He stepped back, pulled them down her thighs and left them on the floor, where he hoped they would stay until morning.

"Did you plan to seduce me when you came to the bar?" he asked against her lips.

"Yes."

"Are you after my money?" He sensed such a woman wouldn't be insulted by such a question.

"Only your bourbon, Mr. McQueen."

"You want to see my collection?" he asked. "I promise it's nothing but booze. I don't own a single etching."

McQueen and his world-class bourbon and whiskey collection had recently been profiled in *Cigar Aficionado* magazine, inspiring a few phone calls from collectors trying to buy some of his rarer vintages, but she was his first official bourbon groupie.

"Eventually," she said, spreading her legs a little wider for him, inviting his fingers a little deeper. "Once you're done showing me everything else you've got."

McQueen showed her. First he showed her right there against the wall. Then he took her up to the master bedroom, a room baroque with ornamentation and ostentation. Even the bed was gilt. He never actually slept in the room if he could help it. He found other uses for it, however. And that red dress of Paris's looked about as good on his floor as the priceless gold-and-green Persian rug it lay upon.

When it was all over, Paris reached for her red dress, and it occurred to him that if he let her leave now, he wouldn't be likely to ever see her again. Something told him he shouldn't let her go. Something told him if all he did was sleep with her, he would forfeit something, a victory or a prize.

"Don't leave," he said as he obliged her by zipping the dress up for her. She had such a lovely back and the light of the bed-side Tiffany lamp danced over her dark skin like a tongue of fire. "I haven't shown you my collection yet."

"Oh, yes, I'd almost forgotten," she said, cool as could be. He wasn't used to women this quiet and unimpressed by being in the bedroom of a billionaire. Too cool.

"I don't know what to make of you," he said, narrowing his eyes at her as she wrapped the red ribbon around her hair and pulled the long locks over her shoulder, Venus at her toilette.

"Make of me? Are you putting me in a pie?"

McQueen laughed. "I'd rather keep you in the bedroom than the kitchen. Come on, tell me about yourself."

"My name is Paris. I was born and raised in Kentucky. I moved to South Carolina for school. I got married a couple years ago, inherited money when my husband died, and now I'm back. I have no children. I am no one special. You only think I'm mysterious because you've noticed I'm not terribly interested in spending the rest of my life with you and that is one mystery a man like yourself can't solve."

"That hurts."

"No, it doesn't."

McQueen raised his eyebrow. "A rich widow. That explains a lot."

"What does it explain?"

"Why I don't impress you. You have your own money."

"You tell yourself that's the reason," she said with a smile sweet as the pie he should put her in, and goddammit, Mc-Queen wanted her again already. She made him forget he was forty-five. "I won't contradict you."

"I'm going to impress you before you leave," he said. "Watch me."

"I'm watching."

He dressed in his suit minus the jacket and tie and led her from the bedroom, down the hall and to a bookcase. On the bookcase were unread leather-bound volumes of all the classics.

"Very nice," Paris said. "Did your decorator provide the books? Or did you order them from the pretty book whole-sale warehouse?"

"This isn't it," he said. "I'm going to show you my prized possession." He pulled on the middle shelf of the bookcase, revealing that it wasn't simply a bookcase, but a door. He switched on a floor lamp inside the door and waved Paris inside. As she gazed around the hidden room, he watched her face. She revealed nothing—no shock, no surprise, no disappointment.

"Cozy," Paris said, but from her tone she might have meant "airless." He watched her take note of the old stone fireplace, the antique sofa with the worn jade fabric and the carved ebony arms. She walked to the wall and pulled back the curtain to reveal...nothing.

"You covered your window with a wooden board?" Paris asked, tapping the board.

"That's a mirror," he said. "I don't want anyone looking in here. And really, what's more terrifying than peeking in the window of a house and seeing yourself?"

McQueen retrieved the key he'd hidden in a small silver

vase on top of the fireplace mantel and opened a satin bronze cabinet with the Twelve Apostles embossed on the side.

"Is that a tabernacle?" Paris asked.

"It is."

"You store your alcohol in a cabinet designed to hold communion wafers?"

"My grandfather had a dark sense of humor where the Catholic Church was concerned."

"I assume he was Catholic?"

"Until he fell in love with a girl who left him for the Carmelites. Never stepped foot in a church again after that. Said no man with any pride would enter the house of the man who stole his wife."

"Pride indeed. Sounds like his lady picked the right man. You exist, so I assume he got over his lover's defection?"

"Got married, yes, but he never got over it. All the McQueens are heathens now, but I do consider this room my little sanctuary. Every man needs one." He took a bottle out of the cabinet and handed it to her.

"This is it?" she asked, cradling the bottle carefully in her hands.

"That's it. You ordered Red Thread at the bar tonight. That, my dear, is the first bottle of Red Thread ever distilled, ever bottled, ever-ever."

"How did you come by this bottle?"

"Private sale. One million dollars. The provenance is perfect. Virginia Maddox herself sold it shortly before she died to pay her medical bills. One of a kind."

"No wonder you won't sell it," she said.

"Not for all the money in the world. This is the holy grail of bourbon. You don't sell the holy grail."

"Unholy grail," she said under her breath, but not so far under he didn't hear it.

Her eyes softened as she touched the red ribbon tied around the bottle's neck. It was a tattered old thing.

"It's a miracle that thing has stayed on there," McQueen said. "Piece of ribbon from the 1860s."

"Slave cloth," Paris said.

"What?"

"The ribbon was cut from slave cloth. Thick wool. Slave cloth was made to last a long time. Slaves didn't get new clothes very often. What they had had to last, had to hold up to hard work and many years. The girl who wore this ribbon? This was probably the only nice thing she had, the only thing she thought of as hers."

"I'm sorry. I didn't know that ribbon... I didn't know that part of the story, that the ribbon came from a Maddox slave."

"Now you know."

"You ordered Red Thread at The Rickhouse. But you would have been a baby when Red Thread burned down. What exactly is your interest in it?"

"It interests me for many reasons. But here, you can't trust me with that bottle. I might drop it. Wouldn't that be a shame?"

She passed the bottle back to McQueen. He put it carefully back into the cabinet. When he turned around, Paris was halfway to the door.

"You aren't leaving, are you?" he asked.

"Leaving for the bedroom," she said.

"So I did impress you?"

"You have a fine collection," she said. "I only wish it were mine."

McQueen followed her to the concealed door and started

to open it for her. With his hand on the knob he looked her up and down and into her eyes.

"Who are you really?" he asked.

"You don't want to know."

"Why not?"

"I told you why. The truth is like bourbon—it'll burn going down."

"I want to burn."

She kissed him, hard enough McQueen forgot about finding out anything else about her except how to make her come again. And after he'd solved that mystery, he fell fast asleep, one arm over her naked stomach, one leg over her leg, his favorite way to fall asleep.

When McQueen woke up, he was alone, and Paris had left nothing behind but the scent of her skin on his sheets and her red hair ribbon on his pillow.

Red ribbon?

Hell on earth, he was a first-rate fool.

McQueen pulled on his pants and shirt and ran to the room behind the bookcase.

Too late. She was gone.

So was his million-dollar bottle of Red Thread.

2

McQueen slammed his hand down onto the intercom button and ordered his night shift security guard to lock the gates.

"Already done," James answered. "Someone tried to get out without the gate code. She's in my office. I was about to come wake you up, boss."

He should have been relieved, but he seethed instead, his shoulders tense with his fury, and he nearly wrenched the door off the hinges when he entered the security guard's small shed. Paris sat primly on a small folding chair, her legs crossed at the ankles, her black Birkin bag in her lap.

"Give us a minute," McQueen said to the guard.

"Do I need to call the cops?"

"Not yet. I want to hear her story first. Then we'll call them."

James left him alone in the shed with Paris. She looked up at him placidly.

"Are all your servants black?" she asked, nodding at the door that James had closed behind him.

"They're not servants. They're employees. And no. My housekeeper is white. The security guard who works the day shift is from Mexico."

"The United Colors of Yes-Men."

"And yes-women," McQueen said. He crossed his arms and leaned back against the door. "You're good. You wore me out, and when I slept..."

"I'm not good. You're easy."

"Am I?"

"Interview in the June 2014 *Architectural Digest* with billionaire investor Cooper McQueen. 'What do you like to read, Mr. McQueen?' the fawning interviewer asked you. 'What keeps Cooper McQueen up all night?' And you replied—"

"Raymond Chandler."

"Because, as you said in the interview, 'I'm a sucker for a femme fatale. Give me a girl with a black heart in a red dress and I'm a goner.'"

"You thought you could seduce me because I read Chandler?"

"And your last girlfriend was a dark-skinned Knicks City Dancer from Puerto Rico, so I knew I had a very good shot at you. I'm your type, aren't I?"

"I don't have a fetish for dark-skinned women, if that's what you're implying."

"I wasn't implying anything, but you immediately seemed to think it was what I was implying. Methinks the billionaire doth protest too much."

"Of all the bars in all the world...you walked into mine to steal my bourbon. You know, stealing something worth a million dollars is a felony."

"I know. But I won't call the police on you if you don't call the police on me."

"I didn't steal it."

"You bought stolen goods. Also a felony."

"That bottle wasn't stolen."

"I know it was."

"I told you, Virginia Maddox sold it—"

"It didn't belong to Virginia Maddox. You can't sell what you don't own. And I was happy to buy it from you and avoid an unpleasant legal battle, but as you refused to sell it, I had no choice but to repossess it," she said with the slightest sinister hiss.

"How do you know all this? How do you know everything you think you know about Red Thread?"

"I am Red Thread," Paris said with the slightest sigh like she was admitting to a bad habit.

"Red Thread is dead."

"A nice rhyme. You should have been a poet." She raised her chin toward the filing cabinet. On top of it sat the bottle. "Look at it. Read the label. Tell me what it says."

McQueen knew what the label said, but he took the bottle anyway and held it label side up toward the light.

The label was faded and yellowed, close to peeling. It was a hundred and fifty years old, after all. The font was an elegant script that said "Red Thread—Kentucky Straight Bourbon Whiskey." Beneath those words it read "Distilled and bottled—Frankfort, Kentucky." And underneath that in tiny script he read, "'Owned and operated by the Maddox family, 1866.'"

"There we go," Paris said.

"Where do we go?"

"Owned by the Maddox family."

"You aren't the Maddox family."

"Are you saying that because they were white and I'm not?"

"I'm saying that because I've looked for the Maddox family

for years, and I haven't found a single one of them, by blood or by marriage, who had anything to do with Red Thread. The whole Kentucky line died or disappeared after the distillery burned."

"Why did you look for us?"

"First of all, I don't believe you are a Maddox. You're going to have to show me some proof."

"You're holding the proof in your hands. One hundred proof."

"Funny."

"Oh, yes," she said with an exaggerated Southern drawl. "I'm a card. Why were you looking for us?" she asked again.

"I wanted to buy Red Thread. What's left of it. I've been wanting to open my own distillery for years. Red Thread is part of Kentucky history. I'd like to be part of Kentucky's present."

"Some things are better off history."

"Bourbon isn't one of them."

"It's too late anyway, Mr. McQueen. Someone else beat you to it."

"Beat me to what? Buying Red Thread?"

"Reopening the distillery. Under a new name, of course. And under new management."

McQueen understood at once.

"You," he said. "You're Moonshine, Ltd.? I tried to contact you."

"That's my company, yes."

"You own the old Red Thread property?"

"Owner, operator and master distiller."

"You?"

"You don't think a woman can be a master distiller? I have

my PhD in chemistry. You can call me Dr. Paris if that sort of thing turns you on."

"I get it," McQueen said, nodding. "I do. This is the first ever bottle of Red Thread, the original bottle. Part of the company's history and you want it because you own Red Thread now. Makes sense. I'm even sympathetic. I might even have loaned it to you to put on display when the company re-opens for business. But now you've pissed me off. And if you don't tell me one very good reason why I shouldn't call the police, I'm picking up the phone in three seconds. Three... two..."

"I can tell you what happened to Red Thread," she said. "I can tell you the whole story. The whole truth."

Well.

That got his attention.

"You know why it burned down?"

"I know everything. But if I were you, I wouldn't ask. By the time I'm done telling you the story, you'll hand over that bottle with your compliments and an apology."

"Must be one hell of a story, then."

"It's what brought me here, the story."

"Your story?"

"My story. I inherited it."

"I think I'd rather inherit money than a story."

"I have that, too, not entirely by my choice."

"You don't want to be rich?"

"God favors the poor. But don't tell rich people that. It'll hurt their little feelings."

McQueen sighed and sat back. He buttoned the middle buttons of his shirt, crossed his leg over his knee. He should call the cops. Why hadn't he called the cops? Embarrassed he'd fallen for the oldest trick in the book? Beautiful woman in red goes home with him, fucks him and robs him while he sleeps. He could laugh at himself, but he wouldn't let anyone else laugh at him. Yes, he could call the cops.

Or...

"They call bourbon the honest spirit," he said. "You know why?"

"You aren't legally allowed to flavor it with anything. Water, corn, barley, rye and that's it. You see what you get. You get what you see. No artificial colors. No artificial sweeteners. No artificial nothing."

"Right. So let's drink a little honesty, shall we?"

"If you're buying," she said.

"I'm always buying."

He picked up the bottle and slipped it into his pants pocket. He opened the door of the security shed and Paris stepped out into the warm night air. Almost 2:00 a.m., he should be in bed now. He'd hoped to be in bed with her. One of these days he'd learn. Not today apparently.

"Boss?" James asked, dropping his cigarette on the ground and crushing it under his boot.

"A misunderstanding." McQueen had his hand on the small of Paris's back. "Don't worry about it."

"Got it. Sleep well, Mr. McQueen."

As they walked back into the house and up to his drinking closet, McQueen considered the possibility that he might be making the worst mistake of his life.

"Sit." McQueen pointed at the jade sofa and Paris sat without a word of protest.

McQueen took the key from the silver bowl and put the bottle of Red Thread back into the cabinet.

"I shouldn't have trusted you." McQueen locked the cabinet and slipped the key into his pocket.

"You're a rich white man. Not your fault for assuming the entire world is on your side. It must seem like it most days. Usually you'd be right, but times, Mr. McQueen, are a-changing."

"That sounds like a threat."

"Sounds like Bob Dylan to me."

He needed a drink, a stiff one, so he poured each of them a shot. The entire time he kept an eye on her as he unscrewed the cap and measured out the bourbon. Now she seemed calm, but it wasn't the calm of surrender. This was a cat's version of calm. A calm that could turn into an attack or a run in an instant.

When she had her shot in hand and he had his, he lifted it in a toast, a toast she didn't return. Instead, she merely sipped her bourbon.

"Pappy's?" she asked.

"It is. You have a good palate."

"You can taste the leather in it."

He couldn't, but it impressed him she could.

"You weren't exaggerating. You do know your bourbon," he said.

"They used to say that about the Maddoxes," she said. "Ever since Jacob Maddox started the distillery and made himself a wealthy man in five years…they said it about all of us—the Maddoxes have bourbon in their blood."

"I've seen the Maddox family tree. There is no Paris on it."

"Perhaps you were looking at the wrong branches," she said coldly.

His words had hit a sensitive spot and her eyes flashed in a familiar way. It was not his first encounter with her sensitive places, after all.

"Now that we both have an honest spirit in our hands," McQueen said, "tell me something."

"Anything," she said, although he doubted the sincerity of that declaration. She was proving to be altogether miserly with her explanations and answers.

"Did you sleep with me just to steal my bottle?"

"Does that sting? I bet it stings." She winced in feigned sympathy, shaking her head and clucking her tongue like a mother tending to the skinned knee of her child. Right then and there he made a realization—he didn't like this woman, not at all.

"I think I could fuck you a thousand nights and never actually touch you."

"Don't feel bad," she said. "You're not the only one with rock fences around you. Built by the same people, too, as a matter of fact."

"Irish immigrant stonemasons hired by my great-grandfather?"

Paris's eyes widened slightly. Then she laughed. Finally. He knew he'd scored a point on her. True, most of the rock fences in Kentucky were built by slave labor. His was not, however, and somewhere he had the paperwork to prove it. While he didn't know the game he and Paris were playing, he knew that while he wouldn't win it, if he played it well enough, he might not lose it.

"You're funny. And you're handsome." She tossed the compliment at him like a dollar bill at a stripper's feet. "If it makes you feel any better, I didn't have to fake anything with you. If I hadn't wanted to sleep with you, I wouldn't have. It was convenient that you were attractive. Otherwise, I might have simply hired someone to break into the house while you were away. Does that help?"

"I feel so much better now," he said. "While we're being honest…is it true? You're widowed?"

"I am. Widowed at thirty-four."

"Awfully young to lose a husband."

"Not my husband, although he died too young for my liking. He was twenty-eight years older than I am."

McQueen nearly choked on his Pappy's. The youngest woman he ever slept with was eighteen years his junior and that relationship had lasted about as long as a bad movie.

"Twenty-eight. I guess that's what they call a May/December romance."

She smiled and it was a debt collector's smile, and something told him she had come to make him pay up. "Twenty-eight years? That's a January/December romance in a leap year."

McQueen chuckled and raised his glass to her.

"What?" she asked.

"You get enough bourbon in you and you sound like a real Kentucky girl."

"I am a real Kentucky girl. Born in Frankfort a stone's throw from the Kentucky River. That's not an exaggeration. With a good arm, you could hit the river from our porch."

"That's not a good neighborhood."

"It was the only neighborhood we had. If you have a roof over your head and food in the fridge and nobody breaking down your door, it's a good neighborhood."

McQueen tried to take another drink of his bourbon and found his shot glass empty. He set it down again on his knee.

"So you slept with me and stole a million-dollar bottle of bourbon. You must really want that bottle."

"I don't want it, no. But I need it." For the second time that night he saw a glimpse of the real woman behind the mask of the femme fatale, the woman in red. A determined woman.

"For what?"

"To finish something someone else started." She glanced down at the bourbon in the glass she'd balanced on her knee. "You know what a bourbon thief is, Mr. McQueen?"

"It's a sampling tube," McQueen said. "You stick it in the bunghole of a bourbon barrel and extract the contents for tasting."

"Isn't that one hell of a visual metaphor?" Paris asked.

McQueen laughed big and long and loud.

"What's your point?"

"Do I look like a bourbon thief to you?"

"You look like a woman who's never stolen anything in her life."

"I haven't. That bottle belongs to my family. You will return it one way or another."

"Apparently I'm going to give it to you by morning in exchange for a story. That's quite a feat."

"It's quite a story."

"Go on, then."

McQueen looked at her as she crossed her long legs, pulled her hair over her shoulder and met his eyes without a hint of fear even though she was on the hook for a million-dollar heist. It made him nervous, what she was about to tell him, but he wanted to know. Knowledge was power and power was money, and no man ever got rich buying stock in ignorance.

"On December 10, 1978, two very important events in the history of Red Thread occurred—the Kentucky River broke its banks and crested at a record forty-eight feet, and the granddaughter of George J. Maddox, the owner of Red Thread Bourbon Distillery, turned sixteen years old. That was the beginning of the end of Red Thread."

"What was? The river flooding?"

Paris gave him a smile, a smile that made him momentarily rethink his decision to not call the police.

"Tamara Maddox."

3

Tamara Maddox wanted to ride her horse the morning of her sixteenth birthday.

And whatever Tamara Maddox wanted to do, Tamara Maddox did.

In all fairness to the girl, spoiled as she was and she knew it, anyone would have wanted to get out of that house and any excuse would do. They'd been fighting again, Granddaddy and Momma. If only they yelled, that would have been one thing, something Tamara could roll her eyes at, laugh at, ignore by turning the volume up on her radio. But no, they whispered their fights behind closed doors, hissing at each other like snakes. Neither of them had the courtesy to tell her what they were fighting about, so Tamara assumed they were fighting about her.

Fine. If they wanted to fight on her birthday, she'd leave

them to it. She had better things to do. And the urge to go riding only grew when she saw a blue Ford pickup truck with a white cab wheezing its way down the drive to the stables. What was Levi doing here on a Sunday? She hoped it was because he knew it was her birthday, but even Tamara Maddox wasn't spoiled enough to think that was the case. Still, one more reason to go riding when one reason—she wanted to—was more than enough for her.

Tamara changed out of her pajamas and into her riding clothes—tan jodhpurs, black boots, a white blouse and a heavy coat—braided her long red hair and raced out to the barn. It was cold today—only forty-five by the thermometer in the barn—but she'd ridden in worse weather. Plus, the rain had stopped finally, and she'd been going stir-crazy inside the house. All she needed was an hour outside in the air with Kermit, her pale black Hanoverian pony, and everything would be all right again.

And if it wasn't, at least she'd see Levi today, and if that didn't make a girl feel better, nothing on God's wet green earth would.

Levi barely acknowledged her when she ran into the barn. Nothing new there. She had to work for his attention and she worked for it very hard. In the summer she'd often catch him shirtless as he mucked out stalls and threw hay bales around. In winter she had to content herself with the memories of his lean strong body that she knew was hidden under his brown coat with the leather collar and a chocolate-colored cowboy hat. Mud crusted his boots. He had dirt on his cheek. And if he got any more handsome, she would die before she hit seventeen. She would simply die of it.

Tamara walked up to him as he was carrying a bale of straw and knocked on his shoulder like she was knocking on a door.

"Nobody's home," Levi called out before she could say a word.

"I would like to ride my horse right now, please and thank you."

"Nope."

"Nope? What do you mean nope?"

"I mean, nope, no, no way. You can't ride your horse right now, please and thank you." Levi walked away from her, straw bale in hand, as if that were the end of it.

Tamara chased after him and determinedly knocked on his shoulder again. He dropped the bale.

"Why can't I ride today?"

"It's been raining for days. It's too wet."

"It's not raining now." She tapped on the glass of the window. "Look—it's dry. Dry, dry, dry."

"What part of *no* do you not understand, Rotten? The *N* or the *O*?"

"You shouldn't call me Rotten," she said, hands on her hips in the hopes he'd notice she had them. "It's not nice."

"I'm not nice. And I wouldn't call you Rotten if you weren't so damn spoiled rotten, so whose fault is it really? And again— the answer is no—*N* and *O*, no. Even you can spell that."

He might have been right about her being spoiled rotten, not that Tamara wanted to admit that. Most days he was the only person in the county—other than her mother—who had it in him to say no to her.

"Oh, I can spell. I can spell frontward and backward, and *no* spelled backward is *on*, as in I'm *on* the back of my horse and *on* the trail for a ride."

"And *on* my last nerve," Levi said. He took his hat off and brushed his sleeve over his forehead. She wondered sometimes if he did this sort of stuff just to torment her because he knew she had a crush on him—not that she did much to hide it. He was a first-class gold-medal tormentor, that Levi. He was twenty-eight and she was only sixteen as of midnight last night, which meant there was no way in hell Momma or Granddaddy would let her date him even if he was more handsome than the men on TV. He had curly black hair and a crinkle-eyed devilish smile he aimed at her often enough to get her hopes *and* her temperature up. He had a good tan, too, all the time, even in winter, making her wonder how he kept his tan so good even in February…and whether all of him was that tan. These were important questions to one Miss Tamara Belle Maddox.

And when he called her Rotten, it made her want to jump on top of him every time he did it.

"You know, today's my birthday," she said. "You have to be nice to me on my birthday."

"I don't have to do anything but die and pay taxes. Unless you're the grim reaper or the IRS, you don't get any of my attention today. Today is my day off. I'm only here because this is the only time the farrier could come and see to Danny Boy's shoes."

She stared at him, eye-to-eye. Or as close to eye-to-eye as she could get. She'd come in at five foot six this year and he had to be at least half a foot taller than her. Still, she did her level best to stare him down.

"Levi."

"Yes, Rotten?"

"I am the grim reaper. Now let me go riding or I'm going to tell Momma I caught you engaged in unnatural acts with Miss Piggy."

"You mean your momma's horse or the pig on *The Muppets*?"

"Does it matter?"

"It matters a helluva lot to me if I'm engaging in unnatural acts with one of them. I need to know who I'm sending flowers to after."

"You are the meanest man ever born," she said, shaking her head. "Where's the pitchfork?"

"You finally going to clean out Kermit's stall without me having to tell you twenty thousand times?"

"No. I'm going to stab you with it so many times we can use you to drain noodles."

"It's on the wall where it always is. Now if you'll excuse me, I have to do anything that involves not talking to you anymore."

Levi stepped away, but she stepped in front of him.

"Levi…" she said, her voice cracking in her desperation. "Please let me go riding today. It's my birthday and I'll clean the stalls and it's my birthday and I'll do whatever you tell me to do and it's my birthday and—"

He sighed—heavily—and lowered his chin to his chest.

"What crime did I commit in a past life that brought me to this point in my current incarnation?" he said with a heavy sigh.

"You're talking weird again," she said.

"Karma," he said. "I'm talking about karma. Which you would know nothing about as you are obviously so young and so dumb and so naive that the only way to explain it is that this is your very first incarnation. You are a baby soul in this universe. Only cause for your soul to be so wet behind the ears."

"You know you love me," she said. "You know I'm your favorite."

"I don't even like you, Rotten. Not one bit."

"Oh, you like me. You like me many bits."

"Love you or hate you, you can't go riding. I have spoken."

"You have to let me go. You work for us. You have to do what I say."

He stared her down and that stare felt like a rolling pin or worse—a steamroller. She gave him a steamroller back.

"You don't sign my paychecks, Rotten. I work for your granddaddy, not you."

"I wish you worked for me. I'd pay you to kiss me and fire you if you didn't."

"I realize I'm the last man who needs to be stereotyping anyone, but apparently everything I ever heard about redheads is true."

"Levi."

"What?"

"They're fighting again."

Levi gave her a tight-lipped look like he wanted to be nice to her but it went against his grain.

"What is it this time?" Levi asked.

"I don't know. They won't tell me. But I know Momma wants to move out and Granddaddy doesn't want us to."

"Didn't y'all use to live in your own house?"

She nodded. "We did until Daddy died."

"You want to move out?"

"I'd rather live in here in the stable than in any house when they're fighting like this."

"That bad?"

"Yeah," she said, then she grinned at him. "Plus, you're out here. I'd trade Granddaddy and Momma both for you."

"Good God, go. Go away. Shoo. Ride your damn horse and leave me alone. But if Kermit gets a leg stuck in a mudhole and throws you and breaks your neck, don't come crawling to me to fix it. Your head'll have to hang there on your shoulders all lopsided."

"Merci, mon capitan." She grabbed him by the arms, kissed both his cheeks and saluted him like she was a junior officer and he her French captain.

"You are out of your damn mind," he muttered as she raced to Kermit's stall.

"Can't hear you," she sang out. "I'm riding in the wind with joy at my feet and freedom in my hair."

Levi unlocked the door where he kept their saddles. They were too expensive, she knew, too tempting for thieves. Also, Levi knew if he didn't lock them up, she'd steal them to go riding whenever she wanted, which wasn't what she wanted, though she would protest otherwise if asked. Half the fun of going riding was bugging Levi until he let her go.

Once she'd saddled Kermit, she led him out to the riding trail that began at the end of the paddock. She hadn't been too keen on the idea of moving in with her granddaddy after her father died. She'd loved their old house, a rambling brick Victorian in Old Louisville, but there wasn't much horseback riding in the city. No horses meant no stables. No stables meant no grooms. No grooms meant no Levi. Oh, yes, she'd gotten used to living out here in the Maddox estate, Arden, with her granddaddy pretty quick after laying eyes on her grandfather's groom. But more and more her mother and grandfather had been fighting their ugly whispering fights, and Tamara hadn't been kidding when she'd said she'd rather live in the stables than the big house.

Once out in the cold air, Tamara decided maybe a shorter ride was a better ride. Muddy trails meant a slow pace and a nervous pony. Her ears burned with the cold and her nose dripped. She swiped at it with her sleeve and was glad Levi wasn't around to see that unladylike maneuver. She and Kermit picked their way down the main path that led through a couple hundred acres of trees. Fall had stripped the leaves off the trees, but there was still something beautiful about the barren forest. Not barren at all despite appearances. Not barren, but only sleeping. She sensed the sap under the bark, and the wood drinking up all the water in the ground from the days and days of December rain they'd had. Even bare the trees seemed brutally alive to her. They were bursting to wake up and release the green in them, counting the seconds until spring when they could stretch and bloom and eat warm wet air like candy.

Tamara found her favorite rock, a big chuck of limestone she liked to lie on in better weather, and used it to dismount. After tying Kermit to a tree trunk, she squished her way through ankle-deep mud and muck to the edge of the river. It was high today, higher than she remembered ever seeing it, and darker, too. Faster. It smelled different, a thick, pungent odor like dead fish and dirty metal. It made her nose wrinkle. As the water tripped over the rocks, it turned white like ocean waves. She'd inherited ocean fever from her father, not that he'd ever admitted that was where he went on his business trips. He'd never had to tell her, though. She'd found the sand in his shoes. When she told him to take her with him next time, he'd winked at her like that had been his plan all along.

Instead, he'd shot himself in the head somewhere in South Carolina three years ago while on one of those business trips, and she still didn't know which beach that sand had come from.

"Come back, Daddy," she said to the river. This river met up with the Ohio, which met up with the Mississippi, which met up with the ocean. And water could turn to vapor and rise up into the sky. There was nowhere water couldn't go. If she gave the water her message, maybe it could find her father. "I miss you. You were supposed to take me to the beach, remember? You were supposed to take me with you."

She sent the same message once a week at least. So far no answer, but today maybe…maybe the river heard her. Maybe today the river would find Daddy.

Tamara returned to Kermit, rubbed his chilled flanks, kissed his velvet nose before mounting up to finish her ride. Without Kermit and Levi, she might very well go haywire in her grandfather's house. Girls at school envied her the brick palace she lived in, but they didn't know about the fights. They didn't know about Momma's rules. They didn't know about Daddy and the cloud his death had lowered around Arden House, shrouding it so that screams became whispers and whispers became silence. Her mother and grandfather were keeping secrets from her, secrets that set them to fighting nearly every day, even on her birthday.

Even on her birthday.

The rain had returned by the time she made it back to the stables, her hands cramped in her gloves and her cheeks chapped raw from the cold wind. She unsaddled Kermit and brushed him down, showering him with all the pets and scratches any horse in the world would want. She left to fetch a fresh bale of straw for bedding and found Levi waiting for her in Kermit's stall when she returned. He'd turned the heater on in the stables and had taken his coat off. In his long-sleeved flannel shirt and jeans he looked more handsome than he had even an hour earlier. An hour from now he'd look even more handsome than he did right this minute. She wasn't sure how he accomplished this feat, but she was quite happy to observe it in action.

"Here." Levi held out a small red box no bigger than a deck of cards.

"What's this?" she asked, taking the box from him.

"Your birthday present."

Tamara's eyes widened.

"How did you know it was my birthday?"

"You said so about ten million times today."

"You got this for me today? While I was riding?"

"Well…no."

"Then you already knew it was my birthday. So you must have gotten it earlier. Unless you keep presents for me hidden around here all the time. You do, don't you?"

"George told me he bought you a Triumph Spitfire for your sweet sixteen. I don't give a damn it's your birthday. I just wanted to borrow your car."

"I'll trade you the car for a kiss."

"Forget it. I'm keeping your present."

He reached for the box and Tamara yanked it away, nearly biting off her fingertips in her urgency to pull her gloves off her hands. They were shaking by the time she got the box lid open. One of the girls at school—Crissy, God help her with a name like that—said girls should always play it cool with guys, not act too eager. Well, Crissy had never been given a birthday present by the most handsome man in the entire world, and Tamara couldn't play it cool if she were sitting in an igloo.

From a bed of yesterday's newspaper, Tamara pulled out a little gold horse on a little gold chain.

"You like horses," he said before she could say anything about it.

"I like you," she said.

"An hour ago you were threatening to turn me into a spaghetti strainer."

"I only threaten to turn people into strainers if I like them. Is this a bracelet?" The chain was only a few inches long.

"Necklace," he said.

"If you put this short chain around my neck, I'll choke to death."

"Exactly."

She glared at him.

"It's an ankle bracelet, Rotten," he said. "Unless you have really fat wrists, then it's a regular old bracelet."

"I don't have fat wrists."

"All I'm saying is if you did happen to have unusually fat wrists, it could be a bracelet."

"I weigh one hundred pounds, Levi." She draped the ankle bracelet around her wrist to show how loose it fit on her.

"One hundred pounds of wrist. I'm not saying it's a normal place to carry extra weight, but it happens. Maybe you could do some wrist exercises or something…"

Tamara kissed him.

It wasn't a cheek kiss this time. She wasn't playing junior officer to his *mon capitan*. She kissed him like she meant it. Because she meant it. God Almighty, did she mean it.

Levi gripped her by the upper arms and pushed her back gently, but still, it was a definite move to put distance between them.

"Sorry," she said, flushing slightly. "Got a little twitterpated there. You know, because I like horses."

"You know you can't go around kissing guys like that."

"Like what?"

"Like me. You can't go around kissing guys like me."

"Why not?"

"You're sixteen, Tamara."

"I was fifteen yesterday."

"That's the opposite thing of what you should say."

"What should I say?"

"Maybe that you won't kiss me on the mouth again. Or anywhere else. I think that would be a good start."

He crossed his arms over his chest.

"But it's my birthday."

"You don't get to do everything you want to do just because it's your birthday." He sounded wildly exasperated with her, and wildly exasperated Levi was her favorite version of Levi. "Try telling a police officer you're allowed to kill anybody and everybody you want just because it's your birthday. That duck won't fly."

"I didn't kill anyone. I kissed. Two S's, not two L's. Makes all the difference."

"Rotten, I'm way too old for you. I work for your granddaddy. He'd have my hide if he caught me messing around with you."

"I want a kiss, Levi, not a marriage proposal. I've never been kissed before. Not really. And that didn't count because you didn't know it was happening."

"I think I knew. Parts of me sure did."

She bounced up and down in her boots.

"Just one? Please? A real kiss?"

"What do you consider a real kiss?" he asked.

She shrugged her shoulders, shook her head. "I don't know. Like the way they kiss on *The Young and the Restless*?"

"Which one am I? The young or the restless?"

"You're the restless, obviously," she said. "Because you're so so so old, and I'm so so so young."

"Will it shut you up if I kiss you?"

"Can't talk with a tongue in my mouth, right?"

He took the box from her hand and tossed it on the pile of hay. He took her hand and pulled her flush against his body.

"Finally," he said, smiling down at her. "Now we have a persuasive argument."

4

Tamara hadn't expected him to go through with it. She'd only expected she would tease him and beg him to do it until he kicked her giggling and pouting spoiled rotten self out of the barn. Making him mad was the next best thing to making him laugh. When he actually took her in his arms, she froze in surprise. He didn't kiss her—he did something better and worse at the same time.

Levi pushed her up against the rough wood of Kermit's stall wall and held her there with his entire body.

"Your grandfather pays me to take care of his horses," Levi said. "I am not paid to indulge you."

"Then do it for free."

Levi gave her a flat hard stare that scared her. Everything scared her right now. Being in such close quarters revealed the disparity in their sizes. Her shoulders spanned half his width. He stood a head taller. She could push against him with everything she had in her and she wouldn't be able to budge the solid pillar of his body that held her pinned in place.

Oh, but she didn't want to push against him. That was, in fact, the very last thing she wanted to do right now.

A teardrop of rainwater slid from Tamara's temple down her face. Levi pressed his lips to that drop. They warmed her cold skin, and she'd never felt anything like that in her life, never felt something so sensual and threatening all at once. She closed her eyes and prayed for more rain, so much rain it would trap them in the stable. So much rain it would form a moat to keep the world out. So much rain everyone on earth would drown in it but her and Levi.

"Levi." She pushed her hips against his. He had something she needed and her body had to tell him that.

"You are playing with fire, little girl," Levi said into her ear.

"I'm not a little girl anymore," she said, looking up at him. It was a brash thing to say, but it had to be said. Her voice quavered as she spoke the words. Tamara studied his face. She'd never seen him this close-up, inches away, close enough to smell him, close enough to see the freckle on his bottom lip. She could have counted his eyelashes.

Levi pushed his hips back into hers, and she felt something hard against her, something that demanded her attention.

Oh, dear. She had made a terrible miscalculation. Levi wasn't a boy. Levi was a man. An adult man twelve years older than her. Older, wiser and so much bigger than she was. She really ought to stop him. She really ought to. Yes, she should do that.

"I love you," Tamara said instead.

"Do you?" Levi asked, barely batting an eyelash at her declaration, which made her madder than being pinned to the wall. How dare he not take her seriously when she told him she was in love with him.

"I do. I swear I do."

"You don't even know who I am. You don't know who you think you love."

"I don't care. I know I love you. You're perfect and handsome and I think about you all the time and I want you all the time and I love you."

"All the time?"

She nodded. "All the time."

She pressed her mouth hard against his, kissing him like she had a loaded gun pointed at her head and only kissing could save her life. It felt so good she sighed, and when the sigh parted her lips, Levi's tongue slipped between her teeth. She'd been kidding about the tongue in her mouth, but Levi wasn't laughing. Not anymore and not about anything. Levi dug a hand into the back of her braid and pushed her mouth harder against his. His tongue tasted so good she wanted to suck on it. When she did, he made a noise in the back of his throat, a dirty noise that made her want to make him do it again.

Levi pulled back from the kiss like he was ripping off a Band-Aid. And yet she remained pinned in place. He had her pushed so hard against the wall she could lift her boots off the ground and not fall.

"Do you have any idea how many girls I've fucked in my life?" he asked her. "Or do you think my entire life is brushing your grandfather's horses and putting up with you?"

She didn't know how to answer that. She panted and shook her head. "I don't know."

"You want to know?" he asked. His voice was menacing now, not seductive, and yet she felt utterly seduced. She didn't want to be anywhere but here against this wall. "You want to know how many girls I've fucked?"

"Yes," she said because she thought that was what he wanted to hear.

"Every girl I've ever *wanted* to fuck, that's how many," he said, and she believed him. Maybe yesterday she wouldn't have believed that. Yesterday he'd have been just the horse groom with the pretty eyes and sexy smile. Today he was a man with muscles and a body and hands big enough to span her waist like they were doing now. "Every girl I've ever wanted to fuck...minus one."

Tamara inhaled sharply.

His hands slid from her waist to her thighs. He lifted her off the straw-covered ground and wrapped her legs around him. She clung to him as if for life, hands grasping his shoulders, her boots wound together at his lower back and locked tight. The seam along the crotch of her jodhpurs rubbed against a soft and swollen part of her, and every time Levi pushed closer, she flinched with pleasure. Her head fell back when he did it again. When she raised her head, she saw him looking into her shirt. She had larger breasts than any other girl her age at her school, not huge, but full. She couldn't hide them and neither could her bra. Tamara took her hand off his shoulder long enough to unbutton her shirt to the center of her chest. He wanted to look at her and she wanted him to see her. He lowered his head and kissed the top of her breast where it spilled out over the lace-trim edge of her white bra. Against her neck she felt his hair and loved, loved, loved the soft tickle of it on her skin.

"You like this?" he asked, grinding against her again, flint against tinder.

"Yes." She could scarcely catch a breath with his chest pressed so hard against hers.

"You're not scared?"

She shook her head no.

"You a virgin?" he asked.

"I told you, I've never even had a real kiss."

"You can fuck without kissing."

"That had never occurred to me."

"I don't recommend it," he said. "I like to do both at the same time."

"That's quite…"

"Quite what?" he asked.

"That's quite a thought," she said. "I like that thought."

"I like your thoughts. I'd like to give you more of them." Again Levi pushed against that raw sensitive place between her legs and she let out a little cry that he silenced with a kiss. At first she froze in fear, but she thawed almost instantly. Then it went beyond thawing and into an immediate burn.

His mouth moved over hers and she sighed with unfathomable pleasure.

With her eyes closed she could do nothing but taste him and smell him and feel him against her, and it was even better than seeing him. He tasted like he'd taken a nip or two of her granddaddy's Red Thread bourbon. A good taste like apples and licorice, but hot, not on the rocks. His lips were soft, too, but insistent, like he was trying to win an argument by kissing her. She happily conceded defeat. Oh, and he smelled perfect to her. Sweat and aftershave and the leather and oil of horse tack. He smelled like a man who worked hard, even on Sundays. Sundays should be a day of rest, a day to spend in bed kissing. Kissing, and more than kissing…

It was the strangest thing, being kissed. His mouth was on her mouth. His tongue was between her teeth and nowhere else. His hands were on her hips holding her up. And yet she felt the kiss in all sorts of places she didn't expect. She felt it in her stomach, down deep. She felt it inside her pelvis and all along her thighs. She felt it in her breasts, which were pressed against his chest. A layer of shirt and bra separated her body from his and yet her nipples were hard and wanted touching and sucking. She was almost out of her mind enough to ask him to do it.

Tamara reached up and ran her hand through his hair. He might not like that, but she wanted to touch his hair, had wanted to touch it since she first saw it two years ago when she and her mother moved into the big house at Arden. Now that his mouth was occupied kissing her, she had the chance to do anything she wanted to do without hearing a protest song about it. She ran her fingers through his hair, loving its soft, thick texture. There was so much more of him she wanted to touch, too. She stroked his cheek, his strong neck, his shoulders. She'd give anything to get his clothes off and touch every part of him that touched her.

Tamara knew about sex from school, about things she'd heard from girls who'd gone all the way and had lived to tell the tale. But no one had ever told her what to do in this situation, when she felt an erection outside her clothes and wanted it inside her body. She didn't want to be a virgin anymore, and she wanted him to be the one to have it for what it was worth. To have *her*.

"Please do it, Levi…" she said into his ear.

"Only because it's your birthday." Levi cupped her breast and squeezed it and that was it—it was happening. Not even a stampede of the four horsemen could stop them now. He pushed the bra cup down, baring her nipple. He pinched it and she died. He lowered his mouth and licked it and she died again. Then he covered her breast with his hot mouth and sucked it and she died and was born again.

"What in God's name do you two think you're doing?"

Levi let Tamara down to the floor so fast her knees nearly

gave out under her. The horse anklet she'd draped over her wrist fell to the ground and into the hay. She yanked her coat tight around her chest and looked at Levi, but he wasn't looking back at her. He stared straight ahead.

There were three people in the universe and all its dimensions whom Tamara Maddox was afraid of. God and the Devil were two of the three and even God and the Devil ranked a distant second behind the one woman who could scare even Tamara Belle Maddox—she who got what she wanted when she wanted it because she wanted it—and that was the woman standing in the stables staring black ice at both her and Levi.

"Nothing, Momma."

5

"Nothing? That was not nothing."

Her mother's voice hit her like a bucket of cold water. Levi let her go and turned and stood in front of her, giving her a chance to straighten her clothes.

"We were just kissing, Momma," Tamara said, moving to Levi's side. "It's my birthday."

"Mrs. Maddox, I swear it was a quick little birthday kiss," Levi said. "Nothing more."

"You are dead, boy," her mother said. Her mother had never been fond of Granddaddy's stable hand, but right now she wished him dead and buried, and she looked perfectly willing to do it herself.

Levi's chin rose and his jaw set.

"What did you call me?" he asked.

"You heard me, boy. And if you ever lay a hand on my daughter again, what I call you will be the least of your problems." She grabbed Tamara by the arm and dragged her from the stables.

"Momma, stop—"

"Not a word," she said. "You wait until I tell your grand-daddy about this."

"What's he gonna care?"

Her mother had hellfire in her eyes and her face was set in granite. She looked as scared as she did angry.

"He'll care."

Her mother marched her from the stables, up the path and through the back door of the big house. She was so angry her hair vibrated like jelly, and considering the amount of White Rain she put in that blond aura every morning, any movement was a bad sign.

Well, this was perfect, wasn't it? Couldn't Tamara have one single day without her mother blowing up at her about something pointless? Yesterday she'd blown her top over Tamara saying "shit" at the dinner table. And Friday when she'd come home from her school in Louisville for Christmas break, Tamara had gotten screamed at for hauling nothing but dirty clothes back with her. Why her mother cared, Tamara didn't know. Not like Momma did any of the laundry. Cora, the housekeeper, did all the work. Her mother didn't work. Her mother never worked. Her mother might not know how to spell *work* if they were playing Scrabble and the only tiles she had were a *W*, an *O*, an *R* and a *K*. She'd probably say *crow* started with a *K*.

Inside the kitchen Tamara kicked off her muddy boots while her mother watched her. Tamara did her level best to ignore her, a feat she'd nearly perfected in the past three years since Daddy died and "angry" had become her mother's default expression, her go-to response to anything. In the beginning Tamara had taken each little slight, each cold reply, each insult, like a brick to her face. But after a few months Tamara had put those bricks to good use and built a wall—high, deep and wide—between her and her mother until she had a fortress of her own and her mother seemed like nothing so much as a villager throwing pebbles at the queen's castle. Of course, even when her father had been alive, her mother hadn't been much of a treat to live with. She and Daddy had whispered jokes to each other about her mother when she got in those moods. Daddy liked to say the Devil owed him a debt and Momma was how Satan paid him back.

Once Tamara's boots were off, her mother grabbed her by the arm and dragged her down the hallway. Arden was a massive home, a hundred-year-old Georgian-revival brick box. Every room a different color like the White House. Following her mother, Tamara passed her pink princess bedroom and the blue billiard room and the green dining room all the way to the red room on the right—her granddaddy's study. Upstairs her granddaddy had his office and for the life of her she couldn't figure out the difference between an office and a study except one had a desk and the other one didn't.

Inside his study her grandfather sat on a red-and-gold armchair, holding a tumbler of bourbon—probably a bourbon sour from the looks of it—in one hand and a newspaper in the other.

"I need to discuss something with you," her mother said.

"You always do, Virginia," Granddaddy said, turning a page in the newspaper without looking up.

"Granddaddy, Momma—" Tamara began, but her mother cut her off.

"You get to your room right now, and don't you dare step foot out of it until I tell you."

"What's going on here?" Now Granddaddy was paying attention. He laid the newspaper on his lap in a neat heap of pages. In the overcast afternoon light he didn't look much more than fifty years old, although he was well over sixty. He had a full head of hair and a face that reminded people of Lee Majors. Women called him the Six-Million-Dollar Man behind his back because they said that was probably how much money he kept in his wallet. Even sitting in his chair he looked big and strong and in control—the opposite of her twig-thin angry little mother.

"I caught your stable boy kissing my daughter," her mother said.

"Levi? Kissing Tamara?"

"I asked him to, since it's my birthday," Tamara said quickly. "That's all. Nothing else happened."

"And this is worth my time?" Her grandfather addressed the question to her mother, not her.

"It was more than a kiss. That boy was all over her."

"It was just a kiss," Tamara said, yelling the words, over-enunciating them like her mother was both slow and partially deaf.

"It was Levi Shelby, are you hearing me?" Her mother outyelled her. "Levi *Shelby*. I told you and told you not to have that boy around here. I told you and you didn't listen and you still aren't listening and you're gonna pay a big price for not listening to me someday."

Her granddaddy took a big old inhale and let out a big old exhale.

"I'm listening to you, Virginia."

"So what are you going to do about it?"

"Nothing," Tamara said. "There's nothing either of you have to do about it. It's my birthday. I asked Levi to kiss me. That's all that happened."

"Go to your room right this second," her mother ordered.

"But—"

"Go on, baby," Granddaddy said, waving his newspaper like he was shooing a dog from the room.

"Go." Her mother pointed a long white finger tipped in a long red fingernail at the door. Tamara left. She shut the door behind her and trudged down the hall, but slowly, slow enough she could hear them still talking. Her mother said, "This is all your fault," which was a classic Momma thing to say. How was Levi kissing her or her kissing Levi her grandfather's fault?

Tamara went into her bedroom and sat on the bed, waiting and trying not to cry. She'd been given the only downstairs bedroom when they'd moved in and as a "treat" to her they'd had it painted pink, since that was a color sure to please a girl. It didn't please her. It was Pepto-Bismol pink and it caused her more stomachaches than it cured.

Finally her bedroom door swung open and slammed shut. Her mother stood before her, hands on hips. Tamara stared at the floor.

"So…how long has this been going on?" she asked.

"What's going on?"

"Answer me," her mother said.

"Nothing's going on. I told you, I asked Levi to kiss me because it's my birthday. He did. That's all."

"Did he touch you?"

"Well, his lips touched me."

"Did he touch you under your clothes?"

"No, Momma." Tamara groaned and rolled her eyes. "We kissed. That's all. I'm sixteen. Am I not allowed to kiss boys?"

"You aren't allowed to do anything. Nothing. Nothing without my permission or your granddaddy's."

"Fine. Get Granddaddy in here. We'll ask him if I'm allowed to kiss a boy on my birthday."

"You can ask him about Levi Shelby, but you're not gonna like his answer."

Her mother stood with her arms crossed, her high-heeled brown leather boot tapping on the hardwood floor. Once, Virginia Maddox had been a real beauty. Tamara had seen the pictures. But she wore too much makeup and dyed her Farrah Fawcett hair until it was dry and cracking. Most days she looked well-put-together, but on days like this Tamara could see the seams showing.

"Tamara, I'm going to tell you something you're not going to like to hear, but you better hear it."

"What?"

"You have one role to play in this family," she said. "Only one. Your uncle Eric is dead. And your daddy, Nash, is dead. You are the only Maddox left after your grandfather's gone. I know you think this makes you special. And I know you think this means you can get away with murder if you feel like it. But it doesn't. It means the opposite. It means you don't get to do anything and everything you want to do. It means you have to fill your role because there's no one else to do the job you need to do. And you better believe if you don't shape up and grow up and do what your grandfather tells you to do, you will end up with nothing. I will not let you screw this up, not after all I've put up with."

"I'm only sixteen. What am I supposed to do?"

"You know. You've always known."

Tamara sighed. "I know. I have to get married. I have to have babies." She knew this. She had known this for years now. Two years ago she wanted to get a Dorothy Hamill haircut and her mother had told her no way—girls who wanted husbands did not have short hair. "I have to keep Red Thread alive, blah blah blah."

"Yes, you do. And you have no choice in the matter."

"I don't have a choice in any matter. You don't give me a choice. Granddaddy doesn't give me a choice. I might as well be in prison for all the choices I have."

"You want a choice?"

"I'd love a choice," Tamara said.

"Fine. Here's your choice. You can pick between Kermit or Levi. How's that for a choice?"

"What do you mean pick between them?"

"I mean, I'm going to fire Levi or I'm going to sell Kermit to the glue factory. So what's it going to be?"

"You can't do that. You can't make me fire Levi or kill my horse. You can't..." Tamara's voice broke on the words.

"Oh, I can. I can and I will and not even your granddaddy will try to stop me. And you know what? It's for your own good and you don't even know it."

"It's not for my own good. It's for your own good."

"Pick, princess. You wanted a choice. I'm giving you a choice."

"I'm not going to choose between Levi and Kermit. I will not." Tamara stood up and crossed her arms over her chest. "I absolutely will not do that."

"Both, then. Levi gets fired and I sell Kermit. Hell, maybe I'll take your granddaddy's revolver out of his desk and put that damn horse down right now."

"Momma—" Tamara choked on her tears. She took a step forward, arms out, beseeching her mother to relent.

"Oh, don't even try that baby-girl routine on me," her mother said, shaking her head so hard her dangling gold-and-diamond earrings clinked like tiny bells. "You won't talk me out of this. You don't even know what you're getting into with Levi. So decide and decide right now. You got three seconds to tell me—Kermit or Levi. One…"

"But Daddy gave me Kermit."

"Your daddy gave himself a bullet in the brain, so your daddy don't get a say in this. Two…"

"Momma, no. Please don't make me."

"Kermit or Levi. Tell me now."

"You," Tamara said. "You go take Granddaddy's revolver and you put yourself down, and me and Kermit and Levi will ride off into the sunset, you nasty old bitch."

Her mother slapped her. Hard. So hard Tamara gasped and nearly fell on her side.

"Momma…" Tamara choked out a sob. She pressed her hand to her cheek and felt the heat of pain and shame.

"One of these days, Tamara, I swear…you're going to get what you want and it'll be the last thing you want."

Her mother turned and left, slamming the door behind her hard enough the pictures rattled in the frames. Tamara panted on the bed, her cheek stinging, her whole body burning with rage. And where was her mother going?

"Kermit…"

Tamara ripped her bedroom door open and tore down the hall after her mother. She knew her mother was going to shoot her horse. She knew it. The carpet scalded her naked feet as she raced toward the front door. It was too late; her mother was already out of the house. But she wasn't heading to the stables, but to her Cadillac parked in the U-bend of the drive-way. The car door slammed. The headlights flickered on and Tamara watched as the car—seemingly driverless behind the steamed-up windows—wended its way toward the main road.

Kermit wasn't who Momma was after. Levi. Momma was

going after Levi. What would she do? Go to the police and report him for molesting Tamara? Go to his home and fire him to his face? What was happening? Where was she going?

"Momma…come back," Tamara whispered under her breath. If Tamara apologized, she could talk her mother out of it. If she swore to be good, if she swore she'd never go out to the stables again alone with Levi there…

"You're letting the heat out, baby girl."

Tamara turned around and saw her grandfather standing in the doorway of his study looking at her.

"Momma left. Do you know where she went?"

"I asked her to give us some time alone to talk. I think you two have had enough of each other for the day."

"She said I had to pick between Levi keeping his job and Kermit. She said she'd shoot my horse. She can't do that, can she?"

"You try to stop her."

"She can't fire Levi. Not for kissing me. Kissing isn't a crime." Burning tears, hot as steaming tea, ran down her face.

He walked over to her, so big and so strong, and wrapped her in his arms, his warm Granddaddy arms. He held her as she cried against his chest, not holding back, letting the tears flow and flow. Maybe her tears could touch his heart. Maybe her despair would convince him of just how evil her mother was acting. If her grandfather put his foot down with her mother, he could save Kermit and Levi. If… On and on she cried, on and on until she was half-sick from it and coughed.

"Enough of that now. Enough." He stroked her back and her hair.

"I'm sorry."

"Don't be sorry. You go and take a long hot bath and put on your nightgown. I'll bring you something to help you calm down and we can talk this out." He put his fingertips under her chin and lifted her face.

"What's gonna help me calm down? A hammer to my head?"

"I'll find us something real good. No hammers." He winked. "Go on now. I'll come to your room when you're done. You and I need to have a long talk."

"About what?"

"Your mother and I made a decision about you today. We both decided it was high time you started earning some of what you've been given. Your mother's idea, not mine. But if she says I gotta, I gotta. You know how your mother is."

"What am I supposed to earn?" Tamara asked. She was only sixteen. Not like she could get a job or anything. What did they want from her?

"It's high time you earn your place in this family. Your mother thinks you're getting a bit too big for your britches. She told me to take you down a peg or two."

"I'm down all the pegs I can go down."

"Now, you and I both know that's not true. Lot of girls would kill to wear your boots, Tamara. You're a lucky girl and you take a lot of what we give you for granted. Your mother wants you to step up a little, start doing more around this house, doing more in this family, doing more for me."

"I'll do whatever she wants, I promise. Long as she doesn't fire Levi or kill Kermit."

He cupped her face in his big warm hand.

"That's my girl."

6

Bonnie Tyler's voice crooned on the radio and Tamara sang along. "It's a Heartache" was her new favorite song. She was long overdue for one, having worn out her 45 of "Dreams" by Fleetwood Mac weeks ago. Tamara sang along softly as she dried off with a plush pink towel. Granddaddy was a smart man. Taking a long hot bath had definitely made her feel better. When Momma came back, Tamara would tell her how sorry she was. Then she'd offer to be grounded from riding Kermit for as long as her mother said. That should take care of that. Kermit could stay and Levi could stay. Tamara would avoid the stables for a month, two months, six months…whatever term her mother deemed sufficient. It would all blow over once Tamara took all the blame.

She heard the door to her bedroom open and shut and she reached out her hand fast as she could to lock the bathroom door. She didn't even have any clothes on yet.

"You finished, baby?" Granddaddy called out.

"Not yet."

Tamara pulled on her panties and her nightshirt. The shirt didn't go two inches past her bottom, so she had to put on the stupid ugly old-lady housecoat she'd gotten for Christmas last year that her mother insisted she wear over her nightclothes. Tamara usually ignored that order. The thing was ugly as sin and it would be a sin to wear it. With a mandarin collar that buttoned at the throat and a hem that landed all the way down around her ankles, it looked like a nun's habit in pink. But it was either this or go traipsing around the room in her underwear in front of her grandfather. Neither one of them wanted that.

She quickly braided her wet hair and with towel in hand emerged into her bedroom. Granddaddy sat on the window seat with a bottle in front of him and two glasses.

"Is Momma back yet?" Tamara asked as she walked over to the window. The soft rain had turned to a hard rain. It had rained all week and Tamara wasn't sure if she'd ever see the sun again.

"She's not coming home tonight."

"What? Why not?"

Was her mother that angry with her? That wasn't a good sign.

"She knows you and I need to have a long talk." Granddaddy uncapped the bottle of Red Thread he'd brought in with him. "She's going to stay at the little inn in town. Just you and me tonight."

"Are we safe here? The news said the river's overflowing."

He shook his head as he poured a finger of bourbon into one glass and two fingers of bourbon into the other. He set the two fingers in front of her.

"Don't you worry about that. This house has stood for over a hundred years with the river right behind us. We'll make it another hundred."

"If you say so," she said, not sure she trusted his judgment as implicitly as he did. Granddaddy was the richest man in the state and everyone knew it. People bent to his will all day long—she'd seen it with her own eyes. He'd get pulled over for speeding and the cop would look at his license, laugh and let him off with a warning. Restaurant owners would bring him drinks on the house. One hotel he stayed at in Louisville assigned him his own personal concierge to fetch and carry for him. People were one thing, but something told her the river wouldn't bend to his will quite so readily. The river had been here before Granddaddy and it would be here after.

"You've had quite a day, haven't you, little lady?" He took up twice as much room as she did on the window seat.

"Happy Birthday to me, right?"

"Want to tell me what's going with you and ole Levi?"

"Nothing's going on with me and ole Levi."

Granddaddy raised his eyebrows and his glass. He took a sip and so did she, wincing. She'd had a taste of bourbon here and there—the house was full of the stuff—but she hadn't had nearly enough to get used to it yet. She hadn't even figured out coffee yet.

"Your mother claims she caught you two rolling in the hay."

She flushed crimson. Bad enough talking about Levi with her mother. If she had a shovel, she would dig her own grave with it right now.

"There was hay, but no rolling," she said. "I asked him to kiss me on my birthday, and he kissed me on my birthday. Tomorrow's not my birthday, so he won't kiss me tomorrow."

"You sound a little disappointed about that."

She shrugged and sat back, her arms clutching her pillow. When she exhaled through her nose, the window turned into a cloud.

"You like him?" her granddaddy asked her. He reached out and pinched her toe. How drunk was he? Very, she guessed. Very very. "Tamara, answer me?"

She laughed at the toe pinch. "Yes, I like him."

"How much do you like him?"

"I don't know. A lot?" She finally met her grandfather's eyes. He was smiling, but the smile didn't make her feel any better. This was the last conversation in the history of conversations she wanted to be having with her grandfather.

"A lot, huh?" Granddaddy sat back and kicked his boots off. They landed on the little pink rug by her rocking chair and left a boot polish stain. She didn't care. She was so sick of pink she was ready to burn the house down to get rid of it all.

"A lot. More than a lot, whatever that is."

"I've noticed you and him talking before."

"Only talking."

"He dotes on you."

"He does not. He's mean to me. He tells me I'm lazy and he makes me muck the stalls and he says I'm spoiled rotten. He even calls me Rotten. I don't think he's ever called me by my name."

"I used to call your grandmother Ornery because she was the orneriest woman I ever met. Drove me crazy when she was younger. I couldn't keep my hands off her."

"Granddaddy, really. I don't want to hear any of that at all, now or ever."

"You're old enough now to hear about things you don't want to hear about."

"I still don't want to hear about them."

He sighed and nodded.

"Such a pretty girl you've turned into," he said. "I'm surprised Levi's the only boy we've had trouble with over you."

"Y'all send me to an all-girls school, remember?"

"It's a good school."

"It's an all-*girls* school," she said again.

"I went to an all-boys school, Millersburg Military. Best school in the state."

"Great. Can I go there instead?"

"And you wonder why we try to keep a close eye on you," he said, giving her a smile. "Maybe we should have kept a closer eye."

"Momma's only mad because she hates Levi for no good reason."

"She has good reason."

"I know he's older than me, but he's not that much older. And he's good with the horses. And Momma said either I had to let her fire Levi or she'd give Kermit to the glue factory. I can't live without Levi. I can't live without Kermit. Is she trying to kill me?"

"You won't die without Levi."

"Maybe I will," she said. She might. Stranger things had happened. "I don't get why Momma hates him anyway, other than I think she hates everybody."

Granddaddy sighed another one of his Granddaddy sighs. She smelled cigar and bourbon in that sigh. She wanted to open the window.

"There's something you don't know about Levi you need to know. Long time ago, Levi's mother used to work for me. She cleaned the Red Thread offices."

"She was a janitor?"

"Cleaning lady."

Tamara felt a stab of pity for Levi. Growing up the son of a cleaning lady must not have been easy. She knew his mother was already dead, but he'd never mentioned that she used to clean for Granddaddy. "Momma hates him because his mother used to be a cleaning lady?"

"Tamara, honey, his mother was black. You didn't know that?"

Tamara narrowed her eyes at her grandfather.

"What?"

"She was."

"But he's—"

"He's light skinned. But he's not white."

There wasn't a word to express Tamara's shock.

"But how—"

"His daddy was white," Granddaddy said with a shrug. "Happens sometimes. And you never know which way the baby will go—light or dark or a mix of both."

"But he's got blue eyes. That's a recessive trait. We learned about it in biology. I had to do a Mendel chart on eye color. He'd have to be white on both sides to have blue eyes."

Granddaddy chuckled again and she didn't know what he found so funny. She didn't find this a bit funny at all. Her mother hated Levi because his mother was black? That was the worst thing she'd ever heard in her life.

The worst thing.

Ever.

In her life.

"Most of them have a little white way back. Our doing, of course. That doesn't make him white, though. My parents were both right-handed and here I am, a lefty. You think my momma was stepping out with the milkman?"

Tamara ignored the question. Her mother had called Levi "boy" and Levi had seemed to take more offense at that than Tamara thought made sense. She got called "girl" all the time,

but even she knew there was a big difference between calling
a white boy "boy" and a black boy "boy."

"That's why Momma hates Levi?"

"She is not very happy about his parentage, we'll say that."

"I don't care if he's part black or part red or part green. I
don't care who his mother was, or his father. If his father was
Hitler and his mother was Diana Ross, I wouldn't care at all."

She might care, but only because she really liked Diana
Ross.

"But I care who your mother is. And who your father is."

"I don't."

"You do and you know you do. You're a Maddox and that
means something. You're special, Tamara."

"I don't see why. Not like I had any choice in it."

"Doesn't matter. The Queen of England was born the
Queen of England. She can't change being queen, but she can
decide what kind of queen she's going to be—a good queen
or a bad queen. And you have the same choice."

"Okay, I'll be the Queen of England, then."

"You'll be something better than that. You'll be my queen.
And you will run the whole kingdom of Red Thread. You
and me, Tamara, we're special. We're the only two people on
this earth with Jacob Maddox's blood in our veins. Did you
know that?"

"I know," she said, but she still didn't see that it made them
very special. She'd never met Jacob Maddox, the man who'd
founded the Red Thread Bourbon Distillery. He'd been dead
forever. And apart from starting the family business, she didn't
know anything about him.

"I wish there were more of us. But your grandmother was
fragile up here," he said, tapping his forehead. "And her health
wasn't too good, either. After two sons, we had to stop. Then

she had her stroke and I can't remarry, not that I'd want to," he said, although she sensed he did want to, wanted to very much. She would if she were him anyway, and God knew half the single ladies in the county were counting the seconds until Granddaddy was back on the market. "Your uncle Eric died over in Vietnam before he could get married and start his family. And your daddy, of course…"

"Right. Daddy." Daddy was dead and had been dead for three years, five months and sixteen days. But who was counting?

"We'd hoped he and your mother would have a big family, but that wasn't to be, either."

"I don't think they liked each other too much," Tamara said, which was both true and wasn't. Granddaddy had liked to tease her mother sometimes about the babies she hadn't contributed to the Maddox family tree and Daddy would tell him to back off and leave her alone, which Granddaddy would counter with "If you didn't leave her alone, we wouldn't have to have this conversation." She'd never figured her mother and father out. They were friendly and yet they seemed like the last two people on earth who should have been married to each other. "He must not have liked me much, either, since he killed himself."

"He loved you," he said, although Tamara wondered. Did men who really loved their daughters shoot themselves in the head and leave them to fend for themselves with a crazy mother?

"I loved him, too. I miss him." She clutched her pink pillow even tighter to her chest.

"I know you do. We all do. I can't even tell you how many times I've thought about how good it was to hold him in my arms after he was born. And Eric, too. My boys. My beautiful boys. I'd give anything to have that again—a new son of my own. Anything at all. Do you feel like that about something? That you'd give anything to have it?"

"I'd give anything to have Daddy back."

That answer seemed to surprise him.

"Well, yes. You and me both, sweetheart."

She wasn't sure she believed him and she felt bad about that. Granddaddy talked about her uncle Eric all the time—handsome, strong, smart, the son of any man's dreams. But Nash? Her father? Granddaddy almost never talked about him unless someone else brought him up.

"I wish Momma would come back, too," she said. But from the looks of the dark and the wet and the new rain coming down, it didn't appear her mother was coming back anytime soon. She found her grandfather looking at her, studying her. He'd been doing that more lately, watching her. Sometimes it didn't feel like his gaze was on her so much as his hands. She liked it when Levi looked at her. But not even he looked at her like this.

"Angel, I know it's not easy being a Maddox. Sometimes we have to do things we don't want to do. Your grandmother wanted to go to college instead of getting married. But her family had money trouble, so she got married. You do what you have to do for your family. Like Jacob Maddox."

"What about him?"

"My grandfather Jacob Maddox got married for money, too. Married a lady named Henrietta Arden. That's why this house is called Arden, because we wouldn't have it but for her."

"Did we get all our money from his wife?"

"No, ma'am. She got ole Jacob out of debt, but the real money? He made that all by himself. Back before Red Thread existed, Jacob had a hemp and tobacco plantation. That was the original Arden. Jacob, as it sometimes happened in those days, fell in with one of the slave girls. Her name was Veritas, but they called her Vera for short. They did love to give out fancy names to their slaves, and she was a fancy girl. Her mother had worked in the kitchens before she died and Vera had taken over her work. The house girls had to dress nice and look nice and act nice. Vera always wore a red ribbon in her hair. One morning Jacob decided he'd rather have Vera for breakfast than steak and eggs."

Her grandfather chuckled again over the rim of his glass before taking another sip. Tamara was getting real tired of that chuckle.

"But Henrietta was not especially pleased when Vera's belly started getting real big and it wasn't because they were overfeeding the girl. One day Jacob went out of town on business, and while he was gone, what did Henrietta do? She sold little Vera. Sold her for a good price. The man who bought her got a good deal—two for the price of one."

Tamara only stared at the bourbon in her glass. She didn't want to drink it anymore.

"You can't sell people," Tamara said quietly.

"Oh, but you could back then. They say Jacob saw every shade of red when he came home to find nothing left of his favorite girl and his baby but the red ribbon she always wore in her hair and a thousand dollars he hadn't had before. But he didn't cry long. You know what he did with that money?"

"Started Red Thread?"

"That's right. He started Red Thread. He bought a still, bought some corn and got to work making this family the wealthiest family in the state. But you know what? He must have loved that girl Vera, because when he started the bourbon distillery, he put a red ribbon around the neck of every bottle in her memory. Put her red ribbon on the very first bottle. We still have that bottle locked up in my office."

"Can I see it?"

"Maybe later," he said. She wasn't allowed in Granddaddy's office upstairs. No one was. "It's been handed down from one Maddox son to the next. It'll be your son's someday."

"We still have the ribbon?" Tamara asked, wanting to see it for some reason, wanting to have it. She should have it, and her granddaddy shouldn't.

"We do. That red ribbon is what made us our money. Wives would tell their husbands, 'Honey, go and buy some of that Red Thread bourbon because I want that pretty ribbon.' Jacob Maddox was a smart man. Must have been a romantic, too. Red ribbon on every bottle? He must have loved that girl."

"Or maybe loved waving that red ribbon in his wife's face," Tamara said.

"Well…maybe he loved doing that, too."

"What happened to Veritas?" Tamara asked.

"Oh, hell, I don't know." Granddaddy waved his hand dismissively. "They sold her, and she wasn't too happy about it. They say she swore at Mrs. Maddox, vowing she would come back someday and cut us off at our roots. She would end our line if it was the last thing she did. As you can see," Granddaddy said, pointing at himself with his thumb, "that prophecy didn't quite come to pass. Although we haven't had the luck with babies as I'd hoped we'd have."

"I guess not," she said, feeling sick at her stomach. Was it the bourbon? She'd barely sipped it. Or was it Veritas screaming curses at Tamara's great-great-grandmother all those years ago? Poor Veritas. They hadn't even let her keep her red ribbon when they sold her.

"The Maddoxes are blessed and cursed all at once," he said,

pouring himself another shot of the Red Thread. "God gives us wealth and prosperity with one hand and takes away the children we need to carry on the line with the other."

"It's too bad," she said. She felt for her grandfather. He'd had a brother and sister, but his sister had polio and didn't make it past thirty and his brother hadn't lived past age ten— scarlet fever.

"A man shouldn't have to bury his own sons."

And a girl shouldn't have to bury her father. That wasn't right, either. Nothing seemed right tonight.

Her grandfather lifted the glass to his lips. He lowered it before he took a drink.

"Are you going to let Momma fire Levi?" she asked.

"Your mother seemed quite intent on it."

"Because we kissed?"

"For starters."

"If you don't fire him, I promise I won't ever kiss him again."

He smiled and laughed. "You know you don't mean that. I think you want to kiss him again. And I don't think you want to be good, either."

"Does anybody want to be good?"

"You oughta want to be good."

"But I'm not good. I asked Levi to kiss me. He wouldn't have done it otherwise."

"I don't know about that. I think he would have done it eventually."

"Please, Granddaddy, don't let her fire him for something I asked him to do."

"I'm probably gonna have to let him go to shut your mother up. She is not a happy camper today."

"She's never a happy camper. She should quit camping."

Tamara giggled, but it was a miserable sound even to her own ears. A few tears hit her cheeks and she couldn't swipe them off fast enough.

"What, angel? What's wrong?" he asked.

"I don't want Levi to get fired. That's all. And I don't want Momma to send away Kermit to punish me." And she didn't want her father to be dead and her mother to be so angry all the time. She should have asked for those things for her birthday instead of the stupid car. "I'll move to Arizona. That's what I'll do. I'll go live with Grandma and Grandpa Darling and then Levi can keep his job and Kermit can stay here with Levi."

It was a good idea. No, it was a great idea. Soon as she said it, she knew that was what she'd do. Soon as her mother came home, she'd tell her the idea. She'd go away for a semester, live with her other grandparents, and her mother would miss her so much that she'd give up this crazy awful idea of firing Levi and selling Kermit.

"Come here, sweetheart. Come over here." He held out his arms to her and reluctantly Tamara crawled into them and rested her head against her grandfather's chest. He felt warm and solid and harmless. She could smell the bourbon on his breath and the cigar he liked to smoke in the evenings. Grandfather-type smells. "I'm not letting you move to Arizona. No, ma'am."

"Why not?"

"Because you're a Maddox and you're my girl. Listen...do you have any idea how lucky you are?" he asked, rubbing her back. "You almost weren't a Maddox, you know."

She raised her head and looked up at Granddaddy in shock.

"What do you mean?"

"I mean, you were born six months after your momma and daddy got married. You know that much, right?"

"Well…yeah. I can do math."

"Now don't get me wrong, Nash loved you. But he did not want to marry your mother. It was the last thing he wanted to do. I had to twist his arm a little."

"How?" She hadn't ever heard this part of the story.

"When talking to the boy didn't get his head on straight, I threatened to disown him. Your mother was carrying the next Maddox and there he was, being stubborn as a mule. He finally gave in after we made a little trade. There's an island off the coast of South Carolina where we grow our trees. All the trees that make up the barrels we use for aging Red Thread. He said he wanted the island, so I gave it to him as a wedding gift. Then he married your mother. And so you were a Maddox the day you were born. You could have been a Darling, no Daddy, no Granddaddy, no nothing. That's why I say you're a lucky girl. Things could have gone very different for you, angel."

Tamara couldn't say a word. Her father had been so against marrying her mother he had to be bought off with an entire island? And if he hadn't given in, she wouldn't have had a father? Her grandparents on her mother's side did okay for themselves. Grandpa Darling had been a bank president here in Frankfort until he retired and moved out to Arizona for the weather. As religious as they were, they probably would have kicked Momma out for having a child out of wedlock. Was that why her mother put up with Granddaddy? Because she knew he'd been the only thing standing between her and poverty?

"Daddy didn't want to be my father?" she finally asked.

"Oh, he did. But not until you were born. The second you

were born, everything changed. Love at first sight. You were his girl from day one."

That made Tamara smile. She'd always known her mother and grandfather had been disappointed she'd been a girl. At least one person in this family had been happy she'd been born a girl. Other than her, that is.

"Aren't you glad you're a Maddox?" Granddaddy asked. She knew what she was supposed to answer.

"Yes, I am."

"Being a Maddox means something in this state. Something important. We are the first family of Kentucky in a lot of ways. We've been here since before the state was a state. We've had governors in the family, senators. Since before the Civil War we've had the distillery. Only four distilleries were allowed to stay open during Prohibition and we were one of them. Even the federal government wouldn't dare shut us down. And we make bourbon and bourbon is a perfect drink. Nothing like it. The problem with perfection is that's not something we little human beings were born for. Perfection comes from heaven and we're here on earth. So when you have something perfect like our family and our legacy and our bourbon, we have to pay a toll on it."

"A toll?"

"That's what the angels' share is. We put fifty-three gallons of bourbon into each barrel to age. And the angels come drink their fill of it. Like paying taxes. So by the time we open that barrel up to sell the bourbon, nearly half is gone. That's why we lose so many Maddox boys in this family. Things aren't supposed to be perfect this side of heaven. And now that there's only two of us left in the world—you and me—we better stick together before the angels come and get us. Right?"

"Right," she said, nodding against the warm flannel of his chest.

"You know, your mother only wants what's best for you. You worry her and that worry keeps her up at night."

"Why's she worried?"

"Because you're the only Maddox grandchild. She wants you to do right by the family, and she's worried you won't."

"I'll do whatever I'm supposed to do. She doesn't have to worry."

"She wants me to leave everything to you in my will. She thinks I won't do it because you're a girl, and we've always left the company to the oldest boy in the family." He picked up her braid and tickled her nose with the end of it.

"Is that why you two fight all the time?" Tamara looked up at him.

"You know about the fighting?"

"You two don't hide it very well. You're fighting because Momma thinks you're going to disown me for being a girl?"

"We fight for a lot of reasons, but none that need to worry you. And you don't need to worry about anything. As things stand today, when I die, you'll inherit everything. The company, the house, the land, all of it. Now, I'm hoping by the time I kick the bucket, you'll have had a baby boy or two, but you make no mistake, Granddaddy's going to take care of you."

"You're not going to die anytime soon," Tamara said. "You're going to live for twenty or thirty years, and I'll get married someday and have kids. Then we'll have a boy in the family again, since that's what everyone wants."

"I'm not getting any younger. But even at my age a man has needs, things he wants to accomplish, things he wants to achieve. Now I've got money enough for a hundred men, you know what I really want?"

Tamara didn't know.

Suddenly Tamara didn't want to know.

"What I want is another son and to see him grow up."

"It must be hard for you with Grandma in the nursing home."

"I'm sure it's harder for her than it is for me. If there's anything left of her in there anymore. Not sure that there is."

Tamara knew better than to suggest he get divorced. If there was anything that would tarnish the family name, it would be her grandfather divorcing his invalid wife so he could get remarried to any one of the fluttering young things who multiplied like fruit flies around him whenever he went out on the town.

"I wish there was something we could do," she said. "I wish there was a way we could fix everything."

If she had a magic wand, she'd wave it and her father would be alive again, and her uncle Eric, whom she'd never met. Her mother would be kind and loving instead of bitter and angry. Her grandmother would be healed and could walk and talk again instead of sitting all day in a wheelchair in a fancy nursing home that smelled like a morgue. And she'd wave it one last time and she and Levi would magically be together and that kiss they'd kissed today would be the beginning of a very good story.

"Actually, there is something we could do," her grandfather said. "Something you and I can do. And even better, it's something your mother wants us to do. And if you're game for it, we'll make sure Levi keeps his job here and you don't have to go to Arizona and you can keep Kermit and your momma will be very, very happy for once in her damn life. How does that sound?"

"Sounds good to me," she said. "Whatever it is, I'll do it."

"I know you will, angel," he said.

Then Granddaddy kissed her.

7

Tamara's entire body, her entire being, recoiled as her grandfather's bourbon-laced mouth came down onto hers. She tried to wrench herself from him, but he grasped her upper arms and wouldn't let her budge. A sound came out the back of her throat, a sound like squealing tires, and a scream that couldn't escape.

His lips felt huge on hers, as if they could and would devour her in a bite if he tried. His stubble scraped her face painfully and it itched like poison ivy. Panic set in. Tamara thrashed and writhed in his arms like a cat in a trap, but he had her and wasn't letting her go.

She became aware of her feet then, sliding across the hardwood floor and then the rug under the bed. They were moving not of her own accord. With a tug and a pull, her grandfather dragged her bodily to the bed.

"Calm down, girl," he said, soothing her like a wild pony. "Calm down. I'm not gonna hurt you."

But he'd already hurt her. Nothing he could do or say would unhurt her.

She tried yanking her arms free of his hands, but he merely tightened his grip. It felt like he was cutting the circulation off to her lower arms he held her so firm and fast. She went limp as a corpse. If he dropped her, she could maybe get away. But despite his age, he was still strong as a stallion.

"Please don't, please don't, please don't…" She chanted the words like a magic spell, but they had no effect on him. He hoisted her off her feet with all the ceremony and gentleness he used when throwing bags of horse feed into the back of his truck and pushed her onto the bed. With one hand he held her arms over her head onto the pillows; with his free hand he loosened his belt buckle.

"Tamara, you have got to calm down." He used his most grandfatherly tone on her—chiding and slightly exasperated. She'd gotten stung by a bee when she'd been little and had screamed so hard everyone thought she was dying. Those were his words back then when trying to get her to surrender her hysterics. "You'll hurt yourself if you keep fighting. Calm down and, I promise, it'll be over fast."

"Please don't do this. I don't want to do this."

"Yes, you do, baby." He nodded his head, but still he straddled her hips and sat on her thighs to still the frantic kicking of her legs. "You said you did."

"I don't want to anymore." She wept the words and choked on them. She could hear her own voice and it sounded alien to her, foreign. She'd never heard herself scream like this, never heard herself cry like this, never heard herself pray to every god and goddess anyone had ever put their faith in to save her from what was about to happen to her. "Please…" She thrashed and squirmed. Tears scored her face, sticky and hot.

"We only got to do it a few times." He ran his hand through her hair, gently, ignoring her thrashing, ignoring her pain.

"I can marry somebody. I can find somebody. I'll have his baby right away. I swear to God I will." Maybe she could bargain her way out of this. She'd marry any man on earth right now to get away from this moment, from this man.

"It's gotta be me, angel. It has to be me. But once you're pregnant, we'll get you married and get you set up in a nice house. And you can have anything and everything you want. That sounds all right, doesn't it? You won't have to live with your momma anymore. I know you'll like that. You can even marry Levi, and won't that make your momma mad." He chuckled then like he'd made a joke. A joke.

Somewhere inside Tamara, somewhere deep inside, something clicked. Or maybe it didn't click. Maybe it snapped. A switch flipped. A light went on. A match was struck. A fuse lit. Something burned, something smoldered.

Something exploded.

…you better believe if you don't shape up and grow up and do what your grandfather tells you to do, you will end up with nothing. I will not let you screw this up, not after all I've put up with.

It's high time you earn your place in this family. Your mother thinks you're getting a bit too big for your britches. She told me to take you down a peg or two.

This was why Momma left and didn't come back. This was why. Because her mother had sold her, sold her out to her own grandfather. Sold her body to him in exchange for Red Thread. Her mother…that coward, that bitch, had driven away, leaving her alone with him so she didn't have to hear her daughter's screams. And her grandfather, this vile piece of shit, was going to rape her until she was knocked up and he could marry her off. He wanted a baby boy so bad he was going to make her have it for him. He would fuck her until she gave him one. If the first baby was a girl, he'd fuck her again and again and again. All for his dirty kingdom. If she could, she'd burn to the ground, right here and right now. She wanted fire, fire everywhere. She wanted her grandfather burning in hell and her mother burning right next to him and the house burning down, taking all of Red Thread with it.

Tamara pushed against her grandfather's chest as hard as she could. Then she saw something.

A brown pool of water crept in under the door. She noticed it first. Her grandfather was too preoccupied undoing his pants to notice anything. But when he turned his head, he saw it, too.

"What the hell?" he said, his brow furrowed in frustration and confusion. For one second he looked the other way. For one second his mind wasn't on her and what he was doing. For one second the water rapidly rushing into the room was more important than anything, even this.

That one second was all Tamara needed.

With her free hand she grabbed the lamp off the nightstand and smashed it against his head. He screamed and blood burst from his temple. In a daze he slumped onto his side, his hand over the bleeding wound, swearing and blinking, and Tamara wriggled her way out from under his bulk. Frantically she looked around for a weapon—anything would do—and saw a heavy silver candlestick on top of the dresser. Two inches of water surrounded her ankles as she stood up off the bed. Two inches and rising fast. The candlestick was heavy and square— art deco, a gift from her grandmother—and when she slammed it down onto her granddaddy's head, it made a soft and awful thudding sound. He keeled over, not moving, not a muscle.

A gust of wind brushed across her body, lifting her hair.

Ice-cold wind like someone had left the door open to winter and called it inside.

Tamara stood there and giggled a little. She'd gone to a slumber party two weeks ago and they'd played Clue. Miss Scarlet in the bedroom with the candlestick...

Noises came from the side of the house, jarring her from her delirium—something falling over, something else cracking and wood splintering like a door coming off the hinges. The water in the house was a foot high now, muddy and stinking and ice-cold. The shattered remains of the lamp covered the bed like glitter. In the window seat sat the bottle of Red Thread. Tamara picked it up and smashed it against the wall. The red ribbon around its neck fell into the water. She fished it out and grabbed her grandfather's hand, twisting the ribbon around his index finger. He moaned and Tamara gasped. The water reached her knees.

Tamara grasped her grandfather by the ankles and dragged him off the bed. She couldn't get any traction at first, but terror gave her strength. She tugged and lugged and pulled. His penis hung out of his unzipped pants like a fat earthworm. If she had garden shears handy, she would cut it off his body.

With one final yank on his belt loops, Tamara heaved him off the bed into the cold dirty water. And then, because she knew she had no other choice if she wanted to survive this night, she grabbed two fistfuls of his Lee Majors hair and shoved his head under the water.

Some part of his brain must have registered what was happening to him. He thrashed hard after the first inhale of muck, but she had the advantage now and wasn't going to lose it. She held him down until he stopped moving and, to be on the safe side, long after he stopped moving.

When it was done, she stood there looking at him there

in the water, floating, seaworthy as a garbage bag. He didn't look like a person anymore.

From the other room came a screeching sound—the river rearranging the furniture. Tamara ripped the silky pink cover off her bed and shook the broken glass out of it. Wrapping it around herself like a shawl, she waded through the now knee-deep water to the door. The house had gone mad. Chairs floated. Papers and books bobbed on the surface like toy boats. The smell of sewage permeated the air. Somewhere a light flickered and Tamara had a new fear then—electrocution. She heard a squeak and saw movement in the water—a gray rat swimming down the hall to save itself. Panicking, Tamara forced her way past a china cabinet now turned on its side and floating and made it to the stairs. She rushed upstairs to the bathroom and hit her knees in front of the toilet. For what felt like an hour she wretched and vomited. She threw up so hard her throat tore and she urinated on herself. She could taste blood in her mouth.

Then the lights went out.

Tamara blinked, letting her eyes adjust to the dark. With the pink blanket around her again, she dragged herself to her feet and felt her way down the hall to her grandfather's office. It faced the highway instead of the river. If the water kept rising, it would be the last room to flood. The door wasn't locked, and if it had been, she would have busted the door down for the pleasure of breaking something. Inside the office she saw a black box on the desk. In the dark the telephone looked like a cat curled up and sleeping. Should she call for help? She didn't know. She'd been warned once not to touch the telephone in a storm, but it wasn't lightning. Carefully she picked up the receiver. The line was dead. She was all alone in the house with her grandfather's dead body.

Tamara went to the window. The lawn was gone. The manicured horse pastures crisscrossed with white board fences—gone. Cobblestone driveway—gone. The stone fence built long before the Civil War by slave labor—gone. Now there was only water. Water water everywhere. Only the stable up on a high knoll had been spared. If the water kept rising, it would be the next to go. And so would she.

When she was a little girl in Sunday school, she had learned the story of Noah and his ark. From what she remembered from her lessons, God had promised He would never destroy the world with a flood again and He'd given the rainbow as a sign of His promise.

It seemed as if God had changed His mind.

Tamara turned from the window and found her grandfather's pack of cigarettes on his desk and the matches in the top drawer where he kept his fancy pens and stationary. She didn't light a cigarette, but she did light the candles she'd found in the top drawer. The sight of the candles on the desk gave her an idea. She started digging through the drawers. If God destroyed by water, she would destroy by fire. Tonight she wanted to destroy everything. Business papers. Letters. Her grandfather's Last Will and Testament if she could find it so she wouldn't inherit anything because she didn't want it. She didn't want a brick of this place. She didn't want a dime. In a drawer she found a handgun and bullets. Granddaddy's revolver her mother had threatened to use to shoot Kermit. Tamara opened the window and held the gun out over the water. Except…no. What if she needed that later? She closed the window, kept the gun. The police might come for her. She wouldn't let them put her in jail for what she did. She'd rather die first than take the blame. Her mother had set her up, left her alone so her grandfather could have his way with her. Her mother would burn for this, too.

Tamara dug every sheet of paper out of the drawers. She tossed his ledger books into the wire wastebasket, an appointment book, anything she could get her hands on. Anything she could burn, she would burn.

Papers weren't enough. Accounts weren't enough. She wanted to burn the very heart of Red Thread. The bottle. The first bottle and Veritas's red ribbon. Where was the bottle?

She picked up a candle and walked around the room, looking along the walls, across the tables. In the corner of the room she saw a girl holding a candle. Her. Her reflection in the glass front of Granddaddy's liquor cabinet. She raised the candle to the cabinet and peered inside, spying row upon row of amber-colored bottles tied at the neck with a red ribbon. The glass bottles danced with the light of her candle flame, and for a moment it appeared they all held fire inside them. Tamara set her candle down, wrapped the pink blanket around her arm and with her elbow smashed in the glass.

Tamara dropped the blanket on the floor and stood on it out of the way of the broken glass. She'd been hurt enough tonight. Red Thread wasn't ever going to hurt her again. She dug through the cabinet looking at every bottle by candlelight. One bottle was from this year. Another from 1970. Another bottle was old enough its ribbon had faded to a dull pink, but it wasn't old enough to be the bottle she sought.

Then she saw it.

In the very back of the cabinet on the bottom shelf in a glass box all its own was the bottle. The first bottle. She pulled out the box and slid the glass lid off the top. From a nest of red velvet, she lifted the bottle out. Around the neck hung a limp and ratty ribbon, rust-colored with age. She set it on the counter, smiling. She didn't know what she should do with it. Drink it? Pour it into the river water? So many choices, each

one better than the last. She had to think of something good,
something that would hurt Granddaddy and Jacob Maddox
even in their graves.

Tamara would wait, think it over. In the meantime, she
should hide the bottle again. She went to put it back in its
velvet bed and noticed something else in the box with the
bottle—an envelope. An envelope her grandfather had hidden.

She pulled it out and examined the front. The handwriting…
she knew this handwriting.

Her father… Daddy.

He'd written this letter. It was addressed to her grandfather.
She kissed the words on the paper because she missed him so
much. Tamara took the letter, took her candle and walked to
the desk chair, where she sat to read it, the bottle long forgotten.

Dad,

By the time you receive this letter, I'll be dead. I can't
stay on this earth another day. Every single day of my life
has been a lie. I do not love my wife. I have never loved
my wife. I have never loved any woman and never will.
It is my greatest regret that I chose your money over my
soul and allowed Virginia to be trapped in this prison of
a marriage with me.

You can have your money. If you've seen my soul anywhere, I'd like to have it back.

I am not taking my life to punish you so much as to
free Virginia from this farce of a marriage and from the
Maddox family. I fear she will make the same choice I
did, taking your money and selling her soul, but I will
die with a clear conscience knowing I have at least tried
to free her. I'm tired of pretending that Tamara is my
daughter. Even Virginia is tired of pretending. Did you

know she told me that Tamara was Daniel Headley's daughter, conceived at Eric's going-away party? I laughed when she told me. Virginia is more a Maddox than I am. You've taught her well.

You should know… I love Tamara as if she is my daughter, and my last wish for her is that my death will free her and Virginia both. Let them go, Dad.

It is not easy for me to die knowing what I know about Levi Shelby. I know you've had your affairs, but I never dreamed you'd stoop so low to seduce a cleaning lady who couldn't tell you no any more than the rest of us could. Levi seems like a good young man. I assume he's turned out so well because he was raised outside this family and without the taint of the Maddox name and the poison that is in every bottle of Red Thread. I hope he never knows who he really is, for his sake. But considering he is the only son you have left, I know his days as a man free and happy are numbered. But better him than my Tamara as your heir. Our family is cursed, they say. I will testify to that. I will be at peace only when I am no longer a part of it. Virginia recently said to me that over her dead body will she allow you to leave a single cent of our family's money to Levi. Feel free to leave every cent of it to him over my dead body instead.

Do not consider my death as you losing another son.

Consider it you losing everything.

I go to join my beloved Eric now, my brother and my friend. He knew what I was and who I was and loved me in spite of it all. I have missed him. It will be good to see my brother again.

Your son,

Nash

Tamara folded up the letter and slipped it back in the envelope.

One by one she pulled the papers out of the trash can, the books and the ledgers. She didn't burn a single thing.

Instead, she went into her mother's bedroom and took off her clothes, all of them. She opened the window and saw the river under the bottom sill. The cold air wrapped around her naked body and she felt clean again. She threw her soiled pajamas into the black night water along with the hateful pink housecoat. They floated away—good riddance. When she looked down into the water, she saw her reflection twisting and stretching. The face wasn't her face anymore, but another girl's face. And that girl was in the dark water with a red ribbon tied around her hair. It couldn't be her... Tamara wasn't wearing a red ribbon in her hair. Where had it come from?

She raised her hand to her hair. No ribbon. She looked at her fingers and saw they'd turned red. Blood. She was bleeding from a cut on her head. That was all. She must have cut herself with the glass from the lamp while fighting with Granddaddy. She laughed at herself for thinking she was someone she wasn't. Silly girl. She closed the window and dressed in her mother's clothes and wrapped herself in her mother's blanket, which smelled of bourbon and cigar smoke.

She went back to Granddaddy's office and pulled a chair to the window. In the distance through the trees she could see flickering lights—flashlights or headlights or both. Someone was alive out there. Someone would find her eventually.

But it didn't matter anymore that someone find her. She'd found herself in her daddy's letter. But not her daddy at all.

"I am not a Maddox," she whispered. The ecstasy of the knowledge smoldered inside her, glowed, burned. She'd never spoken five more beautiful words in her life. She didn't have

Maddox blood in her veins, that vile blood that had raped Veritas, that had sold her and her baby. She wasn't one of them. She wasn't cursed. And that was why she'd lived and Granddaddy had died. The curse had struck him and spared her. Because she wasn't a Maddox. She wasn't a Maddox at all.

But Levi was. And yet he hadn't been good enough for her grandfather. He'd wanted a white son, all white, and she'd been the chosen vessel for the chosen boy. A ripe teenage girl under his own roof. No wonder he had made her and Momma move in with him. No wonder.

Tamara smiled. She had an idea. Her mother had said she would let Granddaddy give a penny of Red Thread to Levi over her dead body.

Her mother hadn't said anything about her live body.

More tired than she'd ever been in her life, Tamara closed her eyes and snuggled deep into the blanket to rest. She'd need all her strength to make it through the next few weeks. The water had stopped rising. She would survive this night. When the police came, she would tell them this story—that her grandfather had been drinking and she'd gone upstairs to sleep. Why upstairs? She'd need an answer for that. She'd gone upstairs to sleep because she wanted to sleep in her mother's room so she'd know when Momma came home. There. They'd fought and Tamara wanted to apologize, so she waited upstairs on her mother's bed. She'd fallen asleep and then woke up when the lights went out. She'd gone downstairs to check things out and found the house full of water and Granddaddy floating there facedown. It was too late. He'd drunk so much he'd passed out, and he'd drowned in the flood. What could she do except go back upstairs and wait to be rescued? She'd broken the glass of the liquor cabinet because she tripped in the dark. She had an answer for every question they'd ask. For now, for tonight, she was safe and she was free. And tomorrow she'd start figuring out how to shoot Granddaddy's gun.

Although she'd had only a sip or two of Red Thread, Tamara felt drunk and happy. Happy because she was alive, yes. Happy because she wasn't a Maddox, indeed. But happiest most of all for one very good reason.

Tamara Maddox had a plan.

8

Paris

"You were right," McQueen said. "Maybe I don't want to hear this story, after all."

"Too late. The train has left the station. No stopping it until the end of the line." Paris crossed her legs, long beautiful legs. He didn't even want to look at them anymore. Nor her face, either. But she looked at him, stared at him. Her face was a sealed bottle, corked and capped and covered in foil. He could get nothing out of it.

"Tamara tied the red ribbon around her grandfather's finger," he finally said. "Smart."

"You're familiar with the tradition?" she asked, seeming pleased with him.

"I don't know where it started," he admitted. "But they said Red Thread drinkers would take the ribbon off the neck of the bottle and twist it around their fingers if they managed the manly feat of drinking an entire bottle in one night. A badge of honor."

"A badge of dishonor," she said, scoffing. "Drinking an entire bottle of bourbon in one night? That's something to be proud of? Makes as much sense as keeping the panties from the prostitute you paid to lay you. Where's the glory in that?"

McQueen laughed, but it didn't feel right, laughing after hearing that story.

"Depends on the prostitute, I guess," he said. "I know those old bottles. They aren't that hard to drink in one long night. What? Ten shots? Twelve?"

"George Maddox had a nickname in certain Kentucky circles. They called him 'The Baron.' The good ole boys called him that. He called himself that. One of the last great bourbon barons. He took his title seriously. That man could polish off a full bottle of Red Thread in a night. And then he'd take that little red ribbon off, put it on his finger and wear it into the office the next day. Big man. He liked to show that he could hold his liquor. It was a point of family pride."

"He has a pretty sick definition of pride. Raping his own granddaughter. Even if Tamara wasn't his granddaughter—"

"She wasn't his granddaughter, no, but the whole world thought she was. Any baby she had would be a Maddox in the eyes of the world—even more important, in the eyes of George Maddox."

"But still…he raised her like a granddaughter. And he did that to her? Really?"

"He did what I said he did." Paris gave him a look that said *Doubting Thomases will not be treated kindly.* "George Maddox was a wealthy and powerful man and had the audacity to think he deserved both his wealth and his power. He'd inherited the money, and the power that came with the name, also inherited. The world gave him everything he ever wanted except a son to pass it all on to—the right son, a white son. He thought the world owed him that, as well. What does the world owe you, Mr. McQueen?"

"Nothing," McQueen said.

"Good answer," Paris said. "If you really believe that, you might have a soul under all that money."

"Tamara's around my daughter's age. I can't..." He shook his head, attempting to dislodge the image of a man his father's age touching his daughter. "Was she arrested?"

"No, she wasn't. I don't think the police even questioned her. With that red ribbon around his finger, everyone assumed, naturally, that he'd been drinking heavily. The investigation was open and shut. George Maddox was drunk, went to take a piss, unzipped his pants, fell and hit his head. When the floodwater came in the house, he drowned. George Maddox was a pillar of the community. No one wanted to know any different. No one wanted to know why they found his corpse in his granddaughter's bedroom with his pants around his knees. They didn't ask questions. Tamara didn't answer any. They buried him. The end. Except it wasn't the end." Paris smiled a satisfied smile like she'd thought of a good secret.

"You don't sound like a fan of the Maddoxes."

"What is it they say? You can't choose your family? Although, in a way, I suppose I did choose them. But that's another story."

McQueen stood and took her now empty shot glass from her.

"What's your poison?" he asked.

"Can you make an old-fashioned?"

"With my eyes closed."

He walked to the bar, a polished and carved mahogany number that had once stood in an Old West saloon. Saloon, the dealer had said. All signs pointed to brothel, including the brass plaque on the back that read Property of Mollie Johnson, Queen of the Blondes. He'd bought the bar despite all the little scratches in it that had most likely come from fingernails. He himself had eight claw marks on the back of his shoulders, courtesy of the widow Paris, so he had a fondness for the damage left by the fingernails of well-pleased women.

"My father insisted I get a real job in college," McQueen said. "Didn't want me mooching off the family money until I'd proved I could make my own way in the world." He returned to the sitting area with her old-fashioned and his bourbon, neat with a splash of cold water. "So I got a job in a dive bar."

She took the drink from his hand, sipped it and nodded her approval.

"They taught you well in the dive."

"Thank you." He sat back on the leather armchair opposite her. The only thing between them was a coffee table and the truth.

"You ready for more?" she asked.

"I don't think so."

"You think hearing this story is bad, try living it."

"You're trying to make me feel guilty," he said.

"You are guilty," she said. "Now I'm trying to convince you to make your restitution."

"Tell the story, then." Restitution. As if he owed anyone anything. He paid his debts in time and in full. But if she wanted to keep talking, he'd keep listening. God knew it was the most interesting evening he'd had in a long time.

"George Maddox was many things," Paris continued. "Most of them bad, but he didn't turn Red Thread into a two-hundred-million-dollar property by being a fool. He was a smart man, and a ruthless man. He knew how to get people to dance for him. Yes, he left everything to Tamara in his will. Of course, he'd fully expected to get something in return for his largesse, but he died before the blessed event could take place. To all the world, Tamara Maddox was the one and only living Maddox. As you and I know, this was not the case. The will was read once Mr. Maddox was in the ground. Everything went to Tamara, but it was held in trust by her mother until that time she was married or she turned twenty-one, whichever came first. George Maddox had likely planned to get Tamara pregnant and then have her married off—very quickly—to one of his handpicked cronies. And the child Tamara would give birth to would be the real heir because George Maddox had fathered it."

"What if it had been a girl?"

"If at first you don't succeed, try, try again."

"I think I hate George Maddox."

"I think I agree with you," Paris said.

"So Tamara's father wasn't Tamara's father."

"Nash Maddox was gay," Paris said. She took another sip of her drink. "You didn't get to be gay and out in Kentucky in the 1960s. You got married to a woman, you lived that lie and you took that secret to the grave with you. Nash did."

"My son is gay," McQueen said. "Told us last summer."

"Do you love him any less?"

"No, of course not."

"You gonna force him to marry a woman?"

"Never."

"George Maddox did. He threatened to cut Nash off unless he got married. They had Virginia Darling standing by, the daughter of one of George's business partners and best friends. They'd grown up together—Virginia, Nash, Eric and Daniel Headley. The parents considered it a given she'd marry one of the Maddox boys. Everyone expected it. Everyone wanted it. And so it came to pass. At age nineteen Virginia Darling found herself a couple months pregnant. No choice then. She had to get married. Nash had to get married, too, or his father would send him packing without a penny to his name. Nash lasted in the marriage as long as he could. He killed himself when Tamara was twelve years old."

"I might have killed myself, too."

"I don't blame Nash at all. Tamara didn't, either, once she knew the whole truth."

"Was she okay after that night?"

"I wouldn't use the word *okay* to describe her," Paris said. "I would use the word *determined*. Soon as George Maddox was dead and buried, Virginia Maddox fired Levi. He was gone in a day. You have to remember back then if someone wasn't in the phone book, there wasn't much chance of finding him. No internet."

"The Dark Ages."

"Exactly. So it took Tamara a while to get her plan in gear. She played the grieving granddaughter well. She held herself together at the funeral, went back to school and got excellent grades, graduated at the top of her high school class a year and a half later. Mother and daughter barely spoke to each other after that night. And all that time Tamara was looking for Levi while her mother was looking for a buyer for Red Thread."

"She wanted to sell the company?"

"Virginia Darling knew how to paint her nails, knew how to dress like a lady, knew how to keep a house. She didn't know how to run a company. Nobody expected anything of her other than to get married and that's all she'd done with her life. She didn't want to run the company, and there were dozens of buyers at her door the day after George Maddox was in the ground. Tamara had to hurry up and find Levi."

"I suppose Levi could have contested the will. Did she find him?"

"Virginia Maddox accepted a buyout offer on Red Thread from a rival bourbon maker. The next day Tamara finally found Levi. It was fate, it seems."

"Fate. Sounds romantic."

"You must not know anything about mythology, then, Mr. McQueen. In all the old myths, the Fates were the villains."

9

1980

Her name was either Cheryl or Sherry—he could never remember which—so Levi compromised and called her Cher. Not that Cher/Cheryl/Sherry seemed to be paying a bit of attention to anything he said. Maybe she didn't remember his name, either, since the only words coming out of her mouth at the moment were "God," "Harder" and "Oh, baby."

Levi had Cher on her back with a horse blanket between her and half a dozen hay bales. Whatever her name was, she was only a couple years older than him—thirty-two, he remembered her saying—but she'd certainly done better for herself in life than he had. The pants he'd pulled off her were Gloria Vanderbilt, her panties were fine silk and lace and were currently dangling off a well-turned ankle. The diamond engagement ring likely cost more than his truck, but in his unspoken opinion, his truck was a helluva lot more useful.

"Harder," she said again, and Levi obliged her. It was hot

in the loft, airless and stank of horse sweat and human sweat. The sooner he finished, the better. So he dug his boots into the hay trying to find traction and pounded into her until she stopped barking orders. The rubber he wore made it difficult to feel much of anything, but when she came, her fingernails made sure he knew it.

He wasn't done yet, but she didn't put up any objection while he took his turn. She lay there with her eyes closed, a pretty girl if not beautiful, and patiently took it until he came with as little fanfare as possible. Cher had been loud enough for the both of them.

When it was all done, he tossed the rubber while she pulled herself together.

"Best horseback riding lesson I've ever had." She shoved her feet into her boots and Levi helped her onto her feet.

"I aim to please."

"Same time next week?" she asked, strolling to the ladder that led down to the stalls.

"If your fiancé wants to keep paying for private lessons, I'll keep giving them to you. Although one of these days he's gonna want to go riding with you, and he might wonder why you don't know a horse's head from its ass."

"You know why he gave me riding lessons, right?"

"Enlighten me."

"While I'm up here fucking you, he's at his office fucking his secretary."

"Nice system you two worked out."

"Everybody's happy." She started down the ladder steps but stopped and turned toward the window.

"What?" Levi asked as he buckled his belt again. Somewhere around here he had a clean T-shirt. He found it under his copy of the *Tao Te Ching* and pulled it on.

"I think your five o'clock is here."

"I don't have a five o'clock lesson today."

"Then who's that?" She pointed out the dingy window that looked down on the gravel parking lot. He'd been too busy with Cher to hear anyone drive up.

Levi walked to the ladder and squatted down to see out the window. First he saw the car, a baby blue Triumph Spitfire, a little girl's sort of sports car. Then he saw the little girl it belonged to.

"Fuck," Levi breathed.

"What? Someone you know?"

"Someone I don't want to know." Levi shook his head. Goddamn. "Go on. I'll see you next week."

She rose up on her toes on the rung and kissed him quick on the mouth before heading down the ladder with ease. Levi didn't follow at first. He kept staring out the window. What the hell was Tamara Maddox doing here? There was no way this was a coincidence. The girl didn't need riding lessons. She could outride him, not that he'd ever told her that. Not that he planned on telling her that. He hadn't planned on telling her anything ever again.

He had to tell her something, though. Out in the parking lot, Tamara leaned back against the hood of her little blue car and shoved her hands deep into her jeans pockets.

She was waiting. Well, she could wait a little longer. Levi took the first few rungs of the ladder, jumped down the rest of the way and landed easy on his feet. The stables had running water and a tiny closet of a bathroom for the little kids who couldn't hold it long enough to make it to the main building, where the owner of Happy Trails sat in his air-conditioned office talking on the phone all day. Levi splashed cold water on his face, ran wet hands through his hair, made sure he didn't have hay sticking out of his jeans. He didn't care if he looked good for Tamara or not, but it gave him sweet satisfaction to keep her waiting.

Levi took his hat off a nail right outside the bathroom door and shoved it on his head before emerging into the bright June sunlight. The second Tamara saw him, she came to attention, standing up straight, no longer leaning on the hood of her car. She pushed her sunglasses up on top of her head and smiled.

"Hey, Levi," she said.

Levi walked past her and kept walking.

He walked straight to the pile of straw bales stacked behind the woodshed, picked one up by the cords and carried it back to the stables.

Tamara didn't speak to him again, but she followed him. She'd done that all the time back when he worked for her grandfather, trailed behind him like a duckling, quacking questions at him. *Why do you work for Granddaddy? Do you want to go to college? Do you ever want to get married someday? Do you think my black boots or my brown boots are prettier? Can I ride your horse?* He ignored half her questions, told her lies to the other half. He worked for her granddaddy because his career as a ballerina hadn't worked out. He was already married— seven wives, one for each night of the week. All her boots were ugly and she could ride his horse the second she was as tall as he was and he would happily stretch her out on a rack if she wanted to speed up the growing process.

Today she didn't ask a single question as she followed him into the stables. He dropped the hay bale in a stall, pulled out his pocketknife and cut the cords. When he stood up, Tamara had a pitchfork in her hand.

"I won't turn you into a spaghetti strainer, I promise," she said, wearing a halfhearted smile.

"Then what are you doing with that thing?" He nodded at the pitchfork.

"Helping." She speared the straw with the fork and tossed a good quantity of it on the bare stall floor.

"I never thought I'd live to see the day Tamara Maddox did hard labor without someone holding a gun to her head."

"Congratulations," she said, spearing the hay bale again. "You lived longer than you thought you would."

He didn't help. No, this show was too good to interrupt. He stood outside the stall and watched her.

"Can you bring me another bale?" she asked. "Please?"

"That's enough."

"It's too thin. Kermit got twice that much bedding."

"Kermit's owner is a rich girl, not the cheapskate who runs this place."

"Ex-owner. I don't have him anymore."

Tamara used her feet to even out the hay on the floor.

"What happened to poor Kermit? Miss Piggy finally got to him?"

"Momma sold him. She sold all the horses after Grand-daddy died."

"Why? I'm not the only man in Kentucky who can muck a stall. She couldn't find anyone else to take care of them?"

"She did it to punish me."

"For what?"

Tamara met his eyes for a moment, then went back to work smoothing out the hay.

"What do you think?" she asked.

Levi felt the tiniest little pang of sympathy. He squashed it under the heel of his boot.

Still, he left her in the stall, walked out to the woodshed and returned with another bale of straw.

"Thank you," Tamara said. He watched her pull a knife out of her boot. Not a little pocketknife. A serrated four-inch blade, a nasty little knife. She cut the cords with it, slid it back in her boot and went to work spreading the bedding.

"When did you start carrying a knife with you?" Levi asked.

"After Granddaddy died. Maybe I'll stab Momma to death with it someday."

Levi laughed. "Nice to know your mother's an equal opportunity bitch, then. And here I thought it was just me she loved treating like shit."

"Not just you."

"That's a big knife, kid. You could hurt yourself with it."

"The world's a dangerous place," she said.

"Then move."

She gave a little smile. "You always were good with the wisecracks, Sam Spade," she said.

"You're not too bad yourself, Pam Pitchfork."

Levi opened the stall door again and took the pitchfork from her hand. It was the closest he'd been to her since that day, and he could smell light perfume on her skin, something like baby powder and vanilla. She looked older than the last time he'd seen her. She looked good. Pretty white shirt with blue trim, bare arms, tight jeans and long brick red hair in a loose braid over her shoulder. She was even prettier close-up, like that was the best way she should be looked at, face-to-face, eye-to-eye. She had a good straight nose and lips full enough to give him bad ideas of his own.

When she was sixteen, she'd been too pretty for her own good.

Now she was too pretty for his own good.

"Tamara, what the hell are you doing here?"

"I've been looking for you ever since Momma fired you."

"How'd you find me?"

"It wasn't easy. Momma would have killed me if she knew what I was up to. Every time I spent the night at a friend's house, I'd borrow their phone and call a stable or two. I knew you'd work with horses, but I called every number in the Yellow Pages and couldn't find you. I'm not allowed at Red Thread by myself, but last week was Granddaddy's secretary's retirement party and I used that as an excuse to get into Granddaddy's office. Nothing had been touched. I found your mother's old pay stubs and her employee file. There wasn't much in it, but there was a phone number. I called it and someone named Gloria answered. I told her you used to work for us and you'd left some stuff that I wanted to return. She told me where you worked."

"My aunt Glory. My mother's sister. I'll tell her to keep her mouth shut in the future when people call looking for me."

"I needed to talk to you, Levi."

"And get me in trouble again? I'm lucky your mother didn't call the cops on me for kissing her precious baby. Thanks to you, I make half the money I used to make working for your granddaddy. I have a nice loft to sleep in, though. You want to see it?" He pointed up to the stable loft, where he slept most nights. He couldn't afford his own place anymore and at age thirty he wasn't about to move in with his aunt and uncle, even though they'd offered.

"I'm sorry about that."

"Sorry about kissing me?"

"Sorry about getting you fired. I never meant that to happen."

"And now here you are apologizing to me like a grown-up. You have changed, haven't you?"

"I had to grow up after Granddaddy died. But even before… I felt bad about getting you into trouble with Momma. I hope you accept my apology."

"Accepted. Now you can go. You're boring the hell out of me. I liked it better when you were a spoiled rotten brat."

"Yeah," she said. "Me, too."

Levi exhaled heavily. A visit from Tamara Maddox was the last thing he needed this week. He'd almost gotten to where he could fall asleep at night without thinking about her and that kiss that lost him the best job of his life. Hating Virginia Maddox had been easy, kept him going. Hating Tamara had been harder, but he'd managed somehow. But never had he ever imagined that her mother would sell her horses to punish her. As cowed and quiet as she seemed now, he had to wonder if her mother punished her in worse ways than that.

"Can we go for a ride?" Tamara asked. "I want to talk to you about something. If you're not busy. And I can pay for using one of the horses. I haven't gotten to ride in a long time."

"My boss is a cheapskate, but he won't charge a Maddox for borrowing a horse for half an hour."

"Is that a yes?" She grinned at him.

"Fine. Yes. I got nothing else to do. Might as well listen to your teenage bullshit for a few minutes."

Tamara grabbed him by the shoulders and kissed him on both cheeks.

"Ah, *mon capitan*. I knew you still loved me."

"Where'd I put my pitchfork?"

Tamara ignored his threat and went from stall to stall looking for a horse to ride. She picked a sorrel mare with four white socks named Scarlett. Levi wasn't about to ride his favorite stallion, Rhett—Tamara would read too much into that—so he saddled Ashley, the one gelding in the stables, instead.

"You haven't lost your seat," Levi said as they passed the woodshed and took the easy main trail. The entire Happy Trails estate was about three hundred acres of woods and fields and horse trails.

"Guess riding a horse is like riding a bike."

He'd opened her up to flirt by complimenting her seat. Nothing. Not a word. How unlike her.

"Guess so."

"You like it here?" Tamara asked.

"It's all right. I get five dollars an hour to give riding lessons to rich girls like you and not so rich girls who want to feel rich. Ten dollars for a private lesson. When I'm not working, I can ride all I want. I don't much like living in a stable loft, but I save a lot of money on rent. One more year and I can buy a place of my own."

"You said Granddaddy paid you better?"

"A lot better. More money for less work. But we know how that turned out."

"You know, you never told me how you ended up working for Granddaddy," Tamara said.

"Not much to tell. Mom got sick my senior year of high school. There went college. I had to work, so I got a job. I mucked stalls at Churchill. After Mom died—"

"How did she die?"

"Mouth cancer. Killed her slow, but it got her eventually. Your grandfather stopped by for the wake. No one was more surprised to see him than me. But he shook my hand and said Mom had told him I had experience with horses, and that sure surprised the hell out of me. Mom hadn't worked for him in years. I told him I did and he asked if I'd be interested in coming to work for him at his place. I said yes. The end."

"Granddaddy and your mom kept in touch?"

"Must have, I guess. No offense but your grandfather didn't seem the type to care much about a cleaning lady. Still don't know what possessed him to come to the funeral. But I didn't complain. It was a good job while it lasted."

Tamara didn't say anything to that.

"So what's the richest girl in the state want with the poorest stable hand in the state?" Levi asked as they crossed a wooden bridge into the deeper darker parts of the woods.

"I'm not the richest girl in the state. Not yet, anyway. Everything's held in trust until I turn twenty-one or get married."

"You'll be twenty-one someday."

"Not soon enough. Momma's selling Red Thread. She accepted an offer this week."

"Isn't that where y'all get your money?"

"We have lots of money. We'll have more money if we sell the distillery. But we shouldn't sell it."

"Tell your mother that, then. I can't help you."

"Momma and I don't talk anymore."

"Why not?"

"Because I hate her and she hates me."

"I know why you hate her—who wouldn't? But why does she hate you?"

"She thinks it's my fault granddaddy's dead. I let him drown downstairs and didn't go check on him."

"Did you let him drown?"

"I didn't let him drown."

"Don't feel bad your mother accused you of murder. She accused me of rape."

"Raping who?"

"You."

"I think I'd remember you trying to rape me."

"I'd remember it, too."

"No, you wouldn't. You'd be dead."

"Tell that to your mother."

"I will someday. Momma has a lot to answer for."

"Yeah, well, don't we all?"

The old Tamara would have said, "Not me." The old Tamara would have said, "Speak for yourself." But this wasn't the old Tamara. This was the *older* Tamara and she only nodded like she had something to answer for, too.

He trotted up to her and met her eye-to-eye.

"Look at me. Why are you here, Tamara? You're real good at asking questions and terrible at giving answers."

"I'm trying to figure out what to say."

"Tell the truth. That shouldn't be too hard."

"The truth is the hardest thing to say."

Levi noticed something he hadn't seen before. Around Tamara's neck hung a little gold cross on a little gold chain. He reached over and touched the cross, lifted it off her skin. Tamara's body stiffened at the contact, but she didn't shy away.

"You never wore that before," Levi said, instantly regretting saying that. "Is this why you're on your best behavior now? You got religion?"

"God saved me during the flood."

"But you carry a knife with you. You don't think God'll save you again if you need Him?"

"I can save myself."

Levi let the cross fall back onto her skin.

"Even your religion is made of eighteen-karat gold."

"God saved me," she said.

"Nobody saved you. A grand total of two people died in that flood. One old lady who had a heart attack, and your grandfather, and the heart attack might have had nothing to do with the flood. You got lucky like everybody minus two people in town. You might be rich and you might be pretty, but you ain't that special."

"You only said 'ain't' because you know that word bugs me."

"Ain't that the truth?" Levi said, grinning. She didn't grin back. "Come on. Either put up or shut up. I don't have all day."

"I'm trying here, Levi. Give me a second."

"Second's up."

He kicked his horse gently in the side and Ashley obeyed the command, turning them away from her. Yeah, he was being an asshole. He knew it. But he didn't like being around Tamara anymore. Too many memories. Too many temptations. He'd never told anyone the truth of that day when Virginia Maddox had fired him. She'd humiliated him like he'd never known he could be humiliated. She'd told him if he got within a mile of her daughter, she would call the police, tell them she'd seen him trying to rape Tamara in the stables. He'd go to jail for the rest of his life because "no way any judge would believe the word of the son of a colored cleaning lady over Virginia Maddox." Oh, he had wanted payback then and the way he wanted to have it was by fucking Tamara, getting her pregnant and then standing there by her side and telling her mother what they had done. Then he'd leave Tamara and laugh his way into the sunset. But those were mad thoughts, the sort he never allowed himself except in the deepest hours of night when he woke up hot and alone with nothing but fantasies of sex and revenge in bed with him. And here she was, right next to him, as beautiful as he remembered, as tempting as he remembered, as dangerous as he remembered.

"It's yours," Tamara said.

"What is?" Levi asked, not looking back at her lest he be

turned to a pillar of salt, which was what his uncle called a man who thought only with his cock.

"Red Thread is yours. Or it ought to be."

"I was a damn good groom, but I highly doubt your grandfather saw fit to leave me his entire company in his will."

"He didn't. But he should've."

"And why is that?"

"Because you are George Maddox's only living son."

10

Levi didn't know if he should laugh in Tamara's face or slap her until she came to her senses. She looked clear-eyed to him, so he went with laughing.

"That's cute. Nice joke, Rotten."

Tamara didn't laugh. Tamara didn't smile.

"It's not a joke. Granddaddy is your father. See?"

She dug a piece of paper out of her back pocket and held it out to him.

He looked at the paper in her outstretched hand before finally reaching out and taking it from her.

"What the hell is this?" he said, scanning the note. The ink was purple and obviously some sort of Xerox copy of a handwritten letter.

"My father's suicide note. Except he wasn't my father. A man named Daniel Headley, *Judge* Daniel Headley, is my father. And according to this note, Granddaddy was your father."

Levi's eyes could barely focus on the words. His heart pounded like horse hooves on dry turf kicking up an ugly cloud of dust.

It is not easy for me to die knowing what I know about Levi Shelby. I know you've had your affairs, but I never dreamed you'd stoop so low to seduce a cleaning lady who couldn't tell you no any more than the rest of us could...

But considering he is the only son you have left...

...the only son...

"This is bullshit." Levi crumpled up the paper and tossed it at Tamara. She caught it against her chest.

"I know it hurts. It hurt me to know Daddy wasn't my father... But it's not bullshit. It's true."

"It's not true. My mother would not—"

"Your mother was twenty-five when she worked for Granddaddy, and he was thirty. He was handsome then, and if you look anything like your mother, she was beautiful."

"She wouldn't sleep with a..." Levi looked up into the trees, silenced the scream rising in his throat.

"Wouldn't sleep with a white man? A rich white man who she worked for? Why not? You and me, we almost—"

"That's completely different," Levi said, but he couldn't think of why except Tamara was beautiful and George Maddox was nothing but a smug old rich bastard. Levi grew up knowing he'd been born out of wedlock. He'd been taunted for it at school, and even though he hated Jay Shelby, the man his mother had married when Levi was six, at least he finally had a father's name they could put down on school forms. "She would have told me."

"Did you tell your mother about all the girls you slept with?"

"She would have told me."

"Did she tell you? Who did she say your father was?"

Levi didn't answer because he had no answer. His mother had never told him a name. Levi had asked, but he'd never asked *her*. Instead, he'd asked his aunt Gloria, who said she didn't know and that Levi shouldn't worry about it. He had a mother and an aunt and an uncle who loved him and that was more family than a lot of people had. But he hadn't missed the look of fear in Gloria's eyes when he'd asked the question.

But no...

"No fucking way," Levi said. "My mother would have told me if my father were the richest son of a bitch in Kentucky. Your grandfather lied to your father and your father believed him."

"You said it yourself—Granddaddy went to your mother's funeral even though she hadn't worked for him in years. He gave you a job paying you more than you'd earn anywhere else. He was keeping an eye on you. Why would he do that?"

"I don't know, but I know I'm done talking about this with you. Now get out of here and never show your face here again. All you fucking Maddoxes can go to hell."

"You are a Maddox," Tamara called out after him.

Ignoring her, Levi spurred his horse and headed straight back to the stables. Tamara, seasoned rider that she was, followed close behind him, keeping up even as he took sharp turns on back trails to evade her.

Back at the stables he put Ashley back in his stall and didn't bother to unsaddle him. Before Tamara could say another word to him, he was in his pickup and driving away.

Last thing he saw as he peeled out of the parking lot, throwing gravel as he went, was Tamara on the back of her horse looking proud and elegant and made of money. She looked like a Maddox. She looked nothing like him.

Levi almost stopped to throw up on his way to his aunt

and uncle's house outside Lawrenceburg. He'd gone on a few drinking benders in his life and had his share of hangovers, but his stomach had never churned like this, like a water-wheel in a running river. His eyes ran and his breaths were quick. He ached like he had a fever and he would have driven into the Kentucky River to cool himself off if he'd been any-where near it.

When he arrived at the little white farmhouse on the edge of his aunt Gloria and his uncle Andre's property, Levi en-tered through the back door without knocking. He didn't see his uncle's truck or Gloria's Chevy. He went upstairs, stripped naked in the bathroom, took a long ice-cold shower and rested his head against the slick pink-tiled wall.

He wanted to think of a thousand reasons why Tamara was wrong, why she would lie to him or why her father would lie to her. But the only thought in his head was this one—*this explains everything.*

It explained why Virginia Maddox hated him so much.

It explained why his mother never told him who his fa-ther was.

It explained why George Maddox came to the funeral and offered him a job.

It explained his blue eyes.

And it explained why he let himself think for one second he was allowed to fool around with a rich white girl like Ta-mara Maddox. Because in his heart of hearts he knew they were the same.

When Levi finally turned off the water, he heard footsteps and his uncle Andre's voice calling his name.

He dried off quickly and pulled his clothes back on. He took a few cold drinks of water out of the sink and tossed his towel into the hamper because Gloria would have his hide if he left the towel on the floor. She worked at a bank and was no one's maid, she liked to remind him.

Levi walked down the narrow staircase and found his uncle standing by the front door, flipping through mail.

"You come for dinner tonight?" he asked without any other kind of greeting. They were family. Family didn't need any hi's and how-are-you's.

"I need to talk to you."

Andre looked at Levi, looked him dead in the eyes.

"Son, you look like you've seen a ghost. You're whiter than usual and that's saying something."

"I'm not kidding."

"I see you aren't. What's wrong?"

"Is George Maddox my father?"

Levi was impressed. Andre didn't bat an eye at the question. Then again, Andre had spent four years fighting World War II and had seen horrors he'd never speak of no matter how much liquor you poured down his throat. What was one more?

"Let's go in the kitchen," Andre said, which was as much of a yes as Levi needed. "I could use a beer. So could you."

Andre poured two glasses of beer and Levi didn't touch his. They both sat at the round oak table on opposite sides playing chicken. Andre blinked first.

"Your mother never told us who your father was. She said he was a married man and he already had children. That's all we know for certain. That and he worked where she worked."

"At Red Thread."

Andre sighed. "Your mother was a beautiful woman when she was younger. Sons don't like to hear that about their mothers, but it was true and we have the pictures to prove it."

"I've seen pictures from when she was younger. I never said she wasn't pretty." His mother loved her white go-go boots, her miniskirts, her silk shirts in wild colors. She was a beauty and in his younger days he'd been proud of having the prettiest mother around.

"She was pretty, yeah. She was also pretty wild. I was half in love with her myself, but I don't regret picking Glory over Honor."

An old family joke. Two sisters—Gloria and Honora. Glory and Honor.

"Mom wouldn't have... Not with George Maddox. Not a chance," Levi said.

"She worked the night shift. I imagine the owner and company president stayed late at work a lot. She talked about him a few times. I remember her saying he and his wife didn't get along too well. I heard she died not long ago. Thought she'd been dead for years."

"You're stalling."

"I'm stalling."

"Tell me what you know."

"I know what she told Glory, which is what I told you. She said she didn't think he'd leave his wife for her, but he gave her gifts, money—"

"Me?"

Slowly, very slowly, as slowly as anyone in history ever nodded, Andre nodded.

"Goddammit." Levi sighed.

"These things happen." Andre lifted his beer and drank half of it. He wasn't much of a heavy drinker anymore, which meant he was enjoying this conversation about as well as Levi was.

"So what happened between them?" Levi sat back in his chair, covered his face with his hands and breathed.

"The usual. He lost interest, started seeing someone new.

She quit when she found out she was pregnant. And six months later a baby boy was born, snow-white and blue-eyed."

Levi wasn't white as any snow anymore, but he wasn't black by any stretch of the imagination. Not even brown. Not on the outside, anyway. But the inside of a man didn't matter to 99 percent of the population.

"Why am I hearing about this now? Why didn't she tell me this before she died?"

"If it was George Maddox, then that's your answer. Money's bad enough, but money and power is a dangerous combination. When you turned out so light, she was afraid your father might try to take you away from her. She was afraid his family might try to kill you to cover up what he'd done from his wife. She was afraid of everything for a long while."

"Still doesn't explain why she wouldn't tell me."

"Your mother knew you too well. She thought you might do something stupid. Get drunk and start a fight. Make your existence known to people who had very good reasons to not want you in the world."

Levi thought of Virginia Maddox and her hatred of him that seemed to stem from nothing and nowhere. Always he'd assumed her loathing of him was simply bigotry, snobbery. She knew his mother was black and she hated him for it. But now he knew better. It wasn't because of his mother that Virginia Maddox hated his guts. It was because of his father.

"So how did you find out after all this time?" Andre asked.

"Tamara Maddox came to see me today."

"She the granddaughter?"

"She is. Sort of. She found her father's suicide note somehow. In it he calls me George Maddox's son. And I guess I am."

Andre tapped the table, wiped a swatch of foam off the inside of his glass.

"I guess you are."

Levi stood up, stood over the kitchen sink and tried not to puke into it. Gloria wouldn't have that, either.

"I can't believe Mom and George Maddox…"

"Why not?" Andre asked. "Didn't you get canned for fooling around with that Maddox girl?"

"With Tamara."

"Kissing cousins," Andre said and chuckled.

"Not quite. Turns out Tamara isn't her father's daughter, after all. Tamara's not a real Maddox, and I guess I am." Levi's lip curled in disgust. He couldn't look at Andre anymore. "Son of a bitch. She worked for him making fifty cents an hour. What was she supposed to do? Tell the boss man no?"

"Your mother told Glory she was in love. He didn't force her as far as I know. She was young and pretty and did what young pretty things do sometimes. But she loved you, too. She married that piece of shit Jay Shelby so you could have a father and a name."

"She divorced him as fast as she married him." His mother's marriage had lasted all of two years, but Jay Shelby had given him some measure of legitimacy, and a last name other than his mother's maiden name.

"Probably her plan all along."

Levi turned around, crossed his arms over his chest.

"I don't know what to do with this," Levi said. "Other than carry it."

"What's there to do with it? What's Tamara Maddox doing mucking all this mud?"

"Tamara said the company should be mine. That's why she came to see me, to tell me what she knew."

"She wants you to have Red Thread?"

"Her momma's trying to sell it and she thinks she shouldn't because it doesn't belong to them."

"It belongs to whoever George Maddox left it to."

"And that's Tamara. It's not like I can waltz into a lawyer's office, tell them who I am and smile while they hand me the keys to the place. I have no idea why Tamara told me all this. No idea what she's got to gain by it."

"Maybe she's one of the good ones. I heard rumors they exist."

Levi snorted a laugh. His uncle had little use for white people. It was "us" and it was "them," and the more "us" stayed away from "them," the better "us" had it. But on occasion he'd admit there was a good one or two of "them." He liked Johnny Carson. He liked Frank Sinatra. He thought *All in the Family* was funny, but mainly because it showed the world how ignorant white people were most of the time. He'd laughed so hard when Sammy Davis Jr. kissed Archie they'd thought Andre was having a heart attack. You could count the good ones on one hand, according to Andre.

"One of the good ones? I don't know," Levi said. "She's not one of the bad ones. She's only...spoiled. Spoiled rotten. She didn't seem like that today, though. She seemed... I don't know, but I think her mother's not been too good to her. Easy to believe. Her mother's one of the bad ones, that's for damn sure." Levi ran a hand through his still-wet hair.

"She's the one who fired you, right?"

He nodded. "Called me every name in the book, threatened to have me arrested, threatened to have me cut up in tiny pieces and scattered in every ditch from here to Ohio. And all that two days after George Maddox died. You'd think she'd have better things to worry about."

"Maybe she knows something you don't know. Maybe she

knows George Maddox did want to leave you something in the will."

"What do you think I should do?"

Andre shrugged, tapped his now empty glass on the table again.

"Maybe you should hear this girl out."

"Tamara can't do anything for me. She doesn't even get the company herself until she's twenty-one. Her mother's in charge of it all till then."

"And you say she doesn't like her mother?"

"Sounds like Tamara hates her mother as much as I do."

"Go talk to her, then. Be smart about it. But hear what she has to say. She might know something worth knowing."

"I don't want their money."

"The hell you don't. You want to keep living in a stable and coming here for your supper all your life?"

That was the last thing Levi wanted. And the first thing Levi wanted was his own farm, his own horses, his own stables. "You think I should go after his money? Really?"

"All I'm saying is if you're gonna have a cracker for a daddy, might as well be a Ritz cracker, right?"

Levi laughed. "Right."

Andre stood up and carried his glass over to the sink.

"After the Civil War, they made us a lot of promises. A lot of promises they didn't keep. A lot of promises they should have kept."

"Forty acres and a mule," Levi said. He'd heard all this before. He'd much rather have a horse than a mule.

"I got my forty acres," Andre said, looking out the back window at his farm. "You go get yours."

II

At dusk, Levi drove back to Happy Trails and parked outside the stables. He felt like shit for leaving the horses untended. Wearing a saddle for two hours wouldn't do them any harm, but they wouldn't be happy about it, either.

Inside the barn Levi found something he hadn't expected to find. Both Ashley and Scarlett were back in their stalls, their saddles off and polished to a mirror shine and their coats brushed and their manes trimmed. The bedding looked fresh and neat. Scarlett, Ashley, Rhett, Plato, Aristotle, Queenie and Zeppelin—all seven horses had clean stalls and oats in their trays. Nothing but contented horses wherever Levi looked. Paul, the owner, never gave the horses oats in the evening. Must have been Tamara. Well, goddamn. She really did miss her horses, didn't she?

On the ladder leading up to the loft Levi found a piece of paper nailed into the wood.

He ripped it off the nail and read.

Levi,

I'm sorry I upset you. When you are ready to talk, come
to the Red Thread warehouse. I have a key. I'll be there
every night at ten until ten thirty waiting for you. It's
safe there, trust me. Momma never goes near the warehouse. She can't stand the smell of the angels.

Tamara

The smell of the angels? He'd been right. Tamara was crazy.
Had to be, didn't she? If she really thought Levi had a claim
on the Maddox money, there'd be no way to prove it except
with that letter that showed she had no claim on it.

Trust me, Tamara wrote. There wasn't a Maddox on earth
Levi trusted as far as he could throw them. And that included
himself when it came to Tamara.

Levi didn't go that night. He refused to cave that easy. He'd
cave, yes, but when he did, he'd cave hard.

Three days later he made the drive back to Frankfort. Although it was the city closest to Happy Trails, Levi usually
drove the extra fifteen minutes and back to Louisville when
he needed something. Last thing he'd wanted was to run
into Tamara or her mother in town. And here he was driving
there for the sole purpose of talking it out with Tamara. If
he'd had worse ideas in his thirty years, he couldn't remember what they were.

Red Thread wasn't one building; it was several. They covered a good parcel of land from the road to the river. One
forked road led to both the distillery and Arden, which was
hidden behind a thicket of woods. Take the left fork to the
private Maddox property. Take the right fork to Red Thread.
Levi turned right, which he'd never done before. He'd had

nothing to do with the distillery at all when he worked for George Maddox, but the warehouse wasn't hard to find. It was the biggest building on the Red Thread property, an ancient and hulking seven-story wood box with narrow slits for windows and an arched wooden door painted green.

Tensing, wary of guards and guard dogs, Levi eased the green door open. According to his watch, it was 10:10 p.m., and if Tamara kept her promise, she'd be here. He looked around and saw barrel after barrel sitting on slanted wooden ricks. Endless barrels receding deep into the cool cave-like recesses. And the smell…pungent, like baking bread, but cold.

"Hey, Levi," she said, and Levi followed the sound of her voice upward. She sat on a wooden staircase in a slant of a security light reading a big leather-bound book. "I'm glad you came."

She had on gray sweatpants, a red-and-white baseball T-shirt and flip-flops. Pajamas. Funny, he'd expected a girl like her to sleep in silk nighties. Or maybe that had been wishful thinking.

"I'm here. Make it good," he said. "It's past my bedtime."

She pursed her lips at him. She never did buy his protestations of innocent and godly behavior.

"I'm sorry I upset you."

"That's what your note said. I can't imagine you're dumb enough to think you wouldn't upset me with what you told me."

"I knew it would upset you. But I'm still sorry."

"Fine. Forgiven. Now what?"

"I don't know," she said. "But I have ideas."

"When you have ideas, I get very nervous."

"Imagine how I feel."

"How do you feel?" he asked. He saw the title of the book she'd been reading. The Bible. Not what he expected.

"About what?"

"About what you found out in your daddy's note."

She shrugged and wrapped her arms around her knees, pulling them to her chest so she could rest her chin on them.

"I was sad," she said. "I loved Daddy. *Love* Daddy. Judge Headley's a good man, and he's always been like an uncle to me. But it was hard to read the truth."

"I'm sure it was."

"He's married, been married twenty years. He never seemed like the type to cheat, but I've given up thinking I know anybody. I don't even know myself sometimes."

"I don't know you, either. You're different now."

"I'm not a kid anymore."

"You did chores you didn't have to do. I'll say."

Tamara grinned. "I miss the horses. I miss my Kermit."

"I'm sure he's somewhere missing you, too."

"If he's alive."

"I'm sure he is. He's a sturdy old boy. Did your mother tell you who bought them?"

"No. Momma and I haven't exchanged ten words in a year and a half. Cora does all the note passing for us. Momma wouldn't tell me who bought Kermit if I put a gun to her head. And believe me, I've thought of that."

Levi climbed the steps and took a seat beside Tamara. He'd told himself he would maintain his distance from her. That resolution hadn't lasted long.

"She shouldn't punish Kermit by taking him from you for something I did. Bad enough she punished you."

"Tell Momma that."

"I'd rather not. She'd call me names and threaten to kill me again. It's cute when you do it. Not so much when she does."

"Momma shouldn't have treated you the way she did. You deserve better."

"We don't always get what we deserve. The world doesn't work like that."

"It will someday," she said.

"Yeah, you keep telling yourself that." Levi leaned back and rested his elbows on the step behind her. "What the hell is that smell?"

"It's the angels' share," Tamara said. She turned around to face him. "You know, it's the bourbon that evaporates while it's aging in the barrels. Smells weird, right?"

"Can't tell if I like it or hate it."

"I can't, either. It's kind of gross and yet I keep sniffing it."

"You're the heir to the biggest bourbon distillery in Kentucky. You can't call it gross."

He'd meant to make her laugh, but she didn't.

"I'm not a fan of our bourbon," she said. "Don't tell."

"Not a soul," Levi said. "I always thought it was pretty good myself. Tastes like apples. Apples and licorice."

"Proof you're a Maddox right there," Tamara said. "Everybody tastes the apple in Red Thread. They say only Maddoxes can taste the anise. A Maddox tongue is made for tasting the bittersweet."

"Lucky me. What do I win?"

"You don't sound happy. Lot of people would be happy to wake up with Maddox for a last name."

"No," he said. "I'm not happy. Did you really think I would be?"

"I guess it was a shock."

"It was and it wasn't."

Tamara wrinkled her nose, something he remembered her always doing when he said something to her that confused her. She was about to launch into a series of annoying personal questions. He decided to cut her off at the pass.

"You know anything about Plato?" Levi asked.

"The gooey stuff?"

He glared at her.

"I know," she said. "The philosopher. I'm young, but I'm not dumb."

"Well, Plato had this theory—anamnesis. He believed all knowledge was innate. It's like…fish. Fish in a pond. The fish is knowledge. You own the pond. And you're up on the dock trying to catch the fish. You already have the fish in a way, since they're in your pond. But until you catch a fish, you don't really *have* the fish. That's why sometimes when you're learning something, a math formula or something, it suddenly clicks and it's not like you're learning it but discovering something you already know."

"I've felt that before," Tamara said. "Like when you find that one puzzle piece in a jigsaw puzzle you've been working on for days, and then you finish the rest of the puzzle in a few minutes. It all comes together and you wonder how you didn't see it before when the piece was right there."

"That's it exactly. That's what it was like when you told me who my father was. Like I'd known without knowing and finally I had that fish in my hands, squirming and gasping for air. I wanted to throw it back. But that's where the metaphor breaks down. You can't ever throw it back once you catch it. And as soon as you see the pattern in the puzzle, you can't unsee it."

"You're something, Levi Shelby," Tamara said. "You're a

stable boy who knows more about Plato and stuff like that than any of my teachers did."

"I read."

"Why?"

Levi boggled at her, shook his head, bulging his eyes out like a Tex Avery cartoon wolf.

"You know what I mean," Tamara said, laughing. She put up two fingers as if to push his eyes back into his head. "Why do you read about Plato and stuff like that?"

"Some of us can't afford college."

"Lots of people who don't go to college also don't read Plato for fun."

"It's not for fun. Not really. There was this man Mom used to clean houses for. Every Thursday. The Thursday House was my favorite house. It belonged to this college professor, Dr. Amos Golding. Taught philosophy at NKU. She'd bring me with her and give me stuff to play with while she worked. Dr. Golding was home one semester, on sabbatical. He started talking to me, and we got to be friends. He was in his forties and I was five, but still, I was crazy about him. I had all these fantasies that he was my real father. I think that's why I read so much. He's the one who told me I didn't need college as long as I read something every day. Something hard. Something that made me think."

"Were he and your mom…close?"

"He was very kind to her, respectful. Flirted a little. And he wasn't married. She'd worked for him several years, so there was this little part of me that believed it was him, and he couldn't do anything about it, since he was Jewish and Mom wasn't. We tell ourselves lies to survive when we know the truth will kill us."

"It didn't kill you."

"Not yet," he said.

It was then Levi noticed that Tamara had put her hand on his knee. She seemed to notice it at the same time he did. She squeezed it like they were old friends and it was old times. He looked down at her hand on his knee and she quickly pulled it away.

"It's okay. I've had more time to get used to this news than you have," Tamara said. "Now we have to decide what to do."

"I don't think there's anything we can do, is there? Raise a big public stink? What good'll that do us? Do you think the courts would really give me Red Thread based on that letter you found? Half the judges in this state probably have kids with their secretaries or housekeepers. They aren't about to set a precedent like that."

"We don't need the courts. We have a judge on our side."

"Oh, yeah, Judge Daddy. Does he know you're his daughter?"

"If he does, he never told me. But it doesn't matter. He'll help us."

"Us? When did 'we' become an 'us'?"

"Aren't we in this together?"

"I don't know what 'this' is. And I don't know why I'd be in it with you."

"You're the only living child of George Maddox. You deserve to inherit his money, his house, his company. All that."

"Why? He fucks my mother and I get to be a millionaire? Not sure that's how it works."

"Come on, Levi. You know we have to do something to make this right. You lost your job because of me. I want to make it up to you."

"Tamara, as much as I'd love to blame you for me getting into trouble and as much as I did blame you, the simple fact of the matter is I am twelve years older than you are. I knew better than to kiss you and I did it, anyway."

"Because you wanted to kiss me."

"Because I wanted to shut you up."

"By kissing me."

"By any means necessary."

"You know you liked it. And you liked me. You still like me or you wouldn't be here."

He gave her a long flat look. A steamroller look. She remained upright.

"I'm leaving, Rotten. Very nice to talk to you. Some of us have to work tomorrow."

He rolled up off the steps and walked past her. Tamara grabbed his hand and he turned around.

"Don't," he said. But he didn't pull away.

"I can help you. Let me help you."

"How can you help me?"

"Tell me your wish," she said, looking into his eyes. She had blue eyes, too, but he liked hers a lot more than he liked his.

"My wish?"

"Your wish. Your dream. If I was a genie and I could grant you one wish, what would you wish for?"

"A horse farm of my own. Nothing fancy. Fifty acres. A hundred maybe, if we're dreaming big. A few horses. A nice farmhouse." It came out so fast he couldn't stop himself.

"A wife? Kids?"

"I don't need a genie for any of that."

"What if I told you I could give you all you wish for? Horses. Land. House."

"You don't look like any genie I've ever seen before. What's the catch?"

"No catch."

"There's always a catch. How are you, who won't inherit anything until you're twenty-one, going to give me a house and a hundred acres of land?"

"Easy," she said. "I'm going to marry you."

12

Tamara was proud of Levi. He didn't laugh in her face. She expected that he would.

Now, he did laugh near her face, but not quite in it.

"Laugh all you want," Tamara said. "I am going to marry you."

"I'm flattered, Rotten. I really am. I had expected a lot of nonsense tonight from you, but a marriage proposal? Now, that's special. You still watching *The Young and the Restless*?"

He sat back on the steps, leaned on his elbows again, crossed his legs at the ankles. She watched his every movement, surprised and pleased to discover she wanted him as much as she ever had. Nice try, Granddaddy. He'd only bruised her. He hadn't broken her.

Levi waved his hand.

"Go on," he said. "I'm all ears. This is a good show—the *Tamara Makes a Fool of Herself* show. Very entertaining. You should be on *Carson* with this routine."

"I'm seventeen," she said, undaunted. The show must go

on. "That's a problem, but not a big problem. A girl can get married at seventeen if she has a parent's permission."

"Like your mother will let you marry me with anything less than a machine gun to her head and probably not even then."

"Not my mother. My father. Judge Headley will marry us."

"And why will he do that?"

"I'll tell him I'm pregnant and it's yours. He's done it before. When his daughter's best friend got pregnant at sixteen, he married her to her boyfriend."

"Her boyfriend probably wasn't thirty years old. I am."

"He'll do it. I know he will. He believes in marriage. And—even better—he's a big-shot judge. No one will question it if he marries us."

"You're smarter than you look. This might be the cleverest murder plot in history. You're trying to get me killed, right? This oughta do it."

Tamara rolled her eyes.

"I'm trying to get you rich. You think you'd take me a little more seriously."

"Why? Why do you care?" Levi sat up straight. "Why would anyone in their right mind try to give money to someone they don't have to give it to?"

"Because it's the right thing to do. You're Granddaddy's only child. It's your birthright. I'm not his granddaughter. I'm not blood. I shouldn't inherit anything. We get married and we both win. We inherit everything, you and me. Then we get divorced in a few years and split it fifty-fifty. Half of a fortune is better than nothing, right?"

"Can't spend that money if I'm dead. And your mother will kill me."

"She won't. Once we have the money, everyone will do what we say. She tries anything and we have her arrested."

"You are a child, Tamara Maddox. I'm not marrying a girl who still eats Frosted Flakes twice a day. And don't pretend you don't."

"But, Levi—"

"What?"

"They're great."

Levi leaned over, put his head between his knees and half laughed, half groaned.

"Levi? You're behaving oddly." He was, too.

He slapped his knees and stood up.

"Well, this has been worth the price of admission," he said. "Now if you'll excuse me, I have to run along. The real world is awaiting my return."

Tamara reached for him and took his arm. He looked at where she touched him. Why did he keep doing that? Did he like it? Or did he hate it? Didn't matter. She didn't let go.

"Levi, please."

"Please what?" he asked.

"You kissed me on my birthday because you wanted to."

"I don't go around kissing people I don't want to kiss."

"You were going to…"

"Fuck you? Probably."

Tamara blushed. "Do you have to say it that way?"

"You're planning on telling this judge of yours I knocked you up and yet you can't handle talk about us fucking? Yeah, I wanted to fuck you that day. It doesn't mean anything."

Tamara lifted her chin, met his eyes. "It meant something to me."

"What did it mean, Rotten? Tell me."

"Momma sold all the horses to punish me for kissing you. And you know what? I still don't regret it."

"Dammit, Rotten."

"Sorry," she said.

He sighed and leaned back against the wall. He shook his head.

"Poor little rich girl. What I wouldn't give to have your problems…"

"Marry me, and all my problems will be your problems."

"That sounds like a marriage vow to me."

"It could be. We could write our own vows," she said. "I'll vow to clean the stalls without you telling me two hundred times and you'll vow to let me ride my horse whenever I want, even when it's raining."

"Not safe to ride in the rain. A good husband wouldn't let you."

"Then you can vow to keep me from getting myself killed."

"What about this baby of ours we're supposed to be having?" he asked. "Isn't it going to be a problem when you say you're pregnant to get us married and no baby ever shows up?"

"I'll say I lost it a couple months after we're married. People lose babies. They lose them all the time."

"Oh, yeah, of course. I lost two babies last week. Hole in my jeans pocket. The babies fell right out somewhere on the trail. I gotta get that hole sewn up."

"You make everything a joke."

"Only if it's funny."

"I don't know why you're making this so hard. It's nothing but a wedding ceremony, and then we can go our separate ways if you want. Nobody'll need to know we don't live together."

"You really think if we get married, I'm going to be content to not fuck you? If I marry you, I fully intend to fuck you."

"Do it, then."

"You really mean it, don't you?" Levi said. "You really want us to get married."

"I do."

"That's cute."

Tamara laughed. "I didn't mean... Yes, I do. I do want us to get married. I do want to say 'I do.'"

"And all because you are so noble and pure and honorable that you think poor little bastard me deserves to inherit even if it means you losing half of what you'd inherit someday."

"Right." Tamara grinned. "Also, me getting married means Momma loses control of the money and the company."

"Nice fringe benefit," Levi said.

"You know you hate her."

"I do, I do. But I do not hate myself, Miss Rotten. Not even a little bit, although if I married you, I probably would."

"Why? Because I'm white?"

"Ring-a-ding-ding," Levi said.

"I'm right?"

"Right and white. She gets it in one."

"I hate to tell you this, but you look as white as I do, Blue Eyes."

"Yeah, and I have blue eyes because one of your blue-eyed forefathers raped one of my brown-eyed foremothers. My mother was black. All the family I have left is black. I'm not about to leave them for you."

"You wouldn't have to leave them."

"You think my family could come to your family parties? You think my family could be invited to our wedding? Where we getting married? The country club? The governor's mansion? Do my aunt and uncle get to come to our big white wedding?"

"No," she said. "But neither do mine."

Levi started toward the door, but Tamara stopped him with one sentence. She hadn't wanted to play her trump card, but if he left her no choice...

"I'll marry someone else, then."

Levi turned on his heel.

"You'll what?"

She shrugged. "I'll marry someone else, then. If you're too stupid to see what a good idea this is, that's your loss. I'm still getting married."

"To whom, might I ask? I'll send a card."

"Doesn't matter. I'll find somebody. Momma's spending my money like it's going out of style, anyway. If you don't want to marry me, I'll find someone who will so I can get my inheritance before it's all gone. I wanted to cut you in because Granddaddy cut you out. But if you don't want to marry me, that's fine. But don't think you're my only option."

"You stupid crazy girl. Do you even know any man other than me?"

"Not many. Granddaddy has some friends who are divorced or widowed."

"You can't marry a man old enough to be your grandfather."

"I can marry anybody I want to."

"You can run through the forest with antlers on your head during deer season, too, if you want. Your funeral."

"If he's old enough, it'll be his funeral. Then I'll be free. Free and rich. And you'll still be living in a stable loft, giving riding lessons for five bucks an hour."

"Goddammit, you're too smart for this, Tamara."

"You said I was dumb."

"You're playing dumb. You're acting dumb. Marrying some stranger to fuck with your mother, that is dumb."

"I have reasons for doing what I'm doing that have nothing to do with my mother. And I'm going to do it with or without you. I'm going to have a good time spending your money on myself."

"You're going to have a better time lying underneath your fat sweaty sixty-year-old husband while he fucks you raw every night. If he can still get it up, that is."

"If that's the price I have to pay, I'll pay it."

"You must still be a virgin, then, if you believe it."

"I am a virgin."

"You sound proud of that. Most girls wouldn't be."

"You would be if you were me."

"Glad I'm not you. Then I'd have just asked someone to marry me and gotten turned down."

"You didn't turn me down. You only think you did. I still haven't heard a flat 'no,' only a pile of jokes and excuses. Now, I'm getting married and it's going to be you or it's going to be somebody else and that somebody else is going to be real grateful to get to spend your money. What's your answer? I'm not going to ask again. I don't have time."

Levi raised his hands to his head and yanked back on his hair, giving his face a ghoulish look for a moment. It made her laugh.

"In the Pantheon of Vexatious Young Women, you are Zeus." He released his hair and hung his head. Defeat. Tamara stepped forward and put her hands on his stomach. He didn't try to take them off, which meant only one thing—she had him.

"And in the Pantheon of Vexatious Men, you are Hera."

Hera—the goddess of marriages who blessed hearth, home and the wombs of young brides. Zeus's wife.

"You're going to talk me into doing this, aren't you?" Levi asked.

"I already have."

"Not yet. I'm still on the fence."

"Would this get you over the fence?" Tamara stepped forward and put her arms around his neck. She brought her lips to his mouth and kissed him. She wasn't sure at first if he'd kiss her back. She wasn't sure at first if she wanted him to.

But he did kiss her back, hard enough she knew he wanted to scare her away from him. One last fight before giving in. She kissed him back twice as hard. Someday he'd thank her for this, thank her for talking him into marrying her.

"You ruined me before," he said. "You're gonna ruin me again."

"I said I'd make you rich."

"That's not what I meant, Rotten. Not what I meant at all."

She shivered despite the heat of his body against hers. Why was he so warm? He felt like a furnace against her skin.

"You're playing me," he whispered against her mouth, nipping her bottom lip with his teeth to get her attention. It worked.

"I thought I was kissing you."

"You're playing me like a piano. And you are Rachmaninoff."

"I must be a natural, then," she said. "Never had one lesson."

Their mouths met again, tongues touched and mated. He was hard against her and she liked it. She loved it even, and considering all that had happened, she loved that she loved it.

"I don't want a child bride," he whispered into her ear. "I'm not that kind of man."

Her fingernails dug into the fabric of his shirt over his shoulders. On bare flesh she would have broken the skin.

"I'm not a child. I haven't been since the flood," Tamara

said, pulling back from the kiss. She laid her head on his chest and could hear his heart racing and knew she'd done it. They were getting married.

"I'm only doing this so you don't marry some dirty old man."

"I only want to marry a dirty young man." She grinned up at him.

"All right, then. You got me. We'll get married. I don't want to do this. And I know I'm going to regret it."

"You'll regret it more if you don't."

"And that's the reason I'm doing it. Damned if I do, and damned if I don't. But if I'm going to burn, I might as well burn in a big fancy bed in your mother's house."

"Soon to be our house," she said. "I can hear her spinning in her grave already." Tamara had never heard a sweeter sound.

"She's not dead," Levi said.

"Not yet."

"So when do we do this?" he asked, pulling away from her.

"Soon as possible. Before my mother manages to spend every penny of mine that's supposed to be yours."

"Soon as possible? Which means…?"

Tamara smiled.

"You free tomorrow?"

13

They were married two days later in Louisville. Judge Daniel Headley presided in his Ohio riverfront office with his secretary and his law clerk acting as witnesses. The ceremony was brief and somber, with Headley acting like he was presiding over a funeral, not a wedding. The rain outside didn't help lighten the mood nor did the judge's reserved demeanor. He had a kind face but wasn't the sort who smiled easily and often. A serious man. He was only forty or so, but he seemed older in this setting, with row upon row of leather-bound legal tomes on hulking ornate mahogany bookshelves and a polished brass statue of Lady Justice standing on a shelf behind his great boat of a desk. Levi knew she wore a blindfold because justice was supposed to be blind, meted out with no regard to race or sex or religion or wealth or lack thereof. From what he'd seen of the world so far, he figured Lady Justice did quite a bit of peeking out from under her blindfold.

The vows were simple and perfunctory.

Do you, Tamara Belle Maddox?

I do.

Do you, Levi Joseph Shelby?

I do.

When Judge Headley pronounced them husband and wife, Levi gave Tamara a kiss as perfunctory as the ceremony.

It was done, then. Papers were signed and witnessed. Hands were shaken. Muted well wishes were given before the judge's secretary and law clerk took their quiet leave of them.

"Have a seat," Judge Headley said, gesturing to the two chairs in front of his desk. "Let's talk about the future."

"Do we have to right now?" Tamara asked. She reached over and took Levi's hand in hers. He had to hand it to her, the girl put on a good show.

"We do, in fact," the judge said.

"We should," Levi said. "Better now than later."

Levi ran his hand down the front of his shirt, straightening the blue tie he wore to match his blue suit. He should have gotten a new suit. The last and only time he'd worn this one had been to his mother's funeral.

"You seem like a sensible man," Judge Headley said. "I'm sure you'll understand when I say I'm not happy about this."

"It's not what I'd planned, that's for certain," Levi said. He could play the part, too. "But we have to do what's best for Tamara."

"Yes." The judge nodded. "Yes, we do. A child needs a father. I know if Tamara's father were still with us, this never would have happened. I blame myself. I should have been more of a father to you after Nash died. I know that's what he would have wanted."

"It's not your fault," Tamara said. "Don't think that this is a bad thing. This is the happiest I've been in a long time."

"Well, I know your granddaddy's up in heaven smiling. He

wanted nothing so much in the world as to see you bringing another Maddox into the world. I would have liked for you to wait a couple years, but what's done is done and many marriages that start out on the wrong foot end up working out. My own sister doesn't like to celebrate her wedding anniversary for similar reasons, and she's managed not to shame the family too much since then." The judge gave Tamara a little wink.

Tamara smiled at him. "I'm sorry," she said. "We didn't mean for it to happen."

"I know, sweetheart. I was young once, too. But your mother's going to want to kill you and me both when she finds out."

"I left her a note," Tamara said. "It's in her medicine cabinet so she'll find it when she takes her sleeping pill tonight. How's that?"

"Let's hope she doesn't get a headache or a stomachache before you two get yourselves somewhere she can't find you. If I know Virginia, she will raise heaven and hell about this. I'd suggest—highly—leaving town."

"We'll be gone," Levi said. "I'll take care of Tamara."

"What about the will?" Tamara asked. "What'll happen with that?"

"It's in probate. You two are legally married and expecting a child together. That will certainly speed the process up. Do you know when you're due?"

"Seven months," Tamara said. "If it goes all right."

"Let's pray it does. I think we're looking at about three months until the will can be fully executed. In the meantime, everything is as it was."

"Will Momma be able to sell the company?"

The judge shook his head. "Not with ownership under

dispute. But you'll still get your five-hundred-dollar monthly allowance. Will it be enough for you to live on?"

"I told you, I can take care of Tamara, sir." Levi sat up even straighter. He didn't want this judge or anyone thinking he couldn't provide for his wife. A hundred and twenty dollars wasn't much to live on, barely minimum wage, but Levi would bus tables if he had to before he'd borrow money from anybody.

"I was under the impression you lived in a stable loft." Judge Headley raised his eyebrow.

"Only to save money, sir. I have a thousand dollars saved up."

"You're going to be a very wealthy man when all this is said and done." The judge picked up a fancy blue pen and tapped it on the desk. "I'd hate to think that was the motive behind this blessed event."

"It's not," Tamara insisted. "After Momma fired him when she caught me kissing him, I had to sneak behind her back to see him. I went to see him. I wanted to see him. I wanted to be with him."

"I want Tamara to be safe," Levi said. "Considering the circumstances, I think she'll be better off with me than with her mother."

"If I didn't know her mother so well, I might disagree. But I do..." Judge Headley's voice trailed off and Levi felt a pang of sympathy for the man. He, too, had been a victim of Virginia Maddox. Tamara said he'd been married when Tamara was conceived, a drunken night at a going-away party. He seemed like the sort of person who'd carry his guilt with him all his life. "You two find a safe place to hole up while I take care of things on my end. Let me know how to reach you. There'll be forms and papers to sign when it's all said and done."

"I'll let you know where we land," Tamara said.

"It's getting late," Levi said. "We best be on the road."

The judge had worked them in after his day in court ended. Now it was close to dinnertime and then it would be night. Levi's first night as a married man. He had no idea where they were spending the night or even if they were spending it together or if they *should* spend it together.

Judge Headley stood up and came around his desk.

"You take care of my little girl," Judge Headley said, holding out his hand to Levi to shake.

"I will, sir. Thank you. I know this is a mess, but we'll get it all straightened out."

"That's what I want to hear. Tamara, you be a good girl. Don't talk back too much to your new husband."

"I promise I'll talk back just enough." She put her arms around his neck and hugged him, hugged him a long, long time. He was her father, after all, not that Judge Headley knew it. Levi looked for the resemblance and saw it. They were both rich, both attractive, both white.

"I'll call your momma tomorrow," Judge Headley said. "You call me as soon as you're settled."

"We can do that. Thank you." Tamara kissed him on the cheek.

"Drive safe, you two. It's cats and dogs out there."

"Rain's good luck on a wedding day," Tamara said. "Didn't you know that?"

The judge leaned back and looked pointedly at the rain coming down like God was emptying buckets the size of mountains.

"If you survive the storm, you'll have all the luck you need," Judge Headley said.

Tamara and Levi left the office.

It was all done.

Over.

Levi was a married man. That was an unanticipated turn of events. He'd gotten used to the idea of never getting married, but he'd done it now. He'd married a rich white girl and he wished right then he believed in God so he could say, "God help us." But they were married and the judge was on their side like Tamara had said he would be. All day from the time he woke up to the time he got in his pickup to the moment he saw Tamara standing in the foyer of the judge's office building in the prettiest lacy white off-the-shoulder dress he'd ever seen, he'd thought something would stop them. Logic. Good sense. A bus plowing into him for his own sake. It seemed like such a crazy idea for them to get married that they wouldn't blame Mother Nature herself for sending the rain on their madcap parade. But nothing and no one had stopped them.

So here they were.

Married.

"Levi?"

Tamara's voice broke through his panic. Levi had stopped to lean back against the wall. His hands were on his face and his breaths were short and shallow.

"I'm all right."

"You don't look it."

"I got married."

"Hey, me, too."

He laughed, but it wasn't a happy laugh.

"I am the village idiot in a city of fools ruled by a mad mayor in the service of a lunatic king."

"Levi, you married into the Maddox family. You *are* the mad mayor. Consider it a promotion."

He lowered his hands from his face, lowered his head to meet her eyes.

"You look beautiful, Rotten."

She grinned broadly.

"I know I do."

"That is not what you're supposed to say when someone pays you a compliment."

"Am I supposed to pretend I don't know what I look like? Look at you. You look so handsome I can't even look at you straight on. I have to catch you out of the corner of my eye or I'll go blind. It's like looking at an eclipse. I need special glasses."

She turned her head left and right, pretending to see him only out of her peripheral vision.

"The village idiot takes a wife." Levi sighed. "And they were idiots together. The end."

"Good story." She put her arms around his neck and kissed him. "Ready to go? It's our wedding night."

"It's five thirty-seven," Levi said, glancing at his watch. "It's our wedding early evening."

"We can still go to bed, can't we?"

"First we're going to my aunt and uncle's house so you can meet them." He took her by the hand and opened his umbrella.

"Do I have to?"

"They're the only family I have, and it's bad enough I got married without telling them. They'll never forgive me if I don't bring you to see them."

"But after, can we—"

"Not tonight, Rotten," he said. "It's been a long day."

Her face fell and she stopped talking. They headed out in

the rain, Levi still holding her hand, but only to keep her under the wide black umbrella with him.

"Where's your car?" he asked.

"Leave it. We'll take your truck."

"Leave your car? It'll get stolen."

"I don't want it anymore."

"We're not leaving an expensive car behind to get stolen because you're bored with it and too spoiled to take care of your own property."

Tamara put her hands on her hips. Not a good sign. "I'm not bored with it. It's registered in my name, Levi. And it's the only one of its kind in the state. People see that car and they remember it. And we're going to have to hide for a while and that car might as well be a big neon arrow pointing right at me. The cops will probably see it and call Momma and it'll get back to her. If it's stolen, fine. Someone who needs it more than I do can have it. Let them have it."

As much as Levi hated to leave a perfectly good car behind, he had to admit she made a point. A baby blue Triumph Spitfire wasn't something you saw every day. His blue '72 Ford F-100 was one of a million on the roads. Nothing special about it at all.

"You really think your mother's going to send a search party after us?"

"I think my mother would send the whole army if she could."

Tamara didn't smile when she said it.

So they left the car.

Levi loved his truck, but as soon as Tamara was in it, sitting all prim and proper in her white dress on the striped gray seats, he felt a little ashamed of it. She'd traded in a sports car for this? He ought to have cleaned it up a little more. Tamara didn't seem to mind it, though. Most girls didn't when he stopped and thought about how many pairs of panties he'd hung from that rearview mirror.

But Tamara wasn't a girl he picked up in a bar and never saw again the next day. Tamara was his wife, and he did not anticipate her having any desire to spend her wedding night in a truck bed. Not that he was going to fuck her anytime soon. Seventeen years old? A virgin to boot? He'd rather fuck a hornet's nest. At least only the one part of him would get stung.

"So…" Levi said, casually as he could. "Where we staying tonight? And tomorrow night? And all the nights thereafter? Hotel?" he asked. "Motel? Rent a cabin in the woods? Riverboat? Steamship? Buy plane tickets and keep flying?"

"I know somewhere we can go to save money," Tamara said. "In case things take longer than Judge Headley says they will."

"Judge Headley. He is your father. You gonna call him Judge Headley all your life?"

"I don't know how to think of him as my father. You ever going to call Granddaddy your father?"

"George Maddox is dead. Judge Headley's still alive. You could tell him."

"And ruin his life? He's married, you know. He was married when Momma got pregnant with me."

"He doesn't seem like the sort of man who'd cheat on his wife. Even drunk."

"I don't think you can judge a man after knowing him an hour. I don't think you can judge a man after knowing him sixteen years."

Levi glanced over at Tamara, felt a pang of sympathy for her.

"Your granddaddy sure gave us the shock of our lives, didn't he?" Levi asked.

Tamara looked at him, startled.

"You know, because he's my father," Levi said, surprised by her surprise. "You think you know someone…"

"I thought I knew Granddaddy. And Momma. I wish I didn't know them."

"You really hate her, don't you?"

Tamara turned her face to the falling rain.

"You don't even know the half of it."

They drove the rest of the way in silence, Tamara's head resting against the window. Levi focused on driving, dodging rain-choked potholes and Kentucky drivers who acted like they'd never seen water before. The *slap-slap* of the windshield wipers lulled him into deep thought. He hadn't meant to hurt her by telling her to back off the wedding-night talk. He didn't want to tell her he already regretted marrying her. It wasn't personal. It wasn't that he didn't want her. He did want her and two nights ago he'd have pushed her over a bourbon barrel and fucked her blind had she let him. But two nights ago they weren't married and he hadn't been thinking with his brain.

The simple fact of the matter that Levi could not deny was that he knew as soon as he touched her he couldn't walk from this…this whatever it was. This marriage. This scheme of Tamara's. He was adrift on a river, no boat, no paddle, and he could not see what was ahead. Tamara was supposed to be the one with the wedding-night jitters, not him.

"Is this it?" Tamara asked as he turned down the long gravel drive to Andre and Gloria's house.

"It is." He paused a moment. "Andre and Gloria are black. You should know that if you don't already."

"I assumed so. I hope they like me."

It was a sweet thing to say and Levi smiled at it.

"Don't worry about it. I don't like you, and I still married you."

Tamara gave him the meanest look he'd ever seen on a pretty girl's face.

"Be polite. Say 'yes, ma'am' and 'yes, sir.' Compliment Gloria's cooking. Don't ask Andre about the scar on his arm. He got it in the war. And whatever you do, don't swear or use the Lord's name in vain. Gloria's very religious. She doesn't like it. Washed my mouth out with soap more times than I can count."

"I don't swear. You swear."

"I don't swear around Aunt Glory. You don't, either."

"I do know how to behave in polite company. It'll be nice to be in it again."

"You're as rotten as ever, Rotten."

"More rotten than ever," she said. Levi believed it.

He eased the truck up the drive, watching Tamara out of the corner of his eye. He'd been prepared to despise Tamara if she put one toe out of line around his aunt and uncle, if she treated them like anything less than they were, which were the best people in his life and about the only real family he had left. Now he repented of those cold thoughts. Tamara was a seventeen-year-old girl married to a thirty-year-old man. She was swimming in deep waters and the last thing he should do was tie a millstone around her ankle. He parked in front of the house, helped her out of the truck, opened the umbrella and took her inside without knocking.

Andre and Gloria weren't in the living room. He heard voices from the kitchen. Tamara clung to his hand with a viselike grip, and he almost teased her to lay off if she wanted him to use that hand on her later. Then he remembered he wasn't using that hand on her later. Although he wanted to.

But he didn't want to. But he did want to. Goddammit, why did he do these things to himself?

They stepped into the kitchen and came up short in surprise.

Levi found Andre in the kitchen, and Gloria, too. But they weren't alone.

"Heard you had a busy day, son," Andre said.

"Mr. Shelby," said one of the two police officers standing in the kitchen, guns strapped prominently to their sides. "You're going to need to come with us."

Levi sighed.

Apparently Virginia Maddox had indeed gotten a headache today.

14

"Levi!" His aunt Gloria rasped his name like a curse of her own. "What on earth have you done?"

"I got married," Levi said. He looked at the cops. "Married by Judge Headley, district court judge. Call him if you don't believe me," Levi said.

"You can't arrest him." Tamara hadn't let go of Levi's hand, but she took a step forward before he could pull her back. "He's my husband. We're married."

"That's not for me to decide," the officer said. He was tall and broad with a military-looking buzz cut and the officer next to him could have been his twin. "I have to bring him in. Let's go."

"We're not going anywhere," Levi said. "Except outside to discuss this."

Levi wasn't about to let Andre and Gloria get caught in this mess.

"Tamara, you stay with Gloria. Officers."

Before they could escort him out, Levi pushed open the

back door. The cops had parked right behind the house in the one spot Levi couldn't see the car from the drive. Did they really think he'd have run for it, leaving Andre and Gloria alone to account for him?

The rain had stopped finally, but the earth was soft with water under his feet. He leaned back against the porch.

"You gentlemen have a warrant for my arrest?" Levi asked.

"This isn't about that," Officer #1 said. His tag said J. Miller and the other officer's tag read J. Spears. Levi made a note of the names in case things got very ugly. "You gotta come with us, though."

"For what reason, might I ask?"

"You might ask. We might not answer," Spears said. "Come on."

"I'm not going with you unless you have a warrant for my arrest. If you don't, go get one. If you do, show it to me."

"That girl's mother seems to think you kidnapped her. That's something we need to talk about."

"I know my rights. You can't bring me in without arresting me. Are you arresting me? Did you see me commit a crime?"

"You married an underage girl."

"Legally married. She's seventeen, and if our marriage is illegal, then go arrest Judge Daniel Headley, too."

Levi heard the back porch screen door open and shut and Officer Miller looked up.

"You all right, son?" Andre asked from the porch. He stood tall and proud with his hands behind his back like a soldier at attention.

"I'm fine. I stopped by to let you meet my new wife. These officers are delaying the honeymoon," Levi said.

"Maybe all of us should go down to the station and talk this out," Andre said. "You and me and your new bride and a lawyer. Miss Tamara says she knows lots of lawyers. Lots and lots and lots and lots of lawyers."

"I'm not leaving with them until they arrest me for a crime," Levi said.

"If you don't come with us to the station, you could come with us to the hospital." Officer Spears took a step forward.

"What's at the hospital?" Levi asked. "Other than good-looking nurses."

Officer Spears grinned. It was the opposite of a pretty sight. "The morgue."

Levi saw the punch coming but didn't have time to block it or deflect it. He took it right to the face. Red light exploded behind his eyes and everything hurt, even the parts the cop hadn't hit. He inhaled and tasted blood in the back of his mouth.

The second punch came on the heels of the first and got him in the ribs. He cried out, hunched over. If he fought back, he was a dead man.

Out of the corner of his eye he saw Officer Miller striding toward him, baton in hand. Levi knew the lights were about to go out, and he only hoped they'd come on again someday.

He heard a struggle and voices and thought Andre had done something foolish. When his vision cleared, he saw white lace before his eyes and thought they might be angel wings. If heaven was real, he was going to feel like a real ass when he got there.

"You touch him again and I'll have your badges," Tamara was saying before Levi could shut her up.

"Tamara, get back in the house." Levi coughed hard between words.

"I'm not going anywhere." She stood in front of him, between him and the officers, her hands on her hips with her chin high and her eyes on fire.

"Miss," Officer Miller said. "You need to get—"

"That's Mrs. Levi Shelby to you. That's my husband. We are legally married. I know my mother sent y'all out here. Well, my mother has nothing more to do with me, and I have nothing to do with her. I'm a wife now, not a daughter. And when did the police ever have enough free time they can run errands for ladies with nothing better to do than cause trouble? Are y'all the marriage police?"

"Tamara, get back in the house right this minute," Levi said, coming slowly to his feet.

"I'll get in the house when they leave." She took a step forward and Spears and Miller looked at each other. "I know you think Victoria Maddox is important. I know you think she's rich. But she's neither of those things. But I'm both. Red Thread belongs to me now that I'm married. I inherited everything. It's mine. Not hers. She's got nothing. No money. No power. You two are the lapdogs for a dead queen. Do I need to call Mayor Bond? My granddaddy was drinking buddies with Governor Hutchings. I'm sure they won't be happy to hear that two police officers beat up the husband of the richest woman in Kentucky. What do you think the newspapers are going to say about it when word gets out? And you better believe it's going to get out."

Levi finally made it to his feet. He grabbed Tamara's hand and pulled her back behind him where she belonged. He could tell she didn't like it, but she stayed.

"You heard the lady," Levi said. "She's not lying. Everything is hers now that she's married. You really want to lose your badges over some family drama?"

The officers didn't look scared, but they didn't look so smug or certain, either.

Officer Miller spoke first. "There's been a misunderstanding. We were told Miss Maddox had been kidnapped and was being held against her will. Considering the circumstances, we believed her mother."

"What circumstances?" Tamara demanded, spitting out the words.

"He means because you're white and I'm not," Levi said.

"You look pretty white to me," Officer Miller said with a smile Levi wanted to slice off his face with a kitchen knife. "Guess looks can be deceiving."

"My mother is out of her mind," Tamara said.

"You oughta give her a call, young lady," Officer Spears said. "Straighten this out before she misinforms anyone else."

"I'll call her the second you two drive away." Tamara was at Levi's side again. No keeping her behind him.

"Then we'll be on our way." Officer Miller tucked his baton back in his belt.

Without another word they ambled to their police cruiser, got inside and drove off. Levi dropped his head down onto the porch ledge and breathed through the last tremors of pain. He would be hurting for a couple days at least, but it could have been so much worse and that's what scared him. Not the injuries he had, but the ones he could have had.

"Levi?" Andre's voice penetrated through the haze of pain. "Why don't you two come in the house, and we'll get you cleaned up."

"Coming," he said, slowly straightening up.

When he reached for Tamara's hand, he found it shaking. Every part of her was shaking.

"It's fine, Rotten," he said, pulling her against him, holding her head against his chest. "They're gone."

"They beat you up," she whispered. "They can't do that."

"You married into a black family," Levi said. "What did you think would happen?"

"Well, you married into the Maddox family. Stuff like that doesn't happen to us." Tamara tentatively touched the bleeding wound on his forehead. "They could have killed you," she whispered.

"Yes, they could have killed me. Don't ever forget that."

Tamara stepped back, looked at him and up at Andre.

"If they'd killed you, I'd kill them," she said, and the way she said it, Levi almost believed her.

"You would have had to stand in line, Miss Tamara," Andre said and brought his hands around from his back. In his right hand he held a pistol pointed at the ground, a pistol he'd been concealing.

"Jesus Christ," Levi said, almost collapsing under the weight of his relief that it hadn't come to that.

"Behave yourself." Andre glared down at him. "Your aunt will skin you alive if she hears you talking like that."

"I'm sorry," Tamara said, still staring up at Andre. "I didn't mean for this to happen. My mother—"

"I told him to hear you out," Andre said. "I didn't tell him to marry you."

"What was I thinking?" Levi asked.

"The better question is what was you thinking with?"

"We're gonna have this conversation now? Are we?"

Andre's eyebrow rose a little higher. A muscle in his jaw twitched. "No, we aren't. You need a doctor, son?" Andre asked.

"I'll make it," Levi said. He took a heavy breath, rubbed the side of his chest.

"Come on," Andre said. "Gloria will get supper for us."

Andre left them alone in the backyard. Tamara brought her hands to his face again, searching out his wounds.

"I'm fine," he said. "Nothing broken, only bruised."

"You sure you don't need a doctor?"

"I'm sure."

"You can eat?"

"I can eat. But we're not staying here. We need to get to a hotel or something where your mother can't find us. This could have gone very bad. I can't get Gloria and Andre in trouble."

They should probably leave the state tonight. They could make it to Indiana or Ohio easy. Ohio cops would laugh it right off if Virginia Maddox told them to go fetch and carry for her.

"Can you handle a long drive?" Tamara asked. "A few hours tonight and then all day tomorrow?"

"Why?" he asked as he pulled himself together enough to walk up the porch steps and into the house.

"Because I told you I know a place where we can go. Somewhere nobody will find us. Somewhere no one will look," Tamara said.

"Where is it?" he asked. Her eyes glinted like sunlight on water, ever changing. She didn't smile.

"Do you trust me at all?"

"More than I did ten minutes ago."

"Then trust me, we should go there."

"Where is there?"

"A place my mother doesn't even know exists."

Levi nodded.

"Sounds like the best place on earth."

15

Paris

"What aren't you telling me?" Cooper McQueen asked.

"Why, whatever do you mean?" Paris looked wounded, innocent. He didn't buy it for a second.

"There's something you aren't telling me that you should tell me, and you should tell me right now."

"Mr. McQueen, what I'm not telling you could fill up a bourbon barrel."

"I want to know who you are. I want to know why you're really here."

"Why do you think I'm telling you this story?"

"To torture me."

"Ah, well…" she said with a smile. "I suppose a girl can have more than one reason for keeping you up all night." She leaned forward and rested her chin on her hand, her elbow on her knee. "Are you scared?"

"Scared? Of you?"

"Of what I'm telling you? Are you scared of this story?"

"Should I be?"

"What's your biggest fear?" she asked.

"Wasting my life," he said, surprised the answer had come to him so readily. "What if everything I've done has been for nothing? What if all this—" he waved his hand to indicate the room, the house, the fortune he'd inherited and earned "—is worthless?"

"Well, then, yes," she said, and he hated the smile she gave him. It was the smile of a woman winning a contest where he didn't even know the rules and winner took all and loser lost everything. "You should be scared of this story."

"Keep talking," he said. "I'm not scared."

"I'll keep talking. Then you will be."

16

Veritas

All Tamara told him was to drive south on I-95. And it wasn't until three hours into the trip that she revealed they were heading to South Carolina.

"Of course we are," he said.

"Is that bad?" she asked, pointing to the interstate sign. He knew they'd been heading south, but he hadn't known they were going that south.

"You have any idea how much Klan is in the Carolinas?"

"The Klan? Like the KKK?"

"You know any other Klan?"

"I didn't…" She looked at him, panic-stricken. He laughed again, not quite with her, but not at her, either.

"It's all right. I mean, it's not right, but there's Klan in Kentucky, too. But do me a favor and don't tell anybody your husband's passing, and I should make it out with my head still attached to my spine."

"It's 1980, not 1880."

"It's not 1980 down here. Trust me. Time passes a lot slower down here." The sad thing was black people were the only people he trusted and yet they were the people he'd have to avoid lest someone pick up on the truth of him and Tamara. But what was the truth? The one-drop rule had never made any sense to him. If one drop of black blood made you black, why didn't one drop of white blood make you white? And hadn't anyone noticed yet that everybody's blood was red? But such questions of logic didn't occur to the sort of men who thought putting on white sheets, calling themselves wizards, of all the stupid ignorant things, and hanging black men from trees were appropriate Christian activities akin to church potlucks and baptizing sinners in the river.

"If it helps, there aren't any people where we're going," Tamara said.

"What is this place? A desert island?"

"It's not a desert," she said.

"But it is an island?" Levi asked.

"It is. A pretty one where we can be alone and hide out. Nobody will bother us."

"Sounds like Fantasy Island. Is some little guy going to greet us and offer to make our dreams come true?"

"I thought I already did that for you," Tamara said. "Your own stables. Your own horses. You remember?"

"Yeah, I remember," he said, trying not to sigh.

Good dream if it did come true. He only hoped he'd live long enough to enjoy it.

Levi didn't tell Tamara he was too hurt to sleep, so he drove on through the night, using the pain in his ribs to keep himself awake. At about four in the morning he was worn-out enough to sleep. He pulled over at a rest stop, locked the doors, rolled up the windows and lay back to rest a couple hours.

Dawn and his bladder woke him up too soon, and he found Tamara lying on her side in the fetal position, her naked feet pressed against his thigh. She looked too young in this light, like a half-grown kid using his suit jacket for a makeshift pillow with her skinny knees pulled up against her chest.

Levi rubbed her bare leg gently and whispered Tamara's name.

"Levi?" she said, her eyes still closed.

"I'm about to start driving again. You better run to the bathroom if you need it."

"I don't need it." She closed her eyes again and seemed to drift back to sleep. But then she spoke again.

"Levi?"

"What is it?"

"Thanks for marrying me."

Levi only looked at her a moment, at his little girl half-asleep and all out of her mind.

"You're welcome, Rotten."

"Were you scared?" she asked, still sounding like she hadn't woken up yet.

"When?"

"When those cops beat you up."

"Nah. I kind of liked it. Getting the shit kicked out of me for messing around with a white girl? Most black I ever felt. I should get some kind of merit badge or certificate of authenticity now."

"You're joking. I know you didn't like it."

"Yeah, I know, too." Levi tried to swallow the fear. It stuck in his throat. "I make jokes when I'm scared."

"You make jokes all the time."

"I'm scared all the time."

"I'll protect you," Tamara said. He would have teased her, except the way she said it…he almost believed her.

"I bet you will," he said, and Tamara didn't answer. She'd fallen back to sleep.

Levi drove for a couple hours until they took a long stop in Asheville, North Carolina, for lunch and clothes shopping for Tamara. She hadn't packed a suitcase, had nothing on her but the clothes on her back and her purse full of money—two thousand dollars in cash. That made him nervous, but he'd be more nervous if she hadn't had it. Levi didn't buy anything. He always kept a few changes of clothes and a spare pair of boots at Andre and Gloria's and he'd brought all that with him in Andre's old army duffel. It wasn't much of a honeymoon they were on, but it wasn't much of a marriage, either.

"Look at that," Tamara said.

Levi glanced out the window. A Confederate flag, the old stars and bars, hung proudly from the porch of a bleached wood shack with a tin roof.

"Told ya so," Levi said.

Tamara shook her head and sighed. "Ignorant," she said.

"That's what Mom always said. She'd see something like that and pray, 'Forgive them, Lord, for they know not what they do.'"

"A good prayer."

"Yeah, but…they know what they do. They know."

Levi hit the gas and drove on, getting as far away from the house and the flag as fast as he could. Not even a jet engine would be fast enough for him. Not even a rocket engine.

Tamara played navigator with the road atlas and directions on her lap. She did a good job because it wasn't too long before they passed a sign that said Welcome to Beaufort.

"According to the directions, we're real close," she said, peering down at the map on her lap. Levi glanced at it, too—well, not at the map so much as her legs. She had on her new short shorts she'd bought that morning and a loose cotton blouse.

"How far?"

"Twenty more miles about to the island. Twenty miles and four bridges."

"So what is this place?"

"Bride Island," she said, putting the atlas aside.

"Never heard of it."

"It's not on the map under that name. They say that's what the locals call it."

"Are you sure it exists?"

"I'm sure. I got directions from someone down here."

"Who?" he asked as he took the exit that pointed to the Sea Islands. He saw a hand-painted sign that read Jesus is Lord of the Lowcountry and one right after that that said Fresh Tomatoes.

"Someone Daddy knew."

"How do you know he knew him?" Levi asked as they drove past the first pink house he'd ever seen in his life. Solid pink but for the white trim, and then another house farther on that was yellow as the sun. After that a pale green house and another that was sky blue. Then a white house with an orange clay roof. And the trees were something else. Ivy coated the tree trunks and Spanish moss hung down from the branches, brown and hoary as an old man's beard. And palm trees. Skinny tall ones that looked like green cotton balls on top. Short squat ones with trunks like fat pineapples.

"Momma had all of Daddy's things boxed up and put in the attic at Arden. When she's out of the house, I dig through

it. One day I found some work papers with the name Bowen
Berry on them. He's some kind of foreman. He's the one who
told me about this place, about where to go, about the house
we can stay in while we hide out."

"Foreman? There's a factory on the island?" He'd been pic-
turing a tiny dot of sand in the middle of a bay, not something
big enough for a factory.

"Close to the island. A cooperage. That's where they make
barrels."

"I know what a cooperage is. Is that why Nash came down
here for work? It's where Red Thread gets its barrels?"

Tamara nodded as she unscrewed the lid of the mason jar
that held what had been ice-cold water but now was warm as
bathwater. A sheen of sweat covered them both even though
they had both windows of his truck rolled down.

"Why's it called Bride Island?" Levi asked.

"I don't know," Tamara said. "But it sounded like a good
place for a bride, right?"

"Is there an island around here called What the Hell Did I
Just Do Island? That's a good place for me."

"That's probably Bride Island's original name."

"Oh, I better go with you, then."

They had to stop for directions a few times to find the
right road to the right bridge. Tamara bought a basket of
blueberries from a fisherman's wife who pointed them to
their turn. They crossed two bridges after that over one island and another. The bridges here didn't cross open water;
they crossed over swamps. They took the turn the fisherman's wife had told them to take and the road narrowed. At
last they reached an old bridge, pale green and rusting.

"Well, that's not very nice, is it?" Levi said.

Before the bridge was a gate. An iron gate in the middle

of high brick walls and hanging off the middle bars was a big damn chain with a big damn lock on it and a sign warning Keep Out. Private Property. Violators Will Be Prosecuted.

Tamara barely glanced at the gate and the lock and the sign. She dug around in her purse and pulled something out.

"I got it," she said, handing him a key. Levi looked at the key, looked at her and shook his head. He put the truck into Park, walked to the gate and unlocked the lock. He had to step off the concrete and into the dirt to get to the lock. The ground was soft and he sank half an inch into it.

"Where the hell am I?" Levi muttered to himself as he pushed open the gates. Back in the truck, Levi drove through the gates and stopped. He got back out and locked the chain behind them, not knowing who or what they were keeping out.

The bridge crossed over a muddy marsh, and when they reached the other side, the road was nothing but hard-packed dirt. On either side of the narrow road were trees, trees and more trees. He craned his neck, following the reach of the trees to the canopy above forming a tunnel. He couldn't see a speck of sky through the green veil. Levi felt like they were being swallowed by a great beast and driving right into its gullet.

And in the air he smelled salt water.

"Are you sure we're supposed to be here?" Levi asked. It was too much, that gate that looked like it belonged on a plantation, the trees, the moss, the sign that said Violators Will Be Prosecuted.

"We're supposed to be here. We're the only ones who are supposed to be here."

"What on earth does that mean?"

"You don't get it, do you?" Tamara said, a smile playing on her lips.

"Get what?"

"Levi, this is our island. We own it."

Levi took a deep breath.

"Once the will's executed?"

"No, now," she said. "Granddaddy and Daddy made a deal. Daddy agreed to marry Momma in exchange for Granddaddy giving him ownership of the island. Momma doesn't know about this place. Daddy didn't love her, but he didn't hate her. He didn't want her to know the only reason he married her was so he could own this island. When I was born, he made sure the island was mine, too. His and mine. Not that I ever knew my name was on the deed. Bowen Berry told me when I wrote him."

"So it's yours."

"Ours," she corrected. "We're married now."

"I own an island," he said.

"Don't get too excited," she said, looking around at the trees that surrounded them, pressing in close. "It's not a very big island."

"Not a very big island? You don't get out much, do you, Rotten?"

Tamara laughed and Levi squeezed her knee, then he squeezed his own knee. Was this real? How could it be? Only in his imagination could he have conjured trees like this, so tall and proud and graceful. They seemed older than earth, older than time. This was a primeval place, and Levi sensed its sacredness. He didn't tell that to Tamara. What with her Bible reading she'd probably think him a heathen. The ancient Greeks had their sacred groves dedicated to the gods. He didn't believe in their gods, but he could see now why they would dedicate a forest to their sacred deities. What god would choose a man-made temple when they could build their own temple out of trees?

"Goddamn, forget gardens. They should have called it the Forest of Eden instead," Levi said.

Tamara said nothing, only pointed to a break in the road. He turned right, onto another road, darker, narrower and even more tree-shrouded than the first. Spanish moss tickled the top of the truck as they drove through it. Levi couldn't drive more than ten miles an hour on the road it had been so neglected. Tree branches blocked their path again and again, and he had to stop and move them out of the way or drive over them so slowly he could hear the wood crack and pop under the tires. The sun was still up—supposedly—but they couldn't see which direction the light came from. He had no idea where the ocean was, no idea where the mainland was. He felt dizzy, but not disoriented, a warm pleasant feeling like being almost drunk with nowhere to go in the morning.

"There it is," Tamara said right as they turned another slow corner.

Ahead was a little house, not impressive at first, not in the way Arden impressed with all its Old South grandeur. But Levi wasn't comparing it to Arden. Arden seemed a million miles away and would always be George Maddox's house even if it became Levi's property someday. But this could be his house and he loved it from the first sight of it. The bungalow was painted white with robin's-egg-blue trim. Levi noted the ceiling and floor of the front porch had been painted that same heavenly blue. The roof was steeply pitched and two dormer windows looked out from the top floor. Wildflowers grew all around the base of the house, nearly choking the porch. He refused to think of them as weeds even if they were. They were too beautiful to be called ugly names.

Tamara opened the truck door before he could walk around and open it for her. She walked up to the porch, carrying nothing with her. Levi grabbed the bags and his duffel. He set them down on the porch floor, which needed sweeping. Up closer Levi could see a layer of grime, dirt and saltwater residue covering the entire exterior of the house. It didn't bother him to see it. It gave him a sense of purpose. This was his house or would be in time. He would take pleasure in putting it to rights.

He opened the screen door and tried the knob. "Do you have a key?" he asked. Tamara stood next to him, so close their bodies touched. She stretched her arm high to feel along the top of the door frame, enough to reveal a few inches of bare stomach under her shirt. She pulled down a key and handed it to him.

"You don't want to do the honors?" he asked. "I opened the gate. You can open up the house."

She shook her head hard.

"You do it."

"What's wrong?"

She looked paler than usual.

"You go in first," she said. "Please?"

"Why?" he teased. "You afraid there's a wolf in there and you want him to eat me, not you?"

"This house…" she said.

"What about it?"

Tamara met his eyes.

"It's where Daddy died. When he…you know."

When he shot himself in the head.

Levi gave her a good long look, searching her out and finding only a girl's honest face and a natural fear of what might be left behind from that day.

"This is why you didn't want to tell me where we were coming," Levi said. "You knew I'd say no?"

"I want to be here. I do," she said. "I need to be here. I… Can you please go in first? Just in case?"

Just in case.

Just in case there was something left of Nash in the house.

"All right," Levi said. "Wait on the porch. I'll see if there's any ghosts or wolves or worse—mothers-in-law—in there. If I don't come back in fifteen minutes, don't call the cops. Call anybody but the cops."

The key didn't want to budge at first. The brass lock had started to turn green and Levi added *Fix or replace the front doorknob* to his list of things to do. They might be here in this place for a while. Might as well make himself useful.

Levi entered the house and shut the door behind him. Automatically he reached for a light switch, but when he flicked it, nothing came on. No electricity. Well, that was all right for tonight. It was dim but not dark in the front room. On the fireplace mantel he found a lantern and a box of matches beside it. He lit it and saw both the lantern and the matches looked new, as if someone had left them for him to find. Maybe someone had. Lifting the lantern, Levi found the front room in good order, with white sheets covering the furniture. He pulled one off, revealing a sofa the same color blue as the porch, with wood arms and legs carved with butterflies and dragonflies. A chair that matched. An oak table. Lamps plugged into the wall. None of them worked, either, but at some point this cottage had electricity. Maybe he had to call the power company? Maybe he had to find the fuse box? The fireplace was empty but looked clean. No ashes. No old wood. The walls were wood paneling but had been whitewashed not that long ago.

The kitchen was small but tidy, old-fashioned. It didn't look like a rich man's kitchen, that's for sure. No microwave oven. No food processor. The gray Formica table and white refrigerator looked like they came straight from the abandoned set of *Ozzie and Harriet*. The big white porcelain sink had become home to a spiderweb that stretched from the window to the faucet. Levi wasn't superstitious, but killing something his first night in his new home seemed like asking for trouble. He caught the spider in a glass and let it outside. When he turned on the tap, pale pink water came out at first, but after a minute the water ran clear. He filled his cupped palms with the water, splashed his face with it and drank a handful. Better he find out right away if the water was potable or not. Better him to get sick than Tamara. But it tasted fresh and fine now that it had worked the rust out of the pipes.

The cupboards weren't bare, but close to it. Two plates. Two glasses. One for Nash Maddox and a spare in case he broke one?

Or one for Nash Maddox and one for someone else?

The bathroom downstairs looked all right, too. The porcelain bathtub must have been quite a showpiece in its heyday, which was probably somewhere around World War I. The finish had worn away on the bottom, but it was still nice, attractive and clean. Small sink. White wood-framed mirror. A toilet, thank God. Electricity he could live without for a month or two if he had to. Indoor plumbing, however, was a necessity, especially now that he had a wife in tow.

Levi started up the wooden staircase off the front room, carrying the lantern held out before him. Two bedrooms up there built into the roof, one to the left of the stairs, one to the right, vaulted ceilings, wood floors. Nice place. One and a half stories was enough space for two people. And both rooms were furnished, a relief, since it meant he and Tamara wouldn't have to sleep together.

His relief felt strangely like disappointment.

The larger bedroom had a full-size brass bed and a nautical navy blue rug. It was the smaller room that got Levi's attention. The twin bed had a brass frame like the one in the first bedroom, but the rug was pink. Pink? Didn't seem like a color a man would choose if a man were doing the choosing. He took a closer look around and found books on the shelves—*Daddy Long Legs*, *The Secret Garden*, *Black Beauty*, *Anne of Green Gables*. Books for children. Books for girls. A pink cowboy hat hung from the closet doorknob. No, a cow*girl* hat. And a silver horse statue sat on the windowsill, forelegs high in the air and wild mane flying. When Levi turned to leave, he saw wooden blocks above the door frame, letters painted on them.

T-A-M-A-R-A

Well, fuck it all and then some.

Tamara's father had tenderly fashioned a room for her, picking out books for her and rugs and ponies. He'd planned on bringing her here to live with him but had killed himself instead. Had hearing the news that Tamara wasn't his biological daughter killed his love for her? No. He'd read the suicide note. Nash Maddox loved his daughter to the very end. So why had he killed himself instead of bringing her here to live? Levi knew Nash Maddox didn't desire women. He didn't understand it, being a lover of women himself, but he never judged any man or woman for their bedtime predilections. As his uncle Andre told him at age sixteen, "As long as nobody gets hurt and it doesn't spook the horses, do what you want and keep the details to yourself." Good advice that he'd always held on to. Didn't sound like Nash Maddox had spooked the horses. Tamara said he'd been a good father and surely she would have been happier with him here than with her mother. The dead were good secret keepers and Levi made his peace with never knowing the answer. Easy for him to do. Harder for Tamara.

Levi left the room as it was. It would hurt Tamara to see it, but love hurt and he wasn't about to deny her a last sign of her father's love.

But he wasn't her father. They weren't blood at all, Nash Maddox and Tamara. But Nash was Levi's blood. For the first time since learning George Maddox was his father did it occur to Levi that it meant Nash Maddox had been his brother. Now passive acceptance of Nash's life and his death turned to active anger. His own brother, threatened and bullied into marrying Tamara's mother. His own brother, plotting to rescue Tamara from the influence of her mother and grandfather. His own brother, left with no recourse but suicide when that plan failed for whatever reason. Levi allowed himself one private moment to grieve for his half brother. Any man who could love a child who wasn't his own blood as his own was a good man, and Levi wished he'd known his brother, wished he could have saved him. But instead, he'd save Tamara. For the sake of his brother he'd take good care of his wife. He'd protect her from her mother the way Nash wanted. He'd even protect her from himself.

Levi took a steadying breath, letting go of his anger, at least for now, at least for Tamara's sake. Back downstairs he inspected one last room. An office of sorts, small with a wooden desk by the window and nothing much else in it but an armchair and a chest-high filing cabinet. He opened one drawer full of invoices and index cards and a liquor cabinet. Nowhere did Levi see blood or bullet holes or anything Tamara shouldn't see. There was a faded patch on the wood floor beneath the desk where a rug used to be. Was this where Nash had shot himself? Had the blood stained the rug? One pane of glass in the window looked cleaner, newer and brighter than the rest. That must have been where the bullet had gone through. Thankfully someone had replaced the pane. They'd removed the rug, fixed the window and cleaned up. Someone had prepared the house for them. But who?

Levi opened the desk drawers looking for spare keys. The top drawer stuck on the track, and when he yanked it back, a piece of paper was dislodged from where it had been trapped. Levi turned to the window and examined it in the light.

"Nash, you devil," Levi said.

It was a Polaroid picture of two men sitting on a yellow beach chair in the sunshine. One was a white man who Levi instantly recognized as Nash Maddox. The man sitting next to him was black and about Levi's age. Nash looked the way he'd looked when Levi had last seen him a few years back. So he guessed this picture was taken not that long before Nash killed himself. Nash looked good in the picture, with his black hair slicked back and a big grin on his face. The black man in the picture was movie star handsome. His eyes had an upward slant to them that put one in mind of pictures of the old pharaohs. He looked lean and tall and strong and had his arm casually draped over Nash's shoulder. Both men were naked in the picture but for their smiles.

So lo and behold, here was the reason Nash came down to Bride Island every chance he got. Levi could think of no other explanation for them to be together in such a pose in the picture. A black man in South Carolina did not sit around naked on a beach next to a white man without a compelling reason. If they were sleeping together, that was a very compelling reason.

Nash…his brother. His dead brother.

"Why'd you do it, man?" Levi asked the picture. "You look pretty damn happy. What happened?"

Levi wasn't glad Nash was dead, but he was glad no one was around to answer that question. With the Maddox family involved, maybe Levi didn't want to know.

Levi considered burning the picture but thought better of it. There were two men in the photograph, and while one of them was dead and gone, the other might be alive and he might want this picture someday. Levi found a flat tin cigar box full of ballpoint pens and stuck the picture in there, facedown. Whoever the man in the picture was, he was important to Nash, but there was no need for Tamara to see it.

His inspections over, Levi walked to the front porch and opened the door.

"No wolves," he said. "Only one spider and he and I signed a peace treaty. You want to come in?"

Tamara gave him a wan smile. She came toward him and put her arms around him, which was unexpected.

"Thank you," she said, and he slowly returned the embrace. Since she already had her arms around him, he lifted her off her feet playfully, swinging her over the threshold.

"The house looks good," Levi said. "No electricity. Probably needs a new fuse. I'll have to run into town tomorrow and get some stuff."

"Mr. Berry said the place blows fuses a lot. Storm surges and bad lines or something."

"We'll be fine with the lantern for one night. But watch your step on the stairs. Bedrooms are upstairs. Bathroom downstairs." Levi left her with the lantern and brought in the bags and duffel from the porch. The downstairs was pitch-black now. Levi saw only a slant of light sliding down the steps. Dammit. He'd meant to warn her before she went upstairs.

He hurried up the stairs and found her in the girl's room— her room, or the room that ought to have been her room had fate hung a left instead of a right. It hadn't taken her long to realize the room's purpose. She sat on the bare mattress by the window, her fingertips stretched out and touching the nose of the horse statue.

The lantern sat at her feet and in the soft shaking light, with her feet barely grazing the floor in a room made for a child, she looked like a little girl. She had a little girl's tears on her cheeks and a little girl's heartache in her voice when she said his name.

Levi stood in front of her and Tamara leaned forward, wrapping her arms around him.

"He was going to bring me here?" Tamara asked.

"I guess he was."

"Why didn't he do it?"

"I don't know, sweetheart," he said, the term of endearment coming out before he could stop it. "Something happened and he couldn't go on. But he must have loved you a lot to put this place together for you."

"I wasn't even his daughter."

"But he loved you all the same."

She pulled back and looked around. Levi handed her his handkerchief and she wiped at her face.

Then she laughed.

"What?" he asked.

"I haven't read any of those books since I was ten. And I hate the color pink."

Levi laughed, too.

"You can take the other room," Levi said. "It's blue. I'll

take your pink room. I think it suits me." He grabbed the pink cowgirl hat off the doorknob and pushed it on his head. "My color, right?"

"You look like the Mad Hatter," Tamara said. She stood up and took the hat off his head and pushed it down on her own. "I'll sleep here. Daddy made this room for me, after all."

"Come on, Alice." He took the hat off her and tossed it on the dresser. "It's been a long day. Let's get ready for bed."

Both bedrooms also had oil lanterns in them. Levi lit every lantern and candle he could find in the house until every room but the kitchen and office glowed with soft firelight. Tamara declared it her job to make up the beds and unpack their things—she was clearly doing her best to act like a wife. She shooed him away while she made the beds. Sore from the drive and his run-in with Kentucky's finest yesterday, he ran a hot bath, took some Tylenol for his bruised side and soaked himself until the water turned cool.

He pulled on his jeans and dunked his sweat-soaked white T-shirt in the bathwater to rinse it out. He hung it and his towel over the towel bar to dry. He hadn't wanted to put on his dirty jeans, which he'd been wearing since last night, but he also didn't want to walk around the house naked or in nothing but a towel. Wife or not, Tamara didn't need to see that. She was a virgin, seventeen, sheltered as a nun, and he planned on keeping her that way until she grew up a little.

On his way up to bed, Levi blew out the lantern downstairs and walked upstairs to the blue room.

When he opened the door, he found Tamara under the covers.

"Rotten, didn't you say you were sleeping in the pink room?"

"I forgot how much I hate pink," she said from the bed.

"Fine. Good night."

He turned to leave her, but Tamara said his name again.

When Levi turned back around, Tamara had sat up in bed. The lantern was on the bedside table, and although she'd taken out her braid and her long brick red hair covered her, he could see she was naked.

"Tamara, we're not doing this," he said, shaking his head. He should have known.

"Please," she said. "I want to be your wife."

"No."

"You said you wanted to."

"I said no such thing."

"You did in the warehouse."

"That was days ago."

"Three days."

"A man says things in an excited state that he repents of in his tranquillity."

"You're extra sexy when you use fancy words."

"Good. Night," he said again firmly, making two sentences of it. He marched into the pink bedroom. The lantern was still lit. By its light he saw the strawberry sheets on the bed, the pink-and-white-striped quilt, the horse in the window, the children's books, the pink hat.

Levi turned and strode into the blue room. Tamara was still sitting up in bed, waiting and watching as he came over to her. He touched the waves of her hair loosened from the braid she'd worn all day. With a slow hand he brushed the strands back over her shoulder. Left shoulder, then right shoulder, uncovering her nakedness. She stared straight ahead and breathed quick shallow breaths through her soft parted lips.

"Levi?"

"You're right. Pink really is an ugly color."

17

Tamara had opened the window in the blue bedroom. Levi could hear the tinkling of wind chimes and smell clean salt air coming in from the ocean. He was George Maddox's son. He owned an island. This house was little and beautiful. And he was about to make love to his wife.

One hell of a week.

Tamara rolled back onto the pillows as Levi sat on the bed next to her. He cupped her face, turning her to meet him in a kiss. Her lips trembled under his. He hadn't expected virginal shyness from Tamara, but he sensed tension in her and vowed to go as slow as possible. His heart battered the inside of his chest, her fear infecting him. Wife or not, he knew he shouldn't be doing this.

"Tell me to stop if you want to stop," Levi whispered.

"I don't want to stop."

Levi kissed her forehead. Nothing could stop this train tonight. They were on a downhill track with no brakes, and God help anyone who got in their way.

He sat up and pushed the covers off her completely and gazed down the length of her naked body. Her breasts were a good size, a handful for a man with big hands, her nipples pale red, not pink. Her navel was the barest little slit. Her hips weren't very wide, but her waist was narrow, giving her a slim hourglass frame. Long legs and strong calves and toenails painted purple, not pink. He cupped her between her legs, feeling her soft curls against his palm.

"Scared?" he asked. She wasn't aroused yet. Spite and gumption alone had gotten her this far; he could see it in the set of her chin and the fire of her eyes.

"No."

"Yes, you are. You're allowed to be your first time, you know, Rotten."

"That's not why I'm scared."

"Then why, baby?"

"Because it's raining."

It was such an odd thing to say Levi didn't know how to respond. He glanced out the window to see, yes, it had started raining. He hadn't noticed, but Tamara had.

"Do you want me to close the window?"

"No," she said, smiling up at him. "I love the rain."

He'd learned a long time ago that when the woman in his life was behaving strangely, his best bet was to take his clothes off. Levi stood up and unzipped his jeans. He pushed them to his ankles and kicked them off into the corner of the room. When Tamara raised no protest, he slid onto the bed again, straddling her waist. Her eyes were trained on the ceiling, but the moment he took her wrists in his hands, she met his gaze.

"Feel me," he said.

He brought her hands to him, wrapping her fingers around his cock. He wanted her to see it, to feel it, to know what she was getting into, what was getting into her. At first she did nothing but hold it in her hands, lightly squeezing as if afraid to hurt him. Not a chance. Nothing could hurt him now. He was bulletproof, invincible. He owned an island. Who but a god or a king could make such a boast? Tamara touched the tip with a gentle finger, stroked the full length of it. Nothing had ever aroused him like the look of her as she looked at him, making a study of him, every inch, every vein, every contour of the head. As she touched him, he touched her, taking both breasts in his hands. He squeezed them, cupped them, molded them against his palms. Her nipples hardened as he brushed his thumbs over them in soft circles, and the color turned to a deeper hue, brick red like her hair.

Tamara released him, but she found new territory to explore. She touched his stomach, her fingertips spider-walking along the muscles. She moved up to his chest, to his shoulders and all the way down his arms until her hands covered his hands, which were still stroking her breasts.

"It doesn't hurt," she said. Levi looked down at her, puzzled.

"This part's not supposed to hurt."

"I didn't know that."

Levi smiled. He took her hands again and lightly pressed them back into the pillow on either side of her head.

"Then I guess I'll have to teach you."

Bracing himself over her, he lowered his mouth to one nipple. She inhaled sharply and Levi smiled against her skin. He took the nipple in his mouth and sucked on it, lightly at first before pulling it deeper into his mouth. Sounds escaped Tamara's lips, soft gasps and softer sighs. As he nursed at her other breast, he lowered his hips to hers, letting her feel the full length of him between her thighs. Without telling her to do it, she opened her legs for him and he relaxed into the cradle of her hips and discovered as he did so that he'd never felt more at home.

The room was cool from the night wind, but he felt nothing but heat. Heat from his body, heat from hers. He kissed a path from her breast to her belly and lower and lower until his shoulders nudged her thighs wider. He kissed her stomach under her navel and above her curls.

"Levi?" His name sounded scared on her lips.

"This is what it is, Tamara," he said firmly, but not coldly. He couldn't blame her for being scared. "This is what happens, so better get used to it now."

"I know." Once again her eyes found the ceiling the most interesting part of the room. Not wanting to scare her, Levi sat up instead. He pushed her thighs wider and felt no resistance from her. He spread her inner lips apart and looked down at her, wanting to know what his wife looked like inside and out. He couldn't see much in the low light of the lantern, but he could see she was wet finally. He pushed a finger into the hole and Tamara's hips rose off the bed an inch, every muscle in her body seemingly tensing at once. But she had to get used to him inside her sooner or later and sooner suited him more than later. The heat inside her beckoned him, but he used only the one finger on her for the time being. He felt the softness around him, the inner folds ripening, swelling, opening up for him. He pushed up and right inside her and traced a straight line from the opening to the hard stop of her womb, where he could go no farther. As he moved in and out of her, her hips moved with him in slight pulses. Near the entrance he felt a tight knot of clenched muscle, and when he rubbed it, Tamara made a noise from the back of her throat—part whimper, part moan.

With his finger still in her and Tamara's attention still

focused on the ceiling, Levi lowered his head and kissed her curls again. This time she made no protest. She seemed beyond words now, lost to herself. She smelled like heat and tasted tart and he had to hold back from burying his tongue inside her. Without him telling her to do it, she pulled her knees to her chest, rested her heels on his back. She was open now, every part of her exposed to him. He licked the red flesh at her core, sucked her clitoris between his lips and massaged it with his tongue. Against his fingertip that knot inside her throbbed like a heart. He cherished the knowledge of it like a hidden treasure. No one on earth knew about it but him, not even Tamara.

Levi didn't know if he should make her come yet or not. An orgasm might make her tighter even if it did make her wetter. He pushed a second finger into her and then a third without her protesting. His own body screamed at him to be inside her and the word it screamed was *Hurry*. His thighs felt like steel and his cock felt like iron. He was hard all over and she seemed as open and ready as any virgin could ever be. Rising up, he knelt between her thighs and draped her legs gently over his.

"Light on or light off?" he asked.

"Off," Tamara said between breaths.

Levi had hoped that would be the answer. This was the beginning and everything worth beginning began in the dark. He positioned the tip between her folds right at the opening. As he leaned up and over her to blow out the wick, he went into her.

Tamara gasped. Levi blew the light out. The room went black.

At first he felt nothing but heat, burning heat, supple and soft, as Tamara enveloped him entirely. He heard a sound again like a strangled grunt and realized it came from him. He held her by her waist and pushed her down onto him as he pushed up and into her. He moved his hips in a roll, over and over, slowly, then even slower, not rushing or thrusting, not until she was totally open.

Levi didn't know if his eyes were open or closed. In this blackness it didn't matter. He didn't need sight when he had touch. He could feel her all around him, a supple warm heat like melted candle wax. He needed to be closer to her. Carefully he eased his full weight onto her smaller body. He slid his hands under her, cupping her bottom to feel the muscles working.

"Like this," he whispered into her ear. He used his hands to teach her how to move, how to raise and lower her hips, not up and down like a piston, but in a long slow sensual oval that allowed him to reach every inner inch of her. An apt pupil, soon she didn't need his hands guiding her. He matched his rhythm to hers, pushing forward as she lifted to the apex, and withdrawing to the tip at the nadir. They were nothing but the coupling now. No other parts of them mattered. Tamara was ceaseless in her undulations, moving like she was made for him and this act that wasn't an act but the opposite of an act. Masks removed. Pretenses stripped away. Roles abandoned in their abandon.

"Is it good, baby?" he asked her, needing to hear her say yes.

"This is what I wanted," she said. "That day…on my birthday…this is what I wanted. Not—"

"Not what?"

"Nothing." Tamara lifted her head and kissed his mouth. Immediately he forgot the question.

While they kissed and while he moved in her, he imagined

what she felt and hoped it felt as good as he imagined it did—the penetration, the thickness of him spreading her wide over him, her burning lungs, her lips dry from hard breathing, her breasts full and heavy, nerves firing and dancing under her skin. He kissed a path down her neck and chest to her nipples because he knew she wanted them kissed and sucked without her telling him. And when he did, he felt her vagina clutching him in response. Her body was his body. His body was hers. He saw himself through her eyes—older, bigger, beautiful to her in that strange way girls found men beautiful, and knowing things she wanted to know. She envied him his freedom, that he was a man and could do anything he wanted to anyone he wanted, while she had to marry him to escape the prison of her life and the prison of the world's expectations. In another world getting married was considered the epitome of settling down, behaving oneself, fulfilling one's role as a woman in the world.

Oh, but not Tamara. Not his Tamara. She'd somehow made marriage her teenage rebellion. What other rebellions did his rotten girl have in her?

Levi went up on his hands again. He thrust into her harder than he should, but she took him. In the dark he could see the outline of her body, her breasts moving with each thrust, her head back and her hands clutching at his arms, clinging to him, panting and moaning with each thrust. She wanted this as much as he did. More maybe, since she'd never had it before, and because she was seventeen, and when he'd been that age, he would have died without sex and considered it the gift of life when a girl gave it to him. So he gave it to Tamara because she needed it, and even though there were a thousand good reasons they shouldn't be doing this, none were good enough to stop them.

Knowing he couldn't last much longer, Levi braced himself on one arm and touched her where they joined. He wanted to feel it while it happened, feel it on his fingers, feel how soft she was against his hardness. He found her clitoris swollen and throbbing, and he stroked it as he rode her, focusing all his attention on the one goal of making her come during her first time. He had to. His self-respect depended on it. The more he rubbed her, the tighter she contracted around him and the harder she breathed and the more she whimpered and moaned and writhed. Her fingers gripped the sheets so hard he thought they'd tear and her hips rose so high off the bed she almost lifted him with her.

They were there. Together. Everything stopped, frozen, tense, taut as an equilibrist's high wire. And they balanced there on the edge, holding on, not blinking, not seeing, too tight to breathe as they pushed, pushed and pushed into each other until the pressure became unbearable, utterly, utterly unbearable…

…and then it was everything all at once. Tamara cried out. Her head fell back. Her inner muscles fluttered and shuddered all around him as he came, pouring into her as they crashed against each other, out of control, erupting with a thousand little explosions along every nerve in their bodies.

Then it was over. Nothing left but the aftershocks, the catching of breaths, the separation and inevitable contemplation of what the hell just happened.

Levi wrapped Tamara in his arms and rolled them together so he lay on his back and she lay on him, her head on his chest, her legs on his legs. It was real now. They were husband and wife. She'd lost her virginity to him. And he'd lost something, too, although he wasn't sure what it was, only that he wouldn't be getting it back. He doubted he'd miss it.

"So that's what it's supposed to be," Tamara said, and he felt her chest moving against his in laughter. Sweat dripped off her forehead onto his shoulder and his semen dripped out of her and onto his thighs.

It was an odd thing to say, but he'd heard odder after sex. Levi stroked her hair, stroked her back, held her close.

"That's what it's supposed to be." He tried to sound as mature as his years, and he thought he pulled it off. He'd never had sex that felt like that before, like they were the same person, same body and blood. It scared him. He didn't like it and yet he wanted more. Having sex with Tamara was like getting high and sobering up all in the same moment. He shivered in the night air like a man with the DTs and pretended the night air caused it.

"Are you scared?" she asked. She must have felt him shaking.

"Terrified. You're an animal. Hold me."

Tamara laughed, a human sound, normal. He took a deep shuddering breath and willed his heart to settle down, but it wouldn't obey. He felt like he'd awoken from a night terror—drenched in sweat, blood racing, and fear, wild irrational fear. As a boy he'd had night terrors, but he hadn't had one in years, and never while awake. No matter how much he told himself it was fine, he was fine, on and on his heart ran as if it wanted to flee his own body.

"I shouldn't have come in you," he said, finding the source of his fear. "I wanted to stop but couldn't. You're on the pill, right?"

Tamara rolled over onto her side away from him.

"No."

18

As soon as she said it, Tamara knew she'd said the wrong thing. She should have lied, but she couldn't do it, not after what he'd done to her. Not after he'd made her feel like that.

"No?" Levi repeated. "No? You let me fuck you and—"

"We're married. We're supposed to do this."

"You're seventeen years old, and I don't want a baby with you."

She felt the bed shift and she turned over in time to see Levi yanking his jeans on.

"What do you mean you don't want a baby *with me*?"

"I don't want kids. Kids trap you."

"I'm not trying to trap you."

"Why didn't you tell me you aren't on the pill?"

"I didn't think it mattered."

"You didn't think it mattered? Didn't matter? This isn't a real marriage, Tamara. You remember that? You remember why we're doing this? I help you get the company from your mother. I get my horse farm. You remember that conversation?"

"Not a real marriage?" She pulled the blanket up to her

neck as Levi struck a match and lit the lantern. She wished he hadn't done that. Now she could see his face and she'd never seen him this angry. "We—"

"We fucked. That's all. That's it. I've fucked a lot of people. Didn't make me married to them."

"But you are married to me."

"Not for long."

"What's that supposed to mean?"

"It means we're done. Tomorrow we're getting the fuck out of here. We're going back to Kentucky. I'm filing for divorce. You can keep your money, you can keep your farm, you can keep it all because I want nothing to do with this or you anymore."

"But, Levi—"

He waved his hand as if chopping off her words as he walked from the bedroom.

"We're done," he said. "I should have known better than to trust a goddamn Maddox. You're as bad as your mother."

He slammed the door behind him.

"I'm not a Maddox!" Tamara screamed, a primal sound that scared her even as it erupted from her own body.

She sat up in bed, panting harder than she had even when Levi had been inside her.

"I'm not a Maddox," she said again, quieter this time, speaking to herself.

Tamara crawled out of bed, wincing as she did. She ached inside. Sex with Levi hadn't hurt, not in the usual way she thought of things hurting. There wasn't a pain inside her. Instead, she felt hollowed out like he'd scraped her insides and opened up parts of her that had long been walled off until now, letting in light and fresh air. She didn't want to close those parts of her up again, not so soon after seeing the light.

When she stood, she felt a rush of fluid from inside her, coating her upper thighs. Tamara looked around the room, found nothing except the corner of the sheet to use to clean herself. That made it too real for her, wiping Levi's semen out of her. It had been so easy in her mind to plan things like *Marry Levi and get pregnant to punish Momma.* But now it was a real thing, not a fantasy. Oh, God, she could be pregnant. She really could be pregnant. And Levi was leaving her.

She didn't want to cry, but she did it anyway as she pulled on her nightgown. From the day she'd met Levi, she'd wanted him, and having him was even better than the wanting. Didn't he know how hard it had been for her to let him do that to her? Didn't he know what it had meant for her to… No, he didn't know. He didn't know because she hadn't told him. And she couldn't tell him now. He'd think she was lying to make him stay. And if he thought she was lying, it wouldn't matter because she'd never want to see him again, anyway.

Tamara picked up the lantern and carried it with her from the bedroom. Carefully she walked down the steps, afraid of falling in the dark, afraid of spiders, afraid of snakes. She clutched the cross around her neck and stroked it for safety and for luck.

"Levi?"

He didn't answer her. She called his name again. Still no answer. She carried the lantern through the living room, into the kitchen, into the bathroom. No Levi, no Levi, no Levi. She took it into the little office, but she couldn't bring herself to step across the threshold into the room where Daddy had shot himself. Still she whispered Levi's name. He wasn't there, either.

Weeping openly now, Tamara climbed the stairs again. The door to the pink bedroom, her bedroom, was closed. She set the lantern down on the floor by the door. She jiggled the handle and found it locked. Levi had locked himself in her bedroom. No. She was locked out.

"Levi—"

"Go to bed, Tamara."

"I have to talk to you."

"Go to bed. We're done talking."

"But—"

"There is nothing you can say to make this all right. So we're done."

Tamara pressed her hands to the door as if she could magically make it open by sheer wanting.

She knew she should go. She knew she should leave him alone to cool off. But she had his come inside her and they were in the house where her daddy shot himself and she was scared. She hadn't been this scared or miserable since the night of the flood.

"Momma was going to kill Kermit," Tamara said. She didn't say it loudly, but Levi must have heard her because after a minute the door opened a crack, and she nearly fell into the room.

"What did you say?"

Tamara stepped back, afraid she'd made it worse.

"Momma. On my birthday. I had to pick—either she'd kill Kermit or she'd fire you. I had to pick. That's what she did to punish me for kissing you. Your job or my horse."

"Your mother did that to you?"

Tamara nodded.

"What did you pick?"

"I should have picked your job, but I couldn't do it. And I couldn't pick Kermit, either. I told her I was going to get you and Kermit and we'd ride away and she could shoot herself instead. She slapped me and left. I'm sorry."

"For what?"

"For not being able to save your job."

"You think I would have picked my job over your horse? There are other jobs."

"There are other horses."

"Your daddy gave you Kermit."

"Yes, he did."

"Your mother is an evil woman."

Before the night of the flood, Tamara would never have thought such a thing. Was her mother a little crazy? Well, yeah, but Granddaddy made everybody crazy. And who could blame her with her husband dead, too? And they'd fought a lot, her and her mother. She couldn't have said she'd liked her mother all that much most days. But evil? No, Tamara would never have said that about her mother before that awful night. She'd felt sorry for her. Even in that big house with her big Cadillac and the credit cards Granddaddy paid for, there was something about her mother that had always reminded Tamara of a dog who had been kicked by its owner one too many times. But the pity was long gone. Her mother had killed the pity.

"Yes, I think she might be," Tamara said.

Levi exhaled and rested his forehead against the door frame. With the lantern between them at their feet, Levi looked like a ghost of some sort, and she imagined she did, too. Their shadows stretched upward to the ceiling. She'd never been this tall, tall as a man, tall as a monster.

"After your mother fired me, I had this fantasy," Levi said. "I'd come back to Arden at night and knock on your window."

"You knew my window?"

"Last window on the side of the house nearest the road. Yeah, I knew your window."

Tamara started to open her mouth, to say something to that, but decided better of it.

"I'd knock on your window in the middle of the night and get you to let me in. And then, in your own bed, I'd fuck your brains out. I'd do it the next night, too. And the night after. And every night until I knocked you up. And then you know what I dreamed of doing?"

"No," she said, her voice hardly more than a whisper.

"I'd leave you. I'd leave you pregnant and alone to face your mother and you'd have to tell her you were pregnant and it was mine, all mine."

"That was your dream?" She'd had dreams like that, too. Not the part at the end. The part at the end was every girl's nightmare.

He nodded. "My fantasy. My ugly awful fantasy to get back at your mother for what she said to me and what she did. I'm not telling you this because I'm proud of it. I'm not. Uncle Andre would kill me with his own hands if I did that to you or any other girl. And here you are, making me into that person I don't want to be. Don't do that to me. Do anything but that to me, Tamara."

"That's not what I want to do, I swear," she said. "I had this idea, the same idea as yours. Momma hates you worse than anybody in the world. Me having your baby would make her madder than anything. It would kill her."

"And you want to kill her."

"Wouldn't you?"

"Go to bed, Tamara. Get some sleep. We'll talk about it in the morning."

"It? What are we talking about in the morning?"

"What we're going to do, I guess."

"Are you going to divorce me?"

"Eventually, I imagine. That was the idea, wasn't it?"

"Yes, but that was before...you know."

"I know."

"Do you hate me?"

"No, I don't hate you. I'm not happy with you, but it's as much my fault as yours. More my fault. I'm an adult. You aren't. I should have taken care of this and not left it to you. This is on me."

She knew what he wanted to say and it hurt. She knew he meant "You're a stupid kid and I shouldn't have trusted you." And maybe he was right. Maybe he shouldn't trust her.

But she wasn't a stupid kid.

"I'll go to bed," she said. "If we have to... If we have to go to a doctor to take care of it, we can do that."

He nodded slowly. "Yeah, there's always that. It was only one time. We'll see what happens."

"Okay," she said. "We'll see." She looked up at him. "Good night."

"Right. Good night."

Levi started to shut the door and then stopped.

"I know you hate her," he said. "I hate her, too. But don't ruin my life trying to ruin hers, okay?"

Tamara swallowed hard and what she swallowed tasted like guilt.

"I won't. I'm sorry."

"It's not your fault. It isn't. I shouldn't have lost it. It's my job to be in charge of this stuff, you know. Every girl on earth is on the pill. Except the one I happened to marry."

"It seemed like a good idea at the time."

He sighed—heavily. One of the old exasperated Levi sighs she'd always adored.

"Do you really think you could handle having my baby?" he asked.

"What do you mean?"

"You know he could be dark, right? I'm light, but that doesn't mean my children will be. It happens sometimes. There are black women so light they can pass for white and they marry rich white men and every time they have a baby it's a waiting game. Will the baby be light? Dark? You never know."

"Is that why you don't want to have children with me?"

"The list of reasons why I don't want to have children with you could wallpaper this house. But if you want to know the number one reason, it's because I don't want to have children. Period. Not in this lifetime, anyway. I can't trust this world with my children. I know what it does to kids like me."

"But you're light enough to look white."

"But I'm *not* white." He said it the same way she'd said, *I'm not a Maddox.* "I know you think you're paying me a compliment by saying that, but you aren't."

"I didn't think I was paying you a compliment. Didn't think I was paying you an insult, either."

Levi exhaled heavily.

"When I was fourteen, Mom moved us from Frankfort to Lawrenceburg. I started a brand-new high school. New kid at school. New start. Mostly white school. And nobody there knows anything about me. I take tests and get put into the top classes. Girls flirt with me. Guys want me at their lunch table. Coaches tell me to try out for the football team, since I'm half a foot taller than every other boy in my class. I was a new man, reborn. That school handed me the keys to the kingdom. Two weeks after school starts, Mom comes for a parent-teacher meeting. That was the end of Levi Shelby's Renaissance. You know what I hate most of all?"

"What?" Tamara asked.

"Those were the best two weeks of my life."

Tamara stared down at her white feet on the whitewashed floor of the landing.

"I was so mad at Mom for ruining it for me," he continued. "I was going to tell her off after school that day, tell her to never come to my school again. I march home and there I see her—she's on her hands and knees in the kitchen, scrubbing the linoleum. Whole day cleaning houses and she comes home and cleans ours. I was ashamed of myself, ashamed enough I got a rag and got down on the floor with her to clean. But I was more angry than ashamed. Those white kids had made me despise my own mother. I didn't want to be one of them after that. My mother was worth a million of them. And you expect me to bring a child into a world that would do that to a kid? Make him hate his own mother? I'm family to Aunt Glory and Uncle Andre. They don't care if I stick out like a sore thumb at family reunions. I'm their blood. And my own father gave me a job cleaning horse shit out of his stables. Where was my invitation to the Maddox family reunions?"

"But I saw a couple of your girlfriends. You dated white girls."

"I fucked white girls. There's a difference."

"But why, if—"

"Because fuck them."

They were the three coldest words she'd ever heard him speak. Cold and slow.

Because. Fuck. Them. Three slaps to the face.

"Is that why...you know, why you kissed me on my birthday?"

"No." He exhaled, rubbed his forehead. She could tell he didn't want to be having this conversation. "It wasn't like that with you."

"Why wasn't it?"

"Because you were...sweet. But you're not so sweet anymore, are you?"

A fourth slap. The hardest slap yet. She wasn't sweet anymore. You didn't hold your grandfather facedown in cold and nasty floodwater until he stopped fighting and come out still sweet on the other side. He took that from her, too, her grandfather did. He took her sweetness and she'd never get it back. Someday she would have to admit to herself that although she was glad he was dead, she could never be happy she'd been the one to kill him.

"I've spent the past year and a half thinking about how much I hate my family, how much I want to hurt them."

"Them? They don't exist, Tamara. The Maddoxes are all dead but for me, right?"

"I guess." She knew of a few second and third cousins, but they weren't part of the business, they weren't part of the bloodline from Jacob Maddox.

"What are you going to do? Go back in time and murder them all?"

"I wish." She said it so coldly that Levi stood up a little straighter.

"Rotten...what's really going on here?"

"Daddy—Nash, I mean—wasn't my father, but he was the only person in the family who loved me. And then Daddy killed himself because of Granddaddy making him marry Momma."

"I know he did and I know that's wrong, but they're both gone now and there's nothing you can do to take back what happened to Nash." Levi put his hands on her upper arms. His voice was soothing, his touch comforting. But she wasn't soothed, wasn't comforted. "You can't hurt people who are already dead."

"No," she said, stepping away from him. "But I can try."

Levi didn't say anything this time. He only shook his head.

"You can sleep in the blue room," she finally said. "I want to sleep in this one."

"It's pink," he reminded her. "You hate pink."

"Daddy didn't know that. He made this room for me. I'm going to use it."

"Good to hear it." He started for the blue room.

"Why did you do it?" she asked, and Levi stopped.

"Do what?" Levi asked, but she had a feeling he knew what she was asking.

"Me. Why did you do me?" Tamara felt heat rise to her face. She wished losing her virginity had magically turned her into a grown-up who could talk about this stuff without blushing like a kid. Not yet.

"The usual reason a man fucks a beautiful girl."

"Is that all?"

"Finishing what we started on your sixteenth birthday. And we're married now, right? Sort of."

"Daddy and Momma never slept together. He said so in his suicide note."

"Well, then, Rotten—there ya go. You've already beaten her."

"Guess I have."

"I'm going to sleep now. If you need me, you know where to find me." Levi stepped past her into the hallway. The door to the blue bedroom was only a few steps away. "But, Tamara, you come into this room, it better be for a good reason. There better be a snake, a bear or a hillbilly with a gun coming after you. I mean it."

"I know," she said. "I'm not going to jump you in your sleep."

"No, you aren't. And I'm not coming near you, either. If we're going to make this thing work without killing each other before we get your money—"

"Our money."

"If," he continued as if she hadn't spoken, "we are going to live in this little house together for months while we wait, I'd appreciate it if you—"

"What?"

"Just leave me alone, okay?"

Levi looked at her like he wanted to say something else. She waited.

But instead, he went into the blue bedroom and shut the door. Funny, she'd known Levi since she was thirteen and came to live at her grandfather's house. He'd called her young and dumb and crazy and spoiled and rotten. He'd called her a twerp, a brat, a hellion, a wildcat. He'd told her to behave herself, to straighten up, to grow up, to act her age, to run along and let him work. And none of it had hurt. Not a word of it had hurt because he hadn't meant a word of it. But telling her to leave him alone? He'd meant it. And it hurt.

Wounded, Tamara slunk into her little pink room. Her lips were a tight line of tension and misery as she pulled down the covers on the bed and settled into the strawberry sheets. The rain still fell soft on the rooftop. In the dark night with the stars hidden behind the oak trees, the rain looked like Christmas tinsel waving outside the window. She didn't think she'd be able to sleep, but worn-out from the drive and the sex and the fight that had nearly finished her marriage before it started, Tamara fell asleep not long after her head hit the strawberry pillow. She slept, and as she slept, she dreamed.

★ ★ ★

She is in a house she's never been in before. It smells of cooking smoke and chimney soot. She's standing in a kitchen of sorts, but it's not like any kitchen she's ever seen except in the pages of history books. There's no faucet, but there is a pump handle. There's no refrigerator, no toaster, no big yellow-and-chrome KitchenAid mixer on the countertop. The floor is wood and covered in a woven rug. A witch's broom hangs on a hook by the pantry. It's hot in the kitchen, hot in the house, hot as hell with no breeze blowing through the open door.

There is a stove in the kitchen, an iron woodstove. A girl stands at the stove. A girl Tamara's age. No, she's a little younger. Fourteen? Fifteen. She has smooth dark skin and large dark eyes framed by long eyelashes, delicate as black lace. She wears a gray wool dress and a red ribbon in her hair. The hardwood floor makes not a single sound as Tamara walks from the doorway to the stove, where the girl stands and stirs a pot of something on the stove top. It's like she's not here. Not in her body, anyway. But something of her must be here because the girl with the red ribbon in her hair looks up at her. Tamara sees the girl has tears on her face and the tears fall in the steaming copper pot as the girl stirs and stirs with a heavy wooden spoon.

"What are you making?" Tamara asks her.

"Saltwater tea."

"You make it with tears?" Tamara asks.

"I make everything with tears."

"Does it taste good?"

"No. It tastes bitter. All I taste is bitter."

"Can I help you?"

"How can you help me?" The girl with the red ribbon speaks softly as if afraid to be heard.

"Do you need my tears, too?"

"What good are your tears to me? I have enough of my own."

"What can I do? Let me help. I've made this tea before, too."

"Who drank your tea?"

"My grandfather. I made him drink a river full of it."

"I don't want to make this tea anymore. But they want it."

"Who wants it?"

"Jacob and his wife want it. He loves to drink my saltwater tea."

"I'll serve it to him this time," Tamara tells the girl. *"If you'll let me."*

"A whole river full of it?" The girl is so young, too young, and pretty, so pretty. Yet Tamara sees her stomach is rounded as if she, too, has been forced to swallow a river of salt water.

"A whole river."

"I don't want to make saltwater tea anymore," the girl with the black lace eyes says.

"Neither do I. But I don't know how to stop making it."

"Your daddy knows," the girl says, glancing up to meet Tamara's eyes.

"Daddy's dead. Is that how you stop making the tea? By dying?"

"Why don't you ask him?"

Then the girl dips a ladle in the copper pot and Tamara sees the tea is a rusty red.

The color of old blood.

The color of old bourbon.

Tamara woke with a start, tangled up in her sweat-stained strawberry sheets. She got out of bed and walked downstairs in the dark, her hand clinging to the railing, her feet finding her footing, since her eyes were of no use.

Your daddy knows. Why don't you ask him?

She couldn't ask her father anything anymore, but still, she had to look for answers. This house was where her father kept all his secrets. The sand...she remembered the sand in his shoes and the wink he gave her. The room upstairs he'd prepared for her because he'd planned to bring her here to live. If this was where he wanted them to live, then this was where he'd keep his secrets.

The rain had stopped at last and her eyes quickly adjusted to the light of the half-moon that filled the office.

On top of the filing cabinet was another cabinet, a liquor cabinet. Anyone else would store his important papers in one of those filing cabinet drawers. But Nash was Granddaddy's son by nature and nurture. She opened the door of the liquor cabinet and pulled out bottle after bottle of bourbon, of whiskey, of scotch and soda. There in the back behind all the bottles she found a business card. One little business card for one big business.

Athens Timber and Lumber, Athens, Georgia. There was a phone number printed on the card and a name written on the back in her father's handwriting. Tamara smiled. Finally the river had gotten a message to Daddy and Daddy had found a way to get a message back to her.

Tamara tucked the card away in the cabinet, put the liquor bottles in front of it again and shut the door. She went back to bed and fell fast into a heavy dreamless sleep.

Levi said you couldn't hurt people who were already dead.

But maybe she could.

19

Paris

McQueen rose from his seat and took a white linen napkin off the bar. He brought it to Paris, holding it out for her. If she wanted it, she could have it, but he wouldn't force it on her.

"Thank you," she said, taking the napkin from him and using the corner to dab her tears.

"Saltwater tea?" McQueen asked.

"My least favorite drink. Too bitter by far."

"I'll stick to bourbon," McQueen said.

"I'm sure you will."

She smiled slightly and it transformed her face. He saw the real Paris in that smile, the real Paris behind the veneer of the red dress, the role she played, his femme fatale, his Brigid O'Shaughnessy, his Maltese Falcon. He wanted to touch her. For the first time since she'd stolen his bottle, he wanted to touch her. But he dared not.

"Maybe it's not a rock fence around you at all," he said. "Maybe it's an eggshell."

"You'd like to think that."

"I would like that, yes. Very much."

He took his seat again and waited for her to speak. Usually he wasn't the sort of man to wait on others. Others waited on him. But for her he would wait. For her he might wait a very long time.

"Tamara wasn't pregnant," Paris said. She laid the napkin on her crossed knee and carefully folded it. He watched her fingers dance over the linen and soon she'd transformed it from a square into a swan.

"I'm sure Levi was relieved."

"Profoundly."

"And Tamara? Disappointed?"

"No. Only determined. Still determined."

"I imagine." McQueen sat back, put his arm over the back of the armchair and watched Paris turn her swan back into a square. "Should I feel bad I got a little turned on by their first time together?"

"Yes."

McQueen shrugged. He was what he was. He wouldn't apologize for it. Not in his nature.

"I assume Levi didn't go through with his threat to take them back to Kentucky?"

"He did not, no. A week passed on Bride Island. Two weeks. Levi fixed the fuse box and they had electricity at the house, which made the waiting a little easier. Every couple of days Levi went into town and called Judge Headley's office to see if the will had been fully executed yet. Not yet, the judge's secretary said. These things take time. So they waited. And waited."

"Sounds nice, peaceful. Spending a summer on your own island isn't so bad. I've done it myself."

"I'm sure you have."

McQueen winced. Why couldn't he stop saying the wrong thing to this woman? She was a minefield. He knew it. So why did he keep walking?

"Peace and quiet they had aplenty. And too much for Levi's sake. But peace and quiet should always be appreciated while it lasts because, as you and I know, it never lasts."

"What happened?"

"Tamara and Levi had houseguests."

"Houseguests ruined their peace and quiet. Must have been bad guests."

"I wouldn't call them bad, but...well...Tamara did have to kill one of them. Then again, I probably would have, too."

20

Levi told her to leave him alone, so Tamara left him alone.

It was surprisingly easy to do even in such close quarters. While the house might be small—only two little bedrooms, one little office, one little living room, one little kitchen and one tiny bathroom—the island itself was big enough to get lost on for days. Their second day on the island, Tamara had walked the dirt road from the cottage to the island's ocean side and seen a sandy white beach simmering in the South Carolina sunlight. As soon as her feet touched the sand, she knew she'd found her daddy's beach, the one he'd walked on and brought home with him after every business trip. Daddy's beach was now her beach and every single day she came out here to swim and sunbathe and sleep under the big blue-and-white-striped umbrella she'd found in the little shed behind the house and kept tied to an oak tree every night so that it would be waiting for her every morning after breakfast.

Levi did not come with her to the beach. He stayed home, worked on the house. He did good work, but she didn't tell him that. She told him as little as possible. For three weeks she'd let him be and he'd returned the favor. She'd always wondered how her mother and father had managed to stay married even though they rarely talked, didn't sleep together and didn't like each other.

Well...now Tamara knew, didn't she?

Tamara turned over onto her back, trying to dry out completely from her last dip into the ocean. Boats never came within five hundred yards of the island, so she had no qualms about sunbathing in only her underwear. No one would see her, so what did it matter? And it felt good to lie topless in the warming sun as the cool waters evaporated off her body. Too good sometimes. So good it made her remember things she didn't want to remember, like her one and only night in bed with Levi.

She'd expected to enjoy it. She hadn't expected it to get her so drunk on the memory of that night she'd never sober up again. Every time the memory of it came to her—bidden or unbidden—her head spun and the room spun and the world spun so she thought she might spin right off it. When the sun bore down on her with its strongest rays, she felt the weight of Levi's body settling on hers. When the water lapped at her legs, she felt Levi's tongue between her thighs kissing the parts of her she never knew were made for kissing. Sometimes when she slathered on the sunblock, she'd spend more time than she needed to rubbing it on her breasts, remembering Levi's mouth on her nipples, sucking them and massaging them with his hot tongue. And sometimes she fell asleep in the shadow of her umbrella and dreamed of Levi inside her again, deep inside her, not only in her body, but in her blood. When she woke from these dreams, it was as if waking from a nightmare and yet all she wanted was to fall asleep and dream the dream again.

Tamara heard the crack of a twig and sat up instantly. She grabbed her clothes and turned toward the sound.

"Sorry," Levi said, standing at the edge of the forest. "Didn't mean to scare you."

"You didn't," she said, her heart hammering in her chest.

She wanted to ask him what he wanted, but she'd promised to leave him alone. She left him alone by never speaking unless he spoke to her first, never asking him questions, never extending the conversation, letting it die instead.

He walked across the beach to her. She saw he still had his boots on. She laid her clothes beside her on her towel again and rolled back into the sand.

"I don't know how I feel about you lying out topless on the beach," he said. "I'm not sure it's legal."

She said nothing.

"Although I suppose nobody could see you unless they had a boat and binoculars."

Behind her sunglasses Tamara rolled her eyes.

"I went into town today," he continued. "I called Judge Headley's office."

Tamara stayed silent.

"He's trying to move some court dates around, speed up the process a little. He says hello to you by the way."

"Hello to Judge Headley." No matter how often she told herself the judge was her father, she still couldn't think of any man in that role but Daddy.

"He wanted to know how you were doing, how you were feeling. You know, as you are pregnant and all."

Tamara sighed.

"I told him you were fine as frog's hair. I told him you were puking every hour on the hour. But considering how fat you're getting, that was probably a good thing. I also told him you were gassy. Real gassy. Like we had to sleep in separate houses gassy. He gave me his condolences, said pregnancy was very hard on a woman, and I should be as nice to you as I could."

Tamara dug her fingers deep into the sand, clawing at it.

"Thank you for calling Judge Headley and checking on the will."

"Right," he said. "I picked up the mail, too. Apparently your mother sent Judge Headley a letter to us and his secretary forwarded it our way. You want to read it or should I?"

Tamara held up her hand and Levi put the envelope in it. Tamara rolled up and looked at it. It was her mother's handwriting, addressed to Levi Shelby and Tamara Maddox.

Tamara stood up and walked across the sand to the edge of the ocean. She ripped the letter in half and then in quarters and then dropped them into the water.

"What did you do that for?" Levi asked.

"Do you care what my mother has to say to us?" Tamara asked.

"No."

"Neither do I."

She returned to her umbrella, pointedly ignoring Levi's gaze from behind her sunglasses as he watched her every movement. He didn't need to know she was looking at him looking at her.

"Something else came in the mail today," he said as soon as she'd settled back down on her big pink towel.

"You're in my sun," she said.

"The sun is setting."

"You're in my shade, then."

Levi moved a foot to the right.

"You don't want to know what else we got in the mail today?" he asked.

"Not really, but you can tell me if it makes you happy."

"I'll tell you. But first you can tell me something. On a scale of one to ten, how much do you hate me?" he asked.

"The scale only goes to ten?"

"Good Lord, why on earth did I think marrying a teenager was a good idea?" Levi asked to the sky.

"I didn't think you believed in God."

"I don't, but I'm starting to see the appeal. Something to be said for having someone to hash it out with when one's high-strung overwrought born-again spoiled-rotten child bride gets her dander up for no good reason."

"My dander is not up."

"You have been giving me the silent treatment for three solid weeks."

"I talk to you whenever you want me to. I'm talking right now."

"Yeah, I ask you what you want for breakfast and you tell me you already ate. I ask you if you want to go check out Beaufort or Charleston and you say, 'Whatever you want.' When I tell the judge you're so gassy you're blowing holes in the walls, you thank me for checking in with the judge."

"You did tell me to leave you alone. You can't complain when I do what you told me to do."

"Goddammit, Tamara, you are driving me crazy."

Tamara stood up and grabbed up her sundress, shook out the sand and shimmied into it.

"You were born crazy," Tamara said as she yanked her dress into place. "I'm just driving you home."

She closed the beach umbrella, picked it up and started walking away.

"A doctor's bill," Levi said. "That's what came in the mail.

A ten-dollar bill from Dr. Jefferson Goode for 'Mrs. Shelby's pelvic exam and birth control pills.'"

"I'll pay the bill tomorrow," she said, still walking.

Levi jogged across the beach to her.

"You weren't planning on telling me you went on the pill?"

"No."

"And might I ask why not?"

"You told me to—"

"Leave you alone, yes, I did. I shouldn't have."

"Well, you did. So I did. I keep the pills right by the horse statue in my room, which you'd know if you ever came into my bedroom, but since you don't—" she paused and pushed her sunglasses back up on her head to meet him eye-to-eye "—you don't."

"I see how it is," he said. They stood at the edge of the beach where it met the edge of the forest with nothing between the two but a line of tall beach grass that itched her legs.

"How is it?"

"You're punishing me because I hurt your feelings."

"I'm not doing anything except what you told me to do. And if it's a punishment, maybe the fault is with your orders and not my actions. Did you ever think of that?"

"I thought of that."

"So what do you want to do, then?"

"I want to make love to you. That's what I want to do."

Tamara only shrugged. "Whatever you want."

She tried to step away from him, but Levi stopped her with a hand on her arm. He didn't just stop her; he stopped her and pulled her back to him, taking the beach umbrella from her hands and tossing it on the ground. He kissed her hard then, hard enough to penetrate the wall of indifference she'd erected around herself the past three weeks. She'd needed that wall to do what she'd done. But it was done now, more or less. The date was set, the offer made and accepted. Just waiting on the paperwork for signing. Did she need the wall now? Did she want it? Yes and yes. But did she want Levi more?

Yes.

Levi had her by the hips and held her flush against him as he kissed her. Tamara had left her arms hanging limp at her sides, but now she lifted them and wrapped them around his shoulders. She opened her mouth to his and he slipped his tongue inside. Their hands roved frantically over each other's bodies. She grasped the back of his strong neck to steady herself while he pulled one strap of her sundress down and took her breast in his hand. He pinched the nipple as he kissed her, rolled it and pinched it again. She gasped from the pleasure and pushed her hips into his, needing him there, right between her legs. He bent his head and took her breast into his mouth, sucking on her nipple as his fingers slid into her panties.

Tamara wrapped both arms around his head, dug her fingers into his hair to hold him to her breast. Levi pushed a finger inside her and she gasped.

"Take me home," she whispered when what she wanted to say was *Take me here*.

Levi pulled away, but only to drag her toward the truck. He opened the passenger door for her and got in behind the wheel. As he drove, all Tamara could think was good thing this island had no speed limit or Levi would be arrested for breaking the hell out of it.

They reached the house in what she imagined was record time if anyone kept those sorts of records. Levi didn't simply open her door; he nearly tore it off the hinges. He lifted her out of the truck and into his arms again.

"I can't wait," he said and started pushing her panties down her legs as he shoved her back against the side of the truck.

"Stop," she said, yanking her hips away from him. "Stop now."

"What?" he demanded, panting between parted lips.

She nodded at the house, where every light was on and someone moved behind the sheer white kitchen curtains.

"Someone's here," she said.

"Who the hell—"

"Momma."

21

"No," Levi said, embarrassed by the sudden rush of fear that one name inspired. He had no doubt in his mind Virginia Maddox wanted him dead for marrying her daughter. "Here?"

"Who else would it be?" she whispered.

"The judge swears she doesn't know where we are."

Levi started to walk around the house, but Tamara clung to his hand and wouldn't let him go.

"I'll go check," he said. "You stay."

"Be careful," she said, finally releasing his hand.

Quietly he picked his way over twigs and gravel as he walked around the house to the back door. He saw no vehicles parked anywhere. Whoever it was had apparently walked or been dropped off. Who? Why? Tamara had told him the island itself was about six miles across, several hundred acres of forest and swamp. A squatter could easily live on the island for months without either of them knowing, which was why every single day that Tamara left for the beach, Levi waited twenty minutes before walking down there to check on her without her knowing. He'd just started feeling safe and comfortable in this house on this island. Now, who the hell had broken into their home?

Levi carefully stepped up to the back door and peered in through the curtains. There was a man standing in the kitchen by the stove. Levi nearly laughed out loud in his relief. The man in the kitchen was black. Levi had nothing to be afraid of.

Levi opened the door.

"Hello?" he said.

"There he is," the man at the stove said. "'Bout time you came home. I thought I'd have to drink this all myself. Hope you don't mind I let myself in. Didn't mean to act like I own the place. Although I do."

It took Levi a few seconds to translate the man's words into words Levi understood. He spoke with the accent of the Sea Islands. "This" was "dis" and "the" was "dah" and the words rolled around the man's mouth thick as taffy.

"Bowen Berry," the man said. He held out his hand for Levi to shake. "And you the brother who's not a brother who's a brother who's not a brother, am I right?"

It took Levi another second to figure out what Bowen meant by that.

"Yeah, I'm Nash's half brother who is and isn't a brother, I guess. Good to meet you."

The man laughed deeply at his own joke. They shook hands, and in the midst of the handshake Levi made the connection between the man in front of him and the man Tamara had said was the foreman at the cooperage...and the man in the photograph Levi had found in Nash Maddox's office. Levi's realization that he had seen this very man naked on the beach was unsettling to say the least. Bowen clearly sensed Levi's discomfort.

"You gonna let go of my hand or you asking me to marry you?"

"Sorry," Levi said, releasing Bowen's hand. "I was trying to figure out where I'd seen you before. I better let Tamara know it's you. She thinks her mother came here to murder us. You want to stay for a beer?"

"I got something better than that brewing up already." Bowen nodded toward the pot on the stove.

"Tea? At night?" Levi asked.

"This ain't your regular tea." Bowen took the pot off the boil. From a battered old cooler, he pulled out a bag of ice and a plastic pitcher. He poured the ice into the pitcher and poured the tea over the ice. Then he took an amber bottle out of his toolbox.

"What's that?" Levi asked.

"Bourbon."

"You're putting bourbon in iced tea?"

"Putting bourbon in *sweet* tea, man. That's my Truth Serum. You gonna love it."

"Sweet tea and bourbon? Damn, I think I love it already," Levi said.

Bowen grinned and slapped Levi on the back.

"Go get your missus. I'll pour the drinks."

"Nothing spiked for her. She's too young."

"She married to you, she ain't too young for anything."

Levi started to the front door and stopped. He turned around.

"I don't know how to bring this up," Levi began. "But while we're alone...you should know I found a Polaroid of you and Nash. I'll give it to you if you want it, but I don't want Tamara finding anything like that. There's nothing else in the house I need to know about, is there?"

Bowen shook his head, the grin still on his face.

"I cleaned everything out after Nash was gone. Must have missed that. But let me tell you something, cum'yuh, the only thing your girl needs to worry about in this house is you." Bowen pointed right at him.

Levi only laughed. "Well, I'd argue, but considering what we were planning to do before you showed up, I'm inclined to agree with you."

They let Tamara in and she seemed pleased as punch to see Bowen. Apparently they'd been pen pals for a year or more, writing back and forth about the island, about the oak trees, about the bourbon barrel cooperage where Bowen was foreman. Bowen didn't call it a cooperage, however. It was a "cuppah-rahge" and he wouldn't say a word about it until Levi pronounced it right.

"Is this Red Thread in the mix?" Levi took a second sip. They sat on the porch, he and Tamara in the swing, Bowen in a chair with his feet up on the railing like they belonged there. They'd left the front door and back door open to air out the house. Tomorrow Levi would run into town and get some box fans. Lots of box fans.

"It's not." Bowen raised his hand and shook a finger at him. "Red Thread's too rich for my blood. I make my own."

"This is your own bourbon?" Levi asked. Tamara took it from his hand and sniffed it but didn't take a drink.

"This new kid botched a barrel few years back. I fixed it on my own time. I got the corn mash, the barley..." He sat up and mimed mixing up a cauldron of corn and wheat, stirring it like a witch's brew. "Then I cooked it real good and put it in the barrel. It's been in my shed for four years now. Tastes like the real deal. Better, maybe."

"You ever think of starting your own distillery?" Levi asked. "Now that you know the secret?"

"Ain't gonna happen," Bowen said as he took a pack of cigarettes out of his pocket and lit one up. "You gotta have the barrels to make Red Thread. And these barrels are all spoken for. I make them, but I can't afford to buy one. They out of my price range."

"They only make a thousand barrels of Red Thread a year," Tamara said, giving Levi his Truth Serum back. "They use regular white oak from Missouri for the regular bourbon, but the top-shelf stuff has to have barrels from here. Scarcity makes the price go up."

Bowen pointed at the woods surrounding the house with his cigarette clenched between his index finger and thumb.

"These trees make those barrels," Bowen said. "You want apples and licorice in your bourbon, you want these trees. Everybody wants these trees." Bowen sat back again, crossed one foot over the other and took a long deep drink before taking another drag of his cigarette. He opened his mouth and breathed out like a dragon breathing fire.

"What's so special about them?" Levi asked.

"What's so special about them?" Bowen repeated, aghast. "Girl, you didn't tell this boy about these trees?"

"We haven't really talked much about the trees," Tamara said, a very diplomatic way of saying, *I've been ignoring Levi for three weeks to punish him for being an ass.*

"You know the story about the island?" Bowen asked Levi, and Levi knew that Bowen knew that he didn't know. The Truth Serum had made them all loquacious. "You, girlie?"

Tamara shook her head. "Daddy never even told me the name of the island."

"For your own sake," Bowen said. If Nash had meant to

kidnap Tamara from her mother and bring her down here to live, it was for the best Tamara not know about Bride Island, where it was, what it was, so Virginia Maddox wouldn't know, either. "I suppose you two ought to know."

"Know what?" Tamara asked, falling under Bowen's spell and the spell of his Truth Serum.

"The true story of this island," Bowen said. "If you want to know it. If you think you can handle it. It's not pretty."

"I want to know." Tamara sat forward and it hurt to look at her. She was a child, Tamara was. No matter how she acted, how she played it, how she played him, at the end of the day she was still a child who sat on the edge of her seat to listen to ghost stories at night.

"I'll tell, I'll tell. Let me fortify my storytelling apparatus a moment here." Bowen took another swig of his drink.

In the early-evening dark the whites of Bowen's eyes glowed like twin fireflies. Levi put his arm on the back of the swing and Tamara leaned against his shoulder. This was much better than the silent treatment.

"It's not a story for innocent ears." Bowen set down his glass and took a long drag on his cigarette before blowing out a fine smoke ring.

"My ears aren't innocent," Tamara said.

"I was talking about him." Bowen winked at Tamara.

"I think I can handle it," Levi said. Bowen refilled his and Levi's glasses from the plastic pitcher. Tamara sipped her plain sweet tea, the ice clinking against the sides of the glass.

"Long, long ago this wasn't Bride Island," Bowen began. "This was nothing but swamp island, nothing but ratty little stub trees, copperheads, rattlesnakes, marsh rats, alligators and enough damn pluff mud to drown a horse in. It wasn't a pretty place, not like now." Bowen pointed at Tamara. "Back...oh, a hundred and many years ago, a rich Frenchman—a *comte*, which is like a count, which is like an earl, I think, whatever da fuck that is—he bought this island. He had three sons, you see."

Bowen lifted his hand holding up three fingers, which Levi could see by the light of Bowen's cigarette.

"The first son, he knows he gets the money and the title when Daddy Count dies, so Son Number One sticks close to home. Son Number Two does what number two sons always did—he joins the army and becomes an officer and secretly hopes for Daddy Count and Son Number One to meet an untimely end. But Son Number Three? Nobody knows what to do with a third son. Join the church? Join the circus? No, Son Number Three does what third sons have been doing all their lives—he leaves home. Go west, young man. He went far west. All the way across the ocean west, all the way here. Daddy Count owned some land in the New World. He bought it from a crook who didn't tell him this prize piece of land was a stinking dirty swamp. When Son Number Three arrives after two months on a boat, he's not a happy boy. What's a man to do in a swamp?"

"So what did he do?" Tamara asked.

"Son Number Three—Julien St. Croix. How's that for a name? *Croix* means *cross* and maybe he was born to carry such a cross. Give the boy credit, he didn't turn tail and run back home. Land is land, after all, and he knows there's gotta be money here somewhere. He's a smart boy. Went to school, knows the world. He thinks, swamp…water…crops…rice. They grow rice in swamps in China. Why not grow rice in swamps in America? So he does."

"With slaves?" Levi asked.

"What do you think?" Bowen pointed the burning tip of

his cigarette at Levi. "'Course he did. And St. Croix made himself barrels of money. But a man can't live off money alone. A man needs a legacy. He needs a wife. So he writes home and tells Daddy Count how much money he's made and how he needs a wife now so he can have sons of his own to inherit this golden swamp of his. He remembers a girl he loved as a boy and wonders if she'll marry him. Daddy Count writes back and says her family needs money. St. Croix writes back and offers to pay off their debts. Daddy Count says that's good, but his bride won't come to America unless St. Croix builds her a house to live in. A fine house. No cabins in the swamp for her. So St. Croix builds a fine house for her right here on this island. Big house fit for a queen. St. Croix writes back and says he's ready for his bride, and Daddy Count makes the deal and puts the girl on a ship and sends her this way. But the ship sinks and the bride dies. These things happened back then."

Bowen shook his head and played like he was wiping a tear off his face. Had he entertained Nash at night with dramatic retellings of stories, too?

"But the deal's done," Bowen said. "Daddy Count paid for a bride, paid off those debts. They send their other daughter instead. The little girl in the family. The only daughter they had left."

"How little?" Tamara asked. Levi looked at her and saw her eyes wide and listening, eager as a child for her bedtime story.

"Fourteen," Bowen said. "Though they told her to tell people she was sixteen. Like anybody care about propriety down here in the swamp. She wasn't much more than a child, but she was the only girl they had left to trade. And they were happy to be rid of her. What else is your little girl good for if not getting you out of debt?"

"And they sent her across the ocean to marry a man she'd never met?" Levi asked, aghast.

"They sold her," Tamara said, and her voice was hollow as a dry barrel.

"I can't say they sold her," Bowen said. "But I can say St. Croix bought her."

"What happened?" Levi asked. "Did the girl make it?"

"Her name was Louisa, named for a king, I think, though Louisa is a damn funny name for a king, ain't it? Anyway, the ship comes in and they put out a little rowboat to bring Louisa to St. Croix. They say she stood up in the boat when she saw the man on the beach waiting for her. They say it was love at first sight. They say the boat was still fifty feet from shore when she stepped out of it. And they say it wasn't love at first sight for St. Croix, but it must have been something because he ran into the water to meet her and carried her all the way out of the water in his arms. Ain't that a pretty picture?"

"Stupid girl," Tamara said, shaking her head.

"Stupid in love. Or maybe she was too damn sick of boats she'd rather drown than stay another second on one. But the first idea is more romantic. I'm a romantic."

"Are you?" Levi asked.

"Can't you tell?" Bowen said, grinning, but it looked like a grimace to Levi. "Now, back to thirty-four-year-old—he might have been thirty-five, come to think of it—Julien and his little Louisa. They were married in St. Croix's house the night she arrived, nobody but slaves and her old lady chaperone to witness. Now, Louisa was a sweet girl, innocent, with a good heart, and St. Croix called her Loulou, and don't you think that made her melt like butter when he did? Little Loulou liked it here, liked the sunlight and the ocean. They say when she smiled the sun came out and when she laughed the birds flew down to hear it and when she sang the angels put down their harps to listen. And when she cried, St. Croix took her upstairs and an hour later both of them would be smiling again. She was so young, you see, no one had gotten around to telling her ladies weren't supposed to enjoy that sort of recreational activity. St. Croix doted on her, spoiled her. When Loulou asked for the foreman to stop whipping the slaves, St. Croix put a stop to it. When she asked for a girl her age to keep her company, St. Croix brought two ladies, a momma and her daughter, over from France to do her hair and dress her and powder her nose, all to please her husband. And when he asked her one day why she was sad and sighing, she said it was because she missed the oak trees at her home in France. She loved the ocean. She loved the sky. She even loved the swamp. But why is it there were no real trees on this island?"

All was quiet on the porch. Levi heard nothing but the breeze, the wind chimes and the ocean roar in the distance. A fly buzzed past his ear and Levi ignored it. Tiny fires glowed in tin cans—homemade citronella and rosemary candles to keep the mosquitoes away. Starlight, moonlight, firelight and one tiny red light from the tip of Bowen's cigarette—the perfect light for telling ghost stories. And Bowen sure told his tale with relish, like a boy trying to scare the shit out of his little brothers. And Levi was scared, but he wasn't sure why. Maybe it was the sounds of the owls calling back and forth or the branches moving to and fro as unseen animals settled in to sleep. Or maybe it was the look on Tamara's face, like she wasn't hearing someone else's story, but her own.

"St. Croix wasn't about to let his sweet bride sigh another sigh, not when he could do something about it. He wrote his man and asked for oak tree saplings, the best there was, spare no expense. Three months later here they come on a ship, two dozen of them. These were the finest trees money could buy, sturdy and strong and from the deepest, greenest forests in France. A rare sort of French oak. St. Croix planted his oak trees and they took. They were ten feet tall by the time his bride was showing with her first child. By the time their son was five years old, the trees were big enough for a boy to find worth his time. And they were happy, St. Croix, his bride and his boy. Happy and rich, which is a rarer combination than we'd like to think. Of course, it couldn't last. The ocean lasts. Trees last. The sky lasts. A third son and his child bride happy and in love? That won't last. How could it? God is a patient judge, but when He issues His verdict, justice is swift."

Levi had been getting pleasantly drunk, but at those words he sobered up. He pulled Tamara closer to him. Her body was stiff at first like she didn't know him. But then she softened and let him hold her tight.

"One fine spring day St. Croix's son—Philip was his name—climbed the tallest of the oak trees and a branch broke under his foot and down down came the little boy. The sand is soft, but not when you fall thirty feet on it. He was dead before his momma could get the scream out of her mouth. St. Croix came home from the rice paddy to find his bride cradling their son's body in her arms. She wouldn't let him go. And the next day she carried him into the ocean and let the water take them both away. When her body washed up two days later, the doctor said she was carrying her second child. His son's body never came back. St. Croix went mad as rich men with broken souls will do when God dares to contradict them. He took his slaves off rice duty and made them drain the swamp. After that they had to plant trees. Oak trees, seeds and saplings from the tree that killed his boy. Every day for years they planted those trees, tended them, cultivated them. Then there were trees as far as the eye could see... Why did he plant those trees? Who knows? Maybe he did it because he loved his wife and she loved the trees. Maybe he thought he could bring his boy back if there were enough climbing trees to tempt his soul. Oh, but he was a sad sight, St. Croix was, wandering this island in his dirty clothes, unwashed hair, unshaven face, arms black from the soil up to his elbows. He planted, too. Planted half the trees on this island himself. And when there was no inch of this island that didn't have a tree on it, he walked into the house he had built for his bride, poured out every bottle of scotch he could find, every bottle of brandy, every bottle of fine Irish whiskey, poured it on the carpets imported from Persia and the drapes that came from the finest houses in Paris. Then he lit the drapes afire, and he and the house burned to the ground. Goodbye, third son. Goodbye, bride. Goodbye, little boy who loved to climb trees. St. Croix's body was nothing but ash and the boy's body never turned up. Only Louisa's body is buried here. Married and buried, all on this island. It's a damn shame if you ask me, but that's what happens when you build your castle on the backs of other men. St. Croix wanted paradise and this island became his hell. Your great-great-grandfather, Miss Tamara—Jacob Maddox—is the man who bought the island from Daddy Count's second son, who wanted nothing to do with the place that broke his brother. And I can't blame him. And this island has been Bride Island ever since because of that St. Croix's pretty little bride, and Louisa Island would sound kind of funny, don't you think? And, of course, St. Croix was already taken."

"That's quite a story," Levi said. "All true?"

"Every word of it. You see, *my* great-great-grandfather was the man who dug her grave and watered the oak St. Croix planted by it. Nothing left of that family but one tombstone. But us?" Bowen slapped his chest and grinned like a town mayor at a ribbon cutting. "We're still here, alive and kicking." Bowen lifted both hands and both legs in the air and waved them. He was certainly alive and definitely kicking. He was also drunk.

"Is her grave still here?" Tamara asked. "Can I see it?"

"It's still here if you can find it. I have no idea what's become of it. Overgrown now, the whole grounds are." Bowen shrugged and downed the last of his bourbon. "But you can find the house pretty easy if you look. What's left of it, which ain't much." Bowen stubbed out his cigarette, slapped his thighs and stood up. "Now if y'all will excuse me, I must be heading home. It's been a pleasure."

"Wait, where's the house?" Tamara asked him.

He pointed north and deep into the woods. Levi saw Tamara staring into the darkness. He put his hand on her knee, fearful all of a sudden, fearful like she'd go right now this instant and he'd never see her again.

"You aren't going house hunting," Levi said. "Not tonight."

"Tomorrow," she said.

"No. You go when I go," Levi said. "Tomorrow I'm going with Bowen to the cooperage. If we own this island, I want to know everything there is to know about it."

"I know everything I need to know about it," Tamara said.

"I don't. Now go in the house. Get ready for bed."

"Do I have to?" she asked.

"Yes, ma'am, you have to. I'm escorting Bowen home."

"I am home," he said. Levi looked at him. Bowen grinned. "I can walk there in the dark with a blindfold on if you made me."

"We'll walk there in the dark together. With a lantern."

"You ain't no fun," Bowen said, rolling his eyes. He stepped off the porch, wobbling as he went, but he made it more or less as vertically as he needed to be.

"Can I walk with you?" Tamara asked.

"Bed," Levi said. "Go to sleep."

"But—"

"Bed now," he said. Tamara turned and walked into the house, slamming the door behind her. Levi watched her through the door, watched her disappear upstairs to the bedroom.

"You have it bad," Bowen said. Levi looked at him and grinned.

"I have a pretty wife and a house and an island. I think that's the very definition of having it good."

Levi lit the camp lantern and he and Bowen set off down the little dirt road to the main dirt road.

"You want to see the cooperage, I'll come get you tomorrow morning."

"I do," Levi said.

"I won't get you too early." Bowen winked at him, his face aglow in the light of the lantern. Levi swatted at a mosquito and the light danced in his hand, flashing a yellow aura over the knotty oaks and dripping Spanish moss. Levi saw eyes peering out from behind a tree. A raccoon? He hoped so.

"Can I ask you something?"

"You can. Can't promise I'll answer it," Bowen said.

Levi asked. "The bedroom upstairs. Tamara's bedroom. Nash wanted to bring her here?"

Bowen stopped walking. He looked up at a break in the trees where the stars were looking down.

"He did."

"Why didn't he do it, then?"

"That house you're staying in belonged to old Robert Maddox back in the day."

"Who's that?"

"Guess he'd be Tamara's granddaddy."

"You mean great-granddaddy."

"Right," Bowen said. "Robert built that little place in the twenties. A hunting and fishing cabin. George Maddox didn't use it much, but Nash sure did."

"What did he use it for?"

"Different kind of hunting. Different kind of fishing." Bowen grinned at Levi and arched his eyebrows. "I was his big catch."

"I see."

"I stayed with him when he came down here and he came down here as much as he could. We'd settled in together real nice. It was safe out here. Safe is hard to find for men like us. Nash wanted a divorce, wanted to start over. And he wanted Tamara, too, but knew her momma would put up a fight. But what's that they say? Possession is nine-tenths of the law. He was going to take Tamara and get her settled down here, fight it out for her in a South Carolina court that's going to side with money over Momma."

"If Nash wanted her down here, if he wanted to get divorced and start over with you…why didn't he? Why did he kill himself instead?"

They'd made it to the end of the little dirt road and stood in the middle of the big dirt road.

Bowen crossed his arms over his chest and looked up at the night sky. The only light came from their lantern and the stars above that shone through a break in the canopy of trees. A million stars. Levi had rarely seen so many. He knew some people looked at the vastness of the universe and it made them feel insignificant. Not Levi. He looked up and saw only the beauty and was thankful he had eyes to see it.

"George Maddox was your daddy," Bowen finally said.

"I know he was," Levi said.

"You wish you didn't."

"Too late now. Ignorance may be bliss, but who really wants to be ignorant?"

"You do," Bowen said. "I'm telling you right now that you do."

"What about Nash? He was my half brother. I want to know why he died before I ever got to know him."

"Then you have to know your daddy was a bad man."

"So I hear."

"He's worse than you heard. Nash would come down often as he could, anything to get him away from that wife of his. Then he'd start feeling guilty about leaving Tamara alone, so he'd pack up and go back. One week the guilt gets him worse than usual and he goes back a day early to surprise Tamara. Instead, he finds his wife in bed with Big Daddy."

"Virginia Maddox was sleeping with George Maddox? Her own father-in-law?"

"Not a lot of sleeping going on, I don't imagine."

Levi's mouth opened a little.

"George Maddox fucking his daughter-in-law."

"Oh, he had his reasons, I'm sure. Then again, they all have their reasons, don't they? Reason number one being 'I wanna.' Second reason? He was an evil man. And he knew Nash hadn't laid a hand on his wife their entire marriage, and George wanted another boy. Nash wasn't the sort of son he wanted. Neither were you. But if George got a baby out of Miss Virginia, everyone would think that baby boy was Nash's baby boy. George wanted another son and he was willing to do anything to get it. But if Nash were dead…"

"If Nash were dead, then nobody would think Virginia Maddox's baby was a Maddox baby. Goddamn." Levi scraped a hand through his hair, rubbed his face. "He told you all this?"

"In a letter he left me."

"Did he… He didn't say anything about me, did he?"

"In his letter? Nah. But he talked about you before. He kept tabs. Said his daddy hired you to manage the ponies, but Nash knew the truth about it. George wanted you around to scare Nash into behaving. You were plan Z, you know."

"Plan Z?"

"Plan A was Eric inherits. Plan B was Nash's child. Nash's child was a girl, so plan C was Big Daddy and Virginia's boy. Don't even ask me what plans D through Y were. I don't want to know."

"And I was plan Z—the last resort."

Bowen nodded. "That you were. If Nash didn't do his job, give George little boy grandbabies, well, there was always you. George threatened Nash more than once that he'd leave every penny of that old Red Thread money to you. I don't think he meant it—plan Z, after all—but it kept Nash in line. You were light, light enough to pass. And Nash knew you loved the ladies as much as he didn't. He knew you'd have no problem giving the Maddox line all the baby boys George could ever dream of."

"I wasn't his son. I was a walking, talking threat, and I didn't even know it. You know something—George Maddox always told me I was welcome to bring girlfriends over to the house to take them riding. I thought he was being nice. Turns out he wanted Nash to see his brother with a girl."

"A girl?"

"All right, lots of girls." Levi had taken George up on that offer and brought his girlfriend of the week over to Arden to go riding. It impressed the girls, yes, but it also reminded a too-precocious Tamara Belle that her crush on Granddaddy's groom was a sweet fantasy and nothing more. Or at least that was what it was once upon a time.

"Before me, Nash had his fair share, too. This island was the Fire Island of South Carolina, if you know what that is."

"I know."

"You and Nash are a lot alike. I can see it. He was a sweet evenin' breeze and so're you. You breeze in at night. Breeze back out in the morning."

"I used to be that. Not anymore. I got a seventeen-year-old wife I have to keep an eye on. No more breezing out."

"You'll breeze, you'll see." Bowen turned and faced the road. "And I will breeze myself home."

"You drunk as a skunk."

"So're you."

"You oughta let me walk you halfway there at least."

"I got my own escort somewhere. Where'd that boy go?"

"Boy?" Levi asked. Oh, my.

Bowen put two fingers in his mouth and whistled so loud Levi winced. Bowen did it again and not one minute afterward a dog trotted out of the woods and down the road. It was a medium-size dog, short white fur with triangle ears sticking straight up and an eager smiling dog face.

"There he is. Come here, White Dog." Bowen slapped his thigh and the dog ran to him.

"That's a white dog, all right," Levi said, scraping his hand over the dog's coarse fur. He was all muscle and gristle and blind obedience. "What's his name?"

"White Dog," Bowen said. "Ain't you, White Dog?"

"You named your white dog White Dog? You couldn't think of anything better than that?"

"He's not White Dog because he's a white dog. He's White Dog because that's the shit they put in the barrels. It goes in white dog and comes out bourbon. But we won't put White Dog in no bourbon barrel for four years. We won't do that, will we, White Dog?" He scratched and rubbed the dog's face. Levi only rolled his eyes.

"So you can get home with White Dog's help?" Levi asked.

"Through the woods and over the river. That's that. You sleep well, man. That's my house. Take care of it."

"Your house? I thought Nash left the island to Tamara."

"He left her the island. He left me the house. But you keep it. I don't want it."

"You mean it? We'll pay you for it."

"You come work for me at the cooperage and that'll pay for it. Truth is, I couldn't sleep in that place if you paid me. Too many ghosts around here."

"I don't believe in ghosts."

"You will if you stay on this island long enough. You'll believe anything."

And with that, Bowen gave him a drunken sort of salute and started off down the dirt way. He and White Dog, and they hadn't made it ten feet before Levi called after him.

"For what it's worth, I'm sorry," Levi said when Bowen turned around.

"For what?"

"I don't know. Sorry about Nash. Sorry I'm in your house with my wife, and you're not in it anymore."

"Go home," Bowen said. "Go home to your wife."

"One more question."

Bowen glared at him.

"Stop asking questions," Bowen said. "You're not going to like the answers you get one of these days."

"Did you love him?" Levi asked. "Nash, I mean."

Bowen narrowed his eyes at him. "Why do you care?"

"Because he was my half brother, and I never got to love him. His wife didn't love him. His father didn't love him. I hope somebody did."

"I loved him," Bowen said. "Wish I hadn't, but I did. The Maddox family is cursed, they say, and I believe it. And once you touch one, get inside one, the curse is in you, too. Someday you're gonna wish you hadn't married into that family, breeze."

"I was born into it. If it's cursed, I'm cursed."

"You're cursed."

"You're drunk."

"It keeps the curse away," Bowen said. "It keeps it all away."

Bowen started off down the dark road again and in ten steps he'd turned invisible, nothing left of him but the sound of his whistling as he walked away, White Dog at his side.

Levi adjusted the wick on his lantern and headed back to his house. He didn't blame Bowen for thinking the Maddox family was cursed, but Levi couldn't believe a superstition like that. Curses weren't real. Curses were voodoo. Any bad luck the Maddox family had, they'd brought upon themselves. Eric Maddox had run off and joined the army during a war instead of going to college or signing up in the National Guard like most of the other fortunate sons did. Nash had killed himself when he probably ought to have killed his father—their father. And Tamara…she wasn't a Maddox by blood. If there was a curse, she was immune. And Levi had grown up outside the family, away from George Maddox's influence. No, he and Tamara would be fine.

As he mounted the front porch to the house, Levi allowed himself one smile as he took off his dirty boots to leave on the front porch. Bride Island. Julien St. Croix. Louisa. Little dead Philip. Jesus, Bowen almost had him there. But that was a good story. Almost good enough to make Levi believe this island was cursed and the family was cursed and everything the Maddoxes touched was cursed.

He wasn't cursed. Bowen just wanted to scare him. But Levi wasn't scared. In fact, Levi was home. Right here on this island, he was home. And not a curse to be seen.

The Forest of Eden, that's what this island was. His Eden. And his Eve was waiting for him in bed right this second.

Levi opened the front door and found Tamara standing in the living room.

"Levi, don't move," Tamara said, holding a gun in her hand aimed right at him.

22

"Tamara..." Levi's blood went cold and still as ice.

"It's right at your feet," Tamara said. "Don't move."

Levi looked down. Curled on the floor, frozen in a tight coil, was a copperhead snake. If Levi put his foot out, he could have touched the head of it with his toe.

"Back away, Levi," Tamara said. "Real slow."

"I can't." The door had shut behind him. He'd have to step over or around the snake to get the door back opened. The snake was looking right at him and Levi's heart was pounding from his throat to his guts. He knew if he moved, even one muscle, that beast would spring forward and clamp down on his leg or on his bare foot, and he had no idea where the hell the nearest hospital was, but it wasn't nearly near enough.

"I can't shoot it with you right there," she said. "I might hit you."

Or if she missed, the snake would strike, scared by the sound.

Levi had left the lantern on the porch, too. Otherwise, he

would have dropped it on the snake. All he could do was stand there and sweat and count his heartbeats in his ears.

"It's moving." Tamara lowered the gun and aimed at the snake.

It was moving, but not in any direction Levi wanted it to move. Its head was lifting, eyes still trained on him.

Levi's feet were riveted to the ground. He was five seconds away from hyperventilating. He tried to focus on Tamara standing there in her little baby-doll nightgown holding a pistol he didn't know they had. But all he could see was six feet of copperhead snake sliding his way.

"Get a broom," Levi said.

"It's too close to you. We don't have time."

Levi's body shook so hard he heard his teeth chattering. Tamara took one tiny step forward and Levi sensed the snake tensing. It coiled tighter, lifted its head higher. A mad, bad terrible thought hit him right then. Was Tamara going to kill him? Wouldn't that be nice for her brand-new husband to die so suddenly, so tragically, but would it be tragic if she inherited every penny?

When he spared a second glance at her, he saw her finger shaking on the trigger.

She was going to kill him. A tiny thing like her couldn't handle a gun that big. The recoil would send her flying. Her hand could hardly hold it. She'd aim for his feet and shoot him right in the chest. But maybe that was what she wanted.

"Tamara, don't shoot."

"Levi, I've got to. It's moving."

"Don't. You'll hit me."

The house turned silent as a tomb. There was nothing to hear but his breathing, her breathing and the snake's belly rustling along the floor. The snake's triangular head rose off the floor an inch or two and its long black tongue flicked here and there, tasting the air, tasting Levi's fear.

Tamara stepped right and the floor creaked.

"Tamara?"

"Hush."

Levi hushed.

Tamara tapped the floor with her foot.

The snake seemed to like it. It swiveled its head toward her. The copperhead pushed away from Levi and toward her. Levi reached behind him and opened the door as slowly and carefully as possible, not wanting to startle the snake into striking.

"Run, Tamara," Levi ordered when there was enough distance between him and the snake to speak. "Run upstairs. Run right now."

"There's this verse in the Bible," Tamara began, her voice soft like it came from far away. "Says a believer can pick up a venomous snake and not be harmed. Mark chapter sixteen, verse eighteen."

"The Bible says a lot of things," Levi said. "We don't have to believe them all."

"What if it's true?"

"It's not true. None of it's true. There was no Adam. There was no Eve. There was no ark and no flood and you can't pick up a copperhead and not get bitten."

"There was a flood," she said. "And it killed the wicked. It didn't kill me."

"You aren't special, Tamara. I told you that. You can die like everybody else. Don't even think about it."

"We all die," Tamara said. "So what's there to be afraid of?"

"That fucking snake, for starters."

"I'm not afraid."

"I am. Now do what you're told." The snake had stopped

two feet from Tamara. From Tamara's bare feet, her naked legs. Levi had on jeans, which wasn't much protection, but nothing stood between her and the copperhead.

"Shoot it if you want to shoot it," Levi ordered. "But don't you dare—"

Tamara took a step forward and reached down. It happened fast, but Levi saw it all like a movie slowed to a single frame a second. She grabbed the snake at the neck, right behind its head, and she ran with it, bare feet on bare floors. Then she tossed it on the ground outside the house and turned her head away.

Bang, bang, bang.

She got off three shots.

Levi ran after her and lifted her in his arms out of reach of the snake's bite, if it had any bite left. He swooped her up onto the porch and dropped her on her feet.

"Are you bitten?" Levi asked, running his hands all over her arms and hands looking for puncture wounds. Tamara didn't speak. Her eyes were wide, her pupils fixed. He slapped her lightly on the cheek, snapped his fingers in her face. "Tamara Shelby, did it bite you?"

She shook her head slowly, still in a daze.

"Is it dead?" she whispered.

Levi looked back. Nothing but the snake's tail was left twitching. The head had been blown clean off at the neck.

"It's dead."

Tamara nodded.

"Good." She stood up straight. "That's good."

She didn't look like a child or a girl right then. No, she looked like some sort of angel, some sort of goddess, with the porch light glowing behind her, turning her hair to flames.

She'd picked up a copperhead with her bare hands, then blown him away with three perfect shots. Who was this girl?

His wife, that was who. He saw she was shaking, shivering, not a demon or angel or goddess, but a girl again. A girl who'd looked death in the face and held it in her hands. Levi picked her up in his arms and carried her into the house. He set her down on the sofa, kissed the top of her head, then went back out to bury the beast. In the shed he found a rusted shovel and used it to dig a hole in the soft earth at the edge of the woods. He used the shovel to toss the head into the hole. Its maw was open, its fangs exposed, its eyes open, staring, accusing. Levi covered it with pile after pile of dirt. Then he scooped up the lanky body and tossed it deep into the trees. Some animal would have a nice midnight snack, probably another snake.

When the snake was dead and buried, Levi leaned on the shovel and breathed and breathed.

What was wrong with him? How could he have thought for one moment that Tamara was going to kill him? This was Bowen's doing with his ghost stories and his talk of curses and graves and warning him to never love a Maddox. She had saved his life and there he'd been, worrying she'd destroy him. Levi felt like the worst fool on earth to think that little girl had plotted some sinister scheme behind his back. He ought to grovel at her precious feet and kiss her purple toes for saving him. And then he would wring her neck for picking up a poisonous snake with her bare hands.

He marched back into the house, slamming the door behind him.

"Tamara!" he called out ten times louder than he needed to. "Where the hell are you?"

"Bathroom," came the small scared voice in response. He didn't care what she was doing in there. He threw the bathroom door open and found her at the sink, scrubbing her hands with lava soap.

"Tamara?" he asked, quieter.

"I thought it'd be slimy," she said, her voice rattling like dice in a cup. "But it wasn't slimy. It was real smooth and slick. Like a muscle. It was so strong. I could feel how strong it was in my hand."

"Tamara…" Levi stepped to the sink and took the bar of soap from her hand. Tears covered her cheeks and her hair was plastered on her forehead. He turned on the cold water and rinsed the soap off her hands. "Tamara, you shouldn't have picked that snake up."

"I know," she said in a hollow whisper. "I thought if I missed, I'd shoot you by mistake. And if I missed, the snake might get scared and bite you. And if I missed, it might bite me and then I wouldn't have another chance. I didn't know what else to do. And I thought…" Levi brushed her hair off her forehead and kissed it.

"What did you think?" Levi whispered. "Tell me."

"I love you," Tamara said, looking up into his eyes. "I mean, I have to love you. There's no reason for me to pick up a snake if I didn't love you, is there? I'd have to be crazy or in love. I'd rather be in love."

Her eyes looked crazy—wide-open with her pupils fixed on him like a blind man trying to remember how to see.

"You were scared, that's all. Being scared makes us do crazy things. Andre drove a truck for a long time. Big rig. Some drunk girl ran a stop sign and hit him and her car caught on fire. Andre ripped the door off her car and pulled her out. He can't do that. A man can't rip a door off a car, but he did. Fear gives us powers we didn't know we had. And love. They're the same thing sometimes."

"I loved you before the flood. And I loved you after. You're the only thing I still love from before. You're the only thing I love that I've always loved." She raised a hand to her forehead. "I didn't mean to say all that."

"You can say that to me." Levi took her face in his hands. "You can say whatever you want to me. God knows you always did." He grinned at her, trying to connect to the Tamara he used to know. She was in there somewhere.

"When you made love to me, I felt like I did before the flood. I didn't feel like this."

"How do you feel?"

"Like I have to do things I don't want to do. Like I'm meant to."

"Meant to do what, baby? Meant to do what?"

Levi had his arms around her, and her head rested on his chest.

"There's things God wants me to do and I don't want to do them sometimes. And sometimes I want to do them."

"What is it? What do you want to do?"

"I want to kill my mother." Her voice was steely and low. She meant it. This wasn't teenage hyperbole married to teenage hormones. She wanted to kill her mother. She wanted to do it herself.

Levi kissed the top of her head. If he could make her laugh, it would be like lighting a search fire inside her and he could follow it to the real Tamara.

"If you were trying to piss off your mother by marrying a black guy, you should have found one a little darker than me."

Tamara's shoulders shook. There it was, a little laugh. And there she was, way back in there. He could see her.

"I didn't tell you what she did to me," Tamara whispered. "I didn't tell you."

TIFFANY REISZ

"What? Tell me what she did to you."

"She…said I needed taken down a peg. She told Grand-daddy that. She…"

"Did your mother beat you, Tamara? Tell me the truth now."

Levi searched her face, but Tamara couldn't look at him. It was all the answer he needed.

"I had bruises the next day," she said. "All over me. I could barely move. Even my feet had bruises."

"Jesus Christ."

"That night was the most scared I've been. The snake was nothing, Levi. Nothing."

Tamara met his eyes again.

"You won't leave me alone?" she asked, her voice more scared than it had been when the snake sat at his feet.

"No, baby girl, I will never leave you alone."

"Please be inside me. I'm not so crazy when you're inside me."

She kissed him and Levi kissed her back. He felt as crazy as she did right then and there, mad and wild from fear and relief, mad and wild from the fury at knowing her mother had beaten Tamara for the crime of kissing him. Well, they would show her, wouldn't they?

Levi yanked her panties down her legs and pulled her gown off her arms and pushed his jeans to his ankles. He lifted her up in his arms and impaled her right there in the bathroom. She cried out as he entered her deeply. As light as she was, it was easy to lift her and bring her back down onto him, and he did it again and again, frantic with need, crazy with it. Her back was against the sink and it was a miracle they didn't rip it out of the wall. She was so hot and wet around him, squeezing his cock like a hand, tight and open all at once.

He drove into her, grasping her by her thighs, pounding into her so hard it hurt him. He couldn't imagine how much it hurt her. But she wanted it and wanted more of it. Her arms wound around his neck and she arched into him, hips moving madly, rutting like animals in heat. She came with a moan and with her fingernails digging into his back hard enough to break the skin. He lowered her feet to the floor and turned her, bending her over the sink. Once again he sank into her warm wet depth and fucked her, jerking her onto him and pumping into her at the same time. It was brutal and she loved it. It was brutal and he loved it. The frenzy seemed to last forever. She came again with a gasp that sounded like pain. And when he couldn't hold back anymore, he clamped both hands on her shoulders and rode her, slamming into her, using her for his own pleasure, oblivious to anything but his orgasm, and when he came, it was endless, and he emptied himself into her heedless of the danger and the consequences and the promises he'd made to himself. This was no time for sanity. He could have died tonight. She could have died tonight. Nothing mattered except they hadn't.

When finished, he didn't pull out of her. He rested his head between her shoulder blades and breathed out. Slowly he slid out of her.

"I feel dirty," she said. "I want a hot bath."

"We'll take one together. Not yet, though. Stay right where you are."

Levi gripped her by the waist and entered her again. He didn't even want to come. That was not what he needed. He only wanted to be inside her for a moment longer. Tamara must have felt the same because she leaned back against him, and when he wrapped his arms around her waist, she placed her hands over his hands. If he got lost inside her, he wouldn't worry about finding his way back out again.

"You saved me," Levi said between slow heated kisses. Everything was slow and sultry in the airless room that smelled of sex and the sweat of terror.

"I don't have anyone but you. Not anymore. And you were always nice to me."

"I was mean to you."

"Even when you were mean to me, you were nice to me. You gave Kermit extra carrots and you kept his mane and tail trimmed. Remember the day I fell off and sprained my ankle? You rode out to find me and brought me back on your saddle. I felt like a little princess and you were my knight. You told me dirty jokes to keep me from thinking about how much my ankle hurt."

Levi's heart broke for her. Poor little rich girl, he might have teased her once. But not tonight. Instead, Levi ran a bath and they both got in the tub. Levi washed her long hair and she soaped up his chest and shoulders. They didn't talk about the snake, about her picking it up with her bare hands, didn't talk about Bowen or Bride Island or her mother beating her. They didn't talk about anything at all. They didn't have to, and words wouldn't have made it any better or any worse.

Once they were clean and calm, they went up to bed, careful of their steps. Tonight he'd leave the lantern on the floor and the wick lit to scare off any other intruder animals. Tomorrow and every day after, they'd make sure to keep the screen doors closed even at night. They lay down in the soft glow of the firelight and Levi made love to her again and it was the first time it felt like that instead of the fucking they'd done before. Afterward, she nestled in close, her head on his chest and her arm and leg draped over his body.

All was peaceful, all was right. He kissed the top of Tamara's head, told her she was a good wife, which made her grin with her eyes closed.

As Levi fell asleep, he felt such peace he forgot to ask Tamara why she'd packed a gun with her and where she'd learned to shoot like that.

23

"Fire it up."

"Seems like a damn shame to go to all this trouble just to set it on fire," Levi said, staring down into the bottom of the barrel.

"You have to char the fucking thing," Bowen said. Levi was used to the musical island accent by now, so when Bowen said, "dah fuckin' ting," Levi heard "the fucking thing" like he was supposed to. "That's the fucking point."

"Well, if you say so, boss," Levi said with a grin. He pushed the barrel over the firepot and dropped in a match. The tinder lit easy and flames rose to the very top. The charring was light, lighter than most whiskeys, just enough to open the wood up and wake up the tannins and sugars in the grain so the bourbon would absorb the flavors. Levi had to admit it was fun turning the pristine white oak solid black. And there was enough teenage boy left in his thirty-year-old soul to enjoy playing with fire.

For the past month he'd been Bowen's apprentice at the

cooperage. He'd told Bowen not to tell the other men there that Levi owned Bride Island, that he owned the trees they were using. It wasn't so much he wanted them treating him like the boss, but it was a little unmanly to admit he'd inherited the whole place by doing nothing more than marrying the boss man's daughter. They were good guys, rough and taciturn, and Levi smiled at the thought of them finding Red Thread's soon-to-be new owner was a seventeen-year-old girl. He hoped he was around when they heard that news.

Building barrels was elemental work. The oak trees grew in earth and wind and the boards were aged in the open air until they were thoroughly cured. And when cured, the barrels were charred with fire and sealed up watertight. It took woodworking skills, metalsmith skills, brute strength and precision finesse to make one perfect bourbon barrel, and Bowen was so good at it Levi had to tip his hat to the man. Bowen could whistle while he worked, even as he ran the staves through the saw, making the cuts by hand and by eye, so good at it he could shave a stave with his eyes closed and so strong he could toss a barrel around like a wicker basket.

When the barrel was properly charred, Levi took off the helmet and wiped his forehead with his handkerchief.

"This is work," he said.

"What did you think we did in here? Make toys for Santa?"

Levi laughed. "You have my respect. I used to frame houses on weekends and it's got nothing on this."

"Tomorrow we'll go cut down trees. That's easier."

Levi winced. "Do we have to?"

"Damn hippie," Bowen said, grinning. "Where'd you think your house came from? Is it made of candy, Hansel? We replant the trees. We always replant the trees. No trees, no wood, no barrels, no job. We replant the trees."

"I know, I know. But they're my trees," Levi said, touching his chest.

"They God's trees and you're a damn fool to think He's doing anything but letting us borrow them."

"God loves bourbon, does he?"

"Who doesn't?" Bowen asked.

They might be making bourbon barrels, but nobody drank on the job. Even if they wanted to, Bowen wouldn't let them. He ran a tight ship. One wrong move and a thousand-dollar barrel would be nothing but firewood. Levi had screwed one up himself his first week by forgetting to steam the wood. When he went to put the hoop on the top, he'd cracked the staves instead of bending them. Bowen had put an ax in Levi's hand and set him out back to chop it up. While he did it, Levi felt like a dog whose owner had rubbed his nose in his own shit to punish him. July in South Carolina. Who the hell needed firewood?

Since then Levi had been careful to make no terminal errors. Nearly any hole could be plugged, any flaw could be fixed, if a man knew what he was doing, and Bowen certainly did. The ten men at the cooperage made ten barrels a day and the cooperage operated six days a week. Over three thousand barrels a year, which wasn't much in the grand scheme of things, but it supplied every single barrel to make Red Thread's top-shelf bourbon and sold the rest for a pretty profit to a winemaker in France. Red Thread got their barrels for their mass-market stuff from Missouri. But these barrels were special and Levi did his best not to ruin them. After watching the magic Bowen did putting the barrels together, Levi never wanted to have to ax another one of them again. He'd piss on a Picasso first.

Levi was halfway through sanding a barrel when he felt a tap on his shoulder.

"Special delivery," Bowen said. He pointed out the window, where a truck was parked.

"Finally," Levi said, smiling.

"What you got out there?"

"Present for Tamara."

"A big damn present by the looks of it. You buy her a truck?"

"Different mode of transportation."

Levi pulled off his gloves and tossed them on the workbench. Bowen followed him out of the shop and to the truck. Behind the truck was a horse trailer. Inside the horse trailer was a horse.

"Aww...that's real sweet," Bowen said. "You got the missus a pony."

"That is not a pony. That is a horse. A Tennessee Walker, and he was not cheap."

"Handsome fellow. What's his name?" Bowen asked, peering through the slats at the black-and-white pinto gelding.

"Rex. Unless Tamara wants to change it."

"When you going to give him to her?"

"Right now." Levi tipped the driver and opened the trailer. The driver handed him the saddle he'd bought along with the horse, an English saddle, used, well-worn and comfortable. Perfect for Tamara's sweet ass, which hadn't sat astride a horse in weeks. Levi couldn't wait to turn up on horseback and surprise her. It was quitting time so Levi saddled Rex and rode off over the bridge toward home.

Home. He loved that word. Home had been a touch-and-go proposition growing up. Sometimes he and his mother had lived in boardinghouse rooms or in an apartment of their own. More often they lived with his grandfather or with Andre and Gloria. They never once owned a house of their own, only rented, only borrowed. Not even during Mom's miserable two-year marriage to the man who'd made him a Shelby. These days nothing made Levi happier than saying he was "heading home" and knowing there was a home with a wife waiting for him.

Rex took direction well. He had a smooth rocking gait that even the most inexperienced horse rider could handle. Levi had picked him out because he was a pretty horse with a gentle temperament but big enough and strong enough Tamara wouldn't be insulted. It wouldn't take much more than a week to build a pen and put down some straw for Rex. Levi could take a couple days off work for that or do it in the evenings. Building a little shed for a stable might take longer, but the horse would do fine outside. The area by the house was shady and cool and Levi already had enough oats and hay to last Rex two weeks. Tamara would give him all the exercise he needed.

Levi led Rex down the narrow dirt road toward the house. He heard something he hadn't expected to hear. A car or a truck. Some sort of engine starting. Rex shied at the sudden sound and Levi had to gentle him fast. The sound approached and Levi rode Rex into the woods and stopped under the heavy hanging branches of a tall oak. The truck rumbled past, a big diesel monster, and Levi read the words painted on the side—Athens Timber and Lumber, Athens, Georgia.

"What the hell?" Levi said, and Rex's long black ears twitched in response. Levi tapped Rex's sides and the Walker moseyed as fast as a Walker could mosey toward the house. They arrived in time to see Tamara disappear into the woods.

As dense as the trees were on this part of the island, Levi knew he had to follow her quick or he'd lose her. He tied up

Rex to a tree branch and went running after her. He heard rustling sounds and tried to follow them, but the woods were a labyrinth and around every corner he feared the minotaur—another copperhead, a cougar, a hole he'd break his leg in. How many times had he told Tamara not to go out in the woods by herself?

Levi heard a twig crack and he turned toward the sound. He saw a glimpse of white and followed it all the way to the scrub grass and to the white sand of the beach. There she was, standing at the edge of the water in her white sundress and bare feet.

"Tamara!" He called out to her and she turned and waved at him.

"What are you doing here?" she asked, all innocence.

He strode toward her, not an easy feat in soft shifting sand.

"What am I doing here? What are you doing here?"

"Nothing. Walking."

"I came home to surprise you and saw a logging company truck driving down my road. What the hell is a logging company doing on our island?"

Tamara's eyes flashed with surprise.

"You saw them?"

"I saw them. Now you answer me. What the hell is going on here?"

"Those trees are worth a fortune, Levi. You know that."

"I know that. So?"

"So we can sell them for a fortune."

"We could. We could do a lot of things. We could even sell our bodies on the streets or cut off our arms and legs and be circus freaks, but we're not going to do it."

"We're going to inherit Arden, Red Thread, the whole thing. We don't need this island."

Levi glared at her, chin high and furious. He could have screamed or spit he was so angry.

"You sell this island to a fucking logging company over my dead body."

Tamara pointed at the trees. "I'm selling it over my father's dead body. He sold his soul for this island and he died here. You think I want to live here forever?"

"Maybe you don't, but I do. Do you care about that?"

"I care about what I have to do."

"I will stop you if it takes my last breath." Levi turned away from her, too angry to look at her. He shook his head, kicked the sand. "Goddammit, what more do you want from life, Tamara? We have a house. We have each other. We have a whole fucking island that's like paradise. We're happy here. We have friends here—"

"That's not what I'm here for."

"What the hell are you here for, then?"

"I have a job to do, Levi."

"There are only two people standing here and only one of the two has a job, so try another one on me."

"I have to finish what I started the night of the flood."

"Putting me in the loony bin? Is that the job you have to finish? You're doing a real good job of it by the way."

"I saved your life, Levi. You're alive and going to be very rich because of me."

"You did and I'm grateful. But I'm not so grateful I'm going to bend over and let you sell this island out from under me. I have never loved a place like I love this place."

"Love it? It's a swamp, Levi. It's supposed to be a swamp. A man bought a little girl, married her and drained the swamp because he went nuts after she died. They kept slaves on this island. Where do you think I got the idea of cutting down the trees? It was Daddy's idea. No trees, no Red Thread. That's why he wanted the island from Granddaddy. Ask Bowen. Bowen's the one who told me that."

"He might have had the idea, but he didn't do it."

"Only because he killed himself. He was going to do it. He wanted to punish Granddaddy and this was the best way to do it. He wanted to make things right."

"Make things right? Make things *right*? Tamara, you can't make things right by cutting down hundreds of acres of trees."

"If you know what kind of man Granddaddy was you would know."

"Oh, I know what kind of man he was. The kind of man who'd fuck a girl over to get her pregnant just so he'd have a son of his own. That's what kind of man he was. Don't tell me I don't know what kind of man he was. I know better than you do. Ask me if that matters? It doesn't."

Tamara's eyes went huge, big as the sky.

"You know what Granddaddy did?"

"Of course I know. I've known a long time."

"You knew and you didn't tell me?"

"I know and I don't care. Not one bit," Levi said. Virginia Maddox had lost all his sympathy the day Tamara told him her mother had beaten her. From what Bowen had said, George Maddox hadn't even forced her to sleep with him. She'd probably done it for the money.

"You know," Tamara said again, her voice sounding so far away he barely heard. "And you don't care."

"I care about the island. I care about the trees. I care about the plan we made that you don't seem to remember anymore because you're so damn obsessed with getting back at your mother and your grandfather."

"Your father," she said. "Not my grandfather. Your father."

It was the cruelest thing she could have said to him, and she'd said it.

Tamara turned away from him and stared at the ocean.

"Tamara—look at me."

She took a step toward the water. Levi grabbed her by the arm, yanked her back, seized with a sudden fear she'd punish him by throwing herself in the ocean.

"Tamara."

She looked up at him. All the fight had left her eyes. All the fight and all the fire. Gone. Tamara wasn't home anymore.

"Tamara?"

She stepped away from him, and he released her arm.

"Tamara, where are you going? We aren't done here."

"We're done here."

She kept on walking.

"Tamara, don't you dare—"

But she dared.

Levi ran after her and she stopped, raised her hand to warn him away. He stood two feet from her, panting in his fury and his fear.

"Tamara?"

"Leave me alone."

24

Tamara wasn't sure how long she'd been walking. A few hours? A few days? She didn't know and she didn't care. She cared as little about how long she'd been gone and where she was as Levi cared about what Granddaddy had done to her.

Not one bit.

How did Levi know? She hadn't told anyone. Had her mother told him? Maybe they were in this together somehow. Maybe her mother had found Levi and told him to marry Tamara and keep an eye on her. Maybe Levi was her mother's spy. That would make sense. Yes…her mother had paid Levi off. That was exactly what happened. Levi was in on the whole thing. Her mother had gotten to him first. Levi had married Tamara to inherit the money, then he would make sure she drowned in the ocean and he'd have everything and that was why he wanted to come down here to Bride Island. That was why he wanted the island so bad, because he was going to bury her on it and take the money.

Oh, they were good. What a good plan. She wished she'd thought of it first.

Tamara looked up. Even in the shade of the oak trees, the sun bore down ruthlessly on her head. Blisters coated her heels where they'd slid, sweaty, up and down against the backs of her shoes with every step. Every now and then one of those blisters would rupture and send liquid dripping down her ankle and into her shoe. Flies buzzed around her legs, seeking the blood and the blister fluid, and she let them have it.

She paused by a tree and caught her breath. Last night she'd slept on the beach. She knew that much. She knew a full night had passed since Levi told her he didn't care, not one bit. When was the last time she'd drunk any water? Yesterday evening? Yes, in the house. The man from Athens Timber had come calling, and she'd served him tea while he'd gone over the numbers—when they'd start clear-cutting, how long it would take, how many acres they could clear in a week, how much money they'd offer her for the timber. It was more than she'd imagined. Then again, she hadn't imagined any numbers because she wasn't cutting the trees down for the money. The money meant nothing. The money was irrelevant.

"Are you sure you want to do this?" the lumber man had asked. He'd looked at her like a father looks at a daughter about to marry the wrong man. "I mean, you'll never have to worry about money again if you do this, but we can take half the trees and replant if you like. You could still get rich and have a nice green island."

"Take them," she'd said. "Take them all."

He'd said if that was what she wanted, they'd be more than happy to take them off her hands. He promised to send some paperwork to her post office box soon enough. The only sticking point was ownership of the island. No matter how much she'd told him the island was all hers, only hers, the lumber man wanted Levi to sign off on it, too. No court battles for him, he'd said. No, thank you. They'd had enough of those in their day. Tamara had said, "My husband will sign the contracts, I promise." She'd been drinking tea at the time, the last drink of anything she'd had before walking away from Levi. The sun was about the same place in the sky as it was yesterday when the Athens lumber man had driven away. She was thirsty and she was tired. And she had an awful feeling the trees were working for her mother, too.

Tamara wanted to sit down, but the tiny voice in the back of her head warned that if she sat down, she'd stop moving. She'd stop moving forever. And that wasn't good. She still had things to do. She couldn't stop moving yet. After she finished what she'd started, she'd come back here and lie down in the forest and never move again. After.

But not yet.

She pressed her forehead against the trunk of the tree. The bark scratched at her skin. She rubbed her forehead and brushed an ant off her face.

"I'm tired," she said. "I want to go home."

Home. Did she even have a home? She couldn't go back to the house she'd shared with Levi for almost two months. He knew Granddaddy had tried to rape her to get her pregnant and he didn't care. How could he not care?

Arden wasn't her home, either. Even if she inherited it, she couldn't live there. Every night she spent in that house she dreamed of the flood, of Granddaddy, of what the flood saved her from, of what would have happened if it hadn't. A house of horrors, that's what Arden was. That place had been bought with blood money and she would not sleep there another night.

What she needed was a new house.

A new house all her own.

And somewhere out here, there was another house. Bowen had told her about it.

Tamara pushed off from the tree and started walking again. Her heart pounded in her ears. The blisters on her feet left her wincing with every step she took. She stepped over a tree root, but her foot couldn't quite clear it, and she stumbled, landing hard on her right side.

She heard a horrible sound, a sort of low animal moaning, and realized it was coming from her.

Her arms shook as she dragged herself onto her hands and knees. Her weak ankle, which had never fully healed from the first time she'd sprained it, had twisted again. She'd torn something. She could feel the tear inside her leg.

"Momma..." she cried, forgetting in her confusion and her agony that she hated Virginia Maddox. Her chest heaved and she knew she was about to throw up. But if she did, that would be the end. No food. No water. She couldn't lose another drop of water from her body.

Somewhere she heard music.

Music?

Grabbing hold of the tree root that had tripped her, Tamara slowly pulled herself to her feet. Her right ankle throbbed and she couldn't put any weight on it. But she did find a thick branch and she used it as a walking stick, resting her weight on it as she stumbled forward through the woods and toward the music. Music meant people. People meant water. She'd find the people and drink some of their water, and then she'd head out again to find the house she knew was here somewhere on the island. She'd live in the house Julien St. Croix built for his little wife. She had died, hadn't she? His wife,

Louisa? St. Croix must have been so lonely without his wife. She knew she would be lonely on this island all by herself. She would find Julien and he would fall in love with her at first sight. He'd ask her to marry him, demand it even because men in those days didn't ask, but took. No, no, no, she wouldn't marry him. Not until he freed his slaves. Terrible man, he should know better than that. Terrible man, he should know you couldn't sell people. She would make him let them go. And he would do it, too, because he loved her so very much—love at first sight. He would love her and she would love him, and when they fought, he would take her upstairs to the finest bedroom in their fine house and an hour later she would come downstairs smiling.

She couldn't wait to meet him, her future husband. They'd have their wedding in the house. They could be married tonight even. And soon she'd have a son of her own. And they would name him Philip after the king.

Wouldn't it be nice to be married to the son of a count? Even a third son of a count was better than no son of a count at all. Who would she be? Lady Tamara. That had a nice ring to it. Lady Tamara St. Croix, the countess of Bride Island.

It was going to be such a beautiful wedding.

Tamara looked down. How perfect. She already wore a white dress. Surely Julien wouldn't mind she'd been married before. It wasn't a real marriage, after all, she would tell him. Levi wasn't her real husband. He was a spy hired by her mother. Julien would protect her from them both. That was why he'd planted all these trees on the island. They were all for her. The trees would protect the house from spies. No one could find the house through the trees. No one but her and only because she belonged here. Here with her husband.

"Oh, my..." Tamara breathed as she stepped into a clearing.

There it was. The house. The house Julien St. Croix had built just for her. It was more beautiful than she'd even dared dream it would be. It looked like a little castle made of gray stone. It had a turret on the north end and a turret on the south end. Oh, and there was a garden, too, a flower garden all around it. And the front doors were solid oak, of course. She knew oak by now. She could tell oak on sight. What else would those doors have been? Douglas fir? Tamara hobbled to the doors and they opened. An older lady in a black dress and a white apron, her dark hair hidden under a white mobcap, came bustling down the hallway toward her, wringing her hands.

"Lady Tamara, there you are. We thought you'd disappeared on us. You're late," the servant said. "Late for your own wedding."

"I'm sorry," she said. "I went for a walk and got lost. Am I dirty? Do I need to change?"

"Oh, no…" The servant stepped back, looked Tamara up and down and smiled. "You look so beautiful."

"Is my lord angry with me for making him wait?"

"He would wait for you forever. You know that. But your guests are restless and your father's pacing a hole in the rug."

"Daddy's here?"

"You think your own father would miss your wedding? Come along and see him. He's waiting to give you away."

"Take me there. Take me there right now. I didn't know he was coming to the wedding."

"Wouldn't miss it for the world, he said. Not over his dead body."

Tamara followed the servant down the hallway. She found she could walk again just fine, no pain. In fact, she could run, and run she did, almost skipping in her haste to see her father again. And there he was, handsome as she ever remembered seeing him, regal as a king with his dark wavy hair and his shining dark eyes and his dark, dark boots on his long strong legs wearing a hole in the red carpet from pacing.

"Daddy!" Tamara threw herself into his arms and he held her tight, so tight she could hardly breathe. But she didn't need to breathe. She just needed her daddy on her wedding day.

"There's my beautiful girl." He rocked her against him.

"I didn't think you'd come."

"I came, angel. I couldn't let you get married without me." He pulled back and held her by the shoulders. "You look so beautiful."

She looked down at herself again. He was right. She did look beautiful. She saw her reflection in the mirror across the hall. The dress shimmered like a full moon on a clear night, a sort of silvery white color she'd only ever seen in her dreams. And her red hair lay in thick waves down her back. A white veil covered her hair, and when it was time to walk down the aisle, it would conceal her face as well, only to be uncovered by her husband once he became her husband.

"I didn't mean to keep you waiting," she said. "I was…" She stopped. "I don't remember. I was walking, and I don't remember."

"You're here. That's all that matters. Are you ready?"

"Yes," she said. "If you're ready, I am."

"You love him?" Daddy asked. He looked so handsome in his knee boots polished to a mirror shine and his black trousers and black jacket and cravat.

"I will love him all my life."

"Then yes, I'm ready." Her father grinned broadly as he lowered the veil down over her face. Then he nodded to a footman, who opened the door. The music she'd heard—it came from here, from this ballroom. A string quartet—two violins, viola, cello—played a soft wedding march, and for a moment it was drowned out by the shuffle of feet as the many guests in their fripperies and finery turned to look at Julien St. Croix's young bride on her handsome father's arm.

Oh, how they sighed at the sight of them. She heard the sighs, although she couldn't see their faces. The veil obscured her sight so all she saw were shadows.

"I can't see, Daddy. Don't let me fall."

"Never, my angel."

"Is it true? Is the man I'm marrying the son of a count?"

"A baron, my love. He's a baron. Only the best for you."

"Wasn't Granddaddy a baron?"

Her father didn't answer. Maybe he hadn't heard her over the music. On her father's arm Tamara took halting steps toward the end of the aisle where her groom waited for her.

Her father stopped and she stopped. They were there.

"Be a good girl for your husband," her father whispered in her ear, then kissed her cheek through the veil.

It was time. Her veil was raised, and she smiled at the man who would be her husband.

The smile left her face.

"Levi?"

"You look beautiful, Rotten."

"No," she said, shaking her head. "I can't marry you. I hate you."

"That's not a very nice thing to say to your husband."

"I won't marry you. I'll never marry you."

"It's too late," he said. "We're already married."

"How? I don't… When?" Tamara looked around the room, scanning faces, looking for friends, for her father, who had gone.

"No wedding necessary," came a voice from behind her.

Tamara spun around and a woman in a red dress stepped out from the crowd of guests. "You're already his. Blood of his blood. Bone of his bone."

"Momma?"

"You're bought and paid for," Levi said over her shoulder. "You're all mine."

"No." She shook her head. "You can't sell people. You can't sell people anymore."

"Of course you can," Levi said, grinning the devilish grin that she used to love and now she hated. "We do it all the time."

"You sold me, Momma…" She stared at her mother grinning in all her triumph and glory. "Why did you sell me?"

"What else is a girl good for?" her mother asked. "It's all I was good for, anyway."

"A girl is good for leaving," Tamara said, looking around at the blank faces staring at her as if she'd come from another planet. "And a girl is good for burning your house down."

Tamara pushed a rack of candles over and the red rug she'd walked across caught fire.

Before anyone could stop her, she ran from the room, from the house, from her wedding, from her mother and the husband she should never have married.

She ran out into the garden and saw the house all in flames, beautiful marvelous flames.

"This is what a girl is good for," she said, smiling. She found a stone bench out in the garden and sat down on it to watch the house burn. It caught fire so easily it was like the very walls were whiskey-soaked. The masonry turned a bright yellow and red and crumbled before her eyes into soft gray ash. The chimney tumbled off the roof. The red velvet curtains fluttered with flames and rolled up like scrolls as they burned. The sounds were like those of a rock slide as the house consumed itself and fell to pieces like a child's tower of blocks that had been built so high there was nowhere else to go but down, down, down...

It would take a long while to burn out. She should rest. It had been such a long day. She lay on her side on the stone garden bench and closed her eyes. She'd sleep here, and then when she'd rested, she would walk on again until she found a new home. A light rain started to fall; she felt it on her face but ignored it. The house was already nothing but a pile of smoldering bricks, everyone inside dead and gone. A little rain wouldn't help and it wouldn't hurt. And she was very thirsty. She rolled onto her back and opened her mouth. Water flooded it and she choked.

"Sit up, Tamara. Come on."

She felt a strong arm under her, forcing her into a sitting position.

"I'm sleeping."

"Don't sleep. You won't wake up. Come on."

She swallowed the water in her mouth and wanted more of it, enough to open her eyes.

A man was kneeling on the hard ground in front of her. She recognized the face, although she couldn't quite place him.

"I know you," she said.

"You better know me," he said. "We're married."

"Didn't I burn you?"

"You sure tried, Rotten."

Rotten...as soon as he said the word she knew him.

"Levi."

"That's me. You know who you are?" he asked, raising a glass bottle to her lips again. She tried to take it from his hands but found her own hands shook too hard to hold it.

"Let me do it. You can't even hold your hands up."

"I can do it." Her voice sounded faded and frayed to her ears. She held the bottle still just to prove she could and took long deep sips from it. Slowly she returned to herself, feeling like she'd been wrenched out of a dream and wasn't quite sure yet what was real and what had been the dream.

"Levi," she said, setting the bottle on the stone bench beside her. Except it wasn't a bench, only a slab of rock.

"That's my name. You know yours?"

"Tamara."

"Tamara what?"

She met his eyes and saw anger in them, and behind the anger, fear.

"Maddox," she said.

"Close enough."

Tamara raised a hand to her head and made herself remember things she didn't want to remember. Her name was Tamara Belle Maddox. She was seventeen years old. She was married to Levi Shelby. She wasn't... No, she was definitely not married to Julien St. Croix. That had only been a dream.

"Tamara, do you have any idea how much you scared me?"

"I scared you? That's funny." She gave a little drunken laugh as if she'd been sucking down a bottle of bourbon instead of water.

"Do you know how long you've been gone?"

She shook her head.

"Two days, Tamara. Two entire days I've been out here with Bowen and White Dog trying to find you. Bowen went to get the police."

"No. No police. They'll call Momma."

"I think that's the least of our worries."

"She's the most of our worries."

Tamara rubbed her forehead, where a knot of pain lived and throbbed behind her eyes.

"Two days, Tamara. Did you hear me? Two days you've been gone. You're lucky you're alive."

She looked down at her body, her ankle, red and swollen, the cuts and scrapes on her legs from ankle to knee. Her hands were filthy, dirt under her fingernails and blood on her palms from catching her fall on a rock. Levi gently held a white handkerchief to her face and she saw it come away with blood.

"I am?"

"Tamara, are you all right?" Levi asked. He took her face in his hands and looked deep into her eyes as if seeking out signs of damage.

"No."

"I didn't think so. Come on, let's get you to the hospital."

"I don't need a hospital."

"You just said—"

"I don't need a hospital. I don't need a doctor. I need..."

"What do you need? Tell me. I'll get it for you."

"I need you to not hate me."

Levi's head jerked back, and he narrowed his eyes at her.

"Why do you think I hate you?"

"Because you don't care about me. You said so yourself."

Levi sighed—heavily—and stood up. She didn't like to be sitting when he stood. His size scared her. He could hurt her so easily if he wanted to—especially here in the middle of nowhere. Where was she, anyway? She glanced around, saw a clearing edged with oak trees, saw a line of black bricks, the remnant of a stone path.

"I care about you," he said. His arms were crossed over his chest—his big arms, his broad chest.

THE BOURBON THIEF   269

"You said you know about Granddaddy, about him trying to have a son."

"Yeah, I know. Bowen told me. Listen, Tamara, what your grandfather did to your mother was awful. It was. But it's no excuse to clear-cut this entire island. I've heard of temper tantrums, but that just takes the cake."

"What do you mean what my grandfather did to my mother?"

"Just what I said he did two days ago." His brow furrowed and he looked at her again like she had a screw or two loose. Maybe she did. She was certain he'd said he knew and didn't care that Granddaddy had tried to rape her and get her pregnant. But he hadn't meant her. He meant Momma?

"What did my grandfather do to Momma?"

"I thought you knew. You acted like it." He shrugged, sighed again. "Bowen says that's why your daddy killed himself. He came home from a business trip and found your mother in bed with his own father, with my father."

"Momma and Granddaddy?" Her mind was spinning.

Levi slowly nodded his head. "He wanted a baby boy apparently. He had three sons at the time—one dead, one not interested in having children and one with a black mother. So he was sleeping with your mother, trying to get her to have his baby so everyone would think it was Nash's baby. Considering the kind of woman your mother has proved herself to be, I imagine she went along with this for the sake of staying in your grandfather's good graces. And probably for money, too."

Momma... He'd been talking about Momma. Her mother and her grandfather. That was what Levi knew about and didn't care about.

"Tamara, you know I care about you. You know that,

right?" Levi knelt in front of her again. He took her face in his hands. "You have to know that."

"I didn't know that."

"I married you to keep you from marrying some old geezer who'd use you and hurt you and treat you like his property. You seemed so determined and so…"

"Dumb?"

"Young."

"I'm not as young as I look."

"No, but you're not as old as you think you are, either. I hate to put my foot down, but I'm going to have to do it if you try to sell this island to a timber company to spite your mother and your grandfather, who is rotting in his grave as we speak."

"I wasn't doing it just to spite them."

"Then why? Why should I roll over and let you cut down every tree on this island? Because I don't know about you, but I kind of like it here. This is the first place I've ever lived that felt like mine and felt like home. So if you want me to stand back and watch you destroy it, you better have a real good reason for it."

"Daddy was going to do it."

"No, Nash was not going to do it. Nash thought about doing it, and Bowen talked him out of it. Instead of selling the island, he decided to keep it and bring his daughter down here to live with him and—"

"And Bowen."

Levi's eyes flashed. "You know about that."

"I know more than you think I know. I know more than you do."

"Well, then, why don't you just sit there and tell me every single thing you know that I don't know. Do you think you could do that? Do you think you could tell your husband what the hell is going on with you? Because I am trying to be a good husband over here, Tamara. I am trying my hardest. In case the will doesn't come out in our favor, I got a job. I've been saving money. I blew a big damn chunk of it to buy you that boy over there." He pointed right at a tree where a black-and-white horse stood tied to it, whacking flies off his back with his tail.

Tamara sat up straight. "That's my horse?"

"It is."

She started to stand, but Levi grabbed her and pulled her back down again.

"Sit," he ordered. "You can play with the damn horse later."

"He's...so beautiful. I can't believe you got me a horse." Tamara couldn't stop looking at him. She didn't feel the cuts on her hands anymore or the ache in her ankle. Levi had bought her a horse. It was so sweet she almost felt sweet again.

"Yeah, I got you a horse. Stupid lovesick idiot I am bought you a horse to make up for you losing Kermit. So there he is."

Tamara tried standing up again and didn't make it. She wobbled on her feet and Levi caught her in his arms.

"You're not walking anywhere," he said as he lowered her to the ground again.

"Sorry. I wanted to pet him."

"Stay there." Levi pointed at her.

He walked over to the tree and untied the horse, leading him over to her with his hand on the horse's bridle.

"Rex, meet Tamara. Tamara, this is Rex, a Tennessee Walker."

"Hi, Rex." Tamara raised her shaking hand and pressed it to the horse's velvet nose. It felt good to pat his nose and stroke his long ears. "Hi, there, guy. You're awfully pretty there."

"Don't tell him that. He's a man, not a girl. He's handsome."

"Hi, handsome." Rex batted her hand with his nose, keeping his head lowered so she could reach his face and ears. "You're a nice guy, aren't you?"

"Nicest guy I could find. His last owner was a teenage girl. She went off to college in California and that's why her parents sold him. He lost his girl and you lost your horse. I thought you'd be good for each other."

"We'll be good for each other." Tamara smiled. She wrapped her arms around Rex's neck, and as the horse raised his head, she came to her feet.

"Tamara—"

"I'm good," she said. "I can stand."

She couldn't put her full weight on her right foot, but she could stand as long as Rex stayed right where he was and let her lean against him. She ran her fingers through his black mane, combing out the thick hairs, untangling a knot. A fly landed by his eye and she brushed it off.

"Do you believe in evil, Levi?"

"I believe in free will."

"That's not an answer."

"It is if you think about it."

She thought about it. Maybe it was an answer. Maybe it was the only answer.

"An evil thing happened to a girl once," Tamara began as she hobbled around Rex, patting his flanks, stroking his long back. "And she wasn't very old, only fifteen or so. And she was being held hostage in this house."

"A hostage?"

"They used the word *slave*, but isn't it the same thing? Isn't that what you'd call it if someone stole me and put me in a house and wouldn't let me leave? Isn't it?"

"Go on," Levi said. "Tell me about this girl."

"The man who was holding her hostage raped her and got her pregnant. And when his wife found out the girl was having his baby, they sold her for a thousand dollars. And the man took that one thousand dollars and opened his own bourbon distillery."

"Someone we know?" Levi asked, looking at her over Rex's back.

"Veritas. That was her name, but they called her Vera. And Jacob Maddox, my grandfather's grandfather, raped her and his wife sold her."

"My father's grandfather. Not yours. Mine."

"Now you know why I was so happy to find out I wasn't really a Maddox."

"Now you know why I was so damn angry to find out I was."

"Levi…if I tell you something, will you believe me?"

"I'll try. All I can do is try. What is it?"

"I think she talks to me."

"Who?"

"Vera."

"Vera? Vera who's probably been dead a hundred years?"

"I thought I saw her the night of the flood. And then sometimes I dream about her. The night…after we were together that first time, I dreamed about her. And she told me Daddy knew things. I woke up and went down to the office and found the card for Athens Timber. I thought she was telling me that I was supposed to sell the trees, that that's what Daddy was going to do. Sounds crazy, doesn't it? Now that I say it, I hear how crazy it sounds."

"It doesn't sound crazy."

"It doesn't?"

"It sounds…sweet. Kind of."

"Sweet?"

"I didn't know you had such a tender heart, Rotten. Especially not for a black girl who lived a hundred years before you were born."

"A hundred years isn't anything, Levi. A hundred years is yesterday. If what happened to you happened to her, a hundred years is nothing."

"You want to destroy the trees on this island because of what they did to that little girl?"

"You can't sell people," Tamara said. "You can't. And they did. And because they did, Red Thread exists. It's funny, you know. They always said Maddoxes have bourbon in their blood. It's not true. But this is true—we have blood in our bourbon. Her blood." She looked at Levi and found him looking at her. "You want to keep selling her blood? That's what we're doing. Brewing it, barreling it, aging it, bottling it and selling it with a red ribbon tied around the neck. A red ribbon like the one she wore every day, like the one Henrietta Maddox ripped out of Vera's hair and left to show her husband what she'd done. A red ribbon like the one he wore on his finger to spite his wife. We still have that red ribbon, you know. It's on a bottle at Arden. I've seen it. She's real."

"I believe she was real. *Was* real. She's dead now and you don't have to take orders from someone who's dead."

"What would you do if that had been me?"

"What do you mean?"

"What would you do if it had been me they raped and sold? Would you still love these trees just as much? Would you still keep Red Thread open?"

"Tamara, it was a hundred—"

"It was yesterday," she said.

"You want revenge. That's what all this is about. Revenge for what they did to her."

"Revenge for what they did to all of us."

"They're dead. The Maddoxes who did that to her are dead. How are you going to get revenge against dead people? Dig 'em up and stake 'em through the heart?"

"I asked myself that same question, and I think I know the answer. You destroy what they loved, and you love what they destroyed."

"So we destroy Red Thread?"

"And we love each other." She looked at him and waited, waited and prayed. If he took the side of Red Thread, there was nothing for it—she would leave him—for her daddy's sake, for Vera's sake and for hers.

"Fine," Levi said. He stood by Rex's head and adjusted the horse's mouth bit.

"Fine? What do you mean fine?"

"'If you could not accept the past and its burden there was no future, for without one there cannot be the other.' Robert Penn Warren said that, and he was probably right. When you told me George Maddox was my father, I was about five minutes away from setting a match to the entire state, so how can I say you're wrong to want to cut these trees down? But if all you say is true, if you say my family did that to her, cutting trees down isn't enough. If we owe her for what we did to her, then we pay in full, not half. We'll close the company. Not sell it, just close it. Shut down production. Stop selling the stuff, all the stuff. That way we both win—I get the island and you get to send every Maddox in the ground spinning in his grave like a top for all eternity. How's that?"

"You mean it?" She couldn't believe what he was saying.

"Of course I mean it. I don't feel any better about making

money off the blood of that girl than you do. If we win the case, we'll have plenty of money to live on. If we lose, then fine. I have a job and we'll wait it out until you turn twenty-one. It's not like we're gonna starve to death. I've survived being broke before. Being broke on an island in a pretty house is better than being broke and living in a stable loft, you know."

"You do mean it."

Levi gave her that wicked half grin that never ceased making her heart jump hopscotch.

"Hell, you said Judge Headley has money. We'll tell him you're his daughter, and he'll pay us off to keep our mouths shut."

Tamara laughed. "Don't you dare. I like him too much."

"Just saying, it's good to have a backup plan. I have a certain lifestyle I've grown accustomed to. And I want to provide for my wife. Name-brand Frosted Flakes. None of that generic shit."

"Stay there," Tamara said.

"Where?"

"Right where you are. Stay there."

Levi held up two hands in surrender. "I'm staying. I don't know what you're doing, but I'm staying right here."

Keeping one hand on Rex's back to steady herself, Tamara hobbled forward step by painful step. She came to Levi and wrapped her arms around him and let him wrap his arms around her.

"Thank you, Levi," she whispered.

"You're my wife. We're stuck with each other. Might as well make the best of it."

"I want to make the best of it," she said.

"I'll tell you what Bowen told Nash when Nash was hell-bent on burning this island to the ground to spite his…our father."

"What's that?"

"Bowen told him that being happy is the best revenge. That there was no way that a man like George Maddox was a happy man, not with a wife in the nursing home, a son in the cemetery and another son in love with a black barrel maker. So if Nash really wanted revenge, he'd be happy instead of trying to make a miserable man more miserable. And that's what Nash decided to do. That's why he wanted to bring you down here to live with him. Because he loved you and you made him so happy."

"I wish Daddy were still alive."

If Daddy were still alive, she would be living with him down here. If Daddy were still alive, she wouldn't have been anywhere near Kentucky when the flood happened. If Daddy were still alive, she wouldn't have had to kill anyone, to hate her mother, to destroy Red Thread. She'd still be sweet if Daddy were alive. Right now she missed that more than anything.

"I know, baby. I do, too. I never got to know my own brother. I always wanted a brother or a sister and here I had one all along and never knew it. Too late now."

"You really think we can be happy? After all this?"

"We can. If that's what you want to do, we'll do it. We'll be happy."

"You said you were lovesick." She grinned up at him. "Does that mean you love me?"

"I did not say that."

"You absolutely said that. I heard you say that."

"You're getting messages from beyond the grave in your dreams. I'm entirely certain this calls the testimony of your senses into question."

"It's cute when you talk all funny like that."

"I'm very cute."

"Can you take me back home? I need a bath."

"Can you ride? I can lead Rex if you can ride. But if not, I'll have to go get the truck. We're five miles from home."

"I can ride."

"Okay, but first I gotta do something."

"And what's that?"

"I gotta kiss you like they kiss on *The Young and the Restless*."

"Can I be the restless this time?" she asked.

"You can be anything you wanna be, Rotten."

She rested her entire body against his and lifted her face to his for a good hard kissing. That was not what she got, however. She got a good gentle kissing with soft hands on her arms and her back and soft lips against her lips and soft sighs mingling with her sighs.

Levi rested his forehead against hers.

"You scared the shit out of me, Rotten," he whispered. "Two days. I looked for you for two days and I was ready to cut the whole island down to stumps with my bare hands to find you."

"I'm sorry. I am. It's hard to trust…anybody."

"You can trust me. You have to trust me. We're never going to make this work—not for a day, not for a year, not for a lifetime—if you can't trust me."

"I'll try."

"Good."

"Trust me, too," she said.

"I can do that. I'll trust you more when you don't smell like a swamp."

"Take me home and put me in the bathtub."

"Right this second," he said. "Come here, and I'll give you a leg up."

He stood on the stone block she'd been sleeping on when he found her. Carefully she stepped up onto it, wincing as her sprained ankle screamed at the merest suggestion of weight. She was going to be spending the next week in bed. If everything went the way she wanted it to, Levi would be spending it in bed with her.

"Alley-oop," he said, what he always said when he helped her mount a horse. It hurt and it was hard, but he got her securely into her saddle. She settled in, adjusted her seat and reached for the reins.

"No, ma'am. You sit. I'm leading," Levi said. Tamara grabbed hold of the saddle pommel. "Better. Ready to go home?"

"More than ready."

Levi clicked his tongue and Rex raised his head. As Levi led the horse, Tamara glanced down and saw the outline of a word carved deep into the stone she'd been lying on. One word—*Louisa*. Dirt and moss obscured the rest, but Tamara knew she'd found Louisa St. Croix's tombstone. And this place was her tomb. And there, the line of black bricks, burned to cinders, was the foundation of St. Croix's house.

"Levi?"

"What is it, Rotten?"

Tamara started to tell him what she'd seen, what she'd found. But when she looked up, for a split second she saw a girl, a pretty girl with black lace eyelashes peeking at her from behind a tree. She smiled like she'd played a trick on someone and gotten away with it. Tamara smiled back, the same smile for the same reason.

"Thanks for coming to find me, Levi."

"What else is a stupid lovesick husband for?"

"I knew you loved me."

"Somebody has to, Rotten. Might as well be me."

25

Paris

Somewhere between the witching hour and dawn, Paris unfurled her long legs from where she'd tucked them under her on the sofa, stood up and took a bottle of Four Roses off the bar. McQueen put his hand over the top of his shot glass when she brought the bottle to it.

"I don't need any more," he said.

"For what I'm about to tell you next you do." Paris looked down at him and he looked up at her, and if this had been a game of tug-of-war, she'd have all the rope in her hands and he'd have nothing but rope burn.

"But they were so happy," he said. Paris looked at him with sympathy. He knew that look. It was the look he'd given his daughter the day she discovered there was no Santa Claus.

McQueen moved his hand off the mouth of the glass so she could pour.

"Make it a double."

26

Veritas

Tamara looked out the bedroom window and saw her husband lounging on the back deck, nose stuck in a book.

Unacceptable.

She could have forgiven him reading if it hadn't been a Saturday afternoon and a beautiful one at that, and she could have forgiven him reading if he had his shirt on, but no. He wore nothing but his rattiest pair of jeans, sunglasses and that serious look on his face he got when he contemplated the mysteries of the universe. He ought to be contemplating the mysteries of *her* universe. Tamara pushed up the window and leaned out to tell him that.

"Stop reading and come to bed," she hollered down at him.

"Be gone, wench," Levi said, casually turning a page in his book. "Go and ply your harlot's trade elsewhere. I'm trying to learn something down here. You had your rampant feminine lusts serviced twice last night, and until you muck out Rex's stall like I told you to, you're not getting them serviced again."

"Are you reading Shakespeare?"

"I am, forsooth. How didst thou knowst?"

"Lucky guess."

"I'm reading *Antony and Cleopatra*," Levi said as he pushed his sunglasses up on his head and waved his book in her direction. "A man falls in love with a woman. It is, of course, a tragedy."

"Shakespeare is boring. Read something better, like Jackie Collins."

"I am learning from Shakespeare. And I'm learning more than how to marry money."

"What do you learn from Shakespeare other than how to talk like a fancy idiot?"

"I'm learning a lot from *Antony and Cleopatra*. I learned I shouldn't marry the emperor's niece while I'm still sleeping with the Queen of Egypt. Also, I should avoid naval battles when I'm outgunned. Land battles, Tamara. Remember that. Listen to your oracles and stick to land battles."

"Sounds sexy. Why don't you come to bed and tell me more about it?"

"Did you clean Rex's stall out in the past thirty seconds?"

"Well...no."

"Then excuse me. I have a date with the Nile."

"You're the meanest man alive, Levi Shelby. You make my life difficult."

"There're American citizens still being held hostage in Iran, Tamara Shelby. Go tell them how difficult your life is. I don't want to hear it."

Tamara screamed.

Levi swiveled his head and looked up at her, eyebrow cocked to high heaven.

"Are you done?" he asked.

"I think so."

"I tell you what, you clean Rex's stall today, and tonight... tonight I will take you upstairs to our bedroom and..."

"Yes?" Tamara asked with unabashed eagerness to hear what her reward would be.

"And I'll play Connect Four with you. I get to be black, obviously."

Levi shoved his sunglasses back down on his face, opened his book and returned to ignoring her and her rampant feminine lusts. If Shakespeare had been alive and in her house, she might have hit him over the head with a shovel. She blamed him for being more interesting than her body was. And she blamed Levi for being Levi, who would rather read than do what Tamara wanted him to do, which was "do Tamara."

Once more she stuck her head out of the pink bedroom window.

"I have to tell you a secret," Tamara called down.

"I already know all your secrets," Levi said.

"You don't know this one."

"Is the secret that you're sorry you're so rotten and you drive me crazy and you promise you won't interrupt me when I'm reading anymore? Is that your secret?"

"No."

"Then keep it to yourself."

Tamara huffed and slammed the window shut. Then she opened it again and peeked out. Damn that man. She shouldn't let him work with Bowen anymore. Before they'd come to Bride Island, he'd had a nice body, lean and rangy, and she'd loved watching him mucking out stalls with no shirt on his back when he worked for her grandfather. After two months working the Bride Island cooperage, hauling logs, lifting barrels, cutting and sanding, and doing all sorts of hard heavy work, Levi's shoulders had grown broader, his stomach flatter, and his biceps were everything a girl wanted her husband's biceps to be. Even his hands were different, calloused all over especially on the fingertips, and when he touched her inside, magical things happened. She was about to give up and make some magic on her own when she was hit with inspiration.

Tamara ran downstairs, checking the floor for snakes as she crossed to the kitchen—it had become a habit—and ran out the back door across the sundeck Levi and Bowen had built last week.

"Finally she gets her ass in gear to clean," Levi said as Tamara breezed past him, attempting to ignore him even if she did want to dive onto his half-naked body like Mark Spitz into a swimming pool.

"I'm not cleaning. I'm riding," Tamara said as she skipped the steps and jumped off the low deck onto the ground and kept running.

Levi yelled something after her. She heard the words *lazy* and *ass* and ignored both of them. He had this crazy notion that just because he and Bowen had done the horse-stall building, she was under some obligation to do the horse-stall cleaning. Didn't the horses of Chincoteague Island run free and wild? They didn't need stalls. They didn't need people changing their straw. Levi hadn't been convinced by this argument, noting that Rex was a Tennessee Walker, not a Chincoteague pony, and if she wanted a Chincoteague pony, she could go catch one herself. He'd be standing by with the ambulance and the priest to perform last rites when her attempt to wrestle one of the wild beasts into a bridle inevitably failed. He'd miss her, Levi had said. They'd bury her on Bride Island, and he and Rex would visit her grave twice a year, on Easter and Christmas.

Well, Tamara told herself, she had only herself to blame for marrying the meanest man on earth.

But two could play that game. She might not be a Maddox by blood, but she had been raised by them, and if there was anything a Maddox knew how to do, it was how to be real damn mean.

Tamara took Rex by the bridle and guided him into his stall. It wasn't much of a stall, not much more than a big fancy lean-to, but it kept him and his oats dry when the inevitable rainstorms hit and they hit about twice a week. She loved those storms, especially when they hit at night. The air turned electric and the little hairs on her arms stood up and her skin prickled, and when the thunder boomed, it would wake up Levi and what's a man and his wife going to do in the middle of the night when a storm hits except each other?

No storm was happening right at the moment and yet Tamara's skin tingled in a pleasant sort of way and she felt restive and twitchy, overly aware of her body and the lack of her husband on top of it and inside it. The warm summer breeze tickled her arms and her back and her belly, and the earth under her naked feet was soft and spongy, and it made her want to run fast and jump high and roll in the dirt like an animal. Was this how Rex felt before a storm? They weren't expecting a storm today, so Tamara would have to make her own rain.

As Tamara saddled Rex, she discovered she was grinning ear to ear and so hard it made her face hurt. It was good to be happy again. She felt like herself again, her old self, before the flood. Except life was better after the flood, since Levi wasn't just Granddaddy's groom. He was her husband, her lover and the source of every good thing she had in her life. Which was why she couldn't keep her hands off him and why she was determined to get his hands back on her as soon as possible.

Right this second.

Tamara tapped her heels into Rex's sides and they moseyed out of the stall and up to the deck.

Levi didn't look at her. Not once.

"Husband?" Tamara asked as she steered Rex past the deck. "Don't you think it's a nice day for a ride?"

"I'm sure it is if you say it is." Levi turned a page in his book. "It is also a nice day for a read."

His eyes were hidden behind his dark aviator sunglasses, and a lock of hair fell over his forehead. His hair needed a trimming, but she hoped he hadn't realized that yet. She liked it longer and shaggier. He'd warned her that thanks to his mother's side of the family, his hair would sport Shirley Temple curls if he let it get too long. Tamara wanted to see that with her own eyes.

Tamara led Rex on a quick circuit of the house before traipsing past the deck again.

"I read a book once," Tamara said, grateful for Rex's smooth gait.

"Good for you, baby. Now go read another one."

"I wasn't finished with my story. I read a book once about a lady whose husband was mean and awful."

"Was it called *The Autobiography of Tamara Shelby*?"

"It should have been. This lady was mad at her husband because he taxed the poor people of the city. Taxed them to death. She begged her husband to reduce the taxes and he was so mean he said he'd only do it if she rode naked through the town on horseback. I can't remember her name, though. Can you?"

Levi slammed his book shut. "Rotten, I am trying to read—"

He took off his sunglasses and stared at her.

"Lady Godiva," Tamara said, sitting up straight and stark naked on the back of her horse. "That's it. Now I remember."

"Tamara, you are naked."

She smiled at him.

"Sun's shining. Nice breeze. Good day for a naked ride."

"I just polished that saddle yesterday."

"I'm polishing it again," she said and danced in the saddle. Rex snorted and she wasn't sure if he was laughing or confused. Levi looked vaguely horrified, which was one of his standard expressions and one of her favorites.

"Get down off that horse and into the house right now and put some goddamn clothes on."

"Why?" she asked, tapping Rex's sides again and leading him in a merry circuit around the backyard. "No one's around but you. And you don't care if I'm naked, do you? You've seen it before. Doesn't do a thing for you, does it?"

"Not a damn thing," he said, staring at her breasts.

"And who's gonna come by? Bowen? He doesn't care about naked girls."

"I don't care if he cares. I care. The only three people who are allowed to see my wife naked are me, myself and I."

"What about my doctor? Huh?"

"Doctors aren't people. They're doctors. Now get off your horse and get in the house and put on some clothes."

"Or what?"

"Or I'll drag you off your horse and turn you over my knee."

"I'll take what's behind door number two, then."

She didn't actually think he'd do it. For all the times he'd threatened to turn her over his knee, he'd never once gone through with it. And yet she got a little nervous when Levi tossed his book down, marched over to her and dragged her off the saddle.

Despite all his manhandling, Tamara couldn't stop laughing for some reason. Laughing and squirming as Levi carried her up to the deck and pushed her down into his lawn chair. Tamara flipped over and came up on her hands and knees.

"I'm ready," she said.

"For what? Getting a sunburn on your ass?"

"You said you were going to spank me," she said, kneeling and tossing her hair over her shoulder.

He started to put her on her back, her absolute favorite place to be, when they heard the telltale sounds of popping and crunching, which meant a big truck was driving on their gravel road.

"Goddammit. This is why we don't run around naked. Go," Levi said, sitting up on his knees to let Tamara out from under him. She raced in through the back door and into the bathroom, where she'd left yesterday's clothes hanging. She threw on her jeans and her favorite rainbow-striped halter top, tied up her hair and splashed water on her flushed cheeks. When she looked respectable again, she came out to the front porch and found Bowen and Levi there.

"What's going on?" Tamara asked, dropping into the porch swing.

"We got mail," Levi said. "You did, anyway."

Bowen handed her an envelope. "Came to the shop yesterday. Miss Tandy left it on my desk."

"Judge Headley," Tamara said. She and Levi looked at each other, one of them scared, the other excited.

"Well, go on. Let's see what he has to say," Levi said.

"Should I go?" Bowen asked.

"You can stay," Levi said, crossing his arms over his chest

and leaning back against the house. Tamara's hands shook with both sets of eyes on her. It wasn't a letter-size envelope, but a big envelope. She'd heard good things come in small packages, but she didn't know if that applied to the US Mail. With her stomach in her throat, Tamara ripped open the seal. Something fell out into her lap.

"Keys," she said, looking at Levi.

"Keys? To what?" Levi took the set of keys from her—there must have been half a dozen of them on one key ring.

Tamara took a folded note out of the envelope, flattened it on her thigh and read.

"'Congratulations. You are now the proud owners of one distillery and one house named Arden and a whole lot of money. Come home and sign the papers. I'll have the champagne waiting.' Signed, Daniel Headley."

At the bottom was a postscript Tamara didn't read out loud.

Your mother dropped her objections and the probate court closed the case. But I would keep my eyes peeled for Virginia. Hell hath no fury, after all.

Tamara looked up at Levi. His face wore a mask of shock in comedic proportions. Mouth open, eyes wide, hands in his hair pulling on his face so hard he looked five years younger.

"Well, hot damn," Bowen said. "Guess y'all will miss my barbecue next week. That's all right. I'll save the leftovers."

"It happened," Levi finally said. "I'd almost given up thinking about it. But it happened."

"It happened," Tamara said.

Levi held the keys in front of his face.

"Keys to a fortune," Bowen said. "Must be nice. I'll leave you two to celebrate in your own way. Just remember me in your will. I don't ask for much. Just leave me the cooperage and any spare millions you got lying around."

"You." Levi pointed at Bowen. "You and I are drinking our guts out tonight. We are celebrating. And after that, we're packing. We'll go back tomorrow. Right?"

Tamara didn't answer. She couldn't answer. She could only stare at the letter on her lap. One little piece of paper…it might blow away in a light breeze and never be seen again. She almost wished it would. This was what they'd been waiting for. This was why she and Levi had gotten married. This was why she'd done all that she'd done, so they could have this letter, which said Red Thread was hers, all hers, to do with what she pleased. It had happened—victory, triumph, the culmination of all her work and all her planning and all her hoping.

She looked at Levi.

"I don't want to go back, Levi."

"Tomorrow?"

"Ever."

27

"What the hell do you mean you don't want to go back?" Levi demanded after Bowen had left them to gather supplies for the celebration.

"I don't know," Tamara said. "I just... I don't want to leave here. I'm afraid to."

"Afraid of what?"

"I told you, I don't know." Tamara and Levi stood in the middle of the living room on opposite sides. She rested her forehead on the mantel as she stared into the fireplace. He sat on the sofa arm and stared at her like she'd grown a second head.

"Of all the things you've done and said that make no sense, this makes the most no sense you've ever made. Tamara, this is why you married me. This is why you made me marry you."

"I didn't make you marry me."

"You threatened to marry some old geezer."

"And if you didn't care about me at all, you wouldn't have cared if I'd done it."

"I do care about you. I did and I do. But you drive me up one wall and down the other sometimes and I swear I'm looking down at you from the ceiling right now. What the hell are you thinking saying you don't want it anymore? Millions of dollars and the company you swore to shut down. You just want to give it back?"

Tamara turned around and raised her empty hands.

"Levi, you don't know how good it's been to be here with you. How good it's been for me. I didn't think I'd ever feel normal again, like I felt before the flood, and this past month I have. And that's worth a fortune to me."

"Me, too, baby. Nothing matters more than you being happy. But you seem to think going back home for two weeks and signing some papers will take away all that happiness. Only if you let it. It's not like we have to stay there forever."

"I don't trust Momma. I don't."

"I don't trust her, either, but what's she got to do with us anymore?"

"She doesn't know where we are. But if we go back, she will. And she'll try to take it all away. She's taken you away from me before, and I know she'll try again."

"So let her try. We won't let her."

Levi stood up and stared at the ceiling a moment. She knew he was trying to calm down for her sake. He walked over to her and took her hands in his.

"Let me tell you what's going to happen if we go back," Levi began, rubbing her soft hands with his rough ones. "We'll pack up our suitcases and get in the truck. We'll drive one whole day to get there and spend the night in a hotel in Louisville. The next morning we'll go to the judge's office. We'll sign our lives away on those papers, and then we'll go back to the hotel. I'll call whoever I need to call to tell them that

Red Thread is shutting down. We'll give all the employees six months' severance pay. Nobody could complain about that. People won't be happy, but what seventeen-year-old girl wants to be saddled with a big company to run? It'll be news for a week or two and then it won't be news anymore. We'll go by Arden and you can get your things out of there or you can sell everything in the house in a flea market. God knows I don't care. And your mother will show up sometime when we're there. And she'll tell you I used to rape her in the stables. Or that I used to steal money from the house. Or that I tried to kill her once. And you won't believe her. When you don't believe her, she'll tell me you're crazy. She'll tell me the doctors wanted to put you in an asylum because you're so sick in the head. And she'll tell me you lied about being a virgin and you lied about being trapped in the house with your grandfather's body during the flood. She'll tell me you tried to murder your whole family once. And I won't believe her lies about you any more than you will believe her lies about me. She might even send the cops after me, but that's fine. She's trespassing on our property, so we'll have the cops arrest her and drag her away. And then we will go to whatever farm has your Kermit, and we'll buy him back if we can find him. And we'll have supper with Andre and Gloria and we'll stay the night in their house and try not to bang the bed against the wall loud enough to wake them. Then we'll invite them to come stay with us down here, hug them goodbye and come back here—you, me and Kermit. Let's hope Rex likes the Muppets as much as you do. The only bad thing that's gonna happen because you and I go back home and sign those papers is that Bowen'll kill me when I tell him we'll have to clear land and put up a real barn for all these damn horses. Okay?"

Levi had his hands on her shoulders, steadying her. He looked into her face and nodded.

"What about Charleston?" she asked.

"What about Charleston?"

"We could live there. We could sell, I don't know, half the island's acres to the timber company. We'd have plenty of money then without going back. We could move to Charleston and be together there like we were that week. Couldn't we?"

Charleston. They'd gone there a week after Tamara recovered from her two nights' stay in the forest. He told her she deserved a real honeymoon, and Tamara knew he wanted to take her mind off their fight, off her anger at her mother. He wanted a fresh start for them, so he'd blown what was left in his savings to get them four nights at an old house turned inn—supposedly haunted like every other house in Charleston. They wore their best clothes and ate at fine restaurants, took a carriage ride around town, toured old houses and sat outside their fancy room on their fancy balcony drinking wine and tea. And at night they could hardly sleep in their antique King Louis bed on their silk sheets for how much they wanted each other. The last night there they'd spotted a shelf cloud in the blackening sky, and sure enough a storm hit so hard the whole town lost power. The innkeeper gave them an oil lamp to light their room, and with thunder and lightning and rain pounding the walls and the roof, she and Levi had done things to each other that she could hardly think about now without losing her mind. She'd said words to him she hadn't known were in her vocabulary, and he'd done things to her she hadn't realized people did to each other. She'd spent half the night with her face in the pillow trying to stifle her own moans and screams as Levi turned her inside out. The next morning she'd woken up raw and sore and covered with enough love bites she could have passed for a spotted jaguar. When she chided Levi for making her walk funny, he disavowed all knowledge and insisted that if she'd been violated and sodomized the night before, it must have been the ghost of the inn who had done it because he'd slept all night long like a baby in a cradle. Tamara had said if it was the ghost of the inn who'd done all that to her, she'd be extending her stay.

They'd *learned* things about each other that night.

And Tamara had learned something about herself. Every time they'd stepped foot in their fancy inn, the desk clerk or the porter would say, "Mornin', Mrs. Shelby," or "Evenin', Mr. Shelby, Mrs. Shelby." She'd been Mrs. Shelby-ed half to death those four days by those fine old-world Southerners with their fine old-world Southern manners. All day every day it was "Good weather we're having today, aren't we, Mrs. Shelby?" and then a tip of the hat and "Mrs. Shelby, don't you dare pick up that suitcase, it is twice your size. You let Mr. Shelby handle it or wait for the porter."

Mrs. Shelby. It had sounded funny the first ten times these strangers said it to her, not so funny the next ten. By the end of their trip, Tamara Maddox was long gone, never to be seen again. She was nobody if she wasn't Mrs. Shelby. And Mrs. Shelby wanted to stay Mrs. Shelby. She wasn't going to be a pretend wife biding her time until she had all the family money and she could run off to Majorca or Rome. She wanted to be a real wife to him for the rest of her life.

"Tamara?"

She looked up at him.

"I just… I don't want to lose you. I finally feel like we're really married. Not, you know, just doing this for the money."

Tamara leaned into him and Levi put his arms around her.

"You're not going to lose me just because we go back home

a couple weeks. Your mother's not God. She's a mean woman, and trust me, I know how to handle mean women by now."

"You won't let Momma do something to us?" Tamara asked. "I know she'll try to get between us."

"You think I'd side with a woman who sicced the cops on me?"

"No. But I'm still scared."

"I know." Levi sighed and her head moved over his chest. "I can't say I'm excited about laying off all the Red Thread workers and dealing with that mess. But we'll just do it. We'll rip off the Band-Aid and get it done fast as we can so we can come back here and start our life up again. Then we'll have all the money we need. We can buy a house in Beaufort. We can turn the island into a park. Or maybe just keep it for ourselves. And Bowen will be real happy to make all wine barrels instead of bourbon barrels. He says they're more fun because they're harder to make and you get to talk on the phone to French people all the time. He swears there's a vintner in France who's in love with him and he's ready to go there to find out."

Tamara laughed and wrapped her arms around Levi's waist.

"See?" Levi said. "I've got all the good ideas. Just don't worry so much. Your mother can't hurt us if we don't let her."

"I want to believe that." She linked her hands at the small of his back and squeezed him close. She wanted to tell Levi how much she loved him and how much she needed him, but he knew all that, and telling him again wouldn't make it any more real. But times like this she felt like they were born to be together, and if they couldn't be together, she would die.

"Whatever comes our way now, we'll find a way to carry it. We're married. We're family. We're in this together. Right?"

Tamara slowly nodded. "Right."

"Good. Of course I'm right. I'm always right."

She pinched him. Hard.

"Now, that was uncalled-for," Levi said.

"Oh, it was called for. So was this." She pinched him again.

"You're asking for it, Rotten. One of these days…"

"What? You gonna finally turn me over your knee one of these days?"

"No. I'm going to turn you over my knee today. Right now and there's nothing you can do about it."

He hoisted her up over his shoulder, squealing and laughing, and carried her up to the bedroom. She called him every name in the book as he did it—monster and brute and animal and beast and the very devil incarnate—and he seemed to take them all as compliments. He yanked her jeans down to her ankles, threw her over his lap and slapped her ass so hard she screamed. It hurt so bad, laughing and screaming at the same time. Like being tickled times a thousand. Then he pushed her onto her back and finished what they'd started earlier that day before Bowen had so rudely interrupted them to tell them they were millionaires.

As they lay in bed afterward, half-naked and all tired, they made their decisions.

Levi was right. Running away to Charleston or anywhere else wouldn't solve any problems. Whatever her mother threw at them, they could catch it. They wouldn't let it stick. They wouldn't let it hurt. They'd be smart and not let her anywhere near them. They'd get in and get out as fast as they could. They'd sign the papers and hire a good man to handle closing down Red Thread for good. And maybe while they were there, Tamara would finally work up the courage to tell Levi the whole truth.

Then, as he'd promised, they'd come home to Bride Island.

Tamara stretched out on top of Levi and wondered how he would take the news when she told him.

"You promise you won't let anything get between us?" Tamara asked, tracing a heart on his chest over his heart. "No matter what happens?"

"Nothing's gonna happen, Rotten. And yes, I promise. But, you know…just in case…"

"What?"

"Pack your gun."

28

"Nobody Does It Better" cooed on the radio and Tamara turned up the dial, sat back and let the highway winds buffet her face.

"This song's about me," Levi said as he merged onto I-75 going north. "I told Carly not to write it, that what happened between us was just between us, and if she wrote a song about me, women would be knocking on my door the rest of my life. But would she listen? No, ma'am. She would not."

"I hate to tell you this, but a man wrote this song," Tamara said.

"Okay, so maybe it's not about me."

"It could be, though." She turned her head and smiled at him. "Nobody does it better than you."

"High praise from an ex-virgin."

Tamara laughed. "Just because I don't have anything to compare it to doesn't mean I don't know it's the best."

Levi grinned behind his sunglasses, white teeth showing.

"Don't make me pull this truck over."

"Next rest stop, forty-seven miles." Tamara read the sign on the side of the road.

"Don't tempt me. We're making good time."

"Keep driving," Tamara said. "We're almost there, anyway. I can survive until we get to Louisville."

"Maybe *you* can."

Tamara squeezed his knee and went back to staring out the window. They'd packed up the truck last night and headed out at first light that morning. If they kept their stops to a minimum, they'd make it to Judge Headley's office before five and could get the paperwork signed today. Tamara's fears about going home had lingered right up to the moment they crossed the Tennessee border into Kentucky. Then, like magic, the fear evaporated like rain on a hot sidewalk. What did she have to be afraid of? This was her home. The road curved and rounded corners and everywhere Tamara looked she saw tall green trees and farmhouses hidden among them. As they traveled north, the trees turned to pastures, the small farmhouses turned to large farmhouses. White stables with red trim. White stables with green trim. White stables with black trim. White fences that stretched for miles. And horses and horses and more horses, grazing and running and making the whole world look like a summer scene from a Currier and Ives calendar.

"You're smiling, Rotten."

"I'm happy," she said. "It's so pretty here. I'd forgotten how pretty. And it smells good."

"Doesn't smell like a salt marsh, that's for sure. And we've got hills again. Good to be back."

"Feels like home," Tamara said. "Is it home to you, too?"

"Of course it is. Born and raised here. Mom's buried here. My family's here."

"I'm here."

"That's what I meant."

"You know, we could buy a place in Louisville," Tamara said. "I loved our house in town. It was nothing like Arden. It was a normal house. Only four bedrooms—not ten."

"Normal? Is that why you loved it?"

"It was Daddy's house and he made it a home. I had friends there."

"You miss your friends?"

Tamara sighed and shrugged. "I feel so far away from them now. It used to be slumber parties every Friday night and birthday parties and we'd all go riding together on Saturdays. But Carol and Katie are going to college and Billie's moving to Ohio for a job with her uncle. And I'm..."

"An old married lady?"

"A *young* married lady."

"You can go to college if you want to," Levi said. "I would never stop you going to school or working."

"Momma wanted to go to college. She didn't get to."

"Family wouldn't let her?"

"She got pregnant with me. That was the end of that."

"Speaking of pregnant, Rotten... I hate to tell you this, but your stomach is flat as a pancake. You gonna wear a pillow under your dress when we see the judge?"

"I'll wear something baggy and I'll make myself throw up on your shoes. How's that?"

"Sounds like a plan. I could use new boots, anyway."

"Well, guess what?"

"What?"

"Now we can afford them."

He kissed the back of her hand and kept on driving. The windows were open, and even with the wind blowing in, the

August heat was stifling. The back of Tamara's leg stuck to the vinyl seats and left little square indentions on her skin. She should have worn pants instead of a dress. The air felt swollen with wet heat. Levi chugged Tab to stay alert and Tamara stared at barns and pastures and horses that she hadn't realized she'd missed until she saw them again.

The bank clock read 4:37 p.m., so they drove into downtown Louisville to Judge Headley's office. He hadn't been expecting them until tomorrow, but he didn't seem to mind at all that they showed up a day early.

"There's my girl," Judge Headley said, embracing her. "You're as tan as your husband now."

But Tamara only rolled her eyes at his joke as she sank into Headley's strong arms. This man was her father. Her father was holding her. He didn't feel like her father and nobody but Daddy ever would, but it gave her a modicum of comfort to know she came from this good man who gave such strong and gentle hugs.

"My girl," Levi corrected. "But I'll let you borrow her for a hug."

"You're a generous man," Judge Headley said, shaking Levi's hand with real affection. "Now, I hope you two aren't too tired from your drive. I need y'all to sign a few hundred pieces of paper. Ready?"

Tamara looked at Levi, who cracked his knuckles as loud as he could.

"I'll take that as a yes," Judge Headley said.

"It's a yes," Tamara said. "Let's get this thing over with."

They signed until her signature read "Tammy Shelly" and Levi's looked like nothing more than an *L*, an *S* and a long squiggly line afterward. The whole time, Judge Headley kept up a steady stream of chatter about the will probation process, and how it had looked to be a long nasty battle until one day three weeks ago Virginia Maddox up and quit the fight.

"She just quit?" Levi asked. "Doesn't seem like her."

"She didn't seem happy to quit. But she threw in the towel and said you could have it all. She meant it, too. She's moved out of Arden. She's staying with a friend of hers in Lexington."

"As long as she stays away from us, that's all I care about," Tamara said, capping her Bic pen and tossing it on the table.

"Why'd she give up?" Levi asked, and Tamara wished he wouldn't. "Did she say?"

"Beats me." Headley gathered up all the papers, the deeds and money transfer notices, into one neat pile and started sorting them out. "But it made our jobs easier. We pushed it through, got it done, and now you two have the rest of your lives to enjoy each other. And you don't have a damn thing to worry about ever again."

Tamara leaned over and hugged him again. She could have hugged the whole wide world. Did Judge Headley have any idea how good that sounded to her—never having anything to worry about ever again? She'd done nothing but worry for the past year and a half. Wouldn't it be nice to take a long vacation from worry? Better than a trip on the Love Boat.

When it was all done, Tamara told Levi she was tired and asked if he'd mind pulling the truck up to the front of the building. He didn't mind at all. She knew he wouldn't. He shook Judge Headley's hand and left them alone.

"Thank you," Tamara said. "Thank you for doing this. I know you went to a lot of trouble for me."

"You're like family, angel face. You know that. Your daddy and Eric and I swore when we were boys we'd always be brothers even if blood had nothing to do with it. I can't believe those boys are gone, but you're here. And you'll always be like a daughter to me. Even when you're doing something crazy like getting married and having a baby before you're even old enough to vote. When's the baby due, anyway? December?"

Tamara swallowed hard. "Yeah. Or January, maybe. Hard to tell sometimes."

"Levi happy?"

"He's real happy. Me, too."

"That's good. Junior can call me Uncle Grandpa if he wants."

"About that…"

"About what?" he asked, putting all their papers in a file.

"About my uncle."

"Eric? What about him?"

"You were at his going-away party the night he shipped out, right?"

"Well, now, let me think back. Yes, I was for a bit. Why do you ask?"

"Just wondering. I heard it was a wild party."

"I wouldn't know. I was there ten minutes before I had to get back home again. My mother picked that night to fall on ice and bust her head open. She called over to Arden and I had to leave right then and take her to the hospital. I hadn't even taken off my jacket yet."

Tamara stared at him. "You sure it was that night?"

"Sure as a man can be. I remember cursing my mother from one end of the state to the other—not to her face, of course—for her terrible timing. She cried so hard at Eric's funeral you would have thought it was her son who'd died. She felt bad dragging me away from his party, since that was the last time any of us saw him alive. Only your daddy cried harder."

Tamara sank down into the chair.

"Tamara? You all right?"

"I'm fine," she said. "Just got a little dizzy there."

"It happens," he said. "Maryanne was dizzy all the time with our first. You know, I thought you'd be starting to pop by now. Must be your dress."

Tamara looked down at the loose sundress she wore. It had settled onto her stomach, which was, as Levi had said, flat as a pancake. For now.

"Just the dress," she said. "I can't wear my jeans anymore."

Judge Headley put his hand on her forehead. His skin was soft, not calloused, not like Levi's.

"You feel a little clammy, sweetheart. Maybe take it easy for the rest of the day."

"I'll do that." Tamara *was* clammy. She felt a cold sweat and she shivered inside all the way to her bones. Her lips trembled and her mouth went dry. She wanted water, lots of it and ice-cold.

Judge Headley glanced up at the window. "Come on. I'll walk you out. Your husband's probably wondering about you."

He took her arm and escorted her to the front door. Levi pulled up right to the curb and the judge started toward the door to open it for her.

"Wait." Tamara took Judge Headley's hand in hers. "You said you didn't trust Momma. Why don't you? I thought something happened at the party that night."

"Something must have. The day before the party your mother told me she was in love with Eric. Then two days later she announced she was getting married to Nash. Hard to trust a woman who'd tell one man she loved him and then marry his brother two weeks after he joins the army. But we were all young and stupid. Who isn't, at that age? She's not a bad woman. Just…maybe not a good woman."

He kissed her forehead and opened the door to the truck.

"Ready to find a hotel?" Levi asked. "You think there's rooms at the Galt House? Maybe we could get a honeymoon suite." He winked at her.

"Arden," she said. "Let's go to Arden."

"Arden? You sure about that?"

"Momma's gone. Why shouldn't we go?"

"No reason," Levi said, pulling out into the street. Tamara saw the river in the distance, brown and shining. "No reason at all."

29

They pulled into the circular driveway at Arden an hour later.

"Well, look at that," Levi said.

"Oh, my gosh. That's my car." Tamara leaned forward. Her blue Triumph Spitfire sat parked in front of the house. "I guess I was right. The police must have found it and called Momma."

"Looks in good shape." Levi pulled the truck in right behind it. "Doesn't look like your mother took a baseball bat to it."

Tamara hopped out of the truck before Levi could open the door for her. She ran to the car and found the doors unlocked and the keys in the ignition.

"Nice of her," Tamara said. "I wonder if the car will blow up the second I turn it on."

Levi grinned. "You been watching too many James Bond movies. But just in case, I'll start the car the first time. You ready to go in?"

"Can I go in alone? Just for a while?"

Levi looked at her long and hard. "You think that's safe?"

"I do," she said. "Do you mind? I just want a few minutes."

"You go in and I'll go pick us up some supper somewhere and bring it back. If there's any food in that house, it's probably poisoned." He winked at her. Tamara smiled because she knew she was supposed to.

"Right. That's perfect. Thank you."

Levi leaned down and kissed her on the lips.

"I'll be back soon," he said.

Tamara nodded. She'd packed only one small suitcase and her purse, so she carried them to the front door. The keys were in her purse, and even though this was legally her home in every way, she felt like an intruder opening the door. Tamara looked over her shoulder at Levi waiting and she waved at him. He waved back and drove off.

The air in the house smelled stale but clean, as if someone had used a whole bottle of lemon furniture polish two weeks ago and the scent still polluted the air.

Tamara set down her suitcase and opened it. From under a pile of neatly folded shirts, she pulled the handgun she'd taken from her grandfather's office the night of the flood. Her hand shook as she loaded it. Learning to shoot had taken practice, and as she'd had no teacher, she'd nearly done herself in by accident a time or two in the process. All she could do was drive out to the middle of nowhere and aim the gun at cans set up on tree stumps. The hardest part had been dealing with the recoil. Once she got used to the gun's kick and the terrible sound of it, she found she was a decent shot. Not great, but she didn't need to be great. She wasn't a sharpshooter. All she wanted was to protect herself, and everyone who knows anything knows the things that can harm you are always the things closest to you.

"Hello?" Tamara called out as she wandered the first floor of the house—her grandfather's sitting room with his big oak bar and his big brass lamp. His big box of cigars was gone. They'd been ruined in the flood and Tamara was glad they were gone. If they were gone, he was gone. Gone for good. The rugs on the floor had been ruined, too, but these new rugs were nicer than the old ones. Persian rugs with swirling patterns of flowers and vines in hues of red, green and gold. Masculine colors, but her mother had picked them out. For whom? All the Maddox men were dead but for Levi, and there was no way on God's green earth her mother would roll out the welcome mat or any other piece of carpeting for him. She must have done it by habit, buying new rugs Granddaddy would have approved of. That had been her mother's entire life—doing everything she did for the approval of men.

Tamara went to the dining room and looked around. China cabinet full of fine-boned china. Mahogany table for ten. Sideboard. Curtains drawn. Nothing ripped. Nothing torn. Nothing broken. Everything left in perfect condition. Tamara wouldn't have put it past her mother to break every dish in the house and shred every bit of fabric. Tamara wouldn't put anything past her mother, which was why she'd wanted to walk the house alone without Levi.

But everything was fine. Yet it wasn't fine. How could Judge Headley have fathered her the night of Uncle Eric's going-away party if he hadn't been there long enough to take off his jacket? Easy answer. He hadn't. She reasoned he could have done it the night before. He could have done it the night after. But what was this about Momma being in love with Uncle Eric? She'd never heard that story before. Had to have been an unrequited love. Eric hadn't been drafted. He'd joined the army as a volunteer. What man in love would do such a thing? A man in love wouldn't do such a thing. So it was nothing to worry about.

Tamara wandered into the kitchen. Here was something to worry about. Sitting on the kitchen table was an envelope. On the front it read "Tamara and Levi" in her mother's handwriting and Tamara eyed it like a snake. She eyed it like a snake because it was a snake, more dangerous than the copperhead that had gotten into their house that night. It was the snake that made Tamara want to go in first, without Levi. If her mother were here, lurking, waiting to strike, Tamara wanted to be the one between her and Levi. If anyone or anything had to get shot, Tamara would do the shooting.

Tamara picked up the letter and walked to the sink. Then she dug around in the drawers until she found a book of matches. Tamara set the letter alight and smiled as the paper turned black and curled. As the fire reached her fingertips, Tamara turned on the faucet and drowned the ashes in the drain.

If Tamara knew her mother, and she did, she knew this letter wouldn't be the only snake in the grass. She raced from room to room, and sure enough she found no less than five envelopes—one in the bathroom, one in her old bedroom, one in the upstairs bathroom, one in the library and one in the master bedroom Granddaddy had slept in. If she read the letters, her mother would win. Tamara would not let her win. She'd lost too much to let anyone else win anymore. Tamara burned them all in the sink and washed the remnants away.

When she finished and they were all gone, she smiled.

That was that. She won.

Tamara heard the happy sound of tires on the drive, and she saw Levi's truck coming around the bend in the driveway. She laughed when she saw the horse trailer attached to the end of his truck. Today he'd signed the papers that made him a millionaire and all he had on his mind was buying horses. Tomorrow they'd probably go and find Kermit, wherever he was. She had missed that sweet boy of hers.

Levi drove straight to the stables and Tamara packed the gun carefully away in her suitcase again. There was a pleasant, rarely used guest room on the second floor at the end of the hall. Tamara had no bad memories of it. They could sleep there tonight and figure out what to do with the house in the morning. She walked down to the stables and found Levi inspecting the stalls.

"How bad is it?" Tamara asked him from the doorway.

"I've seen better," Levi said. "There's mold in a lot of the old straw, some dry rot in the doors. But I can get at least one stall cleaned up by tomorrow. I called the farrier, and he said he knew who bought Kermit and the rest of the horses. We can go haggling tomorrow to get them back. Kermit at least if they won't sell the others."

"That's good news," she said, leaning in the doorway of the stall as Levi kicked old straw around, inspecting the floors.

"How's the house? Any ghosts? Any wolves?"

"No ghosts. No wolves. No mothers-in-law."

Levi grinned. "Good news. You want to go riding tomorrow? Real riding?"

"What do you think Rex and I have been doing this past month?"

"A Walker walks. You used to run Kermit like you were in the damn Derby. Can't do that on the island. Too many trees in the way."

"I don't know if we should," she said, watching as Levi raked the old dirty straw to the edges of the stall. "Might not be safe."

Levi looked sharply at her. "Safe? This from the girl who

used to stand on Kermit's saddle and pretend she was in the Ringling Brothers? When did you start caring about being safe on the back of a horse?"

"When I got pregnant."

Levi dropped the rake.

He stared at her.

Tamara tried to smile. "You gonna say something?"

"How?"

"The usual way."

"But you… We went to the doctor and—" He paused and buried his fingers in his thick dark hair and pulled it away from his face. She couldn't read his expression. Was it shocked and happy? Shocked and horrified? Shocked and shocked?

"Remember the snake?"

"I remember the snake," Levi said.

"I'd only been on the pill three days that night. Not enough time for it to start working. Anyway, that's the doctor's guess. He did the math."

"The snake. Right." Levi rubbed his temples. "Wild night."

"Levi, are you happy?" she asked, tears burning the backs of her eyes. "Or are you mad at me?"

"Why the hell would I be mad at you?"

"I don't know. I know you didn't want kids. And I—"

"Oh, my God. Tamara…" He walked to her and took her in his arms. She sank into his embrace like she was sinking into soft earth. He held her close and tight, rocking her against him.

"I didn't mean to, I swear." She'd been good. She'd taken her pills. She hadn't meant for it to happen. But she couldn't be sad about it.

"I know, Rotten."

"I want to be happy about it."

"So do I. I'm scared, but I'm happy." Levi rubbed her lower back and she finally started to relax a little.

"Me, too. Scared, I mean. But happy. Scrappy."

Tamara laughed against his chest, which hurt, since she was crying, too, and it wasn't easy to do both.

"How long... How long have you known?"

"A week, I guess. I was gonna tell you Saturday, but Bowen showed up. I'm two months along."

"I can do the math."

Two months since the snake. Strange to know the exact night. Strange to have a snake to thank for their child. That was the night she told Levi she was in love with him still. And the first time she'd told him had been right here.

"You know, we were in this stall the first time we kissed," Tamara said.

Levi raised his head and looked around.

"We were, weren't we?"

"My birthday kiss," she said, grinning at him. "My first real kiss."

"You were good at it."

"I was?"

Levi slowly nodded, wide-eyed. "Rotten, if your mother hadn't interrupted, you would have gotten that roll in the hay you'd been begging for. I was ready to strip you naked and have you right against the wall, which would have been my preferred choice of birthday present."

"So what's stopping you?"

"It's not your birthday."

"We can pretend it is..."

"Is that safe?"

"My doctor says it is. We can have sex all the way up to

the last month if I feel like it. He said I won't be, but he said we could. In theory."

"Well, if we've got a fast coming in a few months, we better feast while we can."

Before she could say another word, he'd lifted her off her feet and deposited her next to the back wall of the stall, right where she had been on her birthday.

He tilted her face up to meet his and kissed her. They'd made love fifty times or more since their first time and kissed a thousand. But this kiss burned her the way their first had, burned her right to the core. She was weak with relief that Levi was happy about the baby, overjoyed that they'd finally won and at peace that they could finally start their real lives together. It was right they should do this here and now, finishing what they'd started on her sixteenth birthday.

Levi reached under her dress and cupped her bottom, squeezing it in his large hands. He ran them up her back and down again as he kissed her neck, down into her panties, and then they were coming off, down her legs as he knelt in the straw. He lifted her dress up and Tamara thought she knew what he would do, but he surprised her. He didn't kiss her between her legs. He kissed her stomach instead, massaging it with his mouth, pressing tender kisses from hip to hip. A soft sob escaped her lips. They would be happy together. They would be. After, Levi dipped his head lower, pushed her legs apart and found her clitoris with his tongue. He worked it gently until she panted, until her head fell back and her hips strained forward, silently begging for more. He lifted her leg up and rested it on his shoulder as he licked deeper in her, opening her up until she felt wetness release from her in little bursts. He stood up finally and kissed her mouth again as he slipped his middle finger into her and curled it forward, finding that tender sensitive place inside her that made her clench and cry out. He swallowed her cry as he stroked her insides and soon she was as wet as she'd ever been. Wet and burning for him. The last time they were here, she'd been a girl, a virgin, and she'd been too scared to do what she wanted. But she was older now, a wife, his wife, and she reached down and opened his jeans, pulling him free and gripping him hard with her hand.

"You want it?" Levi asked in her ear, his hot breath tickling her bare neck.

"I want it."

"Take it, then," he said, pushing his pelvis into hers.

Tamara guided him and he plunged inside her with a thrust, filling her completely, so completely she cried out again and nearly came from the penetration alone. He lifted her and settled her over his hips and thighs so that her feet were off the ground, pinning her with his cock to the wall behind her. He yanked the straps of her dress down her arms and pushed it all the way to her waist. He grasped her bare breasts in his hands the way she loved, tugging on her nipples, pulling on them, dipping his head to suck them and lick them. Tamara writhed on him, barely able to move, but moving as much as she could. Her vagina squeezed him and Levi gasped. He pushed into her with quick rough thrusts and she came hard, muffling her scream of pleasure by burying her mouth against his shoulder. He drove his own orgasm into hers, hard enough it hurt against the wall, but she didn't care. Soon he'd be treating her like a glass doll, so she had to enjoy his lust for her while she could until she could have it all again. Levi slowed down, pulled out to the tip and slid back. He did it again, drawing it out and pushing it back as Tamara's body throbbed around him. She was going to come again if he didn't stop doing that, fucking her so slow and hard and deep. He didn't stop. Tamara clutched his shoulders and arched her back to give herself room to move. She sank down onto him, moaning as he filled her.

"Show-off," she panted. She knew Levi. She knew he was showing her what she could have had on her birthday if her mother hadn't chosen that moment to ruin her life.

The wood behind her was smooth, painted and slick, and she slid up and down it as Levi worked her up and down on him, her breasts pressed to his chest, her nipples hard as stones and her body ready to burst from the mad ecstasy of being used like this. She couldn't get enough of it, couldn't get enough of Levi. They would be lovers forever and this child inside her was only the first of many they would have. Levi was beautiful and smart and the world needed half a dozen of him at least. And their children would be Shelbys, not Maddoxes, and because Levi was good, they would be good. Their sons would be generous and kind and their daughters would be wise and strong. And they would never ever meet their grandmother. And there on the cusp of perfect happiness, Tamara came again, rocking and shuddering in Levi's arms as he pounded his own climax into her, filling her and filling her until she couldn't take any more.

Carefully Levi let her feet down to the floor as he pulled out of her.

"You all right, Rotten?" He cupped her face, kissed her burning cheeks.

"Never better." She grinned up at him, feeling drunk with her happiness. "I feel…"

"What?"

"Wet." Tamara clamped her legs together. "Very wet."

Levi laughed sheepishly. "We had gone a whole twenty-four hours without doing that."

"I need a paper towel. Or maybe a beach towel."

"There might be a towel in my old office. Stay here."

Tamara straightened her dress and Levi went to the tiny "office" he'd made for himself at the other end of the barn. There'd never been much in his office but for a small desk, a telephone, all the horses' medical records and a first-aid kit. Maybe the first-aid kit was still in there. She might need it. The barn was painted and the wood was sanded, but she had an itching feeling like she'd gotten a splinter in her back.

Tamara started to walk out of the stall, but she caught a glimpse of something on the ground. Kicking the straw aside, she saw a glint of gold. The ankle bracelet with the horse charm on it Levi had given her on her birthday. Tamara had dropped it when her mother had dragged her from the barn. She thought she'd never see it again.

"Levi?" Tamara called out. Levi didn't answer. She ran from the stall to his office.

"Levi, you won't believe it. I found the bracelet you gave me for my big fat wrist. It's been here the whole—"

She stepped into the office and stopped dead, cold and scared.

Levi held a letter in his hands. An open letter. The envelope on his desk said "Tamara and Levi" in her mother's handwriting.

"Levi?" Tamara heard the fear in her voice. "Remember, you said she'd try to hurt us. You said you wouldn't let her hurt us."

Slowly Levi looked up from the letter, looked at her. Then he bent over at the waist like he was about to be sick. The letter fell from his hands. Tamara grabbed it off the ground.

"Levi, what—"

"Read it."

Tamara and Levi—

I left copies of this letter where you two were sure to find one. I have tried in vain for weeks to contact you through Daniel Headley's office. In desperation, I have given up the legal suit in the hopes you two would finally come home. There is no easy way to say this, but just to say it. Tamara, I received your note about your marriage where you informed me that you knew the truth about Nash and that he was not your father. You said you knew Daniel Headley was your father. That is not the truth. The truth is that George Maddox is your real father. And he is Levi's real father.

There is more to this story, but that is all you need to know. If you don't believe me, I have a letter from Nash, his suicide note he mailed me, that will tell you everything I have told you.

Please, Levi, let my daughter go before it's too late.

The note was signed "Virginia Maddox."
And it was already too late.

30

Tamara slipped a hand under her dress and pressed it between her legs into the wetness, cupping herself as if trying to staunch a wound. She pulled her hand away and saw Levi's semen on her fingers. Her husband's.

Her brother's.

She rubbed it off on her dress.

"Tell me it's a lie," Levi said, his head buried in his hands.

"I…" Tamara fell back against the door frame. "I don't know."

"It has to be a lie. It has to be a lie."

"I…"

"Did you know?" Levi grabbed her by her upper arms and stared into her eyes. "Did you know this?"

"No. I swear to God I didn't know."

Judge Headley hadn't even taken his jacket off the night of the party where he and her mother had supposedly conceived her.

I'm tired of pretending that Tamara is my daughter. Even Virginia is tired of pretending. Did you know she told me that Tamara was Daniel Headley's daughter, conceived at Eric's going-away party? I laughed when she told me. Virginia is more a Maddox than I am. You've taught her well.

Daddy laughed.

Daddy laughed at her mother when she told him Daniel Headley was Tamara's father.

Daddy laughed because it wasn't true, not because it was.

"Your mother tried to send us a letter. You tore it up..." Levi's head fell back and for a horrifying second his eyes were nothing but the whites.

"I didn't know what it said, I swear. I didn't know."

"You said she beat you because I kissed you. She didn't tell you why she hated me so much?"

"She didn't beat me," Tamara said. "That's not what happened. She—"

"Oh, God." The cry sounded like someone had ripped the words from his chest. He doubled over again, wheezing. Tamara couldn't see. She was underwater and drowning. There was no surfacing for her.

Bone of her bone.

Flesh of her flesh.

Blood of her blood.

Tamara reached for Levi and he held up his hands in front of his face.

"Don't," he said, not looking at her. She had become Medusa and he would turn to stone with a single glance at her. She had become Sodom and with one look back he would turn to a pillar of salt.

She lowered her hand and pressed it against her stomach, the stomach he'd kissed with love and reverence only minutes ago, but now it was a poisoned cup.

It was like someone had lowered a bell jar over her body, muting all sounds and setting her ears to ringing. Outside the clear wall of glass she could hear the faintest murmuring, and she knew if the glass lifted, it would sound like screams. She could see clearly through the glass and she watched Levi from inside it, her hands raised as if pressed to the smoother curved surface inside. She watched Levi grasp at the wall, needing it to help him stand. She watched him push past her. She called his name, but he couldn't hear her through the bell any more than she could hear him. His shuffling steps turned into a run.

The glass suddenly shattered and Tamara could hear again, although the ringing in her ears remained. She heard sounds of metal and engines. Leaving sounds. He was leaving her. She let him go.

Tamara emerged from the stables into the evening sunlight, blinking and wincing. The light hurt and she shrank from it. Stumbling, she made it to tree cover and she wandered in the little woods where she'd played and ridden her horse as a child. There was the tree she had climbed when she'd fallen off her horse and lacked the height to mount him again. There was the stone she'd lain on half sleeping, half daydreaming the summer after her father's death, the summer after she'd had her first period and pondered her future. On that rock she'd dreamed her dreams of love and sex and marriage and prayed God would give her a husband who could take away the pain of her losing her father by trading it for pleasure.

"I killed my own father," Tamara whispered to the rock. Her hands pressed against its rough gritty surface. She waited for the guilt or shame to come to her, but none showed its face. God killed His own Son. Why should He judge her for killing her father? God's Son was sinless. Her father was not. Neither was she.

"I didn't know," she whispered again, trying to explain herself to whatever being would bend an ear to her confession. "I didn't know who he was. Levi didn't know…"

They had sinned in their ignorance. But their ignorance had been willful. Her mother had tried to warn her and Tamara had not listened. She'd torn up the letter and scattered it in the ocean. She hadn't been pregnant then. It hadn't been too late then.

Tamara heard a sound she knew well and followed it. The sound of water, the river, trickling and skipping over limestone and tree roots. She followed the path down to the dock, where she'd sat with her father and dangled a fishing pole into the brown waters. Her father? Which father? Both Daddy and Granddaddy had been there. At the dock's splintered edge, Tamara lay down onto her side to look at the water and take her comfort from it. *Rise*, she prayed. *Rise and carry me under and carry me away.* She couldn't do it herself, not with a child inside her. But if the river wanted her, and if the river was where she belonged, it would come for her again as it had come for her before. For surely God had spared her that night to destroy her this day. It had not been her time then. But her time had come.

Tamara waited. She needed courage to do what she had to do. She waited and needed courage to throw herself in the river. The courage didn't come. Hours passed. The sun set. Night arrived and still Tamara couldn't do what she had to do. While waiting, she fell asleep, and even as she fell asleep, she prayed she wouldn't wake up again.

Instead, she dreamed.

★ ★ ★

In her dream she isn't Tamara.

Who she is she doesn't know until she looks down at her stomach. Not two months along anymore, she is heavy with child now, ready to burst. She will give birth any day. Maybe today.

She's been ordered to sit at the table in the kitchen and wait for Missus. She sits. She waits. Her stomach aches. Her stomach, her legs, her back. Everything aches. She wasn't made to carry this much weight around. It feels like she's been eating stones and has built a dam inside her body with them.

Phyllis, the other house girl, comes in and looks at her but doesn't speak. She is scuttling about, getting this and that from the cabinets.

"Phyllis?"

"I can't talk to you," Phyllis says in a hiss. "She'll whip me."

"What's she gonna do to me?"

"I can't talk to you."

"She's gonna sell me?"

Phyllis takes the bottle she's fetched and clasps it to her chest.

"I can't…"

She gives Veritas a look of pity. There is no hope for her. Veritas lays her hands on her stomach. It hurts to the touch and she curses the thing inside her. Once Master had her that first time, he couldn't get enough of her. He took her every chance he got, morning and night. He'd even keep Phyllis waiting outside in the dark and the damp and the mosquitoes while he took her in their slave cabin in the bed she and Phyllis had to share. After the first few times, she'd learned how to take it without getting herself hurt or bleeding after. But she hated it every time, especially after when he'd act sweet to her, tell her how good she was, how pretty. He'd kiss her forehead like she was his little girl, tug on the red ribbon in her hair. One day she tried to go without wearing it and he ordered her to put it back on.

Veritas puts her head down to rest. Most days she'd be cleaning right now—changing sheets, beating rugs. She wants to be cleaning and working, not sitting here waiting. Waiting scares her.

A few minutes pass and she hears a commotion outside. A cart or a carriage. The jingle of bells, the rattle of gear and hooves.

Missus's voice carries far, all the way into the kitchen. It might be her last chance to run. But she can't run. Not with her belly so swollen and her legs so sore and weak. Whatever is inside is trying to kill her. No surprise to her. Everything outside her wants her dead, too.

Missus comes in the back door and Veritas lifts her head fast. There's a man behind Missus, an ugly man scarred by years and pox. He doesn't look clean to Veritas and she wished she'd tried to run when she had the chance.

"Up, girl," Missus says, and Veritas pulls herself to her feet. It's not easy to stand.

The man gets close, close enough Veritas can smell him. He smells like he's rotting, like old meat in the sun. He looks her up and down, touches her hair, lifts her skirt to see her legs. She flinches when he puts his hand on her stomach.

"Two for one," the man says. "If it lives."

"I'm sure it will," Missus says. "Unfortunately."

The man looks at Missus, raises his eyebrow. She's not an ugly woman, Missus, but not a beauty, either. Master's handsome, but they said he was out of money when he married her. Missus knows why he married her, but that doesn't make it any easier.

"How much?" Missus asks.

"Nine hundred."

"Not for her. Pretty girl like that? Two for one?"

"Thousand. Take it or leave it cuz it's all I brought with me."

"Go on, then. Leave the money. Take the girl."

"Where you taking me?" Veritas asks.

"To catch a boat," the man says.

"But I—"

"Hush up, girl," Missus says. "You did this to yourself."

The man puts irons on her wrists. They have a heavy rope through a hoop and he pulls her like a dog on a leash out of the kitchen.

"He did this to me." Veritas looks down at her belly. "He did. Not me. I didn't want him."

"Shut your mouth, or I'll cut out your tongue." The man tosses his cash on the counter on his way out the door. Veritas digs in her feet and pulls back on the rope.

"Don't do this," she says to Missus, her face wet with her fears. "Please don't do this, Missus. I didn't want him. He took me and I didn't want him. I never wanted that. Don't make me go. Don't make me—"

Missus slaps her hard. Then she does it again. A third time. Then the man stops her.

"Hey, she's mine now. I paid for her," he says.

She ignores the man and grabs Veritas by the hair.

"You will die in chains," Missus says. "You were born in chains and you will die in chains."

Veritas cries out as Missus rips the red ribbon from her head and takes a hank of hair and skin with it. It is the only thing she has of her mother's and Missus has it in her hand.

Veritas hears a sound like a river rising, bursting through mountains, washing away the world. But Veritas is on top of the mountain and she smiles as it's washed away. The river is speaking and it speaks through Veritas.

"You will have a son, and he will die of a fever. And you will die giving birth to your next child. And your husband will be happy to see you dead and buried," Veritas says. "Oh, he will dance on your grave, you ugly old hag."

"What did you say to me?" Missus hisses.

"I said you will die and your husband will smile at your graveside. And someday I will smile over his. I will come back and cut

*this family down to the roots. Then I will tear out the roots and
everything you had and everything you are will burn, and not even
all the rivers of the world will put out the fire I start in your house.
My child will be a girl and I will name her Paris after my mother,
and when Paris comes knocking on your door, you will let her in,
and she will bring my vengeance in her blood and your death in her
hands. There will be no more Maddoxes because of me. I curse you
all from the branches to the roots. Veritas will rule your house."*

*Veritas punctuates her sentence by spitting in Missus's face. Missus
raises her hand again to Veritas, with a fist this time, and the second
they touch, Tamara is awake again.*

Tamara recoils as she feels the touch of hands on her body.
"No—"

"Come on now. Let's get back to the house."

Arms lifted Tamara off the dock, and Tamara whimpered
in protest. She didn't want to leave the river, not while she
lived. But she didn't have the strength to pull away, to wade
into the water. She could barely walk. How long had she
slept? How long had it been since she ate? How long since
Levi had left her?

"I don't want to go…" was all she could get out between
breaths.

In the house she was placed on a sofa. The sofa was a new
antique, purchased after the flood. It wasn't even September,
but someone had started a fire and it glowed like a grinning
demon behind the gate. Tamara's eyes opened and shut in
slow, dazed blinks.

"I can't be here," she said to herself, but someone heard her.

"You're sick. You need to rest."

"I'm not sick."

"You always said that, baby."

"Don't call me baby," Tamara said.

"But you are my baby."

Tamara opened her eyes.

"Momma?"

31

Her mother bathed her skin with wet washcloths and helped her into clean clothes. Tamara didn't speak the entire time as her mother raised her arms to put the shirt on her, tapped her feet to help her into her favorite old jeans. She was a child again in her mother's care. Tamara wished she could hate it, but she'd missed it. Her mother half dragged, half carried her into the living room and sat her down on the sofa.

"What are you doing here, Momma?" Tamara asked as she stretched out on her back. She had no more strength to sit up straight.

Her mother held out a cup of water, but Tamara only looked at it.

"It's just water," her mother said, taking a sip of it to show her it was safe. "Drink it."

Tamara's hand shook as she took the cup from her mother's hand. Her mother helped her up enough to drink. Once it was to her lips, she drank every drop down in a few quick swallows.

"I thought you were someone else," Tamara said, clutching the cup of water. "I wanted you to be someone else."

"Levi."

Tamara lay back down again but didn't close her eyes. If she closed them, she would see Levi behind her eyes.

"Why are you here?" Tamara asked again. The room was dark but for the fireplace burning. Her mother must have lit it to warm her chilled skin. Tamara looked down at her arms and saw bumps on them—mosquito bites. Had she lain there on the dock all night long? But it was still night.

"I'm your mother. Why wouldn't I be here?"

"Why are you *here*?" Tamara asked again and heard the knife's edge in her voice, serrated and gleaming.

"I thought you should know the truth."

"A little late for that, Momma."

Tamara turned her head. Her mother looked tired, but almost pretty again. She wore very little makeup and had her dyed blond hair caught in a low bun at the nape of her neck. She was in a black short-sleeved sweater and slacks. A good look for her. Classy almost.

"I'm sorry about the letter," her mother said at last. "You and Levi disappeared and I didn't know how or where to find you. I had to wait until you came back."

"We wondered why you gave up the suit."

"It seemed the only way to get you two to come back from wherever you'd run off to. I left a dozen messages with Daniel's secretary. None of them got through?"

"Levi brought me a letter. I threw it in the ocean. He told the judge's secretary not to send anything from you to us. You can't blame him. You sent the cops to kill him."

Her mother raised her hand in protest. "I did no such thing. I told them to bring you home. That's all I told them."

"They would have killed him if I hadn't stopped them."

"I'm sorry." Her mother's voice sounded hollow as a reed, but Tamara believed she was sorry. So was Tamara. "I didn't tell them to do that. I got your note, and I didn't know what else to do. Your grandfather—"

"You mean my father?"

"George," her mother said definitively. "George was supposed to tell you the night of the flood. He was supposed to tell you who he was and who Levi was so you'd know why you two couldn't be together. I guess he didn't get around to telling you, did he?" Her mother looked at her finally.

"No," Tamara said. "He did not." She sighed and stared back at the ceiling, waiting, her hand resting lightly on her stomach, wanting to be close to what little bit of Levi she had inside her.

"I was in love with Eric," her mother began speaking again. "So in love. But he treated me like a baby sister. I threw myself at him and he threw me off. I was only seventeen, so I thought I could make him love me. I went after Nash then, hoping to make Eric jealous. Nash and I got along real well, but he treated me like a sister, too, although for different reasons. When I tried to be with him, he pushed me away just like Eric had. Eric liked older women, wild women. Not dumb little girls. I didn't want to be a dumb girl anymore. I was here at the house one day, nosing around for Eric or Nash. Neither of them were home. But George was. I poured my heart out to him and he poured his heart out to me. He wanted a divorce from his wife. Doctors told her she couldn't have more kids after Nash, but George wanted more than two sons. Especially once he figured out Nash had no interest in getting married, no interest in women at all. But your grandmother was old-fashioned. She wouldn't give him a divorce for anything. Not for love or money. I found out later my sweet mother-in-law wasn't so old-fashioned, after all. What she was was very, very angry with George. That's why she wouldn't divorce him. She was punishing him."

"Because of Levi?"

Her mother nodded. "I didn't know about that then. I just knew I was lonely. George said if he were a younger man and single, he'd marry me himself. I said if he were single, I would marry him, and I didn't care he was older. So he took me to bed that day and a hundred times after. When I found out I was pregnant, I hoped he'd get divorced and marry me. He didn't. He had a different idea. He tried to force Eric to marry me, but Eric wouldn't do it. Eric would rather join the army and get himself killed than bow to his father and marry some dumb girl like me. And Nash...you know about him now. But George talked him into it. I lied to Nash and said the baby was Daniel Headley's. I thought if he knew it was his own father's, he wouldn't have anything to do with me or the baby. But he knew. He knew all along."

"Daddy loved me," Tamara said.

"Of course he did," her mother said. "You were his half sister."

Tears leaked out of Tamara's eyes. She wanted to be sick. She *was* sick. But she kept it inside, swallowing her bile.

"Go on," Tamara said, hoarse with anguish.

"Nash and I got married. I don't know why he finally caved to his father, but he did. Maybe he knew he had to get married anyway, or people would start to wonder about him even more than they already did. Six months later you were born. A girl. George was disappointed, but it wasn't the end of the world. Eric was still alive in Vietnam. Nash was alive. Then Eric was killed. So George demanded Nash do his duty as a husband and give him a grandson. Nash only laughed at him. So George took it on himself to do the job for him."

"Daddy caught you two together, didn't he? That's what Levi heard. That's why Daddy killed himself. If you hadn't slept with Granddaddy, Daddy might still be alive."

Daddy would be alive and Tamara would have been with him down on Bride Island. She would have slept in that pink room on her strawberry sheets and been happy. She would never have even met Levi. If her mother hadn't killed Daddy.

"Slept with him?" her mother said, then laughed a sad terrible little laugh. "That sounds almost romantic. I had a child to raise. I wanted nothing to do with him anymore. Not after he lied to me, got me pregnant, sold me off to marry one of his sons, sold me off like cattle. But George knew about Levi by then. And you know what he said to me? He said to me all the time, 'Behave yourself, Virginia, or I will leave everything to Levi and you will have nothing. You will be out on the streets, and Levi will be swimming in gold.'"

"What did you do?"

Her mother paused and Tamara knew then what had happened. The same thing that happened to her the night the river saved her. But the river hadn't saved her mother.

"I behaved myself."

Those were the three ugliest words Tamara had ever heard in her life.

"George hired Levi to work right here at this house. Hired him to rub him in my face, to keep me quiet, to keep me behaving. Nash was dead. So was Eric. I didn't know why he still wanted me around. He had other women on the side. Not just me. I don't know what he thought I was good for. Your grandmother tried to kill herself after Nash died and all she succeeded in doing was making herself a vegetable."

"Grandma tried to kill herself? Y'all said it was a stroke."

"She took every pill in the house, baby. Gave her brain damage. I think she lived as long as she did to spite George. I don't blame her for that."

"Why did you never tell me this?"

"When your daddy…" Her mother paused, corrected herself. "Nash wrote me a letter right before he died and told me not to tell you he wasn't your father. He loved you like his own, and he didn't want anyone taking that away from you. And truth is, I was ashamed of it all, ashamed to tell you the truth. But when I caught you and Levi kissing in the barn, I knew it was time to tell you. George was going to tell you. If you hadn't killed him, maybe he would have."

"So you knew I killed him?" Tamara asked. "You knew all along? But—" Her mother had blamed her for George Maddox's death but had never outright accused her of murder. If she'd known, why hadn't she told the police?

"He's left-handed. When he put a red ribbon on his hand, he put it on his right hand because that's the only way he could get it on. When they found him, it was on his left hand. Of course I knew you'd killed him. Who else could have?"

"You knew and you didn't ask me why?"

"I was protecting you. You could have gone to jail for murder, Tamara."

"Why did you think I killed him? Go on, tell me."

"I don't know. I imagined you'd fought with him over Levi. It didn't matter. I just knew you did it and weren't sorry about it."

"You want to know what happened? You want to know why I wasn't sorry? You said I had to pick between my horse and Levi's job. You'd kill my horse or you'd fire Levi. I went crying to Granddaddy and he was so sweet to me. He sent me to take a long hot bath. Then he came to my bedroom with some Red Thread bourbon. He had me drink some. And while I drank, he told me his big sob story about how much he wanted a son and how the world had taken away all his babies. Then he said he had an idea how we could help each other make everything okay again. Wanna know what that idea was, Momma?"

"No. Tamara, no—"

"He kissed me, Momma. He kissed me hard and dragged me to the bed—"

"No." Her mother shook her head.

"And he unzipped his pants."

"No!"

"And then the floodwater came into my bedroom and it was like God had heard me screaming. Granddaddy saw it, and when he took his mind off me for a second, I hit him over the head with a lamp. When that didn't knock him out, I hit him over the head with a candlestick. And when that didn't kill him, I pushed his head under the water and drowned him. Because I knew if he lived, he would finish what he started, and he would make me give him a son. That's why I killed him. Not because he was going to fire Levi. Not to save my horse from the glue factory. Not because I wanted to inherit all his dirty money. Not because he told me about you and him. And when I was under him fighting for myself, I knew you had sold me to him. You'd set me up so I'd give in to him and do anything he wanted so we could stay in this house and keep his money. He said you told him to take me down a peg or two. You're gonna tell me you didn't do all that?"

Her mother sighed, heavy and sad. She wiped a tear off her face, nodded.

"I told him that," her mother whispered, her voice hoarse, her eyes closed. "I told him to tell you about Levi. He'd been threatening to leave Red Thread and everything to Levi because he's the last Maddox boy. I thought if you were scared we'd lose everything to Levi, you'd stay away from him. George was only supposed to scare you into behaving yourself."

"He scared me. But I didn't behave myself," Tamara said.

"You really thought I'd sell your body?"

"Hard not to believe it of a woman who'd just threatened to shoot my own horse. You really thought he wouldn't do what he did to me after what he did to you?"

"After?" her mother said, incredulous. "There was no after, Tamara. Of course I didn't think he'd go after you. He was still coming after me."

"Momma... I didn't know."

"That makes two of us, I guess. I would shoot every man, woman and animal on earth to save my daughter from what I went through... Instead, I handed you over to it."

Tamara twined her finger in her hair, a red coil. Her mother took another coil of her hair and caressed it between her finger and thumb.

"You and I have the same color hair," her mother said. "Under this dye. But I've been dyeing it so long you don't even remember I'm a redhead, too. Or maybe I'm not—it might be gray under here. I don't even know what I look like it's been so long since I've seen myself."

"You really didn't sell me to Granddaddy?"

"No, baby." Her mother shook her head. "I would have

killed him myself had I known what he'd planned to do. I would have killed him with my bare hands."

"I did it for you," Tamara said.

"I should have thanked you."

Tamara leaned forward and into her mother's arms. All this time they could have been allies. One more sin on George Maddox's head. He not only took her father away from her, he took her mother, too.

"You hit me," Tamara said.

"I shouldn't have done that," her mother said, pulling back and holding Tamara by the shoulders. "I was so upset seeing you and Levi together. But, Tamara, I swear to God I never sold you out. I told George we were running out of time. I told him to talk to you. I told him to tell you the truth. I told him to beat sense into you if it came to that, but I never ever told him he could have you. If he didn't tell you the truth, you'd be carrying Levi Shelby's baby anytime now."

"I'm carrying it now."

Her mother bent over, her face in her hands.

"Momma?"

Abruptly her mother sat up.

"I'll take you to a doctor tomorrow. I know one."

"No," Tamara said.

"He's your brother. You can't have his baby."

"I'm having it." Tamara made the decision as she said the words.

"Surely he wouldn't want you to."

"He's gone," Tamara said. "He left me. It's not his decision."

"He's your brother," her mother said again. "You have the same blood. It's not natural for you to have his child. It's against everything. It's against God's will."

"If God wants the baby back, God can take it back. I don't

care if it's a sin. I want it." She did want it, this child. Vera had been forced to have a child she didn't want. Tamara would not lay down the cross Vera had had no choice but to carry.

"This sin is mine," her mother said. "This is on me. You can't blame yourself. Neither of you—not you or Levi—can blame yourself for this." She grabbed Tamara by her upper arms and looked her in the eyes. "Do you hear me? I did this. You had no idea who you were and he had no idea who you were. And I knew. I knew who you both were and I never told you because I didn't want you to hate me. And you loved your daddy so much. I couldn't take him away from you by telling you the truth. He didn't want me to tell you. I didn't want to, either. And now we're paying for how selfish we were. We're both paying."

Tamara slowly came to her feet. She put her hand on her mother's head, soft, like a benediction.

"It's not your fault," Tamara said.

Her mother looked up, her face stricken as a new widow's.

"Where are you going?"

"Home," Tamara said. She'd go back to Bride Island and back to their house. And she'd wait there until Levi could look at her again, and if he couldn't, it didn't matter. She would see him in their child's face every day.

"This is your home."

"This wasn't ever my home."

Tamara walked out of the room and into the gloom of the hallway and toward the front doors so grand and silent. And there was her suitcase sitting by the door, where she'd left it. Except she'd closed it up and now it sat open on the floor.

Kneeling, Tamara dug through her clothes, calmly at first and then frantically searching and searching for something she knew wasn't there anymore.

"Baby?"

"It's gone," Tamara said.

"What's gone?"

"My gun. Granddaddy's gun."

"Levi took it?"

Slowly Tamara nodded. So Granddaddy was right, after all. Perfection was for heaven, and when you tried to bring perfection to earth, you paid a heavy price. A perfect face withered with age. A perfect love died from neglect. Bourbon was a perfect spirit, which was why the angels took so much of it while it aged. She and Levi had been perfectly happy there for a while. No wonder the debt collector had come knocking on their door.

And this was the price Tamara had to pay. She would never see Levi in this life again.

She rose from the floor.

"I have to go," Tamara said, turning to her mother. She kissed her on the cheek. Her skin was smooth and cool and smelled of roses.

"Don't." Her mother grabbed her by the arms. "Don't leave me. I'm sick, Tamara. My doctors gave me less than a year. At least you can stay with me until I'm gone. I can see the baby. And you and I, we can make it better between us. We can find a way."

Tamara almost laughed at her. She did laugh at her. Did she laugh the way Nash laughed when her mother told him the baby was Daniel Headley's? Now her mother was dying? She appreciated the lie. She took it as a sign her mother loved her enough to try anything to get her to stay. But Tamara couldn't stay, not in this house. In this house she was a Maddox and her child would be a Maddox. She'd go back to Bride Island, where she'd been a Shelby and her child would be a Shelby.

"There is no way." Tamara shook her head. "Goodbye, Momma. You can live in the house."

"I'll die in this house."

"You wouldn't be the first."

32

Tamara drove to Red Thread in her baby blue Triumph. On her way to the warehouse, Tamara stopped at the grounds-keeper's shed, where all the tools were stored. A fire ax hung on the wall and she took it down. It was exactly what she needed.

She found a book of old matches in the shed, too. She shoved them down into her pocket and that was all she needed. Nothing else. Nothing more. Time to finish what she'd started.

When she arrived at the warehouse, she was glad to see the parking lot all empty and abandoned. They always shut Red Thread down in August. The heat was too much for anyone or anything but the bourbon.

With a shaking hand Tamara unlocked the warehouse door and stepped across the threshold. The scent of the bourbon hit her hard, cold bread baking, pungent, almost rotten and yet sweet. It made her head light and her eyes water. She shut the door behind her but didn't lock it. There was no way to lock it from the inside.

Tamara needed a plan of attack. She'd need a whole army to bust all the barrels in the warehouse. Everywhere she looked were row after row of giant fifty-three-gallon oak barrels resting on wooden ricks. The task seemed Herculean now that she faced it. The ax seemed woefully inadequate. She should have brought a machine gun.

Tamara took a deep breath. She could do this. She just had to be smart. The warehouse had seven floors that held all the very best Red Thread bourbon. The cheaper stuff was in the warehouse right next door, with a wooden breezeway connecting the two buildings. If this warehouse burned, the one next door would catch fire, too. Fire liked to climb and eat. If she gave it enough fuel on the first few floors, it should eat its way all the way to the top.

Tamara went up to the fourth floor and straight to the Red Thread Legacy Single-Barrel bourbons. These were the oldest bourbons, the ones hand-selected by Maddox men, who would come in once or twice a year and go on a tasting spree looking for the best of the batch. They signed their names on the barrels. Here was a row of George Maddox specials. Behind it was a row of Robert Maddox select bourbon. Her great-grandfather had been dead twenty years. One barrel sporting his signature would sell for as much as a car. Tamara picked her first barrel. It had George Maddox's signature scrawled on the lid. She cracked her knuckles for the fun of it, lifted her ax and slammed it into the wood. She took a good chunk out of the wood, but it required three or four more swings until the barrel cracked and the bourbon burst out of the oval slit she'd cut into it. A puddle of rust red formed on the floor.

Every barrel that bore her grandfather's name got the ax. Every barrel that bore her great-grandfather's name got the ax. The fumes from the hundred-and-fifty-proof bourbon scalded her eyes and went to her head. She wondered if she could get drunk just off smelling the stuff.

"Lizzie Borden took an ax…" she chanted while she chopped. "Gave her bourbon forty whacks. When she saw what she had done, she gave her father forty-one…"

She giggled at that. She thought it was a fine rhyme.

When she'd finished busting up all the barrels of Red Thread Legacy, she took a rest, leaning back against the wall to catch her breath. This was hard work, swinging an ax. Already she'd formed blisters on her hands. The acrid smell of undiluted bourbon filled the air and made her want to vomit again. Or was that morning sickness? Was it morning yet? She glanced out a window and found it was still full night without even the hint of morning on the horizon. Maybe she had night sickness instead. Was that a real thing? She didn't know anything about being pregnant. Levi would surely kill her when he found out she was chopping up barrels while carrying his child.

Except he wouldn't get mad at her because he wouldn't know. Because he took her gun and drove away. Since he wasn't there to tell her to stop, she didn't.

"Break over," she said to herself. She wiped off her face using the tail of her shirt. Sweat or tears? Both. She went down to the third floor and started swinging at the barrels by the stairs. Bourbon gushed out from the ragged gashes and poured down the stairs to the second floor.

The work was hard. She felt like she was damaging her body by doing it, breathing in all those fumes and fighting exhaustion to keep going. But she did keep going. For all the pain and the discomfort and the nausea, she took a terrible pleasure in what she did. She imagined George Maddox standing a few feet away from her, his wrists and ankles bound in

Veritas's shackles, another man holding him by an iron neck collar in place. Granddaddy would have to watch what Tamara did. He would have to stand there and do nothing while his own child, his own blood, busted open barrel after barrel of Kentucky's finest bourbon and let it pour out onto the cold dirty ground. And there was nothing he could do about it.

"You did this to yourself, Granddaddy," she said. "You have only yourself to blame. You raped my mother, and you tried to rape me, and you treated Levi like a servant when he was your own son. You fucked us all…" It made her smile to say "fuck" to him. She wasn't ever allowed to swear at home. Not a "fuck." Not a "shit." Not even a "damn" unless it was followed by the word *Yankees*.

"Fuck you," she said and took a swing. "Fuck your father. Fuck your grandfather. Fuck his father. Fuck you, Jacob Fucking Maddox. If y'all hadn't fucked so much, you wouldn't be so fucking fucked."

Tamara raised up the ax to hit another barrel and it slipped from her hands and landed on the floor behind her with a terrible clatter. She gasped and jumped back. It had almost hit her right in the back.

Panting and woozy, she looked at her hands. Her palms streamed with blood. She'd worn off whatever was left of her blisters and the skin on her hands. She stuck them under one of the barrels still leaking fluid and screamed at the sting as the alcohol cleansed her open wounds.

She wept from the sheer agony of it. Not since that night with her grandfather had she known such extreme physical suffering. How could she keep going like this? But how could she stop? She wasn't close to being finished. She'd probably broken open only a hundred barrels if that. A hundred of the maybe forty thousand in the entire warehouse? Not enough.

Not nearly enough. She staggered back and turned to the window. She pressed her sweaty brow against the glass. A hundred yards away, no more than that, she saw the river. To it she whispered a prayer, a petition… *You carried Veritas away. Help me bring her back.*

The river made no reply. It flowed on, silent, lovely and dark.

Tamara lifted her head and made her appeal then to the angels gathered around.

Please?

No answer.

She lowered her head and rested it on a broken barrel. Her shoulders slumped and she could hardly stand. She pushed a hand against her stomach for comfort. Alone as she felt, she wasn't alone.

Tamara tried standing up straight, but she was hit with another wave of nausea. She staggered backward and rested against the wall. She sank down to the floor and lay there. All she needed was a little rest. That was all.

"Tamara?"

Was it God calling her name?

"Tamara?"

Was it Daddy coming to get her and take her to Bride Island?

"Tamara?"

A hand touched her shoulder. Tamara's eyes flew open.

"Levi?"

33

Instinctively Tamara tried crawling away from him. She reached for the ax, but it was too far away. Levi was dead. Who was this man who'd come for her?

"Tamara, calm down, it's me. It's me. It's just me."

"Levi…" she breathed. A slow smile spread across her face. She closed her eyes.

"Yeah, it's me. Who else?"

She forced her eyes opened again. Levi knelt on the floor in front of her.

"You were gone. And you…you took the gun." She gulped the words, trying to swallow them. In her panic and confusion she was breathing in reverse. "I thought you were dead."

"I was driving to the island."

"Why?"

"Bowen. He knew."

"You were going to kill him?"

"No. But I was going to kill someone. But I stopped. I couldn't keep going. I told you I couldn't do it. I couldn't be the man who got you pregnant and left you to face your mother alone. I came back. I had to come back."

"I was afraid you were already dead."

"I didn't think you'd want to ever see me again."

"Yes," she said. "I always want to see you…"

That was the first time it occurred to her that she didn't care what the truth was about him and her and them. She was his wife first before she was his sister. Only a half sister at that. Surely a full wife trumped half a sister. Did one have to be greater than the other?

All those nights together—mornings, too, and afternoons—they had sought each other's bodies. Whenever they could, whenever they wanted, Levi found her breasts and her fingers hunted down his buttons. Once a day wasn't enough any more than eating once a day was enough. They didn't even try. Three times a day, sometimes four, they joined themselves together. Levi didn't ask permission nor did she deny him anything. It was a given. Both of them were a given. When she reached for him, he took her. When he reached for her, she gave to him. The hours apart were a severed time. In the dark one night as he moved lazily inside her, in no hurry to finish and separate themselves again, Levi had told her a theory of Plato's taken from the *Symposium*, of how once all humans had four legs and four arms and two faces. These creatures were powerful enough with so many eyes and so many limbs that even Zeus feared their might. He sliced them in two, Zeus did, sundered them in half. And forever since that time each half goes forth in misery seeking its other half. When Levi was inside her, she believed this fairy tale. Four legs. Four arms. Two faces. One body. Half meeting half. Half making whole. Her half brother. Her half husband. Her half. Their whole. Levi had quoted to her, "Love is simply the name of the desire

and the pursuit of the whole." They'd laughed at the joke as
he slid his fingers inside her. Love, though they did love each
other, had as little to do with it as it had to do with dinner.
She had to eat to live. She had to be with Levi. Same reason.

"I can't stay away from you," Levi said. "I tried and lasted
one day."

"What will happen to us?" she asked. "What will we do?"

Us. We. Those were the words she understood.

"Did you know in the days of the pharaohs the royal family
would often marry brothers and sisters or fathers and daughters? Did you know that?"

"No. They never taught us anything good like that in
school."

"The pharaohs were like gods," Levi said. "They were
worshipped. The blood of the gods couldn't mingle with the
blood of the commoners. Gods aren't easy to come by. They
had to marry their own so they could stay gods."

"We aren't gods. We're just people."

"So were they. But they were gods, too. We can be, if you
want," Levi said. "At least to ourselves. What is a god but
someone who is worshipped? I'll worship you and you'll worship me and we'll be gods together."

"Will you forgive my sins?" she asked.

"There are no sins," Levi said. "Gods don't sin. They act.
What they do is right not because it's right, but because they
did it."

"What do gods do?" she asked. "I've never been a god
before."

"Anything they want."

Tamara felt Levi's hand on her face.

"They smite people," he said. "They part seas and send

down lightning and thunder. They impart justice and mercy and vengeance…"

Tamara opened her eyes. She saw the bourbon on the floor like blood leaking from a corpse.

"Maybe I am a god." She looked at Levi.

"What are you doing?" he asked. "What is this about?"

"It's about our father," she said. "He thought he was a god, too. But he wasn't. He was a devil."

Levi was smart. She did love that about him. That she could say one thing and he could, with one step, transverse a dozen deductions and get straight to the end where the truth lived.

"What did he do to you?" Levi asked, narrowing his eyes at her.

"The night of the flood… Momma didn't beat me. That was a lie. She slapped me, but she didn't beat me. But the bruises I told you about were true. Granddaddy gave them to me."

"He beat you?"

"No," she said and shook her head. "He wanted a son, a real Maddox son."

"Tamara—"

"He wanted one with me. He wanted a son he could pass off as legitimate. A Maddox son. My son. His son."

"A white son."

"Royal blood," she said. "Gods and mortals don't mix."

Levi rubbed his face. His blue eyes were rimmed in red. "Fuck…"

"He dragged me to the bed. My bed. My stupid pink bed. But before he could do it, the river came in the room to save me. The house was flooding. I had a second, and I took it." Levi lifted his head and she looked him in the eyes. "I killed him."

Levi said nothing. Tamara smiled.

"I smote him," she said and giggled drunkenly.

Can gods kill other gods?

"I was so sure Momma had sold me to him like Jacob Maddox's wife had sold Veritas down the river that I stopped talking to her. And she thought I'd killed Granddaddy because we'd fought over you and my inheritance. He'd been threatening to leave everything to you unless she and I did what he wanted. She fired you because she knew you were his son and she'd seen us kissing. She wanted to keep us apart. But I don't blame her for hating you or me or anybody. Granddaddy made her earn her keep, too."

"You never told me this," Levi said. "Why?"

"Because I was afraid you wouldn't believe me. And if you didn't believe me, I couldn't love you, and I wanted to love you. I needed to love you."

Levi looked up to the ceiling. She wondered if he was praying. Did gods pray to other gods?

"They sold a girl to start Red Thread. Raped her and sold her and bought a still. You can't sell people," Tamara said.

"No. No, you can't."

"This distillery was everything to him," Tamara said. "Red Thread was everything. If he ever had a soul, he sold it for this place. He knew I was his daughter. He knew it all the time. That didn't matter. Only this mattered…" She pointed at the barrels, the thousands of barrels that might as well have been filled with liquid gold. "He tried to take you away from me. All that I had. So I'm taking all he had away from him. I took his life first. And now I'm taking his soul."

It took all she had left to get up off the floor. Her hand left a bloodred print on the wall behind her as she fought her way to her feet. A wave of dizziness hit her as she bent to pick up the ax.

"Sit down, Tamara," Levi ordered. He did that sometimes, gave her orders. And she loved it. He was her teacher and her lord. It pleased her to obey him, but only after she put up her fight so he would have to fight back and subdue her.

"I can't. I have to finish this."

"Rotten, sit your ass down on the floor right now."

Her body obeyed even as her spirit rebelled. Gently he took the ax from her hands.

Levi walked a few feet, dragging the ax behind him. He stopped. He turned.

Then he slammed the ax into the nearest barrel so hard the staves exploded.

Then Levi smashed the next barrel open like he'd been born for the job. And maybe he had. Just the way she'd been born to bring down Red Thread for Veritas. Finally. At last.

Down the line he walked, smashing barrels as he went. One. Two. Twelve. Bourbon was everywhere, all over the floor. A flood of it sweet and ripe with scents of sugar and apples and licorice, spiked and potent enough to make throats burn and eyes water. Thousands of dollars of bourbon. Hundreds of thousands of dollars of bourbon. Five-year aged bourbon. Ten-year aged bourbon. Twenty-year aged bourbon. The stuff that sold for a hundred pounds a bottle to English dukes.

It was an orgy of bourbon and destruction. Alcohol erupted from the holes in the casks, broke like ocean waves onto the ground. Wood shattered. Barrels ruptured. And Tamara sat on the floor and laughed and laughed.

Finally Levi came for her and carried her down the stairs to the main floor. There he did the most damage and it delighted her to see it. Sweat soaked his T-shirt and she could see the muscles rising and straining underneath the wet fabric. Did gods sweat? She could believe it. It made him look more powerful. He was strength and beauty incarnate, and she desired him. Her lover, her brother, her husband, her god. When this was all over, they would go somewhere and take a long hot bath together. He would make love to her after they were clean or maybe before. He always made love to her. They would talk about the baby, what to name it if it was a boy or a girl. They were gods now and gods must make other gods. They wouldn't have a family. They would have a pantheon.

Tonight Levi became a god of destruction. There must be a god for that, mustn't there? Destruction and vengeance and justice. And yet it was a mercy that he did this for her. She couldn't finish what she'd started. Only he could finish it for her. He worked in a fury. Hate had walled them both up in this prison. Levi would cut their way out.

Even when Levi was out of her sight, she could hear the ax at work. Metal splitting wood. Cracking. Levi's grunts of effort. He'd spent half the summer in the cooperage learning how to make the barrels. Who else was better suited to break them? Levi had made himself into a machine, lean and sleek and molded for this purpose. He brought the ax high in the air and let the weight of it crash into the barrels. They didn't stand a chance against him. A pool of a thousand drunken nights that would never happen surrounded her. Fights would go unfought. Angry words unsaid. Confessions would remain unconfessed with a little less liquid courage in the world. Children would not be conceived who otherwise might have been. They lay on the floor at Tamara's feet—the fights, the confessions, the children—all of them. They flowed past her like a river, trickled through the cracks between the floorboards and disappeared.

When the barrels had been broken, enough of them anyway to do the job, Levi came back to her. The ax was in one hand. With his other hand he reached for her.

"Come on," he said, waving his hand at her, beckoning her to take it.

"Why did you come back to me?" she asked him.

Levi shrugged. "I didn't know who I was before you. I don't know who I would be after." Levi had a beautiful voice, resonant as an oboe. Was this the first time she noticed that? "But while I was with you, I knew myself."

"We'll stay together?" she asked.

"We will."

"Can we bear that?"

"Can we bear being apart?"

No. No, they couldn't. Who could they love after loving each other? Who could they touch if not each other? They had ruined each other for anyone else. The curse was on them and in them and they must stay together lest they spread the curse to others.

"Will we have to go away and hide?" she asked.

"We can go anywhere we want to go."

"I want to go home."

"Then we go home."

"How did you find me here?"

"I went to Arden to look for you. Your mother told me you'd left, that you thought I'd died. I was on my way out of here when I saw your car in the parking lot. Your mother said to me... She said she was sorry. I think she is."

"She is. So am I."

"We should leave," Levi said. "This smell is something awful."

"It'll get worse," she said.

"Then let's get it over with."

She took his hand this time and let him hoist her to her feet. With his arm around her he brought her out of the warehouse. The door was open now and bourbon leaked all the way out to the sidewalk.

"What did you say this was?" Levi asked. "One hundred fifty proof?"

"About that. Maybe more."

Tamara pulled the book of matches out of her pocket.

"I wish he was still alive," Levi said. "Just so I could rip out his heart."

"This was his heart," she said.

Her hands shook so hard she couldn't light the match. Levi took the book from her and lit it for her. Then he put the match back between her fingers. He nodded. It was time.

Tamara flicked the match into the warehouse door.

Do gods start fires?

The gods invented fire.

34

Tamara dropped the match into the bourbon, and in less time than it takes to blink, Red Thread had ignited.

Flames skimmed the surface of the alcohol, racing and chasing their way into the warehouse. Levi kicked the door shut and locked it as fast as he could. He grabbed her hand and ran with her fifty yards into the trees that ringed the property. At first not much seemed to be happening. But only at first...

Then smoke sneaked out from under and over and around the door. The windows clouded up white and turned red.

They heard a crack, a clamor. Things falling. In minutes the fire had made it to the top floor and burned its way through the roof.

She heard sounds like bombs going off. The barrels were detonating. Around them the night air turned warm. Then it turned hot.

Levi coughed and so did she. Her eyes burned, her lungs. They pulled back farther away from the warehouse. Tamara wanted to be sick but couldn't. She had nothing in her to vomit up.

From within the warehouse came new sounds. Crashing. Breaking. Beams catching fire and falling. Floors giving out. A beautiful sound and a terrible smell. They had to pull back even more. The scent of bourbon was everywhere, stinging their eyes, singeing their nostrils. They covered their mouths and their noses with their shirts.

"Let's go," Levi yelled over the sound of the fire and the wind.

"Not yet," she called back. She had to see one more thing. She waited. It wouldn't take long surely. She waited longer. And yes, there it was. The fire caught the wooden breezeway between the first and second warehouse. It would all go down now. The entire operation. The offices. The bottling plant. The still. From the parking lot to the river, all of it would burn.

Tamara giggled at the sight of what she'd done. Would they even suspect her? A little thing like her? And what would it matter? She owned the warehouse, the company. She could burn it to the ground if she wanted. She could do whatever she wanted. Her laughter grew hysterical. But it wasn't laughter anymore. She was crying. Her stomach hurt. She hadn't eaten in too long. She was dehydrated. She'd overtaxed herself in the warehouse. She'd inhaled too many fumes and they'd gone to her head and made her sick. This time she'd say it. She was sick. Her mother would be proud of her for admitting it.

A cramp struck her like a fist in her lower back, nearly felling her. She clung to Levi. Sweat beaded on her forehead. She was hot, so hot, burning hot, scalding hot.

"Tamara?" Levi looked her up and down.

"Can you put me in the river?" She had to cool down and the river was right there. Right there... She would boil to death if he didn't put her in the water. She thought that was what she said, but she couldn't make out her own words.

"Jesus, Tamara, you're bleeding." Levi's hands were all over, holding her up, searching her face.

The heat was between her legs now. A line of red coming out of her and staining her legs. Levi's eyes were black with panic and fear. That wasn't good. How much was she bleeding?

Did gods bleed?

She was off her feet and in his arms. They were running away, the fire far behind them. She could see the smoke rising into the sky, creating night clouds that blocked out the stars. She'd done that, hidden the sky away. Only a god could do that.

Drink up, she called to her angels. And the angels came and drank. But they were greedy beasts and came after her, too. Their wings closed in around her. They always said the Maddoxes had bourbon in their blood.

That night the angels drank their fill.

35

Paris

Before tonight, the only thing in the world more important
to Cooper McQueen than a good bourbon was a beautiful
woman. He had the woman. He had the bourbon. What he
wanted more than anything now was the truth.

"So what happened?" McQueen asked, meeting Paris's eyes
for the first time in an hour.

"The newspapers described it as a 'river of fire,'" Paris
said. She sat like a lady, like a duchess. Back straight, ankles
crossed, hands in her lap. She turned her head and looked
into the empty fireplace. "Flaming whiskey poured out like
lava. There's nothing quite like a whiskey fire. It doesn't just
burn. It consumes everything. And the smell..." She paused
and laughed. "Well, they say the firemen couldn't get near the
warehouse for the sweet sickening scent of it. All they could
do was form a perimeter around it to contain the fire. Even
six hundred feet away they could feel the heat of it. A hundred

and fifty firemen from four or five counties couldn't handle the immolation. They say even their helmets melted from the heat. The warehouse collapsed and the burning rubble ignited the next building over. And the next. Domino effect. The operation was old. The buildings were mostly wood. Tamara's grandfather's obsession with tradition doomed his legacy. They should have torn down those old wooden buildings decades earlier and replaced them with brick and steel. Nothing doing. On the entire property there was only one fire hydrant. There was nothing anyone could do. They let it burn itself out. By morning there was nothing left."

McQueen cleared his throat. Something in it didn't want to let him speak.

"And Tamara?" he asked. "What about her?"

"Why do you ask?"

"Because I want to know what happened to her."

"Do you really?" Paris asked. She seemed suspicious and amused, as if she didn't believe he had it in him to care about the girl who'd brought down Red Thread. "No one was charged with arson, if you were wondering. Any evidence of arson—which it had been, of course—the fire destroyed it all. Can't take fingerprints off a pile of ash. To this day people talk about the fire and what might have started it. Some people thought it was Tamara's mother doing it out of revenge against her daughter for stealing the company from her. Or a disgruntled employee. Or lightning. That does happen. Lightning from the heavens. Bolt from the blue. You know what they finally classified the fire as?"

"What?"

"An act of God."

"You won't tell me about Tamara?"

"I've told you enough about Tamara. You don't get any more of her."

A sort of fury overcame McQueen. For hours he'd been taunted and teased by this woman. She'd shown up in his bar and had offered him a golden box and had dangled the key in front of him all night long. Even now the key was in the lock. Why wouldn't she turn it?

But his anger was displaced and he knew it. Paris was in front of him. It was easy to take his anger out on her. He sympathized with Levi's fury that George Maddox was already dead and buried. McQueen would have enjoyed ripping that heart out, too.

"Levi was her brother," McQueen finally said.

"He was her husband first, like she said."

"He was her brother first."

"If I told you right now my name was Karen or Susan, how would you think of me a month from now? A year?"

"As Paris."

"*She* saw him as her husband first. So he was her husband. It's like goslings imprinting on the first thing they see. She saw her husband. He was her husband. Those threads were tangled long before her birth. We won't untangle them tonight."

"My daughter is seventeen," McQueen said after a long pause.

"Where is she?"

"Her mother's. Emma and I went on a trip to LA over the summer to visit a college she wanted to see. She took a big stuffed dog with her on the plane to use as a pillow. She's still a little girl. I'm trying to imagine her getting married. She'd be back home again in a week."

"Do you love your daughter?"

"What kind of question is that?" he asked. "Of course I love my daughter."

"I wonder if someone will tell someone else her story someday."

"I hope it's a happier story than that one," McQueen said. A tight knot had formed in his stomach. He'd been drinking all night, but he was terribly sober and wished he wasn't.

"Oh, but it is a happy story. I know that's hard to believe. When justice is done, the people rejoice. When mercy has fallen, the angels rejoice."

"Please… I'm begging you," McQueen said, leaning forward and holding his hands open in supplication. "Tell me what happened to Tamara. Did she die?"

"We all die. Side effect of being born."

McQueen let out an exasperated, "Fuck," and stood up. He walked to the window and pulled the mirror away. He felt imprisoned in this room and the truth stood guard all around him. He stared out at the green lawn, neat as a chessboard. That wasn't right, was it? If somebody had enough money to turn a wild wood into a chessboard, maybe they had too much money.

"You're torturing me on purpose," he said.

"Whoever tortured anyone by accident?"

"Are you trying to make me angry with you?"

"You caught me stealing a bottle of bourbon worth nearly a million dollars at auction and this is what makes you angry? That I won't tell you more of Tamara's story?"

"I listened to every word you said tonight. There were so many chances to end it before it started. If Nash hadn't killed himself… If Virginia had told Tamara the truth instead of leaving it to George Maddox to tell her… If George had acknowledged his son… If Tamara had told her mother what her grandfather did to her instead of keeping it a secret... There were so many times someone could have done something or said something and then..."

"And then what? You think someone could have saved Tamara from Levi? Or saved Levi from Tamara? Or saved them both from George Maddox?" Paris shook her head like she was chiding a small child she'd caught with his hand in the cookie jar. "I told you. Fate was what brought them together. Fate was what brought about the end of Red Thread. And fate is just another name for a train that cannot stop until it reaches its final destination."

McQueen watched one green leaf catch an updraft. It fell up instead of down. When he slept again, later today or tomorrow night, he would dream of Tamara, and in his dream he would see her in a white dress running toward railroad tracks, and a train—red and black and made of unforgiving steel—charging toward her, and if she kept running, she would be hit. And in his dream he would run from nowhere and catch her in his arms at the last second before she ran onto the tracks. She'd giggle and laugh and wriggle like little girls do when you pick them up when they don't want to be. *We were just playing a game, Daddy*, she would say, and he would have to chide her without scaring her because he didn't want her doing it again, but he also didn't want her to know how close she'd come to being hit. *But that's not a good game. Don't play that game. You'll get hurt, baby...*

She was a baby, Tamara Maddox. Only gods and little children think they're the center of the universe. Only gods and little children are right about that.

"There's no way..." McQueen stopped, his throat inexplicably tight. "There's no way to go through that and survive it and be okay after. Is there?"

"Why do you say that?" Paris asked, her voice a doctor's voice now, searching for a diagnosis.

"Because I wouldn't be able to deal, finding that out about the person I married. I couldn't bear it. I couldn't."

"But you aren't Tamara Maddox," she said. "You aren't Tamara Shelby."

"No. I'm not."

McQueen sat on the coffee table in front of Paris. He reached for her hands and she let him take them in his. He caressed her fingers, her palms, traced the long, curving lifeline down the base of her index finger to her wrist. The ring finger on her left hand retained the slightest indention from a wedding band taken off only recently.

"You loved your husband?"

Paris answered in a whisper. "I did, yes."

He stroked her pulse point, the lightly throbbing veins.

"Paris…that was what Veritas named her child."

"She did."

"And you're descended from her. That's who you are, isn't it? That's why you say you're a Maddox?"

"I am a Maddox. Veritas was my grandmother's grandmother. And that makes Jacob Maddox my grandmother's grandfather."

"You drink bourbon." He grinned at her, clutching her smaller left hand in both of his.

"It's in my blood. Of course I do. And let's be honest, it is some good shit, Cooper McQueen."

McQueen laughed and so did she.

He lifted her wrist to his lips and kissed it.

Over the top of her hand at his mouth, he said to her, "Make me an offer."

"I'll tell you what happened to Tamara."

He raised his eyebrow.

"You drive a hard bargain," he said.

"Make me an offer," she said.

"You tell me what happened to Tamara, and you come back to bed with me and stay there until morning."

"It's almost morning now."

"An hour will suffice."

"I like that you care about Tamara," Paris said. "It does you credit."

"I'm trying to buy your body with a bottle of bourbon."

"I would have thrown it in, anyway. Call it gift wrapping."

"We have a deal?"

Paris turned her hand in his and they shook on it.

"Deal," she said.

"Tamara?"

"After."

"You are torturing me."

"Consider it payback for history."

He was white. She was black. And she was right. He had no answer to that but to place his hands on her neck, pull her to him and kiss her mouth. Apples and licorice.

McQueen had said "until morning" and "until morning" he lasted. When it was over and the sun returned, he watched Paris rise from the bed. She zipped her dress up by herself and he wondered if every woman he'd ever assisted with that task could have done it themselves, too? One less reason for men to be in the world if women could zip their dresses up all alone.

"You want your ribbon?" He dangled the scarlet bit of silk from his fingers.

"You can keep it," she said.

"I don't keep trophies from the women I sleep with."

She reached for the ribbon and he pulled it back.

"You're worth making an exception for," he said. "And I get the feeling I won't be seeing you again. Will I?"

"Would you want to even if you could?"

"Are you going to steal any of my other bourbon bottles?"

"I might. You have an excellent collection."

"Come back and drink it with me. It will be nice to share them with a connoisseur."

"I might see you again. Maybe. Maybe not. We'll let the Fates decide. Until then…" She slipped her feet into her high heels and gave him a lady's curtsy. She held out her hand to him and he kissed the back of it.

"You have given me a strange and memorable night," he said.

"You have given me exactly what I came for. And came for. And came for…"

"You can come again anytime."

He followed her down the stairs to the living room and extended his hand to her, giving her the bottle.

"All yours," he said. "Virginia Maddox didn't own the bottle. She couldn't legally sell it. I couldn't legally buy it."

"You're out a million dollars."

"A night with you—best million I ever spent."

"Only a million for a night with me. You got a bargain." And then, without a hint of reverence for the last known bottle of Red Thread in existence, she plucked it out of his hand and dropped it down into her purse.

"What are you going to do with it?" he asked. "Drink it? Save it? Pass it on to your children someday?"

"None of the above."

"Then what?" he asked.

"The answer to that question wasn't part of our deal."

"No, you're right. It wasn't. But Tamara…she was part of the deal."

Paris nodded. "Yes, she was."

"So what happened to her?"

"Funny you ask about her and not Levi."

"You can tell me about him, too, if you want."

"No, he's another story."

"Tamara was just a girl, a girl my daughter's age."

"A girl who killed a man, eloped with her brother and brought down a bourbon dynasty."

"I didn't say she wasn't an impressive girl."

Paris grinned. "That she was." She looked past him and away. What she saw he didn't know, but he would have given anything to see through her eyes.

"Tamara died in her husband's arms," she said.

McQueen's head dropped back. He swore.

"She died in his arms twenty-three years after the night Red Thread burned."

McQueen's head snapped up again.

"What?"

"Tamara didn't die that night. But she did miscarry. It might have happened, anyway. Women lose pregnancies all the time. But after all she went through…you don't have to blame the angels for that. You can blame the shock and taking an ax to a hundred barrels of bourbon, inhaling that poisoned air."

Relief so potent it could have been a hundred and fifty proof hit him in the gut. He hadn't given a damn about the pregnancy, only the girl.

"But she lived. She survived all that?"

"She did. Barely. She bled a lot and had to go to the hospital. And she had to stay at a different hospital for a long time."

"A different hospital? She was committed?"

"Rich women don't go to mental hospitals. Rich women go on vacation."

"But she wasn't pregnant anymore. I assume she and Levi got divorced and she remarried eventually?"

"Why would you think that?"

"Because you said she died in her husband's arms."

"She did. In Levi's arms."

"Why? There was no reason to." He covered his mouth with his hand and breathed. "She was free."

"She didn't want to be free. What was she going to do? Put a personal ad in the newspaper? Find a nice man at church? She'd killed her father and married her brother and burned her family's legacy to the ground. How do you go on after that? You sure as hell don't go on alone. They were like two sailors too drunk to stand up on their own, but if they leaned on each other, they could make it."

"But what about her mother?"

"Virginia Maddox hadn't been lying. She had ovarian cancer and was dying of it, which was how you ended up with your bottle and its perfect provenance. Tamara died of it, too. If it comforts you at all, and it should, Tamara had a good life with Levi, and although she died too young, she was happy until the end. As happy as any woman could be who had to carry what she carried."

"You know that for sure?"

"I do. And now if you don't mind, we'll be on our way." She patted her Birkin bag containing the bottle of Red Thread. The first bottle. The original bottle with Vera's little red ribbon falling to pieces on the neck. Knowing what he knew about it, McQueen would not be sad to see it go.

"Where to now? Off to steal a rare bottle of wine?"

She smiled tiredly. They had been up all night, after all.

He liked her tired. She looked human like this, approachable, vulnerable. He wished she'd stay another night. He wished he had more worth stealing.

"I have a little errand to run. And then I'm going home to sleep."

She started for the door. McQueen put himself between her and it.

"Ever had Fighting Cock?"

"You talking about the bourbon or some sex position I haven't tried yet?" Paris asked.

"The bourbon," he said, laughing. "I keep meaning to try it. Haven't worked up the courage yet. But you could give me the courage."

"Ever licked a spark plug and then taken a shot of whiskey?"

"Not that I recall."

"Same aftertaste," she said. "In other words, highly recommended."

"Come back," he said. "Come back here whenever you want. Tell me more stories. Steal all my bourbon."

"I'll think about it."

McQueen opened the door for her but shut it before she could leave.

"What aren't you telling me?" he asked. "There's more, right? More to the story?"

"There's always more to every story."

"What is it?"

"What do you think it is?"

"You," he said. "Who are you?"

"I already told you that."

"Not everything. Not even close."

"Not everything," she admitted.

"Then what?"

"Ask me who my husband was and I'll tell you."

"Who was your husband?"

Paris leaned forward, put a gloved hand on his chest. She kissed his cheek and he inhaled, wanting to capture her scent forever in his nose. Wildflowers plucked from a field. Not bred for beauty, but beautiful, anyway. Plucked from the earth, wild even in a vase.

"Thank you for a lovely night, Mr. McQueen." Then she opened the front door.

"You said you'd tell me who your husband was."

Paris skipped down the stairs, graceful as a gazelle even in those high heels.

"I said I'd tell you," she called back. "I didn't say I'd tell you now."

Then she was gone.

36

Paris got into her car and it was with some measure of relief that she watched the gates of Lockwood yawn open to allow her to leave. Dawn had come and she put on her sunglasses. She wanted to sleep and she would sleep as soon as she got home. She almost wished she'd slept at Cooper's. He wasn't a bad man, and if he'd heard a word she'd said tonight, maybe he could even be a good man someday. But the world was changing and the Cooper McQueens of the world soon would be nothing but relics, like suits of armor and iron maidens. She did like him, though, and he was handsome. And she'd been alone for too long. Maybe she would see him again. Then she would have to tell him another story.

Good thing she had one.

Paris would tell Cooper McQueen her story, the one that began when she was sixteen and received a letter in the mail. A black girl who went to Franklin County High School in Frankfort, Kentucky, and lived in a yellow shotgun house one hundred feet from the Kentucky River didn't get letters on fancy stationary. That was where she'd start the story, with the letter.

Dear Paris,
I hope this letter finds you well. The information I'm about to tell you might come as something of a surprise, but it seems we are related…

Paris had read the letter three times before she could absorb the news. A woman in South Carolina who owned a horse farm that bred and raised Hanoverians and Tennessee Walkers was telling her, Paris Christie, daughter of a single mother with two other children by another man, that she was related to the sort of woman who bred horses and owned islands? Hell, Paris wouldn't have believed she was related to the sort of woman who bred dachshunds.

In the letter the writer said she'd had her ancestry investigated (who did that?) as she'd been looking for the descendants of a woman who'd been enslaved on an ancestor's hemp farm (white ladies sure had a lot of free time it seemed). It turned out that Paris herself was the last living female descendant in the long line from then until now. Paris didn't know her father very well, but he sometimes sent cards, sometimes a little money. His mother was dead; she knew that because she'd asked her mother about her grandparents on her father's side and she hadn't gotten the answer she wanted.

The letter had been signed "Tamara Shelby."

When her mother married her longtime boyfriend, a man Paris had never gotten along with, Paris had made plans to leave home as soon as possible. The letter had come to her the day after she'd inquired at school about taking her GED so she could graduate early and get on with her life. Paris wrote back to the woman, Mrs. Tamara Shelby, and had asked for more information. Another letter followed containing the name Veritas and the name Jacob Maddox and the words *Red Thread*. Paris went straight to the public library, which was also a stone's throw from the river, which was not an exaggeration at all. She really could throw stones into the river from the library parking lot. She could have jumped in it and swam had she wanted to. Instead, she went inside and got books and newspapers and discovered the letter writer wasn't crazy. Red Thread had been a real company in town off what was now Fair Oaks Lane. A bourbon distillery known far and wide for its fine bourbon and the red ribbons on the necks of the pricey bottles, the fancy stuff. The man who started the company had once owned Paris's grandmother's grandmother. Apparently to Tamara Shelby, who had been born Tamara Maddox, that made Paris her relative.

Well, if she insisted.

When the invitation to come and visit was offered, Paris accepted without asking her mother's permission first. Her mother was a good woman and Paris was a good girl, but they were good in different ways and living under the same roof wore them both out. She let Paris go, and for the first time in her entire life, Paris left Kentucky.

It was love at first sight when Paris laid eyes on Tamara Maddox Shelby that June day when the car pulled up to the front of the house, a gleaming white farmhouse, newly constructed from the looks of it. Tamara Shelby stood on the porch, a woman in her midthirties at the height of her beauty. It was love at second sight when Paris saw Tamara's striking husband, whom she at first thought was Italian with his tanned olive skin and thick black wavy hair with enough gray to give him a distinguished air. But when he spoke, it was in English with a Kentucky accent so familiar he could have been her own cousin. Tamara, it turned out, was thirty-three, and Levi, her husband, forty-five. Paris had been a baby the year she and Levi married. Hard to believe a woman of only thirty-three had already been married for sixteen years.

As rich as they were, Paris expected them to be pretentious. Wine snobs. Horse snobs. Money snobs. But they weren't. They were both from Kentucky and they were kind to her, down-to-earth. She was treated like family by Levi and Tamara, doted upon. She was the child they never had. They loved her. Paris loved them.

At the end of the summer, Paris refused to go home. Tamara and Levi told her she could stay with them, and her mother's new husband wasn't too sad to see her go. They taught her everything they knew about horses, about the island, about the park they were turning it into. She learned to ride. She learned the business of running a farm. She learned how to make herself indispensable to these two people she worshipped almost as gods. They had plucked her from her old life living in a decaying two-bedroom house with a mother and stepfather she couldn't stand to be around a minute more and brought her to paradise. They valued her, Tamara and Levi did. They loved her. And when Tamara learned she was dying of the same disease that had killed her mother, she brought Paris to her bed, wrapped her arms around her shoulders and told her the true story of Red Thread, who she was and who Levi was. The story Paris had told Cooper tonight.

Paris hadn't taken it nearly as well as Cooper had. She'd run away from home, run back to Kentucky, driving all night in the truck Levi and Tamara had given her, Levi's old truck he'd paid a fortune to keep running. She made it halfway to Frankfort before turning around and driving back to the island. Levi was waiting for her when she pulled into the drive.

"I've made that drive, too, kid," he'd told her. "And I came back."

"I don't know if I can carry it," she'd said.

"You'll carry it here or you'll carry it away, but you have to carry it. At least if you stay, we can help you carry it. *I* can help you," he'd said, remembering that the plural would soon become that terrible singular.

After Tamara was gone, gone to wherever gods go after they die, they buried her in a clearing on the island, Levi and Paris and Bowen Berry and a dozen horses standing around her grave. Paris couldn't leave after that. Her heart was in that island and to leave that farm was to leave herself behind. She stayed and she worked. And she learned.

She went to school down in South Carolina. Went to college, went to graduate school and eventually got her PhD in chemistry. Levi didn't say a word about it, although she knew he knew what she was planning to do. He had plans of his own, too. When Paris was thirty-four years old, he gave her the shock of her life by asking her to marry him. She'd been horrified at first—this man who'd been a second father to her proposing marriage. But he promised it wasn't like that. He wanted to ensure that all he had would be hers when he died and that no other Maddox—and she knew by that he meant none of the white members of the Maddox clan—could take it from her.

So Paris had married Levi because she knew that was what Tamara would have wanted her to do.

Out of respect for her husband, who had been her husband in name only, she waited until he was gone before she put her plan into action. She bought a house in Frankfort, Kentucky, a historic Georgian home on Wapping Street that had once been home to a general in the Union Army. Paris moved her now divorced mother in with her and found all their old fights mysteriously resolved. Their only disagreement these days was over Paris's decision not to have children. She was still young enough, although time was running out. Better do it, her mother said. Better hurry. For a long time Paris had ignored that advice. It gave her a grim sort of satisfaction to kill off the Maddox line simply by not having children. But it wasn't only the Maddox line that would die with her, it was Veritas's, too, and truth was, she wouldn't mind being a mother. She might even like it. So before she'd gone into The Rickhouse last night to take her chances with Cooper McQueen, she'd decided to take her chances with God and fate, too. Maybe in nine months Cooper would find out last night had been even more interesting than he'd thought it was. Fate was a train that didn't stop until it reached its final destination. Paris knew this ride was only starting.

Now, that was a story.

Paris drove into town but didn't go straight home yet. One more thing to do before she was done and she wanted to get it over with because Tamara was out there somewhere watching.

Inside the iron gates of the Frankfort Cemetery she parked her car and stepped out onto the soft lawn. A storm must have hit Frankfort last night, as the ground was sodden and spongy and the heels of her shoes stuck in the grass. She nearly lost one trying to pull herself free. From then on she kept to the paved walkway until she found the row she sought.

Famous men were buried in this cemetery. Men like Daniel Boone and Judge John Milton Elliott, who'd been murdered by a fellow judge, assassinated for the crime of ruling against the man's sister in a dispute over land. The murder had made national news and the *New York Times* had said of it that "such a crime could scarcely have taken place in any region calling itself civilized...except Kentucky."

Kentucky was a border state, after all. On the border between North and South, on the border still between old-world and new, between civilization and the sort of place where the names Hatfield or McCoy still meant something.

A few feet off the main path lay a series of mossy grave markers. Paris stepped carefully onto the lawn and walked past the tomb of Eric Maddox, who died in Vietnam, Nash Maddox, who died by his own hand, George Maddox, who died at the hand of his daughter. She walked down the line, descending decades into the past with each step.

1978.

1968.

1965.

1927.

1912.

Before Paris hit the turn of the century, she paused. This was it.

The gravestone was dark granite, two inches thick and about two feet tall. The top of it was a pointed arch and beneath the arch were angel wings carved into the stone.

Decades of wind and rain and neglect had worn the stone down so that the words were hard to read. But Paris could make out most of it.

Here lies the body of Jacob Jude Maddox and his loving wife, Henrietta Mary Maddox. In heaven they shall be reunited with their children...

After that Paris couldn't make out the words or the names.

Henrietta had died first, but Jacob Maddox had followed soon after. Her sire. Her ancestor. Her grandmother's grandmother's rapist.

She tried to feel something for him. Hate? Bitterness? Anger? Begrudging gratitude he'd been horrible enough to do the deed that not only had brought about her existence but had started the company that had eventually made Paris a very wealthy woman?

She had all Jacob and Henrietta's money, Paris did. The Maddox money she'd inherited from Levi, who'd inherited it from Tamara, who'd inherited it from her father, George, who'd inherited it from his father and his father. It was hers, all hers. Jacob was dead and she was alive. Alive and rich. The girl whom he'd raped had given birth to a girl who'd given birth to a girl who'd eventually brought about the existence of Paris Shelby, who was standing on Jacob's grave in five-thousand-dollar Manolo Blahnik heels and carrying a sixty-thousand-dollar handbag, which to her was nothing more than a costume she'd put on to seduce Cooper McQueen. It had worked, for in that overpriced handbag was a bottle of bourbon worth a million dollars.

Two bottles were in her handbag actually. The Red Thread and another bottle of bourbon worth far more than money to Paris.

Paris took out the first bottle, the Red Thread, and unscrewed the ancient rusted cap. She took a whiff. Its scent had faded long ago. It was nothing but dirty water now. Paris didn't drink a drop of it.

Instead, she flipped the bottle over and poured the contents onto the graves of Jacob and Henrietta Maddox, who were, to the best of Paris's knowledge, burning in hell at that very moment.

"A little fuel for your fire," she said, and when the bottle was empty, she dropped it on the ground. With one well-placed kick of her toe, she shattered the bottle against the tombstone. Then she took the second bottle from her handbag and set it on the grave, twisting it into the ground like a knife into a chest.

The label of this bottle read "Veritas Single Malt Bourbon," the first fruits of Paris's distillery. Veritas was one label, the high-end fancy stuff she'd worked her ass off perfecting. The other brand currently aging at Paris's distillery—which had once been Red Thread Bourbon Distillery—was called Truth Serum in honor of old Bowen Berry. Bowen still worked the cooperage on Bride Island and had taught the trade to his nephew, who was learning now to make the bourbon barrels that his uncle had stopped making thirty-five years ago.

"The barons are dead," she said. "Long live the baroness."

If and when she told this story to Cooper McQueen someday, she would tell him that she laughed when she stood on their graves. A better story than the truth, that she didn't laugh. Instead, she cried. Only a little and only for Tamara and Levi and Veritas and herself, too. She cried for herself because she'd been carrying this burden a long time and it hurt to let it down even more than it hurt carrying it.

As Paris walked away, she tied the red ribbon from the Red Thread bottle around her finger.

It was done. It was finished.

Love what they destroyed.

Destroy what they loved.

And with that, Tamara's vengeance was complete.

But Paris's was only beginning.

And it began with a million-dollar bottle of bourbon seeping into the ground. Paris shook her head, finally laughing like she wanted to. Hard to believe she'd conned that bottle out of Cooper McQueen with nothing more than a few fucks and a dirty story. Paris owned him last night and perhaps she owned him still.

Like Tamara always said, you can't sell people.

Oh, but you can buy them.

★ ★ ★ ★ ★

HISTORICAL NOTES AND ACKNOWLEDGMENTS

This story is a work of fiction in its entirety. While the Kentucky River did flood on December 10, 1978, and crested at historic highs of forty-eight and a half feet, no bourbon barons were found dead in its dirty waters the next day. The destruction of Red Thread detailed in the book was inspired by the unsolved fire at Heaven Hill's distillery in Bardstown, Kentucky, on November 7, 1996, which—to the best of this author's knowledge—had nothing to do with an inheritance dispute or revenge. George Maddox's fathering a secret child by a black employee was inspired by the late South Carolina Senator Strom Thurmond, who fathered a daughter by a teenage black maid. This author wishes to honor the memory of the many Essie Mae Washington-Williamses in this world.

Special thanks to Kentucky attorney and writer Lucie Witt for her help with the legal aspects of the book—inheritance and marriage law both—and her special insights into the social and legal and personal challenges faced by Americans in interracial marriages. Thank you also to early readers Alyssa

Linn Palmer, Karen Stivali and Andrew Shaffer. Very special thanks to Tqwana "The Q is Silent" Brown for her thoughtful critique and invaluable insights, as well.

Thank you to all my readers of all my books. As always, my deepest gratitude to my editor, Susan Swinwood, and agent, Sara Megibow, without whom I would have no writing career at all, much less one that allows me the freedom to write books such as this one.